ReGeneration

Book Three of the
Solarium-3 Trilogy

JOHN R. SPENCER

ReGeneration, Book Three of the Solarium-3 Trilogy
First Edition
DeerVale Publishing™ March, 2015

This is a work of fiction. Names, characters, places and
events are either the product of the author's imagination
or are used fictitiously. Any resemblance to actual persons,
living or dead, locations, businesses, companies,
or events is entirely coincidental.

While the author has made every effort to provide accurate
contact and website information at time of publication,
neither the author nor the publisher assumes any
responsibility or liability for errors or changes after
publication, or for any third-party websites or their contents.

ISBN 978-0-9863727-4-2
eBook ISBN 978-0-9863727-5-9

Contact Information at www.Solarium-3.com

Cover by delaney-designs.com

Dedication

*For my dear wife Candy who encourages me,
and for my niece Julia, who waited for
this book so eagerly.*

Overhead Diagram of the Solarium-3 Pods

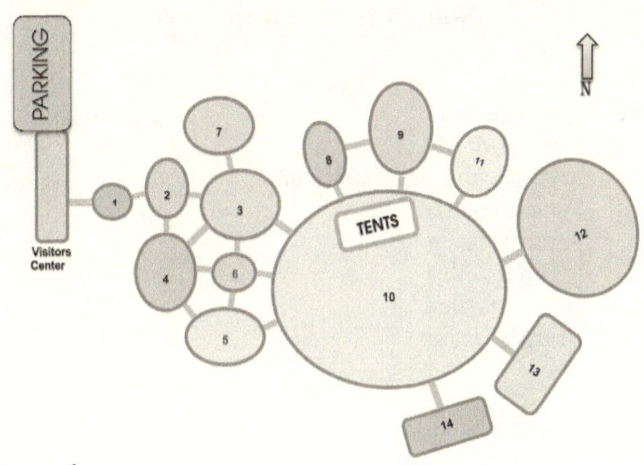

Legend

Pod 1   Entrance Pod
Pod 2   Communications Center (Comm.)
Pod 3   Research Center
Pod 4   Residence (House)
Pod 5   Recreation & Pool
Pod 6   Aviary
Pod 7   Infirmary
Pod 8   Maintenance Shed
Pod 9   Large Animals Housing & Research
Pod 10 Main Agriculture Area, Crop Fields
Pod 11 Small Animals Housing & Research
Pod 12 Ocean, Aquatic Plants & Marine Animals
        Research
Pod 13 Equipment Storage & Main Supply
Pod 14 Fuels & Fertilizers

Solarium-3 Family Tree

The First Generation	Age at Arrival
Clayton Block	44
William "the 2nd" Atchison	47
Pamela Hansen	36
Sarajane Haug	34
Mai Ker Moua	26
Jimmy Algood	29
Bridget Listner	31

The Second Generation	Born
Herald Listner-Block	
Bridget and Clayton's son	March 5, NC 1
Sing Moua-Algood	
Mai Ker and Jimmy's daughter	August 8, NC 1
Piper Hansen-Algood	
Pam and Jimmy's daughter	October 10, NC 3
Nathaniel Moua-Algood	
Mai Ker and Jimmy's son	September 6, 4 NC
Braden Listner-Algood	
Bridget and Jimmy's son	May 2, 6 NC
Kai Moua-Block	
Sing and Herald's daughter	June 10, 18 NC

Prologue

On Pikes Peak, From Haeven

The three men stopped about 20 feet away. Herald began to feel sick again. His half-digested lunch started coming up. He swallowed hard and forced it back. He was not about to chicken out.

The first man came a few steps nearer and stopped. The other two waited further back.

Except for the strange glow around him, he was ordinary looking, with a dark complexion as if he had been in the sun a lot. His clothing was common looking and outdated, plain woolen pants and a dark green, poorly tailored shirt. His face was pleasant but uncommon, with a forceful jaw and cheekbones.

He examined the four Solarians closely, as though he was curious yet at the same time quite certain about them.

"Hello."

He spoke the simple greeting but didn't move or offer a hand. He knew he should not come closer.

"Who are—? I mean, where are—?" Bridget's lips felt as if they were three days' frost-bitten. "Where are you from?" she finally managed.

While Bridget mumbled, Piper was beginning to loosen the hold on her arm.

"Oh, no . . ." Piper said with a worrisome tone.

Her mind was spiraling up and down at the same time. Like Herald, she began to feel her whole universe was turning upside down—or right-side up. Her eyes remained fixed on the man.

"*Really?*" *she asked him with obvious relief, though the man had said nothing more.*

An unexpected smile broadened across Piper's face. The stranger's eyes began to sparkle.

"*Yes, Piper,*" *he finally said.* "*Sorry it's sudden. But I did warn everyone, didn't I? 'When you least expect it'?*"

Piper was laughing almost hysterically with joy. She let go of Bridget's arm and flung herself against the man's chest.

Bridget, Mai Ker and Herald listened dumbfounded to Piper and the man, but they still didn't grasp what was happening. Several more shadowy figures were emerging from the cloud, seeming, as before, faint at first then becoming more solid.

"*I have to say, you've all been very patient,*" *the man said as he comforted the child in his arms.*

"*What?*" *Mai Ker asked, her mind more boggled by the appearance of even more people walking up behind the first three. She wanted to sit down but couldn't. Her legs felt like boards and her lungs kept trying to overfill.*

The man didn't react to her obvious distress, but answered her in a calm voice.

"*I only mean, you've been waiting for me a very long time, haven't you?*"

"*Mom?*" *Herald muttered. He looked from Bridget to the man and back to his mom, as if she should be able to explain.* "*I don't—understand,*" *he said, stepping backward.* "*Tell me I'm not awake.*"

The words were just out of his mouth as dizziness overtook him. He fainted and fell to the ground.

1

"Wake up, Herald."

The consoling voice, though close to his ear, sounded to Herald very far away. Herald blinked. It was the stranger, the first man who appeared from the strange cloud here on Pikes Peak. He was kneeling by Herald, trying to rouse him.

Bridget, also kneeling by her son, became more mystified because no one, in the few moments since this frightening, mysterious encounter began, had spoken Herald's name. She looked in the man's face. How could this total stranger know Herald? More pressing, though, was a much bigger question ricocheting around in her brain. Who *was* this man, and those who had appeared from the cloud behind him?

Herald felt a hand gently rubbing his shoulder. He began to come around. Still light-headed and his stomach in full rebellion, he cautiously opened his eyes.

There was the stranger, still bent over him. It had not been a dream.

"Come on, Herald. Let's get you up," the man said.

Herald laboring for breath, said, "Help me?" He rubbed his eyes and tried to quell the sick gurgling in his stomach.

The man helped Herald slowly to his knees, then to his feet. His stomach made a quick wretch, but fortunately nothing came up. His muscles felt shaky, as if someone had run several quarts of water into his veins.

"Thanks—" His eyes, still blurry, focused on the man's face. "What—I mean, who are you?"

It was the question bouncing around the minds of the other three Solarians, although Piper was fairly sure she knew. Looking around, they found themselves surrounded by a small but growing crowd of strangers standing about, seemingly at loose ends, as if they, too, had just woken up.

The Solarians felt like fish just off the hook, smacked in the head, waiting to be cleaned. Mai Ker, especially, looked as if an invisible board had swung down through the heavens and struck her senseless. Their minds raced. Knowledge, feelings, and memories were being sifted, shaken, and reordered in ways they could not begin to understand.

Then it began. Painfully brilliant flashes of light exploded across the sky, shooting out in every direction from within the circling, luminous cloud that covered the peak. The distorted bolts of light raced instantly from the eastern horizon to the west much faster than natural lightning could have traveled. It was as if some great hand had quickly unzipped the sky, let in the phantasmagorical lights, then just as quickly zipped it back shut.

Watching these strange images of light and color flood the sky, Bridget realized it was not normal lightning. The flashes were more brilliant than lightning, more brilliant than the waning sun that had begun its reluctant journey toward the western horizon, chased by these radiant arms of light that swallowed the sun's beams. To the amazement of the Solarians, the strangers around them—those seeming specters who were now fully flesh and blood—appeared perfectly at ease under the spectacle dancing over their heads.

"I—" Bridget began, but she could get nothing more from her mind, her lungs or her lips. She stared in wonderment at the sky, then at the man Yeshua. She felt her heart infused with new energy. It pounded like a worn-out jackhammer.

The other Solarians felt this, too, but none tried to speak. Not only was the form of the jagged beams overhead different, so were the colors. After only a few moments it became obvious that they were not just colorful lights, but living creatures.

Yeshua, the man who had helped Herald to his feet, stood looking upward, also, with the satisfaction of a builder who has just finished constructing a towering building after years of work.

"They've come," the man said with a gratified expression. He looked at the Solarians to see if they understood. None did. Mai Ker's face asked him a silent question.

"From all the realms," he added, as if this was self-explanatory.

Mai Ker's eyes remained fixed on him, confused.

"To celebrate the dawn," the man said, patting Herald's shoulder and redirecting the boy's gaze upward. "You don't want to miss this!"

The deeply furrowed frown on Mai Ker's face deepened. Riotous, streaming arms and fingers of light danced across the sky. The huge, luminous cloud continued to swirl slowly around the top of the peak. And now this man-from-nowhere was speaking of a dawn in mid-afternoon. She felt a compulsion to ask him some question but had no idea what the question would be.

The gyrating arms of light skipped closer to the ground but stopped against some invisible barrier, then darted from side to side like disoriented bees. They rotated into a widening, nearly perfect spiral that hovered some 200 to 300 feet above the cloud. Whatever these lights were, there was no thunder, just a kind of shuddering, crackly noise that accompanied them, like the sound of a large truck rolling over walnuts that had fallen on a roadway.

Piper was the first to say anything halfway intelligent.

"You're him. Right?"

She took hold of the man's arm again, tugging for his attention as he continued to smile at the strange display of lights. Without looking down, he said, "I am."

Piper smiled. Certainty, and even deeper relief, bathed her face.

Herald glanced at her, then at the stranger.

"Him, who?"

"Yeshua," the man said, still looking up. He was obviously enjoying the magnificent symphony of light conducted by some unseen hand.

What no one noticed was that as he watched the sky, the intense radiance that surrounded him when he emerged from the cloud slowly dissipated, transforming itself into a softer glow that appeared to be connected to the lights in the sky.

Herald, his mind only just regaining full sensibility, gave the man a searching look. He turned to Piper.

"Why . . . I mean, how do you know him?"

"I don't," she answered, "but he knows me."

Herald still half-wondered if he was dreaming, but knew he wasn't. Maybe, he thought, he had suffered a concussion when his head hit the broken pavement. Nothing made sense. He looked again at the lights moving overhead, watching and listening like a four-year-old at an amusement park. The lights, he noticed, moved in a meaningful pattern but he couldn't make out what the pattern was. The lights were obviously alive, but Herald didn't understand how that could be.

Bridget and Mai Ker were also mentally drifting somewhere between earth and sky, their emotions in a jumble. The appearance of this man who quickly took charge of everything by his mere presence was disconcerting. Strangely, they both felt all right, frightened but safe.

Mai Ker eyed Piper. Piper alone seemed to have a sense of what was happening. Her face beamed, smiling back at Mai Ker and Bridget and Herald as if a great gift she had promised them years ago had suddenly materialized—without her help.

Amid the shock and confusion, the Solarians were getting peculiar stares from the newcomers. Obviously preoccupied, the Solarians had forgotten they still had air masks on. That, coupled with the bright orange radiation suits they were wearing, raised a question about who was odder here on the mountaintop, the newcomers or the Solarians themselves.

The man calling himself Yeshua turned to Bridget.

"You can take those masks off. You don't need them—or the suits, either."

Bridget hesitated.

"How can you know that?"

"Trust me."

She didn't.

"You're certain?"

"If anyone is, I am," he laughed.

They had no way to test if he was telling the truth. They had only his word. But the Solarians now felt silly in their suits and masks, looking around at the newcomers who were breathing just fine.

Bridget, always the adventurer, pulled her mask off. She took a couple of hesitant breaths. The air felt different, thinner, but it was fresh. She drew in another breath as if she had never really breathed before. It filled her lungs. She felt instantly stronger.

"It's alright," Yeshua assured her. "Mai Ker?"

Mai Ker's eyes grew a size larger when she realized he had just called her by name, too. *How can he know me?* she wondered.

"How do you—" she began.

"It's alright, Mai Ker. I know all of you. It's alright," he repeated calmly.

Though hardly realizing it, she removed her mask. Her heart told her that not only did he know her name, he knew everything else about her. She, too, took a long, deep breath that so refreshed her she just held it in, as if she must not lose it.

Piper and Herald were more than happy to ditch their masks. The taste and smell of the air, contrary to the stale bottled air that had, so they thought, been keeping them alive, was delicious beyond anything they had known.

Then, unexpectedly, the stranger Yeshua sat down by the edge of the roadway. His eyes looked toward the ground, then he closed them. Herald watched, untwisting and stretching his neck, which had taken a beating when he collapsed onto the rough pavement a few minutes ago.

"What's he doing?" Herald whispered to Piper. He thought she would know.

"Not sure. Praying?" She really wasn't sure.

Herald was fully coherent again. He kept staring, while trying not to, at all these new people he had never seen, and whom he had never imagined existed. The world suddenly looked very different. And here was their apparent leader, sitting, eyes closed, as if no one else existed.

"He's strange," Herald whispered again.

Piper elbowed him to be quiet.

Bridget's heart had slowed. Mai Ker's eyes returned to normal size. The mystifying appearance of these others had startled them like a scream in the dark. But not only did they both feel safe, they curiously felt at home with these complete strangers. "Stranger" was not even the right word.

As their minds swirled, the circulating spirals of light overhead slowed, though they didn't stop. The dancing images, now stretching for miles in every direction, could now be seen to be thousands of individual lights moving in concert. Individually, they were just as indescribable and strange as they had appeared *en masse*. They possessed a beauty that was not of the earth, nor of sky, nor of any imagined Heaven.

Yeshua finally opened his eyes. He looked at each person, including the four Solarians, studying each as if for a job interview. He was about to speak when Piper's intense, penetrating blue eyes became as wide as the saucers of a child's tea set. She looked toward the sky again, and it hit her.

"Oh, Lord. I've met one!" she said in a crisp, musical tone. She knelt down by Yeshua, grabbing his forearm again. "Haven't I?"

He nodded. "Messengers," he told her, "the watchers."

"Where's mine?" she asked excitedly, her eyes scanning the spiraling creatures.

Yeshua laughed happily.

"Yours is near, Piper." He rustled the hair on top of her head, drawing some strands gracefully through his fingers and gently brushing them back into place as if finishing a sculpture. "Your heart has required special care."

Piper thought he meant her emotions. What none knew but him was that he meant her physical heart and the undetected mitral valve defect with which she had been born.

As he withdrew his hand, the warmth of his touch on her head waned like the heat of the sun that continued its post-meridian decline, unnoticed, toward the western horizon. What Piper and the other Solarians did not yet grasp was that they were witnessing the approaching sunset of the entire world, indeed, the entire universe. The sun of a new history would soon rise.

Mai Ker finally bolstered her courage. She moved, like a rabbit in front of a coyote, to where she could watch Yeshua's eyes. Cautiously, she knelt by Piper as if for protection, still watching his eyes, certain they would tell her if he was about to strike.

"But where—where are all of you from? Is your ship in there?" she asked, pointing up the road into the still-rotating cloud.

"Ship?" Yeshua replied very seriously.

"Yes. You have arrived in some kind of ship, haven't you?"

"A kind of ark," he said cryptically.

"Noah's ark?" Piper asked, befuddled.

Mai Ker motioned Piper to be quiet and began to speak again, but the man let loose a hearty laugh.

"No," he grinned. "The ark that has carried these folks," he said, gesturing to the newcomers, "can't be seen by normal eyes. Only the eyes of the Spirit."

Mai Ker was sure he was making fun of her with a joke she didn't understand. But she couldn't think of what else to say. Bridget tried, stepping toward them.

"Well, come on. You're all from *somewhere*. What, another planet?" she asked, almost begging, hoping it might be this simple.

She was answered with another jovial laugh.

"No, no," he chortled. He sat back, his chest bubbling with enjoyment. "Well, this is odd. All that preparation, and everyone still in the dark." He shelved his laughter and stood, becoming very serious. "No. All of these souls," he said, gesturing to the crowd, "they are all very much of the Earth." He looked keenly at the four Solarians. "Me, especially."

"I am sorry," Mai Ker complained, "but I do not understand anything you are talking about." She stood, too, and backed away a few steps. She couldn't look into this man's face for more than a few moments without feeling a mild pain throughout her body. Although he seemed winningly attractive and pleasant, there was something unbearably intimidating about him.

She turned and looked off into the distance, trying to regain her bearings and assimilate what was happening around her. She failed. She knew she was not hallucinating but, like Herald, had to wonder if she was dreaming.

She stared off to the east, mentally retreating, trying to reground herself in what she thought was reality. Oblivious to the others, she rapidly replayed the events of the day. They had set out from the Solarium early this morning on another simple exploration, making the slow trek through the barrens of southeastern Colorado. She remembered driving toward Colorado Springs and the beauty of the great peak that hovered above the city like a giant's catcher's mitt, where she now stood amid strangers who simply could not be here, under strange, ethereal lights that also did not belong. And, just beyond them, the huge, luminous cloud still hung over the mountain like a watery castle washed against the shore of some distant, foreign world.

It all felt imaginary. She remembered looking up some hours ago—she wasn't sure how long—seeing the strange, magnificent cloud with its inexplicable glow. Now the cloud revealed itself to be an opaque vessel that, impossibly, had carried life within it.

She felt a choking in her throat again, the wariness she had felt all day, though she had not known its source. Below her, the ruined city looked more utterly dead than before. At her back was new life. Which was more real?

She decided it was their carefully planned day that was the illusion. How could they have planned for the events they had stumbled into?

When she turned back, Yeshua was walking away toward a small group of the newcomers. Mai Ker, her mind still in an uncontrolled drift, ran after him. New courage welled up in her heart, a desire to face something she did not really want to face.

She stepped in front of him. He was not much taller than many of the others yet seemed to tower over them all. Mai Ker's voice trembled uncontrollably.

"Are we dead?" she asked in a dry whisper.

Yeshua took hold of her arms firmly, but gently.

"No, Mai Ker," he said. "You, you few of the Solarium, have been spared that."

Another problem. Not only did he know her name, he knew of the Solarium. Her eyes fell to the ground. She found herself staring at his feet. She had a sudden desire to drop down and touch them but feared she *would* die in the attempt.

Yeshua, escorting a petrified Mai Ker by one arm, spoke quietly with several of the newcomers who mentally noted the instructions he was giving.

"Salah," he said, "you will lead us down. Thomas, you and I will talk more this evening. We have much to do."

Piper had sat, watching the fanciful creatures of light that still swirled overhead, while Herald did a quick study of the faces of the forty or more people who had now appeared from the cloud. Bridget knelt by Piper, not sure again who was protecting whom.

Piper's sky-blue eyes looked up at Bridget. What was happening around them dawned on Piper with full force. The purpose of their lives and their survival, which had been entirely invisible to them, was being laid bare. The seemingly purposeless grind of their lives had not been pointless. Piper began to see and her whole body tingled. Like the glimmering lights above them, a glimmer of understanding formed in her mind. Their survival had *not* been futile, or meaningless. The apparently random pieces of their lives, like parts of some huge puzzle, began to fit.

She got up and joined Yeshua, who seemed to be keeping Mai Ker on her feet. Bridget followed.

"Daddy always talked about you," Piper told Yeshua.

Yeshua smiled at her.

"Talked about?" he asked her with an innocent but knowing look.

"Hoped for." She tried to suppress the frown, but it came anyway.

He nodded but remained motionless.

"So, you're the one who let my daddy die," she said, a hesitant but sharp accusation.

He nodded again, and again said nothing.

Bridget looked at Yeshua, who returned her gaze. She didn't dare scowl, but her eyes penetrated his. Several moments ticked by, moments when pain, anger and confusion boiled inside her.

"I'm waiting," Bridget said. "We're all waiting," she said indicating Piper, and Herald and Mai Ker. She sensed that the man knew exactly what she meant.

"Yes," Yeshua finally responded, with a patience that seemed out of place amid the tension, "as I said, you've all waited a very long time. That's why I've come."

"So we can wait even longer?" Bridget asked as with a scalpel. She was pushing a dangerous but unknown limit.

He returned Bridget's look with a patient but equally incisive smile.

"The time of waiting is finished, Bridget. The time for knowing begins." He looked around at the crowd, who waited silently. "We should be going down. It's warmer down lower," Yeshua said. "Some of my friends here are from very warm climates. I'm sure this chill doesn't agree with them."

"Wait," Bridget cried. "You're not—you're not going to explain?"

"Of course I am, Bridget. I know the waiting has been unbearable. For you, especially. But it was to teach you patience. That is even more necessary, now."

Bridget's eyebrows creased and rose, but she didn't reply.

"I think Mai Ker is terrified of going back across that dam down there," Herald said as the newcomers assembled around them.

"It'll be perfectly fine," Yeshua said.

Herald smiled.

"That's what I tried to tell her before," he said.

"It will be much safer than before," Yeshua told him.

Yeshua called Salah and had him move to the head of the group, to lead down the road. The third man, Thomas, followed just behind Yeshua. None of the three looked back to see if the Solarians would follow. Several of the newcomers hesitated, though, watching to see if the four Solarians would go first.

"What about the trucks?" Bridget called to Yeshua.

He stopped, turned, looked around the crowd. His eyebrows rose slightly.

"I'm certain no one else here has ever operated any equipment like those. I think two of you must bring them." He turned and continued his descent behind Salah.

Herald looked quickly at Mai Ker.

"All yours, Mai Ker. Key's in the truck," he said as he hurried after the others.

"I'm too young to drive," Piper grinned, dashing after him.

Bridget looked at Mai Ker. Mai Ker shook her head.

"OK. I'll take this one, she said gesturing at the truck she and Herald had been in. "But I'm *not* driving across that dam!"

"Whatever," Bridget said, irritated, climbing into her truck.

She and Mai Ker made awkward back-and-forth turns and managed to get turned around on the narrow road.

"You first," Mai Ker said over her radio.

Bridget puttered forward. They caught up to the crowd quickly and followed slowly behind them.

"But who are they?" Mai Ker pleaded to Bridget over the radio. "I still do not understand. Are they more refugees?"

"Don't think so," Bridget radioed back. As they had for Piper, events were beginning to jell in Bridget's mind. "I don't think so . . ."

Piper caught up to Yeshua near the head of the group. She edged ahead of him and turned, trembling. Her brow furrowed. He stopped briefly, looking at her.

"Something else, Piper?" he asked.

"I've never seen you. So how come it feels like I have?" She wrinkled her cheeks, trying to decide about this man who seemed to be a long-lost father, or brother, or husband.

"Most people recognize others by their looks," Yeshua said, starting to walk again with Piper tagging close beside him. "You, Piper, recognize someone more deeply."

He looked over his shoulder toward Herald, who was also following closely.

"Walk ahead of me, would you, Herald?" Yeshua said.

Herald was still uncertain but did as asked. Each request this man made seemed reasonable, and in some way a command.

"OK, Piper seems to know you," Herald said, "but she's always been kinda strange, you know?" He grinned, realizing the man did know. "But I'm not getting it. Who are you?" He looked around. "And all these?"

"It's alright, Herald. It takes a while to know me. I am the Son." It was a simple statement without the least tone of bragging.

"Son of who?" Herald asked, although distant, tinkling bells of recognition began to sound. Those old

Christmas songs that his mother had never really explained began like a quiet echo among the rocky crevices nearby. The irony of his own name echoed up. "Hark, the herald angels sing . . ."

"Son, but brother of all," Yeshua added. He kept walking.

Although the intense radiance that had followed him out of the cloud had lessened slightly, a different radiance now lit the man's face. It wasn't a smile, it was something far deeper.

Piper tried to watch the broken-up road but kept looking up at that face. She clung to Yeshua's arm as if he might disappear at any moment. To the other Solarians, his face was intimidating and somewhat abnormal, either less than human, or more than human. To Piper, he was both handsome and beautiful. His eyes were alive with a love that spoke of no lust but only purity, of caring, of joy. His not-very-large but distinctive nose stood out strikingly. For the first time, Piper realized he had a fairly short but full beard. It was nearly golden and seemed to blend unaccountably into the very tissue of his face.

"Jimmy's Bible," Mai Ker was mumbling to herself in the second truck. The fright which had first taken her was beginning to pass. Her mind fought to make sense of things. She drove, wondering, trying to stop the emotional earthquake that this man's appearance had triggered inside her.

Then they arrived at the dam.

Mai Ker hit the brake as they came around a bend and the upper end of the reservoir appeared below them. Bridget noticed in her mirror that Mai Ker had stopped so she pulled over, too. The group walking ahead heard the trucks stop and also stopped. Salah and Yeshua looked back.

"A problem?" Salah asked him.

"No. There will be no problem about the dam."

Yeshua walked back to the trucks as Mai Ker and Bridget got out.

"Someone else must drive, now," Mai Ker said in a controlled plea.

"It will be fine, Mai Ker," Yeshua promised her.

"Stop using my name, please?" she begged. This familiarity made her terribly uncomfortable. "OK, you know my name. You don't know me."

Yeshua smiled.

"Actually, dear daughter, I do."

Mai Ker felt the panic simmering again. She broke forward, ran a few paces down the road past the others, and stopped dead.

The reservoir that had been there not more than two hours ago was still there, but barely. The water appeared to have drained nearly to the bottom. The looming, near side of the high concrete dam stood naked and exposed. With the tremendous pressure of the water gone, the manmade mountain of concrete had settled onto itself, as if newly poured. The cracks near the top were still visible but thinner.

To her horror, Mai Ker saw that the cracks extended much deeper than she had thought when they crossed the dam on the way up. Several diagonal cracks reached almost to the bottom of the exposed structure. Strangely, although the dam had obviously settled, the road surface across the top looked as undisturbed as if it had been poured yesterday. And the large, obviously deep cracks were compressed, looking like partly erased pencil marks.

"That cannot be," Mai Ker said with a confused look. She turned toward the rest, shaking her head in bewilderment.

"I can't believe it," Bridget said, coming up to Mai Ker and looking down at the dam.

The rest of the crowd gathered around them, Yeshua standing toward the back.

"Wow," was all Piper could manage.

Herald could manage nothing at all. As they stared, they saw perhaps the strangest thing yet.

"Impossible," Bridget said.

Although the dam stood intact, deep down by either end, much deeper than where the surface of the water had been earlier, there were now two large, natural rock tunnels, one at either end of the dam. Several million gallons of water were bubbling out of the remains of the lake through the two portals.

"No way," Herald finally said. "Those were *not* there. We'd have seen the water coming out, when we went below the dam." He turned and frowned at Yeshua, who was silently watching the whole thing.

Piper wrinkled her nose and sniffed, trying to dry the dripping from her sinuses caused by the cooling late-afternoon air.

"Pretty neat," she said, sniffing again over a broad smile.

"But the water was clear up there," Mai Ker insisted, pointing to the obvious watermark high up on the side of the dam.

"It couldn't have drained that fast," Bridget interjected. "Not through those little tunnels."

"Everything is possible," they heard Yeshua say as he appeared alongside them. "You would be surprised."

"Already am," was Bridget's honest and dumbfounded reply.

As she and others gawked, it was apparent that only 30 to 40 feet of water remained against the bottom of the dam, all that was left of the reservoir. The dam looked solid, safe, and indestructible.

"Would you like me to drive, Mai Ker?" Yeshua asked her politely.

She looked at him, started to nod, then shook her head "No." She tramped back to her truck.

"That was easy," Thomas said to Yeshua.

"No, it wasn't."

"Let the trucks go first," Salah said.

Bridget shook her head.

"Nope, you guys be the guinea pigs. We'll follow. If you make it." She returned to her truck, and shivered.

"No trust," Thomas whispered to Yeshua.

"It will come, Thomas. Sometimes, it takes a while. Remember?"

Thomas gave him an embarrassed look.

"What's wrong?" a 10-year-old boy named Josiah asked.

"Nothing, I guess," Salah said. "At least, not now."

Everyone crossed the dam. It was boringly uneventful. Mai Ker started across last, her eyes wide but her mind firmly closed, certain her truck would not make it. She inched along behind Bridget's truck. At the far side, Mai Ker breathed again.

"Thank you," she said to the air.

Before anyone realized it, the group emerged from the Pikes Peak highway and were coming into the ruins of Cascade. The town was still devastated. Nothing had changed since the Solarians came through earlier. For some reason though, the town felt less empty to the four Solarians. If pressed, not one of them could have accounted for the difference. What was still only wreckage was in some vague way coming back to life. None of the four spoke of it, yet they all sensed it.

In moments, they were at the junction with old Highway 24.

"I don't know the way," Salah called to Yeshua.

"Ask Herald," Yeshua said.

Herald's eyes grew as large as Piper's had earlier.

"You trust me?" he asked Yeshua.

"Well, it's kind of mutual, son."

"I get it," Herald smiled, though he didn't.

Herald gestured at the whole group with a head-nod like he had seen in an old Western movie in the

Solarium archives. It was the knowing nod of a native scout leading settlers on to their new home, of which they knew nothing. In days past, Herald would have felt a deep sense of pride at this moment. As it was, he felt only uncertainty because he still had no idea where he, or they, were headed.

2

Thursday, July 24th, Late Afternoon

"I'm tired, Yeshua, and hungry," the boy Josiah grumbled as they walked down the steep incline of the highway toward Manitou Springs.

As the large group walked along together, the strange rippling lights overhead moved ahead of them slightly, as if they were leading instead of Herald. Constantly changing shape, but subtly, the lights swirled in the air, cascading like a mountain stream of light particles flowing downward with the contour of the mountain.

Yeshua came over to Josiah and picked him up to carry him for a while.

"Your new legs are still growing in strength," Yeshua said to Josiah.

"Perhaps some of them could ride now," Salah suggested.

"I'm not tired," Yeshua replied.

"No. But you can't carry them all."

"You'd be surprised," Yeshua laughed.

"Actually, I wouldn't be at all surprised," his friend said.

"But you're right." Yeshua stopped, looked around, and called the others. "Whoever is tired, climb into the trucks," he told the group which numbered exactly forty-one, not including himself.

Several of the newcomers found their way up into the beds of the pickup trucks. Little 10-year-old Josiah leaped out of Yeshua's arms and made a beeline for the cab of Mai Ker's truck. He fumbled at the door handle.

He was sure it was a handle but it didn't operate like a handle should.

Mai Ker leaned over and opened it from inside. She forced a little smile. Josiah beamed back, climbed knees first onto the seat, and leaned forward with his short arms propped lazily on the dashboard.

"I am ready, now," he smiled at Mai Ker as if giving her permission to drive on.

Precocious, she thought. *Cute, though.* A tussle of dark brown hair sat like a bowl atop his roundish head. His shirt and pants, moderately dark blue and brown, looked to have been handmade, but where or by whom Mai Ker couldn't judge. They were odd, but as clean as if they had just come off a department store shelf. They looked stiff, fresh, new.

Piper continued to stay close alongside Yeshua. Her mind was honing in, trying to understand him. Her hope about whom he was when she first clung to him up on the mountain was becoming certainty. The careful but tender way he had held her, and the sense of grace she had experienced in that moment, was like nothing in her life before. It was a knowing, a sense of being grounded—no, anchored—in the heart of this man who had so unexpectedly appeared. His very touch had reassured her. To Piper, it seemed she was almost an extension of his own body.

She walked along, replaying those first moments on the mountain. Time had frozen since. The encounter that seemed only several minutes to the four Solarians had lasted nearly an hour. But in this new reality they were beginning to experience, time was running in a different warp or along a new tangent. Piper felt it. Time was not the same. Some moments felt like they might last forever, others flew by almost unseen.

From Cascade, the pavement seemed to stream past as they descended the remaining five miles toward Manitou Springs, like gliders coming in too fast for a landing.

Bridget felt like she was on one of those moving sidewalks that were used in large airport concourses.

Although Herald had started out in the lead, he had fallen back as they moved along and was now 30 feet behind Piper and Yeshua. Only now did Herald begin to notice the odd clothing the newcomers were wearing, odd in part because nothing matched what was worn by the others. Mulling back over his history studies and pictures in the Solarium archives, it looked as if each of the newcomers had been cut from the page of a different century and pasted randomly together into a scrapbook.

Salah wore a long, broad-woven tunic that reached just below his knees. It must have been blue at once time but its color had faded away so that it was nearly white. Thomas, by contrast, wore a longer robe-like garment that touched his ankles. It had a red hue but also had a peculiar whiteness about it. Each of the others, men, women, and several various-aged children, had clothing that seemed to fit that person perfectly but was unique when seen against the backdrop of the others.

"Why does everyone look so different?" he finally asked a woman walking near him.

She looked around, looking back at him with a puzzled expression. The question had not occurred to her.

"Different how?" she asked.

"Their clothes, I mean. Like, I dunno, like they couldn't possibly know each other."

"I'm sure they never did," she said "Each of us comes from a different time. And, I suppose, a different place."

Herald, walking along the gradually lessening incline, squinted at her in doubt.

"How did all of you get here?"

"How would you say it?" she wondered aloud to herself. "Reborn? Yes. That's just what has happened." She gave herself a faint smile, understanding something she had actually not contemplated over the last hour and a half. "I had to wonder about myself," she confessed to Herald, "because of how we were before, that is."

"Before?" Herald asked. She didn't reply. "What do you mean, before?"

"Well, dead."

Herald's feet stumbled to a halt. She stopped alongside him, giving him a curious look as if she didn't believe that he didn't believe her.

"Dead . . ." Herald repeated with a tone that said it was not possible. It was not that he disbelieved her, but he couldn't take in that he was talking with someone who was, or at least had been, dead.

"This is getting kinda scary," he admitted. He looked at her more closely. She had obviously lived a long life but seemed not much older than 30. Herald continued to stare at her.

"I don't understand."

"Probably not. But you will."

"Who are you?"

"I am Anastazja."

"No last name?"

"I think we won't need last names now."

Herald looked dubious. She started walking again and he fumbled along beside her.

"Why?"

"I don't think they will count now," Anastazja said.

With no way to contradict this, Herald had to take it as fact. He was certainly not going to argue with someone who had been much older than himself, not to mention dead.

"You're lagging, Herald," Piper called from the head of the group by Yeshua. She gestured to him to come back to the front. "Supposed to be leading," she reminded him.

He gave her another native-guide kind of look and shooed her on with his hand. He had more questions for Anastazja. First, she was obviously not dead anymore. Her skin looked fresh and resilient, no sags, no circles under her eyes like older people have. This he knew mainly from pictures, since in fact he had never actually known anyone very old in his short lifetime. His thoughts wandered to Sing, and Kai, and he wondered what they were doing at that moment and what in the world Sing was going to think when she found out about all *this*.

"You're not kidding me, are you?" he asked Anastazja.

"Kidding?"

"Fooling. You're not fooling?"

"About having been dead?"

Herald nodded emphatically.

"No, son. I am very serious. It was very, very strange. I can't even tell you what it was like." She thought for a moment. "I don't have the right words." She shook her head sternly. "You should ask Yeshua. He could tell you."

She walked on ahead of Herald. Apparently the uncomfortable conversation was over.

They were nearing the western edge of what had been Manitou Springs. Yeshua drifted back in the crowd and came alongside Herald.

"Your leadership seems to be slipping a bit," he said gently.

"Said she was dead," Herald answered, his mind feeling a bit numb. His eyes were dark, his face fretting.

"So she was," Yeshua assured him.

"She said you can explain it to me," Herald said.

"I can, sometime. Now is not the best time. I think

today has been hard enough for you. And for Piper and Bridget. And, well, mostly for Mai Ker."

"Mostly, I think you're right," Herald mumbled. "And then, maybe I don't really want to know. But I have seen a dead person, you know."

"Yes."

"Pretty sad."

"Indeed. I know the feeling," Yeshua said, looking straight ahead. "But not everything is forever."

This went directly in Herald's one ear and out the opposite. He nodded as if he understood, which he didn't. He picked up his pace, taking the jibe about his leadership to heart, and moved back to the head of the travelers.

In the rear truck, Josiah was having a fabulous time riding with Mai Ker in what seemed to him an utterly fantastic vehicle that he could not have imagined when he had lived centuries ago. He kept smiling and chattering simple nonsense to Mai Ker as they drove. Then, out of the blue, he looked over at her and said, "You are pretty, ma'am." Being a very pale Caucasian child, he had never seen anyone with such rich, brown skin.

"Thank you," she said. Since she had not gotten anywhere in understanding what was happening, she decided to ask the boy. "Where did all of you come from?"

He looked at her squarely, then back out the windshield. He shook his head a bit.

"Can't tell you," he said very seriously.

"Why not?"

"No, I mean I can't tell you. I don't know. But it was very strange."

"Arriving here, you mean?" Mai Ker pressed him.

"No. Strange where we were. Or what we were, I mean. I was somewhere, but I didn't have this," he said, gesturing at his arms, legs, and entire body.

Mai Ker's foot went for the brake, but she backed it off and kept creeping forward.

"Can you explain, sweetie?"

"My name is Josiah."

"Sorry, Josiah. Can you explain what you mean?"

"Everyone said we were dead."

This time her foot smacked the brake.

"Shouldn't we keep going?" Josiah asked inquisitively.

Mai Ker, having no reply, started the truck forward again.

"Who told you that you were dead?

"Well, it isn't like someone has to tell you. It's so different, you see. You just know."

Mai Ker's mind spun. She thought fleetingly of Block, and Willy, and Sarajane. And Jimmy. She felt she was going to cry but stifled it.

"OK. So, if you say so, you were dead. But how did you come here?" she prodded the boy.

"Him," Josiah said, pointing through the windshield.

Mai Ker had no doubt who "him" was.

"That Yeshua man," she said.

"Uh-huh."

"He brought you?"

"I guess."

"What do you mean, guess?"

"It's just—it's hard to say it. All of a sudden, we were with a lot of others—dead people, I mean—then it was like he collected me on his arm somehow and *whoosh*—here I was, with this bunch." Josiah's young face became very emphatic as he tried to describe those moments. "I never have seen most of them before! Kind of scary, in truth."

Kind of . . . ? Mai Ker thought silently.

"Alright, then, up on the mountain, what was happening?" Mai Ker asked the boy.

"How do you mean?"

"When you all came out of that cloud."

"We were being restored. Regenerated, someone called it."

"What?" she asked with a frown. This didn't register at all.

"Born over again."

"In that cloud?"

"No, I don't think so." Josiah pondered his next words. "I think, you see, we were regenerating before—and that cloud just sort of carried us here. Do you see?"

"But you were dead? You're not joking?" Her complaint echoed Herald's.

"Joke? Ma'am, why would I joke about *that?*" he almost growled at her.

"OK," she said, "never mind. Let it go. We can talk later, maybe. I can see you are upset."

"Well, wouldn't you be, ma'am?" he said seriously.

Mai Ker erupted into a controlled laugh. Josiah frowned.

"No, honey, no, I am not laughing at you," she assured him. "I suppose I am laughing at myself," she admitted. "Yes, I would be very upset."

"I guess," he said.

HERALD LED the group toward what had been a main street when Manitou Springs was alive and well. He looked back occasionally toward Yeshua to see if he approved of where they were headed. Yeshua looked completely unconcerned and offered no direction.

Eventually, Yeshua caught up to Herald and they walked together toward what looked like an abandoned city park that was essentially an open space scattered with rubble.

"You were feeling pretty low, weren't you, Herald?" Yeshua asked.

"What? Just now?"

"No, months ago. Remember?"

Herald had no idea what he meant.

"C.Q., C.Q., C.Q.?" Yeshua said cryptically.

"Wait," Herald said with surprise, his eyes getting wide, "you have a radio?"

"No, no radio," Yeshua told him. "So who were you seeking?"

"I dunno, nobody. Anybody. Just somebody alive."

"Yes. That would have been me," Yeshua replied. "Anyway, I just wanted you to know I was listening. It was touching. I felt your heart in those simple letters, Herald." He looked around the remains of the park. "Let's settle in here for tonight. The air is thicker, and warmer. It will help everyone think more clearly."

Sure ready for that! Herald thought.

Bridget had parked her truck by a broken-up curb a short distance away and walked over to them. Mai Ker pulled in, too, but sat in her truck, looking around. Before she realized it, Josiah was out the door and running toward the others.

"I'm starving. How about everyone else?" Bridget asked Yeshua.

"Yes. We'll need to arrange for a meal, and some rest."

"How can we feed this mob?" Bridget asked. "We've got almost nothing left. Just some leftovers from lunch."

"We'll see," he told her. "Maybe just get out what you have. I'll take it from there."

The doubt in Bridget's eyes was manifest but she was beginning to believe Yeshua was a man of his word, and meant what he said, and would do what he said. She didn't know why she felt so certain, but she did.

"I know you're tired and overwhelmed, Bridget. It's alright. I'll take care of supper. Why don't you and Herald rest, and talk?"

"I'm both," said Bridget emphatically. "I am tired, but mostly overwhelmed." She sat on the ground right where she stood.

Yeshua smiled. His face, though no longer glowing as brightly, still held a luster that could not be missed. Smile or no smile, he embodied life and strength in a way that would have made Clayton Block look like a child's stuffed toy. Bridget couldn't decide. Either this Yeshua was not quite human, or was a little too human. When he smiled, which he did a lot, there was a passion and power in his face that she had never seen before, even in Clayton.

"That was a long walk," Herald said, sitting on what may have been a tree stump. He leaned down against his mother's shoulder.

"It was good for you," Yeshua told him. "Nothing like staying fit. You'll see." He smiled more broadly. "In time you'll learn to walk as I do, no work at all. This is only the beginning."

Salah and Thomas came and sat beside them as Yeshua wandered away.

"Salah," Bridget said, "what nationality are you?"

Salah looked at her.

"Does it matter?"

"No, just curious. I wondered if you were Greek."

Thomas, who had also joined them in a small circle, laughed this time.

"He's not, but some of my friends used to think I was!" Thomas laughed.

"Why?" Herald wanted to know.

"I'm Hebrew," Thomas said, "but not Hebrew enough for some of my family. And my friends used to complain that I must have been Roman!" He laughed louder. "I was raised a Hebrew, in what you called the Holy Land. But all the land will be holy, now."

"I was Arabian," Salah finally answered. "A very low class, I should add. Not worth horse dung, until he saved me."

"Who?" Bridget asked.

A bothersome tick spasmed on the man's left cheek as he attempted a smile. "That name isn't mine here," he said.

Of course that was true. Soren was the name of the man this shade had possessed, the name of the man I had freed. This spirit was an entirely different person.

"Who are you then?"

"You can call me Nero." The fiend spoke in a way that made it difficult to understand individual words. As if he was in pain.

"What do you want?"

"To dance," he answered. "To drink. To fuck." His words wheezed out of his skeletal frame. "To live."

Violet had told me about the spirits, lost and wandering the Dead Side, usually unable to help themselves in death just as in life. When they broke down enough they became more like animals. Not even understanding their own desires, but fighting viciously for them as if it meant their survival.

In a way, it did. Try as they might, many shades never succeed in making a connection with the living. Of those that do, most have trouble staying for long. They inevitably fall back into exile on the Dead Side. Sometimes, however, they find a way to bond with a host, like Violet attaching to the pocket watch. In these cases, when the shades do lose their grip on the material world, they're sometimes able to reclaim their foothold. Again and again, they can return to the same human being. Coming and going as chance and pleasure allow. It's the kind of fateful oppression that destroys lives.

Expulsion, however, disrupts the connection. Exsufflation results in a forceful split. Not only are body and spirit sundered, but the long-term bond is obliterated as well. Soren had sucked in the white sage, so any permanent hold this fiend may have had on him was gone. The living Soren was safe. More importantly, this desperate creature before me had been cast out. The sage had done its work; this shade would more than likely never see the material world again.

"It's time to move on," I told him. "This is all that's left for you here."

The man's neck jerked before he recovered his composure and approached me. "I wanted to break you and you escaped me."

Could I fight here? How would that even work?

"I was lost and desperate and wondered who you were," he continued, getting closer. "And then, here you are."

I backed up slowly, even if it made my position less threatening. This thing I was looking at wasn't quite human. The thought of it close to me was frightening.

I could just wake up, right?

Nero's eyes glazed over in a deathly white pallor. "You should never have come here."

My foot stuck as I tried to step back again. My arms wiggled like soggy noodles at my side. I couldn't raise them. Nero advanced and my entire body heaved in place.

I was stuck in water again, but that didn't prevent the scabbed spirit from effortlessly gliding forward and snatching my neck into his long hands. Overgrown, twisted, and broken fingernails scratched my skin. I opened my mouth wide and let out an empty scream.

And then I was in my bed, convulsing. The comforter was wrapped around me snugly. I had to wiggle back and forth to free my arms and roll over onto my elbows.

The sun was already up, although the shuttered blinds did a good job of holding back the day. My shoes, shirt, and jeans were where I had left them, right on the floor, and everything appeared normal.

I needed to stop drinking right before bed.

Chapter 13 - Sunday

The next morning was like most Sunday mornings. I slept in a little later than I would've liked, first only getting up to swallow an aspirin, take a dump, and force down a glass of water before passing out again. That is as good a prescription for hangovers as I've found.

By the time I woke up for good it was noon. My apartment still had a slight November chill so I opened the vertical blinds and got a lovely view of the North Hollywood Metro Station across the street. The buses that periodically shuffled in and out were a bit loud but the convenience of the location trumped the distraction—I could hit Hollywood and Downtown with the Red Line without needing to drive or look for parking or suffer valet service. I did like to drive, of course, but I also did a fair share of drinking.

I sat down on the couch, my laptop on the coffee table in

"What do you mean, who?" Salah said with a penetrating look. "Him," he said, gesturing without looking in the direction Yeshua had just gone.

"You were in a battle together?" Herald asked.

"Only the one ancient battle, son, against the archenemy. I died about—let's see—in your calendar, about the year 870. I was losing, and Yeshua saved me."

"How?" Bridget asked.

"Same way he saved you, I suppose," was his reply.

Bridget and Herald were feeling completely lost in the conversation here in this empty, ruined park. They let the subject drop. Almost at once, Yeshua came back. He had a lightweight cloth towel in his arms in which was wrapped three very large loaves of what could only have been, from the smell, fresh bread.

"See if there's some good water around, Thomas, would you?" he asked, setting the loaves onto a broad, platter-like piece of concrete debris.

"Wait, I don't think we want to drink anything from around here," Bridget cautioned.

Thomas was on his feet and moving toward a creek bed.

"It will be fine, Bridget," Thomas assured her.

MAI KER had finally gotten out of her truck. She had settled alongside Piper in a small barren area about 30 feet away from Bridget and that group. Piper was very tired from walking and sat the moment they reached the park.

"You OK, Piper?"

"Fine."

"You're sure?"

"Still a little confused, maybe. You know, about Daddy."

"Just a little?" Mai Ker grimaced. "I'm lost." She focused on Piper. "What's wrong?"

Piper looked over her shoulder to where Yeshua and

the rest sat a short distance across the park.

"He's not like what I thought," she confided to Mai Ker.

"I don't even understand who he is," Mai Ker admitted.

"You will," Piper promised. "But he's not like I thought."

"How?"

"I thought he would be . . ." She fumbled for a word. ". . . more serious? I don't know the word exactly. More," she pondered it, "solemn, I guess?"

Thomas, coming back from the creek carrying some kind of open, metal cylinder he had scrounged up and filled with water, came by the two.

"Speaking of the master, are you?" he asked Piper courteously.

"Yes. I don't understand why he's not more serious-sounding.

"Love is always solemn," Thomas said, "but solemn is not sad, Piper. Many mix them up."

Piper, who had experienced so much sadness at her father's death, wasn't sure there was any difference. She had lived through the days since then with a deep sense of loss and sadness and had come to equate seriousness with sadness.

"Maybe I have mixed them up," she admitted. Her heart was still very tender.

"What is truly solemn, in the invisible places, is expressed with the most exquisite joy," Thomas said. "It's a joy you will learn, in time."

Piper smiled but said nothing more.

Thomas offered some water to her and Mai Ker. Both refused, sure they should not drink it. He walked on to Yeshua and the others.

front of me. I had some contract programming to catch up on. I hoped to get ahead this weekend but I couldn't bring myself to open Visual Studio. It was easy to find distractions. Right now, front and center were the other objects on the table. I was drawn away by a chunk of metal sitting next to an empty rocks glass from last night.

Soren's ring. I must have removed the bulky thing from my pocket before I went at it with Rachel. I hefted it in my palm and examined it. It was heavy. Looked like a small horseshoe that wrapped around the finger, open at the top end just enough to preserve the effect. It was oblong and bulky and not at all convenient to keep on one's finger. But Soren did. Or Nero, anyway.

What was it they said about horseshoes bringing good luck?

I browsed Wikipedia and new age Wicca blogs. Going from encyclopedic style, heavy on references, to trust-me-I'm-mysterious was interesting. But the information was more or less the same. Horseshoes warded off spirits because they were iron of the earth. I leaned back on the couch. Fat lot of good the iron did for Soren.

That shade, that fiend on the Dead Side—it still sent chills down my spine. I glanced out the sliding glass doors to the balcony and enjoyed the light of the day. If I was going to one day be stuck on the lonely streets of a gloomy Downtown Los Angeles, I might as well enjoy the sun when I could. Of course, the bliss didn't last long. I kept thinking about my dream. Then my thoughts drifted to other mysteries. The owl. The man in the plaid trench coat. Livia.

I'd known Violet for four years and there was so much about her that still puzzled me. Now I had finally uncovered new clues to the events of her death. It took all of three minutes before I was googling "double murder", "murder-suicide", and other relevant terms. Violet wouldn't have liked it, but she was on the nightstand in the bedroom.

It took some doing, but newly armed with the name of her mother, I found an interesting parallel. It wasn't an exact match. The daughter's name wasn't Violet but maybe that was an alias. It would certainly explain why I hadn't been able to find the details of her death before.

Ever thorough, and positive I was on to something, I dug into secondary sources to paint a picture of the events of Violet's death, six years ago.

The marriage of Alexander and Livia McAllister was a happy event. Livia was a well-to-do young socialite and Alexander's family had accumulated a sum of money in real estate and stock investments. Young Alexander was raised as the only son and successor of this empire and dearly loved his new wife. The couple were often described as dreamers and idealists who adored each other wholeheartedly, mostly noted because of the contrasting events of their later lives.

They gave birth to a beautiful baby girl and raised her in the

3

Thursday, July 24th, Evening

"If we're going to eat, maybe we should get started," Bridget said. "It'll be dark pretty soon."

Yeshua, sitting on the bare ground near Bridget, tore off a strip of the bread he had brought to them and handed it to her.

"You won't have that kind of darkness anymore, Bridget. There will be light. Even after dark settles on the land, you will always see the Father's light."

Bridget didn't follow this but she was feeling very tired and didn't ask him about it. He seemed to have an answer for everything and she was running out of questions. The sun had long since dropped behind the peaks to the west, the air was beginning to chill, and the dark was in fact closing around them, although, as Yeshua said, there remained a background glow that would continue through the night.

As tired as Bridget felt, she was afraid of having to spend a night OUTSIDE, though she wouldn't admit it. She didn't feel safe. To admit this with Herald close by would not be smart.

"Who else has brought food?" Yeshua asked.

There was silence.

"We have those leftovers," Bridget said. "In one of the trucks."

"I'll get it, Mom," Herald offered and was off.

"Anyone else?"

A second small boy named Iwan stepped toward where Yeshua was sitting. He looked about 12, with sand-colored hair, dark brown eyes, and an engaging smile. He held a hand forward.

"And what have we here?" Yeshua asked the boy.

"I found some dried meat, Lord," the boy said, "here, still in my pocket. Is that possible?"

"No doubt," Yeshua said.

"My mother gave it to me just before the city was overrun. When she was killed."

"Very generous of you, Iwan."

"You're welcome. Thank you, father."

"There is bread too," Yeshua said, handing him a chunk.

No one noticed, but the barren soil beneath Yeshua had begun to change from an acrid black to a softened brown.

A woman came over to him, opening a large pocket near the waist of her large skirt, and handed him what looked like another freshly baked loaf of dark, brown bread. The Solarians were baffled by the food that was appearing.

"I've kept it. It was the last I made, during the siege. Still fresh, though," she assured him. She looked surprised. "Hardly seems possible, after all this time."

"A kindness," Yeshua said to her, "thank you. Who's hungry?" he asked, looking at the Solarians and the rest.

The others all scurried toward him. Herald, returning from the truck, tried for the head of the line but didn't quite make it. In his turn, though, he handed Yeshua the remains of their lunch and received in return a large chunk of bread and a torn-off strip of what appeared to be dried beef.

Piper and Mai Ker came over and joined them to eat. One of the newcomers, no one noticed who, had made a small fire to one side of their rather large circle. But it was not the source of the light that bore in around them out of the darkness.

Piper munched her bread and, having been persuaded

by Salah that the water would be fine, was sipping from a small cup that was being passed around. As the evening grew darker, despite the light from the campfire, she realized that the strange, curling beams of angelic light that had followed them down from the peak were still nearby, but hovering at a distance now, as if under an order not to come so close as to be a nuisance.

Just to the east of them, several spirals of these unearthly light creatures sparkled above the barren wreckage of Colorado Springs. At moments they would seem to cautiously approach, then back away. Piper watched, wondering, trying to see if she might pick out the one she had seen three nights ago. It was impossible. There were too many.

She ate, watching the lights dance. It looked like an entire shower of fireflies beginning to appear in the air as the final glimmer of natural light faded.

"They're the angels, aren't they?" she asked Salah, breaking what had been a restful silence.

"Only a few of his angels," Salah said. "A very few."

Mai Ker's eyes told her there were many more than a few. But having grown up in a culture that believed in many gods and spirits, this didn't trouble her.

"How many are there?" Mai Ker asked with fascinated interest.

"How many?" Salah asked.

"Yes. How many, total?" she asked, watching the supernatural lights.

Salah looked very serious, as if the question could not possibly be answered.

"Countless."

"My people believed in these things," Mai Ker told him. "We believed they ruled all things secretly."

"Well, there is no secret. Only One who creates," Thomas interjected, "and He alone rules. Make no mistake, for many have. He who created everything else, created the angels. They serve him, and they make nothing. Except, sometimes, trouble." He received the cup as it came around to him and took a drink of water.

"All the angels serve him," Piper said musically.

"No, sweetheart," Thomas said gravely, "not all."

Piper continued to watch, intrigued as the angelic lights moved about. Herald finished his meal, then turned toward Salah and Thomas.

"So, they're his angels?" His head gestured toward Yeshua.

"Yeshua? Yes. They stay around him, though not always will you see them," Salah explained.

"They belong to him?"

"Just like you and I do. We are all his creatures."

Mai Ker wondered at this and her mind began to drift again. She was still trying to adjust to the fact of others who were alive, and to reframe her mind to account for this man Yeshua. He simply didn't fit her mental picture of how the world operated. This day, and this afternoon, had been far too full of impossible things. People who should not even exist had appeared, uninvited, from the midst of a strange cloud that didn't belong there in the first place. Then this moderately-sized man who led them, whose presence seemed overly large, kept taking charge of everything and everyone. Surely, she guessed, he was from some divine realm, such as her people had always believed in, yet he seemed so human.

She tried to remember some of the stories Jimmy had read from his Bible. Was this King Saul, she wondered, or maybe that fellow David? This man was a king, she could feel it. But his name was so strange. It sounded a bit like that Hebrew warrior, Joshua. Maybe this was Joshua? The name, at least, was similar.

The newcomers who had appeared with Yeshua, it seemed to Mai Ker, continually talked in riddles. All of them, even the boy Josiah, seemed to know something she didn't. And there were these two odd-looking men, Salah and Thomas, who apparently didn't know each other but were both obviously close friends with Yeshua.

Her mind swept back to their first encounter on the peak. She momentarily relived the fear and the thrill when Yeshua walked toward them from the cloud. So much confusion had erupted in her, so many conflicting feelings. Her mind was a sponge trying to soak all this in but too much continued to drip out the edges.

Despite her fears, Yeshua had managed to break down barriers not only in her mind but in her inmost heart. Whenever he came close, first her heart sank, then it flew free. She couldn't explain that perplexing feeling. It was the feeling of an awkward, embarrassed teenager who suddenly realizes she has grown up. This Yeshua was a complete puzzle and it was wearing her down.

What felt most strange to Mai Ker was that the way she felt this evening was very much like how she had felt when she first realized how much Jimmy loved her. With Yeshua, though, this feeling was magnified out of all proportion, amplified beyond what was human.

That's it, she thought. *It's too big,* this feeling that Yeshua stirred up in her. She needed to regain control of herself. She couldn't. If she couldn't grow slowly into how she felt about him, this feeling might crush her.

She remembered the expression Jimmy often had on his face when he read from his "Word" and spoke of God's love. But that moderate sense of god-like love she had felt from Jimmy was like baby food compared to the feast that was the presence of Yeshua. He stirred in her a desire deeper than love that touched her core like a rich, sweet delicacy filling her to overflowing.

As Mai Ker reveled in these feelings, she realized with a start that little Josiah had slid up beside her on the ground. He leaned tentatively against her side, not looking directly at her. He looked exhausted, exactly as she felt at the moment. Without thinking, she put her arm around him. He felt chilled. She pulled him closer.

She realized, again in a way that seemed quite beyond normal, that she cared for this little guy deeply. Yet she hardly knew him.

What in the name of goodness is happening to me? she wondered.

Without Mai Ker realizing it, Josiah had dozed off, and so had she.

THE TRIP down the mountain had tired everyone except Yeshua, who was still on his feet, walking from person to person, chatting as if it were early morning just before sunup. He did steer clear of those who were obviously dozing or sleeping.

He finally came and settled by Herald, Bridget and several of the newcomers.

"Time for you all to rest."

Thomas looked at him.

"Forgive me, Lord, but I feel like I've been resting for far too long!"

Yeshua chuckled.

"I suppose many of you feel that," he said.

Salah, walking back from a wash-up in the creek, came over to them. Around them in the near-dark, the ruins of the old park remained, its beauty long gone. The burned and exploded stumps of trees had decayed into near dust. But in the creek nearby, they could now hear more clearly, in the evening cool, the burbling water running delightfully down the streambed.

Salah sat. He pulled a flexible water skin from a strap over his shoulder.

"More water," he said. "It's really fascinating, Master," he commented to Yeshua.

"The water?"

"No! That things like this"—he shook the water skin—"that were with me at the end should turn up with me now." He laughed. "What a sense of humor you have!" He laughed again louder. "A water skin!"

He passed the water skin around so the others could have a drink. Bridget could tell it was very old, probably centuries old, and let it pass by, giving a subtle, motherly shake of her head toward Herald. He sniffed the thing, and drank from it anyway.

"Good water," he said, handing it back toward Salah.

"Yes, it is!" Salah agreed. "This mountain stream water, even here in your mid-summer, it's as cold as any from a northern country lake would have been in winters past."

The water skin was passed around several more times. Bridget finally, carefully, took a drink. A quiet peace began to settle over everyone. Most found a reasonably comfortable spot on the ground and stretched out.

Yeshua stayed sitting, watching over the several small groupings of fellow travelers taking their rest. Before long, he noticed that Mai Ker had awakened, from the weight of Josiah leaning into her side. He went over to them. Josiah was out cold, making a faint, childlike snoring sound. Mai Ker gently repositioned him so she could get up.

"Do you need to stretch?" Yeshua asked her. He offered her a hand.

"I—" She cut herself off. She reached for his hand as if it were a live electrical wire. "I'm sorry," she muttered, embarrassed. "I do not know what is the matter with me."

"There is nothing the matter, Mai Ker, that you can't change."

She took his hand. The touch of his hand around hers calmed her but also invigorated her. She stretched her back which was stiff from being stuck in the old guard truck too much of the day.

"Shall we walk a bit?" he asked.

Mai Ker nodded. She let go of his hand and, not waiting, took the lead and walked toward the gurgling of the creek, a sound that tonight was particularly soothing.

"Please forgive me if I do not understand what has happened today," she said as Yeshua followed her. She felt some sort of explanation was needed for her standoffishness. "I did not see this coming."

"None of you saw, beyond the immediacy of the day. It's not just you, Mai Ker," he said. "Perhaps in the scheme of things, you couldn't foresee this."

She turned and looked at him with a face that was half a frown and half a question. He looked into her eyes with that kind of look Mai Ker had often experienced when speaking with Piper.

"Do you see?" he asked.

"No, I really do not," she said, turning away. "I do not see anything. You—all of you—just appearing like that. Do you realize how upsetting it was?" It was an unapologetic question.

"Yes, I realize."

Mai Ker found herself weeping slightly, then catching little hiccupping breaths. She turned partway around and looked up at him again.

"I am afraid of you," she confessed. "I do not know why."

Yeshua gently brushed some of the tears from her face. She tried to get one or two more words out but couldn't. She was overcome with such emotion that her words were formless and, so it seemed to her at this moment, meaningless.

"Maybe we should sit down, here," Yeshua said.

He helped her sit facing the quiet stream. They were silent for several minutes while she regained some composure.

"Tell me why you're afraid."

"How? I do not know myself."

Her mind flew in reverse. She longed suddenly for the Solarium, for its safety, its solid, protective walls. Nothing out here right now felt safe or solid. She remembered a night long ago INSIDE, not long after Sing's birth, when she stood over the large crib, watching as Herald and Sing slept so peacefully together. The wonder of the two infants had felt like a blessing from the heavens, an encouragement amidst all the despair, and yet there was the unfathomable mystery of why they had been born at all. The days and months that followed were filled with non-stop worries, trying to nurture the children, trying to raise them in the strange haven called Solarium-3.

She remembered with a sharp ache how they had almost lost Sing when she was just five. How Jimmy had prayed so ardently, how nothing seemed to fix it, and then how suddenly the illness reversed and Sing got well. Perfectly well. And now Sing was a mother herself, with her own beautiful daughter, Kai.

Something clicked in Mai Ker's mind. Other days and evenings flashed through her memory. She thought about Jimmy's Bible, Jimmy sitting patiently, reading to her and the children. They had all been more or less disinterested, and Jimmy had been so intent, so much in earnest. Now the promises Mai Ker had made fun of were opening in front of her, promises about God's plan, about the Messiah who promised to return.

Mai Ker felt overwhelmed again. New tears poured out and drenched her face. She couldn't help herself. So many conflicting emotions of love, anger, fear, anxiety, hope and promise rushed at her that she nearly fell to pieces right there on the ground.

Yeshua gently placed a hand on her arm. She looked sideways at him, and knew.

"You are— I mean, you cannot be—" She took a little catch breath. She was terrified to say it. "You are *that* one?"

He nodded and moved his hand behind her shoulder because she was about to keel over backward.

"I am."

"But you promised to come back."

He understood what she meant but didn't challenge it.

"And now I have."

Trying to squelch the flood of tears, she burst out laughing, gasping again for air.

"You'll wake the entire camp," he cautioned.

"Who cares!" she laughed. She gulped a glob of tears and saliva pooling in her throat. "So he was—all that time—he was right?"

"Jimmy? Yes."

"Oh God. Oh, good God."

Yeshua let the flood of emotion pour out of her. Then he pulled her toward himself and cradled her against his shoulder. Mai Ker's laugh awakened Josiah. He stumbled over and was standing behind them, watching the scene with confused curiosity. After a moment of assessing the situation, and deciding that Mai Ker was not in fact dying or in physical pain, Josiah walked closer and put his arm around her other shoulder.

Yeshua smiled and patted Josiah's hand across Mai Ker's back.

"You are a good child, Josiah. I'm glad I brought you along."

Josiah didn't speak but just wrinkled his mouth in a smile. He knelt down by Mai Ker.

They sat together quietly for the next half-hour. Everything around them was still, except for the gentle movement of the radiating arms of light beyond the far edges of the encampment.

As the darkness deepened, the new nighttime light in the air around them became more pronounced. It also became apparent that the glow they thought had left Yeshua earlier in the day was still visibly present around him. The glow extended far beyond him, faintly lighting everything nearby, including Mai Ker and Josiah's faces.

Piper had also stirred from sleep. She gazed around and noticed Thomas kneeling, tending the fire. She went over to him, sleepily.

"Did he leave?" she asked.

"Yeshua?"

"Yes."

"Over there," Thomas pointed, gesturing toward the three odd-sized figures seated near the creek bank.

"Can we?"

"Of course," Thomas said.

Thomas stood and he and Piper walked toward Yeshua, Mai Ker and Josiah. They stopped about 15 feet back. Piper saw that Yeshua had leaned back against a large rock by the edge of the stream that had been placed in the park for children to climb on. Mai Ker was leaning against him, and Josiah was leaning against her, three mismatched dominoes, half-tilted.

The evening breeze moved quietly around them like breakers caressing a shore. The moon shone brilliantly overhead, as if it might burst open at any moment. The comforting glow around Yeshua inhabited the darkness like embers of a long burned-out fire that refuse to surrender their light. Had this glow been just a little brighter, Piper might have noticed the most outrageously strange thing of the entire day. On the ground beneath Yeshua, not only had the dirt lightened in color and softened, but the slightest shoots of grass had begun to push up through the soil in a small circle beneath him.

"Is he sleeping?" Piper asked Thomas.

Thomas stood behind her, a kindred spirit.

"He doesn't sleep now."

"He looks asleep," she said. She wanted more than anything to creep over and pry an eyelid open to find out if Thomas was just teasing her.

"He's resting. But he needs no sleep."

"I'm really tired," she said. "I need to go back to

sleep. But I'm afraid it will be cold tonight. I've never slept OUTSIDE."

"It won't be cold, child," Thomas assured her. "You're too close to him."

4

Friday Morning, July 25th

The night passed swiftly and everyone was waking just as the sun was coming up. But it was a different sunrise than any of them, except one, had seen before. The sun rose looking like it had been on a long vacation and was not quite up to any work this morning. There were no clouds near the eastern horizon and the sunrays spilled out as cool beams across the barren land and hills, barely bright enough to form shadows where the near side of hills ducked out of the sun's sight.

What also was different, at least to Mai Ker's sharp eye, was that the sun looked to be a little further south along the horizon than it had been over the last month. She said nothing, though, dismissing this oddity as a trick of her own imagination, confused as it was by the seemingly impossible events of the 24 hours just past.

Yeshua was cooking something for breakfast over the rekindled fire in the middle of the park. Where he got the tinder and logs that were burning—just as someone had last evening—remained a mystery. Certainly no usable wood had survived as far in any direction as anyone could see.

Yeshua was cheerful, whistling quietly, obviously enjoying his task.

"Shouldn't we cook for you?" one of the women in the group asked.

"Oh, feel free to help. But I don't mind. I rather enjoy specialty meals," he smiled.

"You brought more food?" Piper asked him, brushing

sleep from her eyes as she walked uncertainly toward him.

"I can supply what we will need. It won't be a feast. Not quite yet. Don't be too disappointed, Piper."

He knew that Piper knew about the promised great banquet, but his comment obviously slipped right past her in her half-awake state. He chuckled.

"Did you sleep well?" he asked her.

"Like a log."

"Could have put *you* into the fire then," he joked.

She looked at him, not sure if it was a joke or an accusation. He reached out his free hand, pulled her to his side, and gave her a warm, sideways hug.

"It's a joke, Piper. I'm very pleased with you," he said to her quietly when his laugh subsided. "You listened."

"I did?"

"To my messenger."

"Your—?"

"By your ocean."

"Oh," she said. She looked puzzled. "You sent him, yourself?"

"I did. I thought you would know."

"I guess I kind of guessed."

"What's important is, you listened. You did as I asked. You led them, encouraged them. Even though you hit resistance. Right?"

"Yes. But I felt it all day, yesterday. Even on the drive up to the city," Piper told him. "I knew there was something that—" She broke off as if ashamed. "Something we were supposed to find. But really something I wanted. For myself," she admitted.

"Don't feel ashamed, Piper," he said. "It was right for you to want it. You wanted to come to me. That was right to want, and good."

She put her arm around his back, which was a stretch, and returned the hug.

"Taste test," he said, handing her a piece of the stuff he was cooking in a small pan.

"Good," she said, although she wondered who was carrying pans around. It wasn't the Solarians.

Bridget and several others joined them and Yeshua dished out the food, which was either a kind of pancake or very flat muffin. Herald was still sound asleep some distance away and even the rich smell of food didn't rouse him.

Mai Ker was awake, too, and she came and sat between Piper and Bridget. Protection.

As Bridget munched down her breakfast, which was quite delicious, whatever it was, she began to ruminate. She watched Yeshua, now sure who he was. She reflected how they had been alone on the Earth these seventeen years, under the protection of the Solarium. They had been certain, and they had been right, that nothing had survived the immolation of the atmosphere that had consumed the life-breath of the planet. Until yesterday, their own survival had seemed a mere accident of timing and unrelated, plan-less events. But what had seemed to be the end of things to the Solarians, she now began to see, had not been the end at all. It had been only a break, a pause in the playing out of history, an intermission in worldly and cosmic events.

She looked at Yeshua, then at the newcomers who had emerged from the cloud yesterday with him. Here was the unbelievable reality of new life, lives raised from death. When she had talked quietly with several of the strangers last evening after supper, each assured her that what she found so hard to believe was true. They had all died. The shock to Bridget was that they had been dead not just hundreds but, in some cases, thousands of years. And they had been brought back. Most could remember the exact instant of their death and the circumstances, though for some the details were fuzzy. She also discovered last night that these newly raised people were as curious as she about whatever plan was beginning to play out. It was like someone had unfolded a long-hidden roadmap and spread it out in front of the expectant eyes of lost travelers, but no one could read the map.

The greatest mystery for Bridget was not how, but *where* they survived, if "survive" was the right word. They died, yet were still in some sense alive. Obviously Yeshua had a hand in that. Maybe more than a hand.

Through all the years in the Solarium—all the unplanned events, the births of the children and, yes, the deaths—Bridget thought she had grown to a point where she could handle whatever might come at them. The sudden appearance of Yeshua and all these other people, however, was clear off her radar, off the map of her understanding. She vaguely remembered, though, Jimmy reading about this very thing from his Bible. The return of the crucified one, the resurrection of all who had died, and the refitting of the world back into some original design that had been long lost by humankind.

Right in front of her was the fantastic reality that others survived not in a Solarium but in the pods of death. It presented a mystery unfathomable to Bridget but one she could not deny in the face of things. Try as she did, the whole idea of surviving death outside the body was still just an arm's length beyond what she could comprehend.

Maybe, she wondered, *that's why Jimmy was always encouraging faith. However smart we were, some things are just beyond us—even when one of the resurrected ones is staring you in the face.*

She looked over at little Iwan, the one who had been so generous last evening with the little bit of food he had found in his pocket. He and the other newcomers were tied together by some thread that Bridget could not see and, in one sense, didn't want to see. After seventeen apparently lost years in the Solarium, here they were, bewildered and witnessing the most amazing events of their lives.

While this ran through Bridget's mind, Mai Ker was studying the face of Thomas, one of the first two who had appeared behind Yeshua out of the cloud. It was a handsome, rugged face, looking as if it had been chiseled out of stone. He must, she felt, be a close friend of Yeshua, yet he and Salah, though friendly, were obviously not friends before. Why had Yeshua chosen these two particular men to act as leaders, here in this ruined park?

Mai Ker wiped crumbs from her mouth and drank water from another cup that had mysteriously appeared, perhaps from someone's overcoat pocket. She listened to Thomas talking with Herald and Piper. As she listened intently, it dawned on her. The words were strange. They were not English. Mai Ker knew several languages, English itself being a second language to her, and she realized that whatever words Thomas was speaking were of no language she knew. Then something else dawned on her. All of them, from different lands and ages, had understood each other perfectly since yesterday afternoon.

"Why is your language strange?" she asked Thomas, butting in, setting her plate down and scooting closer to them. "I'm sure it is not English. But—explain this, please—I understand every word you are saying."

Thomas stopped speaking, as if he had done something wrong. He looked across at Yeshua who was also listening but who had said nothing for the last quarter of an hour.

"From now on there is only one language," Yeshua finally replied. "The language of my Father, expressed in me."

Herald was amazed to realize, quite abruptly, that it was not English he was hearing. But he, too, understood every word. He frowned.

"That can't be. All I know is English. Well, Mom tried me on French once. Kind of a bust." He looked at Bridget and she smiled.

"Many things that 'can't be' now are," Yeshua said. "Before, you would not have understood these words at all. But you're mistaken. You do know this language. It's embedded deeply in you. You spoke it, though not well, as a baby. Until you had to unlearn it."

Mai Ker cocked her head sideways, trying to digest this latest in a series of surprises. Piper listened from several feet away, trying to hear each word with new ears.

"You mean," Mai Ker interrupted, "we can hear now—" She broke off, lights flashing on in her eyes. "Oh, goodness. I realize it. I am using these different words, too." She looked, unbelieving, at Yeshua. "Am I not?" she laughed.

"You are," he said. "All of you."

"Oh!" she laughed harder. "I cannot, I mean, this cannot—" She began to laugh uncontrollably, but it was laughter of delight not humor.

"All of us?" Bridget asked, listening carefully and analytically to each word as she spoke them, unable to discern whether she was speaking her native tongue or not.

"All," Yeshua said. "It was always in you, in the deeper recesses of your mind. This is the language that underlies all others. Every word you knew before was a shadow of my words, the only real words."

"But, when—" Bridget stopped, embarrassed, suddenly unsure of herself. "When did we start?" She felt jumbled and thought she sounded incoherent. "I mean, when did we change? To this language?"

"Yesterday, on the mountain. The first words I said to you. The first words you spoke to me."

Bridget was shaking her head weakly, finding this completely implausible, but wondering if it could be true. So much of what couldn't be true now was.

Mai Ker held her hand on her chest, breathing in and out, as if these new words were going in and out silently with each breath.

"Words are not what is spoken," Yeshua said. "Your word before you speak it is your true word. The sounds you used to express it were merely learned. A social convention. Any set of sounds will do. You learned at a very young age to associate certain sounds with a certain idea in your mind. But language is not sound, it's what lies beneath the sounds. From this true language, the Father's language, all thoughts and all emotions well up."

Yeshua was speaking plainly but their minds were wobbling, trying to incorporate what he just said.

"The language of the heavens," he told them, "of the invisible places that are not places, the song of all living creatures. Love expressing union." He looked around at the Solarians and the others. "You see?"

Most didn't.

"But then why do these new words sound like our old ones? To us, I mean?" Piper asked.

"What is true is always understandable. Ears must be tuned to recognition. I helped you retune. You speak now the words you've always spoken, but with new sounds."

"I don't understand something," Herald said. It was becoming his litany.

"About language?" Yeshua asked.

"No," Herald mumbled. "What you meant about the invisible places. You mean, they're not real places?"

"You misunderstood. I didn't say they weren't real. I said they were not places."

"Herald, maybe you shouldn't—" his mother started to say, but Yeshua cut her off.

"No, Bridget. It's alright. If he doesn't ask, he won't grow."

"So some place can be real," Herald said as if repeating back a school lesson, "but it's not a *place*." He shook his head. "I can't get that."

Yeshua wanted to laugh but he restrained himself. He knelt on the ground by Herald and gave him an encouraging look.

"Does your mother love you?" he asked.

"Sure." Herald looked at her. "I think so."

"And where is the 'place' of that love."

"But love is a feeling."

"No, it is something much greater. But it's not a place, is it." This last was not a question, but the simplest of statements.

"Mom?" Herald said, looking at her plaintively, knowing he was over his head and sinking.

"Afraid you won't get any help from me on this one," she said, raising her hands as if to block the pleading of his eyes.

"Let's not worry about it today, Herald," Yeshua said. "There is a lot for you to learn. And an eternity to learn it. Just know, for now, there are invisible things that are very real. And the most invisible place that is not a place is where my Father is."

"Like Jimmy used to tell us?" Piper chimed in. "In Heaven?"

"No," Yeshua said. "Beyond even that."

Though still befuddled, Herald could not let it drop.

"So, wait," Herald risked. "You mean the Father, Jimmy's God person, he's *your* father?" Herald had never had much trouble believing in God until this moment. "So, he's—real?"

"Absolutely real."

"You're like a riddle book," Mai Ker interjected.

"Why are you confused?" Yeshua asked them. "He's also—in a different way—your Father, too."

"I do not think you are making sense," Mai Ker grumbled with a tone of frustration.

"I always make sense," he assured them.

"I'm not asking any more questions," Herald said. "But can't you just be a little clearer."

Yeshua smiled.

"Perhaps it's too clear. It will take time. Just keep watching."

"He's right about that," Salah said, yawning, ready for a morning nap.

"Please don't worry about these things," Yeshua said. "You all worry too much."

Piper finished off the cup of warm breakfast drink that, she assumed, someone must have brought. It was like warm sweet tea but not so bitter. Except for Salah, most had eaten their fill.

Yeshua called everyone else around him.

"Some others will be coming soon," he told them. "Not all will appear here, but they will all come, in their time. I'm asking that most of you stay here with Salah. He has my instruction on how to feed you over the next few days."

"Will we be safe alone?" one man asked. He looked about 40 but was actually much older. He was dressed in a very colorful outer cloak over pants that seemed to be made of wool, dyed dark green. Though she couldn't be sure, Bridget imagined him to be a solider of the Orient from about the 15th century, judging from drawings she had seen in books.

Yeshua smiled at the man.

"You won't be alone, Katsuo. And nothing more can hurt you. You have died. You are reborn. You're under my protection."

The man dropped to one knee, either as an expression of thanks or a simple courtesy. He bowed his head in traditional Japanese manner, then rose.

"I will be going with our new friends here to their

home," Yeshua explained to the new people who had appeared with him yesterday. "There are others there, and I must meet with them."

"But, sir, we still don't understand many things. This place, here, it is all unfamiliar to me, to us," Katsuo said, again with a very slight, courteous bow.

"Yes, but all of you understand where you've been and what has happened since your death. Our new friends still have a great deal more to learn about."

"You don't mean—" Piper began to say, but Yeshua stopped her.

"No, Piper. You will not die. We are beyond that time. Death is buried."

Tremendous relief flooded Piper's face. The momentary fear that had passed over the faces of Bridget, Herald and Mai Ker also disappeared.

"I'd like to go along," Thomas said.

"You will. And six others I will name." He quickly named the six, all by first names, and beckoned them closer. "I want you to come and greet the rest of the remnant with me. The others are terribly afraid because they are sure they've lost these four, as they have lost others before," he said gesturing to the Solarians. "So we need to go to them quickly."

The noise of a motor approached behind them. Bridget turned. The old guard truck she had parked along the curbing yesterday pulled up close by the crowd. Salah got out.

"I've inspected this strange horseless wagon of theirs, Lord. You'll be safe enough in it."

Yeshua was amused at Salah's description, and equally amused that Salah thought he could still be hurt in any way. He decided to wait for a better time to explain this to his Arabian friend.

"Just fine, Salah," he chuckled, "just fine."

Herald ran to retrieve the other truck.

"At least we're not walking," Bridget said, relieved.

"Not today. You can't travel fast enough, yet. And we must go in haste. Your friends at home are troubled. You and Herald can drive."

With no formality, the Solarians, Thomas and the other six climbed into the two trucks. Yeshua stood near the truck Herald would drive.

"Mom," Herald said pulling Bridget aside, "I can't drive, not for *him*! I'd prob'ly land in the ditch!" he said in a forced whisper. "I don't want to make him mad."

"You can ride with me," she said to Yeshua. She grinned at her son. "You are always a surprise to me, Herald," she said, kissing his cheek.

THEY TOPPED off both gas tanks from the storage tank in the one truck bed, which was still nearly full.

As they drove out of Colorado Springs east into the sun, Bridget noticed for the first time how placid the sunlight seemed this morning. She looked at Yeshua who was on the other side of Piper in the seat.

"Is it just my eyes?" she asked him.

"No."

"Why is it so—?"

"Different?"

"Yes."

"It's waning, Bridget. It's not just my children who must be made new."

"What's that mean?" Piper asked.

"The whole creation has been waiting, through these many generations. Waiting, for you to come in."

"In?" Bridget asked.

"Into the Father's kingdom."

This spun in Bridget's mind a thousand more questions and she almost pulled the truck to a stop. But she kept driving, staring straight out in front of her, staring at this so-different sun, trying her hardest not to look at this man in the seat beside her.

Finally, she had to ask.

"But what if we're not?"

"Not . . . ? " Yeshua looked at her, knowing her question but waiting for her to express it.

"In. What if we're not—*all of us*—in?"

She dared a little sideways glance. Piper's eyes were also fixed on him now, waiting. He was looking straight ahead again.

"That's what we're going to the Solarium to find out."

There was complete silence the next ten miles. As Bridget thought about this, she became frightened. She wondered what he meant. *Me? The others? Both?*

She didn't dare ask anything else right now. *In the Father's kingdom?* she wondered. She was not sure about herself, let alone the others. She was terrified for Mai Ker. And she couldn't begin to fathom what this meant for the children, living after the great destruction and with so little teaching about any of this.

Mostly my fault, she thought guiltily. *Why did I have to be so pig-headed about it?* Many conversations with Jimmy and Pam flashed back to her. She squirmed a little in the seat. Had she failed not only herself, but the children?

Instantly, she felt regret for not having taken Herald seriously when he first asked about those Christmas carols. He had asked simple questions. He only wanted an explanation about faith. She had always put the whole subject off. Save it for some other day.

Her problem was, this was that day.

If there's mercy anywhere, she thought looking up through the top of the windshield, *please let it be now.* Then she realized she was looking in the wrong place.

5

Friday, Mid-Morning

In the truck behind Bridget's, Thomas was riding shotgun with Herald, Mai Ker seated between them. The other newcomers were in the pickup beds, four in Bridget's truck, two in this one.

Mai Ker was still examining the morning sun, which was now an hour higher. Her eyes carefully registered the difference of radiance. It wasn't exactly less radiant, it was just different. It was more pleasant, warm but not brutal. And it definitely looked too far south for late July at this latitude.

Herald's mind was focused on his driving. He wasn't talking, mainly because he was afraid after the long conversation this morning to ask many questions.

"You excited to see them again?" Thomas asked them both.

"We just left yesterday," Herald said.

"A lot has happened since then," Thomas observed.

"Oh my, that is an understatement," Mai Ker said. She looked at Thomas. "They are the ones who will be excited," she added, "though I am not sure 'excited' is the word. I am sure they are worried sick. We were supposed to be back late yesterday. They will think we are all dead."

"Now there's an interesting thing," Thomas said.

"What?" Herald asked.

"They're worried you've died. And here you are, the only ones who didn't."

Herald slowed down and looked at him.

"Watch the road, Herald," Mai Ker ordered.

"Sorry." He made a quick glance. "What do you mean?"

Mai Ker took his chin and directed it back to the road. Thomas was reflecting on what seemed to him a very great irony.

"Only that all of us who've returned, we died. Didn't think we would. We thought Yeshua would come right back. But we did die. And here you folks thought you would die, and won't."

Mai Ker digested this, looking at him with a peculiar frown.

"Why would you think you would not die?" she asked.

"We didn't understand then. After Yeshua had risen—well, just say we all thought he'd be back a lot sooner. We thought we'd be alive to see it."

"But you are."

"No, we had to die first. Now, I understand it. The witness. Our deaths were our witness." Thomas shook his head. "It is so ironic. We didn't think we should have to die, but it was our deaths that drove his message home." He looked at Mai Ker, then at Herald. "Do you see that?"

"Not sure," Herald said, trying to stay focused on the road ahead. *Mai Ker has had enough upset for one day,* he was thinking.

"Our dying brought the message, the promise, to life. Isn't that odd? See, I didn't understand that, until death was right there, staring me cold in the face."

He suddenly got very quiet. Mai Ker felt a shiver.

"We just wanted him back. Yeshua, I mean. Perhaps you can't understand how—once we saw him risen— how upset we were when he turned around and left again."

"I think I can understand how you may have felt," Herald said.

"Well, I didn't understand it completely until now." A knowing look crossed his face. He nodded to himself. "You just never know what he's up to."

"So why did he leave you?" Mai Ker really wanted to know.

"I don't know his reasons. I suppose, partly, it was so he would be there when we died. And there he was, to welcome us."

"Welcome you . . . where?" Mai Ker asked.

"I can't explain that. Not even sure it's what you would call a 'where.' But he was there, wherever we were."

"How would you know that?" she asked, more confused.

"Well, we were still awake, even though we called it sleeping. And Yeshua was there, the only one of us who was whole."

"Whole?" Herald asked. He glanced at Mai Ker who didn't notice, her face glued to Thomas'.

Thomas saw their serious stares.

"Sorry. Left you hanging there. Whole, I mean, in his new body. We were just half-selves, if you get what I mean. Surviving, but dead, sure enough. Kind of loose spirits hanging about, our bodies gone, our very existence preserved only by his grace." Now he shivered slightly. "It was a fearful state, that I will tell you."

Still the blank, questioning stares. Thomas tried to give them a frame of reference, one that made sense to him but little sense to Herald or Mai Ker.

"Well, he'd given us his promise, hadn't he? If we believed who he was, even if we died, we'd live. At first, I admit it, I thought it was just an expression. But it was miraculous. Don't know how he does things like that. I guess, it's his being God."

Whatever Thomas meant, his meaning escaped Mai Ker and Herald.

"Can we go back to that part about how you thought

he would be back sooner?" Herald asked in an overly polite voice. It would not do to upset their new friends.

"Oh, well as time grew, many more people came to believe Yeshua was the One, the Messiah. We told them he'd be coming back. But years passed, and the brothers and sisters started to die. It was very troubling. Some started to doubt everything we had told them about Yeshua, and everything we'd promised. Got some of us killed. But, that was the plan, you see. Thousands, millions, still to be called into the kingdom. Folks like you. And that takes time. I can tell you, you learn patience fast when you're dead." He chuckled softly.

"What do you mean, it got you killed?" Herald asked.

"Well, we said Yeshua was coming back soon. And when he didn't, they called us liars—and worse. Threatened us, said, deny it all or you're dead. Pretty soon, many of us were."

"How could you give up your life like that?" Mai Ker asked in disbelief.

"Well, what would you have done, ma'am? How could I deny what I saw with my own eyes! After he rose? Talk about embarrassment. When the others saw him, and I wasn't there, I told them they were all crazy. Imagine that. I didn't believe my good friends! Then, when he showed up a week later, I still couldn't believe it! He stood in front of me, made me touch him. I've never trembled so badly before—or since." Thomas caught his breath, remembering that moment. "I should have died right then and there, because I doubted him. Yes, he would have been right to just strike me down, right there. But you see, that's the kind of love that's in him." Thomas looked out of the windshield and realized Herald, taken up in the conversation, was about to drift off the right side of the very bumpy road. "Watch it, son!"

Mai Ker accommodated by grabbing part of the wheel with her left hand and helping Herald hold it steady.

"Maybe we should not talk about this right now. Maybe just let Herald drive," Mai Ker suggested rather firmly.

"Suits me. This whole rig scares me anyway," Thomas said. "Who would invent something like this?"

The three grew quiet. Mai Ker turned inward. Thoughts of Jimmy kept flooding back, as they had unpredictably over the last few hours. It was not that she didn't understand Thomas, or the things Yeshua had said last evening. It was more that she was worried. Like Bridget in the other truck, Mai Ker was worried not so much about herself but about the children. All of them. Jimmy had taught them a little about the Messiah, yes, but once he was gone—so suddenly—faith and God just dropped out of the picture most of the time.

Especially for me, she admitted to herself. *I was so angry at this God person, for taking Jimmy.*

Before his death, Jimmy had tried to convince Mai Ker that his God was trustworthy but there was always a roadblock in her mind. Maybe something from her parents, Jimmy had thought.

When Mai Ker would listen to Jimmy speaking of God, it was as if she was in a dream, with her eyes wide open but unable to see anything but blank darkness. That blindness was real, not a physical blindness but a spiritual blindness. Something dark always interfered, the source of that darkness hidden from her thoughts.

She had genuinely tried to understand but the idea that this God-person could have a son was really going too far, not to mention the idea that this son supposedly became a human being. That was one step too far for Mai Ker. No God could become human, she felt, and not cease to be God.

Her mind whirled with these thoughts as she sat alongside Thomas, a friend of the man they now said was that same son, the man who was somehow God.

She looked at him, and frowned, and wondered.

Can such a thing really be? she asked herself. Her intellect dragged its feet, but now she had met the impossible thing that was possible, God's Son, for certain a man, who had now returned exactly as he had promised his friends. And when she had sat with him last evening, she had felt an incredible peace, an inexplicable feeling considering the day she had just lived through.

Mai Ker felt distressed. Tears of frustration squeezed from her eyes.

Thomas was watching. He could imagine the wheels spinning in her mind.

"Don't worry," Thomas said. "It took me a long time to trust him. It may take you time, too." He lowered his chin slightly and looked straight into Mai Ker's damp, brown eyes. "You'll be alright."

She looked at his face, a face that had witnessed untold miracles but was filled with affection and genuine sympathy.

"You seem sure." She was about to cry.

"I am sure. Because I know how deep his love for us is."

Mai Ker saw the depth of emotion expressed in the lines and muscles of Thomas' face. Inexplicably, she felt so safe alongside him that she blundered on to the one question she really didn't want to know anything about.

"What was it like? Knowing you were going to die?"

"Haven't thought about that for a while. A long while."

"Sorry. It is not my business."

"No, it's no secret. I don't know what you went through at that place, this Solarium, they call it. But I wager you faced death there a time or two."

Mai Ker nodded somberly.

"So you know, at least. For me, death was frightening in one way, but in another way, it wasn't. I realized, at the moment, that I'd known it all along. Right? We always knew we would die. Just not the time."

Herald turned his head toward Thomas but Mai Ker's hand steered his chin forward again.

"Yes. That is true," she said. "I have always known this."

"Except—here's the ironic part—now the whole bunch of you find out you were always wrong. You won't die at all." He smiled at them both. "Don't know if that's good luck, or bad," he considered.

"You're sure we won't die?" Herald asked, without turning his eyes from the highway.

"When you've been waiting as long as we have—for yesterday to arrive—you ask him a lot of questions. One thing about Yeshua, he's not bashful about your questions!" Thomas grinned. "Lucky for me, too. But he told us, once we all came back, death was behind us—for good."

"How could you ask him questions?" Herald said in complete disbelief. "After you died?"

Thomas looked over as if Herald had cabbage in his head.

"Why not?"

"Well, ah, you were *dead?*" Herald said.

"Yes, but we didn't just go poof! I told you, he was right there to welcome us. We weren't what you'd call ourselves, no. But our minds were still intact, that much. And feelings, we still felt everything intensely. I don't understand that part. How can you have feelings without a body? But there it is."

The questions in Mai Ker's eyes had become more intense. Thomas shrugged at her.

"Don't know any more than that," he laughed. "Death was a big mystery before I died. Once I did die, it was even more mysterious."

"Maybe we should just let it drop," Herald conceded.

The inside of the truck grew quiet again, although

conversation could be heard through the back window from the man and woman sitting, back against the cab wall, in the bed of the truck.

Astonishingly, just a few minutes later, Bridget in the truck ahead began slowing. They had already reached Punkin Center. Herald and Mai Ker recognized the rubble of buildings at the intersection. Both trucks stopped.

"How'd we get here so quick?" Herald asked Mai Ker. "It was much longer yesterday."

"Yes," she said, wondering.

"The world's changing," Thomas said. "You're in for some surprises, I think. Just try to enjoy them." He gave a jovial laugh.

Bridget walked back to their truck.

"Anybody need a rest break?"

"We're all good in here," Herald said.

She checked with the man and woman in the back of Herald's truck. They were comfortable so she got back in her truck and they turned south.

Although the ride was going quickly, it was still boring, with nothing around to look at but bleak, barren landscape. The four newcomers in the rear of Bridget's truck were bubbling with curiosity to see the great Solarium they had been hearing about. Most of the buildings they had seen in their lifetimes were paltry, flimsy structures barely able to support their own weight. The Solarium sounded like a truly remarkable place. And it was the place, the one place on all the Earth, Yeshua had told them, where a remnant of humankind had been allowed to survive.

This they all wanted to see. Thomas and the six others Yeshua had invited along had lived distant centuries in the past, so the technology and construction of a place like the Solarium was far beyond anything they could imagine. Just the simple lights and electronics in the truck cabs boggled their minds.

"What is that round dial in front of the driver?" Garan, one of the young men in the back of Bridget's truck asked his new friend Adrian.

"I don't know," Adrian said. "Some kind of counter, I think. It has all those numbers but I can't tell what they mean."

Across from him sat Anastazja and a little girl named Eira.

"The Solarium, it must be like Heaven," Eira said to Bridget through the sliding rear window of the truck cab. Her long dark hair, not fully shielded by the cab, blew erratically in the wind as they drove.

"I wouldn't say that," Bridget said. She almost bit her tongue, but said the rest anyway. "Some days, it was much more like Hell." She looked toward Yeshua, who simply smiled.

"But here you are," Yeshua said. "Not to mention little Piper here. And the others."

"I'm not little," Piper protested.

"Oh, child," he laughed, "you are so very little you can't imagine it."

As Piper expressed her disappointment with a petulant look, Bridget reflected on the fact that, as he said, here they were. She found herself feeling disjointed and a little lost in the great open space around them and in several large spaces inside herself that also felt empty.

"Even when the Solarium seemed like a safe haven, some days it sure felt like Hell," Bridget said.

"And the other way around," Yeshua added. "It is always the people who make it one place, or the other."

He was quiet for several moments. The engine of the truck hummed its steady drone in off-key harmony with the loud, knobby tires. Yeshua recalled a day of heavy footsteps, some his own, and the sound of horse hooves plodding along hard paving stones that led up a steep hill. A shadow of deep pain passed across his face. He stared out the windshield.

"The world was Heaven at my birth, and Hell at my death." The shadow of pain in his expression was driven away by an intense look of deeper satisfaction.

Piper stared up at him. Her petulant look evaporated. Astonished love replaced it. To imagine that this immense, powerful presence next to her could ever have died was out of the question. Such a person, surely, could not be killed. But she saw something in his eyes, even as they looked straight ahead. They were set. They held a steeled determination she had never seen, an absolute and terrifying determination that would sacrifice all to save merely one.

She gently took hold of his arm with both her hands, to reassure herself he was in fact real. He didn't move. And Piper knew in that moment how very incredibly small she truly was.

6

Friday Afternoon

The second half of the journey from Punkin Center sped by faster than the first, despite the badly broken-up roads. A little past noon, both pickups were drawing to a stop in the parking lot of Solarium-3. Coming along the drive from the guard shack, their passengers were largely invisible to the Solarians INSIDE, blocked by the Visitors Center.

The newcomers in the backs of the pickup trucks had been in awe for several minutes, ever since the shiny domes came into view once they were a few miles east of La Junta. Now, as the visitors climbed out of the trucks and stood near the Visitors Center, the great pods looked more enormous than ever looming over them like artificial mountains.

"This was worth the trip," the young man named Garan said. "How in Heaven's name did they do this?"

"You remember the great cathedral they started at York?" his new friend Adrian asked.

"That monstrously large one? Just before we died?"

"Yes. I heard it was like this when they finished. Very big."

"Astonishing," Garan replied.

"Makes you want to kneel, doesn't it?"

Yeshua watched and listened, squelching a slight grin.

"Would you escort us in, Bridget?" he asked politely.

"Sure." The last of the newcomers had gathered around. "This way," she gestured.

To minimize the shock, Bridget had made sure that all their handheld radios were turned off when they were still several miles from home. She didn't want to have to begin explaining everything to Pam over the radio once they came into range.

She led them into the Visitors Center and toward the long hallway that connected it to the pods. The eyes of the newcomers were bouncing everywhere, taking in the dusty, broken display and souvenir cases, the defunct soda and candy machines. For many of them who had lived centuries before the death of the old civilization, the technology around them was captivating. They were more anxious than ever to get inside of the huge pods. Most felt overwhelmed by the sheer size of the place as they looked up at the pods through the glass walls of the hallway that led toward the entrance pod.

The four Solarians expected Pam would be frantic by now but they hadn't counted on the possibility that she had gone nearly mad with panic. As Bridget led the group toward the outer door of Pod 1, they saw Pam, eyes as wide as dinner plates, emerge from the door of the Comm. Center in Pod 2, waving a radio in her hand.

Bridget switched her radio back on.

"Where in God's name have you been?" Pam was shrieking over the radio. "I've been calling and calling—ever since yesterday—I was—!" She broke off at first sight of the unexpected visitors. She stumbled to a stop and fell silent. She began to tremble.

"Oh no, oh no, no . . ." Pam sputtered, almost wilting to the ground.

Bridget tried to calm her.

"We're OK. We're all alright, Pam. Just ran into a surprise."

"A really big surprise, Mom!" Piper called over her own radio.

Pam, stunned at what she saw in the hallway beyond Pod 1, stood frozen. Her mouth gaped, her knees became rubbery. She felt like she might fall any second. Another wave of panic—an entirely different kind of panic—swept over her. She didn't know whether to cry or scream, but in any case could do neither.

"Just let us in, Pam," Bridget pleaded.

"But who—who—?" Pam stopped. Her head felt like it was disconnecting from her body. She was dizzy. "Oh Lord. . ." she whispered to herself, this time covering her mike. "Oh my Lord. . ." she repeated.

"Open the doors, Pam," Bridget ordered Pam, though still in a controlled voice. She didn't want to make her more upset than she obviously was.

Pam stood dazed.

"Mom, are you OK?" Piper appealed over her radio.

Pam didn't actually know the answer to this question. She was mainly just trying to keep her feet under her.

"Can you *please* let us in?" Bridget begged, becoming impatient.

Pam gradually awakened from her trance. She looked out. She saw no weapons, no signs of coercion from the strangers behind Bridget.

"Yes, OK. OK," Pam mumbled as she wobbled back into the Comm. Center. She tried to collect her raging thoughts. She took a deep breath, focused her eyes narrowly on the command console, and keyed in the unlock sequence for the outer door of Pod 1.

"You can open both doors, Pam," Bridget told her.

Not on your life, Pam thought. She stared at the console. Her mind still reeled and she felt she was about to throw up, shaking like a drunk coming out of the DTs. *Who are those strangers? Where in the world did they come from? Are they refugees like before? But surely they are all dead,* she told herself. They were dead. She had seen the bodies. *Who in the world are they?* She grabbed hold of the edge of the console desk and looked straight down, trying to steady the floor, which seemed to move under her feet like a rubber raft on a turbulent lake.

"Pam?" Bridget radioed again. "What's the problem?"

Pam looked up and peered out a high window toward Pod 1.

"Sure you're OK?" Pam asked.

"Pam, just open the doors. Let us in, please."

"But the airlock," Pam said.

"Don't worry. No need. The air's fine," Bridget insisted.

"How can you be so sure?" Pam demanded, unwilling to unseal the inner door until she had locked the outer door and purged the OUTSIDE air.

"Pam, listen to me. Just trust me, OK? We're fine. You're fine. The air's fine. Let us in!"

Bridget's voice was becoming agitated. Yeshua, standing several steps behind her, walked forward and put a hand on her shoulder.

"Give her a second," he said.

Pam walked back to the door Comm. Center and looked out again. She had been fraught with worry for so many hours that she found it hard to trust even Bridget at the moment. She finally noticed that the four Solarians weren't wearing their air masks. She panicked again, glaring at Piper, a mother's anxiety welling up and ready to pounce on someone.

"Piper!" she demanded over the radio. "Where is your mask?"

"It's OK, Mom. Just let us in, OK?"

"I—" Pam tried to think clearly, and Piper's voice helped settle her down. "I have to get Nate and Sing over here to pull the seals."

"We're waiting," Bridget said, trying to maintain her patience. She was completely irritated that Pam would not simply do as she was asked.

Pam hurried back to the console and paged Sing and Nathaniel over the intercom. Both children, who had also been fretting through the night hours over their missing family members, came running from Pod 11.

"Oh no!" Sing said as they came in sight of Pod 1 and stumbled to a stop. "Somebody got them!"

"Somebody *who?*" Nathaniel said. "Who *are* they?" he cried. Fear agitated his voice and he swallowed hard. He stood still, utterly dumbfounded to see the strangers. He began shaking just as Pam had.

Sing also stood frozen, unsure what to do.

"Kids, pull the seals," Pam called. "Hurry up!" Despite her own misgivings about the strangers, her curiosity had now scaled over the top of her fear.

Both children resisted, standing immobile several more moments. They had never seen so many people. Except for the few Solarians, they had never seen anyone at all. These new people, the new faces looking back at them through the Stellar walls, made no sense to their young minds. Curiously, Bridget and the other three Solarians looked fine, if impatient.

Bridget motioned for Sing and Nathaniel to approach Pod 1. They finally moved ahead slowly, then snapped to work and began pulling the seals from the inner door. They worked furiously like two little robots, pulling tape and insulating materials away from the doorjamb, but their eyes remained glued to all the new faces that stared back from the other side of the entry pod.

"This is too scary," Nathaniel said mainly to himself. "Mom," he hollered, "I'm scared."

In the hallway opposite, Mai Ker could see her son's lips moving but couldn't hear him. She could, however, see the anxiety on his face.

The locks clacked open and those OUTSIDE moved into Pod 1, pulling the inner seals off the inner door. Sing and Nathaniel jumped back as the crowd poured

INSIDE. Mai Ker was instantly hugging both her children.

"You two OK?" she asked.

"Why wouldn't we be?" Sing asked. "Mom, who are these—?"

Her eyes fell on Yeshua, who had hung toward the back of the group as they entered.

"Who's *that*, Mom?" Sing stared into his face, looking at his eyes. He seemed as if he was stepping inside his own home. His short-cropped golden beard seemed for a moment to be on fire. The indescribable radiance around him glistened the air as he moved. And she saw in his expression something that reminded her vaguely of her father.

"You will see," Mai Ker told her. She kissed Sing and Nathaniel with welcome kisses. "Where is Kai? Is Kai alright?"

"We're all fine, Mom. You're the ones we've been worried sick over!" Sing said emphatically.

"I know, honey, I know. Everything will be alright, now."

As the group entered, Herald left both doors standing open. Pam protested but Bridget convinced her it was alright. She escorted their guests into the great pod, #10, then over to the elaborate tent complex that the Solarians called home. The eyes of the newcomers were scanning every inch, nook, cranny, beam and fixture as they walked. One woman, Katherine, stumbled over the edge of a sidewalk for not paying attention to her own feet.

The place boggled the minds of the visitors. Things like light fixtures, the huge overhead circulation fans, the complex piping for the rain system, all tied together by the sparkling rays of sunlight pouring through the pod roof, not to mention the immensity of the pod itself, overwhelmed the newcomers.

The spiraling streams of angels who had followed the trucks all the way from Colorado Springs, though difficult to see in the present daylight, hovered OUTSIDE above the Solarium, assembling themselves into a kind of freeform canopy. Remarkably, their presence in no way impeded the sunlight that continued to bathe the whole complex.

"Whooaah . . ." Garan uttered. "Yes. Like a great cathedral."

Adrian, who had been so impressed even from the parking lot, looked around in silent awe.

"What do you think, Garan?" Yeshua asked him.

"Beyond anything I could even dream of," Garan answered. "What do all these things do?" he wondered, pointing at the arrays of mechanical equipment, electronics, speakers and sensors.

"How could they build this?" Adrian asked.

"Time, skill, luck," Yeshua answered.

They had arrived at the tents.

"I suppose everyone's hungry?" Bridget asked.

"We have lots of food," Mai Ker said proudly, the understatement of the day.

"We're at your pleasure," Yeshua said. "Something very warm and filling would be wonderful."

Pam, Sing, and Nathaniel had followed along like stray ponies crowding a herd of wild horses. Their eyes remained wide, their minds even wider. Pam pulled Bridget aside by the front of the main tent.

"I don't understand," Pam began.

"Lot of that going around," Bridget chuckled.

"Who are they? Where'd you find them?"

"They kind of found us."

"But where?" Pam demanded. "Everyone's dead."

"Well, yes, you could say that's how they found us. Except him," Bridget said, pointing to Yeshua. "Somehow, he's been alive all along."

"You're—" Pam stammered. "You're confusing me," she moaned. "And you're upsetting me."

"Do you have any cookies made?"

"Now?" said Pam, looking horrified.

"Sure, now. Why not? I'm sure everyone will love some."

Pam was almost stupefied. *How can Bridget be thinking about cookies at a time like this?* Her heart was only now beginning to slow down a little. Her mind searched the kitchen.

"I only have some leftovers from three days ago."

"That's fine. We can eat them for a snack. Get acquainted," Bridget said.

Pam realized she had been breathing a lot faster than normal the last few minutes. She stopped herself, took a long, slow breath, and tried to force a smile. But she was still just as confused.

"I'll warm them up." Her head was shaking meaninglessly as she went toward the kitchen tent.

DESPITE YESHUA asking the newcomers to stay nearby, they were so entranced with the Solarium complex that they began to explore. Pam had given everyone a quick snack of warmed-up casserole and the left-over cookies but food was the least thing of interest at the moment to their visitors.

Adrian and Garan worked their way back to Pods 2 and 3 to get a closer look at all the strange and amazing machinery and equipment they had noticed on the way through from Pod 1.

"Don't touch anything," was the gentle warning Bridget issued when the two young men asked if they could go explore. "Things have a way of going haywire around here almost on their own," she said over-seriously.

Both men nodded, turned, and walked quickly toward the Research Center in Pod 3. Not being able to touch or try to operate anything along the many stacks and consoles of equipment they didn't even recognize was very difficult. They managed to keep their hands off the computers and scientific instruments set up around the building, though they did cheat a bit by opening up several large printed reference volumes in two of the bookcases. The text, in English, was unreadable to them both, although Adrian had spoken an earlier form of English in his first life. The mathematical equations and various illustrations were interesting but communicated nothing to them. It all may as well have been Greek or Chinese.

A very polite and proper man named Jacob, Katherine's father, found Pam needlessly sorting some dry towels in the kitchen.

"Might I introduce you to my daughter?" he asked from the doorway.

Pam had seen Katherine earlier in the dining tent but they had not been introduced. Pam had been busy just trying to keep her mind from running off its rails.

Katherine, though apparently about the same age as Pam, hovered behind her father, unwilling to step into another woman's kitchen uninvited.

Jacob appeared to be the oldest person in the group of visitors, though his actual age wasn't clear. His grizzled, long-bearded face showed genuine surprise as he looked around at the modern conveniences of the Solarians' tent-kitchen. The beard was unable to impede his near-continuous smile. Katherine had a rustic look that spoke more of strength than delicacy. Her collar-length, nearly black hair might have been hand-trimmed with a knife, though its appearance did not concern her in the least. Part of it was tied in a knot at the back of her head.

Pam looked at Jacob, glanced over his shoulder at the woman, and nodded awkwardly.

"This is my daughter Katherine, Pam." His smile became larger than normal.

"It was so nice of you to offer us lunch. The road here was very tiring," Katherine said, stepping through the tent's doorway with a very slight curtsy.

"Oh, of course," Pam said in her most gracious tone.

In fact, she was nearly paralyzed. Bridget had explained to Pam, in whispers at lunch, how all these people had returned from the dead. Pam, a Christian most of her life, should have found this comforting, or at least interesting. Instead, she found it terrifying. Reading in a book about things like people being raised from the dead was one thing. Standing alone with them in the kitchen, she now discovered, was something entirely different.

Pam forced herself to make it appear as if she was breathing normally. She had no idea of any conversation they could carry on that would not make her sound completely foolish.

"So, Bridget said that Yeshua, this man who brought you all here, that he is the one?"

"Which one?" Jacob asked.

"The Messiah. Jesus."

"Is that what you called him?"

Pam tried to nod nonchalantly, uncertain if she had just made her first blunder.

"We called him Jesu," Katherine said, savoring the name as if it were an entire verse of poetry.

"I just—" Pam found the words hard, the admission harder. "I didn't really think that would ever happen. A promise that would never come true. Especially, after what we—" She stopped herself in mid-sentence, her mind revisiting the horrors of what the Solarians had lived through, and the worse horrors they had found OUTSIDE over the last few months. "Please don't repeat this, but for me, anyway, Yeshua has some explaining to do."

"Oh, I would not disagree with you there, madam," Jacob said. "I think we all feel like we need to know more. I held faith in him all my adult life. And toward the end, during the great sickness that swept through our land, I began to feel the doubts. You know, feeling he had simply gone off to Heaven and abandoned us."

Katherine took her father's arm and rubbed his shoulder gently.

"Father, just because I died so suddenly was no reason to give up hope."

He looked at her reassured, now that she could again stand alongside him.

"I know, Katherine. But losing a child is a bitter thing. It took all of my heart to hold onto the Lord when I felt he had robbed me of you."

"You never lost me, Father. I simply prayed for you, like I always did, from somewhere else."

"Well, enough talk of death and sadness. Goodness knows, I've had far too much of that," Pam broke in awkwardly. "Would you like to look around a bit? We could take a walk to our ocean. Such that it is."

"I always wanted to see an ocean," Jacob laughed. "I suppose this will do," he beamed. He offered one arm to Pam and his other to his daughter. "Shall we?"

YESHUA WAS with Bridget while she set some watering timers for the wheat fields near the south wall of the giant Pod 10. Eira had tagged behind them. She had met the other Solarian children but was still painfully shy and felt much better staying close to Yeshua.

"So, are you going to speak with us?" Bridget asked.

"About what?" Yeshua asked, knowing perfectly well.

"You know, what you said earlier, about the kingdom. Who is 'in,' as you put it."

"Oh, we'll get around to that." He watched Bridget work as Eira watched him and his every move, her young eyes studying him as if he were some ancient, extinct bird who had suddenly reappeared.

"Don't know about anyone else, but I'd like to know," Bridget said, working her way on to the next timer box.

"The wheat looks handsome," Yeshua said, avoiding her question. "There is a great deal we will discuss, Bridget. It sounds like you want to do it all in one day."

"I guess having something done, and over, that feels better to me. I've never been one for waiting."

"You are an honest woman, Bridget," Yeshua smiled. "We'll talk later, perhaps."

He offered his hand to Eira.

"Would you like me to show you around the Solarium, Eira?" he asked.

"You'll want me to come and show you things, I guess," Bridget said, finishing her chore.

"That's alright, Bridget. I can find my way."

Eira took his large, strong hand.

"But it's not as simple as it looks," Bridget protested mildly, feeling put aside.

"True. But then the design was in my mind long before it occurred to John Haskins or his friends," Yeshua smiled. "But please do come along."

Bridget followed as Yeshua gave Eira a tour of the several of the pods, revealing details of materials, design, and interconnections that even Bridget had never known.

"Good Lord," Bridget whispered to herself as she listened in awe.

HERALD AND Sing were talking privately in a small storage shed in Pod 13. The Solarium complex was so abuzz with excitement at the appearance of Yeshua and the others that Herald had found no time to explain to Sing what had happened over the last day and a half until now.

Sing listened, trying to absorb details that seemed impossible.

"Out of a cloud?"

"Not just a cloud, Sing. It wasn't like anything you've ever seen. It was awesome, intricate—I can't ever describe it. Moving, and alive. And then they just sort of popped into view."

He left out the part about him passing out.

"And we were all scrambling, trying to protect ourselves. We thought they must be dangerous or something."

Sing listened as he recounted the whole of Thursday afternoon, the overnight, and the trip back this morning.

"But I don't understand who this man is," Sing said as she juggled Kai in her arms. "And such a funny name. What does 'Yeshua' mean, anyway?"

"No idea," Herald said. "Just a name like any other, I guess."

"He doesn't look like any other."

"Right, like you've seen thousands of men to compare?" Herald laughed.

"Well, I've seen enough pictures, and movies. He just—it's how he walks and carries himself. Don't you see it?"

"Yes, of course I do. You're right. He's . . ." Herald considered. ". . . he's unique."

"And why is he here, then?" Sing felt some impending crisis or decision in the air, though she could not begin to account for why she felt that.

"I'm not sure I know," Herald admitted. "I suppose he just wanted to see the place."

Herald could not see through the shed wall to realize that Yeshua, Eira and Bridget were only 100 yards away.

"Do you still love me?" Sing asked suddenly, as if she doubted it.

"What? What a dumb time to ask something like that!"

She frowned, and looked sideways.

"Of course I still love you. I always will. You know that. There's nobody else!"

"Well, from the conversation at lunch, it sounds like there might all of a sudden be a whole lot of nobody elses!" Sing said, perturbed.

Herald hugged her and kissed her.

"There is only one Sing," he reassured her.

NATHANIEL AND Braden were almost bursting with excited questions as they hung around Piper at the playground in Pod 5. She wanted to relax from her travels, but her brothers were not going to let her. Braden looked at her as though she might have just returned from outer space.

Both boys had been careful to keep their distance at lunchtime not only from this stranger Yeshua but from the other newcomers, too.

"How do you know they don't have some kind of OUTSIDE disease or something?" Nathaniel prodded Piper.

She laughed.

"Nate, you don't get it. They're not sick, or diseased. They were *dead.* They can't get sick anymore."

"How do you figure?" he asked.

"Yeah, what makes you so smart about all this, Piper?" Braden asked. "You don't know any more than we do. Well, OK, except you *were* there yesterday."

"Guys, I love you, you're my brothers, but you're acting stupid. Just have to trust me. I know some things. I don't understand them all yet. But I know things that—well, they never fit together until now. And I'm sure Yeshua will explain them for me."

"So, like, we can touch them, and talk to them and things?" Braden asked as if he were talking about imaginary monsters.

"They're not gargoyles, Braden, they're people. Just like you."

"I guess they don't look sick," Nathaniel admitted.

"Come on, I can see I'm not going to get any rest. Let's go find him. If you'll just listen to Yeshua, just a little, you'll see what I mean. He's not a bear."

"More like a tiger, I'd say," Braden said warily.

7

Friday Evening

After a very filling supper prepared by Mai Ker, Sing, Herald and Pam, and eaten outside the tents picnic style, the Solarians and their new guests crowded together into the living room of the main tent, a very cozy fit. Yeshua had said just before supper that he wanted to speak with everyone together.

Pam, still in mild shock, started the meeting by passing around a large tray of warmed-up cookies, some a peanut butter variety and some oatmeal-raisin. Yeshua took three and passed the tray on. He chewed slowly, obviously savoring the warm cookies.

"You're a great cook, Pam," he smiled.

She smiled back. Bridget had told her quietly during supper who he was. Pam was certain Bridget was wrong. He was not anything like she had imagined, especially his modern-looking clothes. But she did notice as they passed the food around, when his long sleeves pulled up slightly, that there was a very deep scar on each of his hands just below the wrist. And she began to wonder.

"I need to talk with you," Yeshua was now saying. His eyes roved over the eight Solarians. Kai was there, in her crib near the back wall, but he never looked toward her.

"These others who have come with us," he continued, "I've had this talk with each of them, long ago. But those of you here"—he gestured around the pods—"who were my chosen in the Solarium, I want to hear from each of you."

The younger children looked at each other, truly worried. They had no clear idea who this was, let alone who all the others were. The kids had no idea what the man was talking about. Although he seemed nice, there was something intimidating, almost irritating, about him. It was not so much his size but the force of his personality.

Piper saw worry in Braden and Nathaniel's faces. She put a hand on Braden's hand where they sat on the floor to one side of Yeshua's folding chair.

"What about, sir?" Piper offered, breaking the tension.

"You all were isolated here. Cut off. You never had a full picture of everything that went on OUTSIDE, as you called it. And you youngsters haven't had a real chance to get to know me. Have you?"

"I'm afraid a lot of that's my fault," Bridget admitted, her words barely audible.

Pam felt like she should chime in on this, but stayed silent. She still felt cautious and afraid.

"I know," he said as if he really did. "But I will give each of you the chance to talk with me privately." He looked around again. "Not just the children."

Bridget had known since yesterday evening that this moment was going to come and that it would come like a bullet. It was a time for choosing. It was a moment, she knew, in which she would choose her future, and also deal with her past.

"Can I say something?" she asked Yeshua.

"I think we mainly need to speak in private, Bridget."

"I know. But I must say something. Now."

"Please," he said with a calm encouragement. It was her choice, not his.

She hesitated. Her mouth went dry, and she felt a tightness in her chest. She forced herself on.

"I just have to be honest with everyone. I was never much of a believer," Bridget said directly to Yeshua. "Not really. I got dragged to church a lot, when I was little, so I knew about you. In some way, I guess, I believed in you. Or, at least, what I thought was good about you." She stopped, more embarrassed than she had ever been, and swallowed slowly. "But I admit, I didn't really believe in—*you.*"

"I know that," Yeshua said with a dispassionate smile that both relieved Bridget and tested her.

"But, well, I did listen. Especially to Jimmy. And I tried. We had lots of time in here, to think, to ponder things. I—I always came up empty-handed."

"Yes, you did," he answered with a tone of irony.

"Lots of long nights, when it was hard to sleep," Bridget continued. "You know? Because of the worry. It was so hard, with all the tragedy, all the death. I—I never really accepted that. I thought no loving God could let things like that happen."

She stared at Yeshua, and she began to choke up. His eyes carefully focused on hers. His made a slight nod, but he said nothing.

"But I did listen," she said. "Like when Jimmy would read from his Bible, and we'd all talk." She smiled toward Pam. "I used to think Pam was a little nuts. Now she thinks I am." She laughed, but Pam didn't. "Anyway, I believe now."

"Do you mean it's easier now?" he asked.

"No, I don't mean that. It's not because you're here. I don't think. But something's just—changed. In me." She dropped her eyes to the floor of the tent, unable to keep looking straight at him. "When we met on the mountain yesterday. Something changed."

"Many have met me without ever having seen me," Yeshua told her.

"Truly blessed," Thomas interjected.

Everyone else was listening intently, but no one else dared interrupt. It was like a private conversation in public.

"Yes, I saw that yesterday," Yeshua said. "Something did change in you there on the mountain. Before you knew who I was."

"Yes."

"What changed, Bridget?"

She wept quietly.

"All I've felt is loss for so long. Clayton. The others . . ."

"Your daughter," Yeshua said quietly, watching her.

Bridget's heart quivered at the mention of the child she had as a teen, and had to give up for adoption. She looked down again for a long moment, but took a forced breath and went on.

"And then, with all that happened to us here, suddenly I had to lead everyone. It was just too much. I've been exhausted. I just wanted a rest, frankly. I think I would have been happy to die."

"And I wouldn't let you," he said. "Yes, you deserved a rest, Bridget."

"But there's never been any rest here. It's been a damned nightmare."

"Not damned," Yeshua told her.

She took this in, confused, but after a few moments understood his meaning.

"Well," she looked around, "except for the kids. They were the blessing." Her eyes filled again with tears, but she didn't cry.

Yeshua smiled at her. She had finally looked up again. He waited.

"I don't know how," she went on, "but when I saw you yesterday—something in me said, *Here is your rest.* That make sense?"

"Yes it does," he said with a deep, comforting tone.

Herald couldn't hold back.

"Why has it been so hard?" he asked. "Why so much suffering all those years? Why did all those people—the ones OUTSIDE, I mean—why did they have to die?"

"Like these you mean?" Yeshua answered, looking around at the newcomers.

This stumped Herald completely, but he floundered on.

"And the others," he said. "All the others. You know."

"Yes, I do know. I know very well. *I know them all.* Even those who have never known me. And yes, I know what they went through."

He paused, waiting for Herald to reply. Herald stared at the tent wall, in over his head again, and remained quiet.

"You have many such questions," Yeshua said to everyone. "Many. And every question has an answer. But it takes time. Even now, it takes time."

"How long?" Sing asked. She always wanted answers to everything, and now.

"A long time. But time is different now."

"Haven't we waited an awfully long time?" she pressed him, with no idea she was repeating almost exactly what Yeshua had said on the mountain yesterday.

"What do you mean?" Pam asked.

Yeshua was obviously tired of sitting. He seemed always needing to be active. He stood, taking the last half of his third cookie, and walked around among them, casually but not aimlessly.

"Death is taken away. So time will run differently now," he said.

"You mean, like the clock will move slower?" Herald speculated.

"You don't need clocks," Yeshua answered. "They

were a crutch, for a broken sense of time. It was one consequence of breaking fellowship with the Father. Men began to measure time into pieces. Not just days, but hours, minutes. Seconds, milliseconds. As though it mattered. But that was false, putting a pretended bandage over an open wound. When the wound is removed—when it's healed—there's no need for the bandage, even an artificial one."

Herald was completely lost.

"You mean, time won't move at all?"

"It is not time that moves, Herald, it's you. Events and moments will pass, but you won't need to count the minutes of those moments. There is now no end. So there is no need to measure out moments before the end." He paused, letting them think, then again interrupted the train of their thoughts. "Clock-watching was nothing but a preparation for death. And death is gone."

The Solarians and several of their guests sat trying to absorb this. It escaped most. Not surprisingly, it was Piper who finally had an insight.

"Eternal life," she said.

"Yes, Piper. Eternity. Few ever understood. Eternity is not the absence of time, but the absence of worry. No death, no sickness, no worries." He gave them what appeared an almost clown-like grin.

"So, since we aren't moving toward death anymore," Piper said, "we're—well, free from time. For the first time."

"Very free, indeed," Yeshua said, losing the grin.

Mai Ker listened intently. Her eyes began to sparkle in a way they hadn't for a long time. But her mind resisted the emotion she felt.

"So, in eternity, there will be no moments of time?" Mai Ker asked.

"The other way around," Yeshua said. "In eternity, every moment is this moment."

Mai Ker stared at Yeshua, still harboring her faint but diminishing worry. "And, you're serious. We are not going to die?"

"I mean that exactly. Anyway," he said gesturing to his older friends, "most already have."

Garan and Adrian gave each other a nod.

"And, Lord, it was not much fun, if you must know," Garan said.

"No," Yeshua said. "I remember it."

"But everyone dies," Mai Ker objected.

"Until now." Yeshua's eyes bore down on her from several feet away.

Mai Ker spoke as if only to herself. "I won't die. Ever. Really?"

"Depends on what you mean by death," Yeshua said.

"I mean dying."

"There are different kinds of dying, Mai Ker."

"What do you mean? These are more riddles."

"No, these are simple truths. If you do not choose life, the life only I give, your body will live on, but your spirit will die. That is the most terrible kind of dying."

Mai Ker pondered this. What Jimmy had talked about so many times was washing around in her mind, but in her heart there was still an embedded resistance. The momentary sense of joy she had just felt, at the thought of not dying, melted into a formless anxiety of what might come next. "New life, resurrection," she remembered Jimmy saying over and over. But it was all merely fables, she had thought. Happy myths to make life tolerable.

Still, standing not 10 feet from her was the One who had claimed to *be* the resurrection, the very source of life. She had stubbornly challenged everything Jimmy had told her. Now she just as stubbornly dug for the truth.

"So, if we don't die, we won't be resurrected. Like them?" She gestured at their guests who sat watching Mai Ker, confounded by the boldness of her questions. "Is that what you mean?" she pressed Yeshua.

He did not directly answer her.

"You few, you who were my chosen here, will not have to surrender your bodies in the way they did. You are spared this."

"'But we shall all be changed,'" Piper said, quoting one of Jimmy's favorite part of scripture. The words flooded back to her. A look of unbridled joy broke across her face. "That's it. I see it!"

"I believe you do," Yeshua smiled. "You are a brave child," he told her. "You always believed. Even when your trust was weak."

Sing was listening as intently as everyone else but was shaking her head weakly.

"Can't you just explain it simply?" Sing asked. She couldn't stand this waiting.

"Simply? Yes, I can," Yeshua told her, "if you will understand it simply. Everyone who lived was under the curse of death, the loss of the body. Death was an essential medicine, to heal the corruption brought on by sin. When wickedness entered the world—my world—I could not let you live forever like that. Broken, corrupt, sick at heart, wretched. Death was part of the cure. But that age has come to its end. Judgment has arrived, the final winnowing of the weeds from the wheat, the wheat from the chaff." He looked at each of the Solarians. A look of subtle accusation greeted him from Mai Ker and Bridget's eyes. "Don't accuse me. You know this perfectly well, from your science. What you plant grows and bears fruit. But there is always the chaff, the stalks, given to the fire."

He saw changed expressions as their faces were softened by his stern truth.

"Perhaps you will understand this, perhaps not," he said. "You did die. You died a more horrid, a more profound death than anyone OUTSIDE, those who lost only their bodies, and that only for a time. They suffered a few moments at the gate of death. Your suffering bore on for years." He seemed to gather his thoughts and rein in some passionate feeling. "Because in here, you—especially the elders, you three who first came here—you had to watch. Angels of a very different kind, but messengers nonetheless. That, dear ones, was a much more painful kind of death." He gave them an incisive look. "You could have ended everything in here—whenever you chose. You knew the means, didn't you?" Mai Ker, Bridget and Pam were unconsciously nodding. "But you chose to persevere. You chose to have children. You chose life."

The silence in the tent that followed these words was amplified, imperious. For just an instant, the newcomers who had died and been reborn experienced, in their heart-of-hearts, the deep anguish that their brothers and sisters here in the Solarium had been forced to live through.

No one dared speak. There was hushed weeping from several of the newcomers. The depth of the sacrifice their Lord had made; the depth of the sacrifice those of the Solarium had made. It burned an impression in every heart, deep, permanent, like the scars still visible on Yeshua's hands.

All felt it would be sacrilegious to break this silence.

"Yes," Yeshua said after nearly a full minute. "You had to witness what happened, the final struggle out there, all the time struggling for your own lives. Double pain. Triple pain, for you three mothers. You dared to bear the children, to bring them in, to give them life. When there seemed no right reason, except the purest love. That was the most courageous of all your acts."

Still, silence.

"You felt weak, failing, But together, you became strong, like granite." He finally walked back to his folding chair and sat. He folded his arms across his chest and let out a deep sigh, as if releasing some pain of his own which he had carried for an age. "In time, it will begin to feel different, it will begin to make sense. Don't try to force it, right now. Let it alone. Every memory will heal."

Mai Ker alone remained bold.

"Not all."

Yeshua looked at her with piercing eyes and spoke with firmness.

"All."

Pam's courage welled up.

"But why?" she asked him. "Why all the death?"

"Because it was my choice. Sin was raging, further and further out of control. You were my stewards of this world. Always, from the beginning. As corruption grew, you narrowed my choices. Evil had to be dealt its final blow, its own death. Yes, I could have let the old epoch roll on indefinitely. I could have let the misery extend, and deepen, and rot. I could have left death loose for centuries to come. But I didn't. I chose."

"But you made us suffer," Pam said.

"It was needed, Pam. And what you witnessed, you will see it as I did, in time."

Pam was doubtful, but held her tongue.

There was silence again for several minutes. The only sounds were quiet rustling as several adjusted themselves on chairs, benches, or on the tent floor. There was so much to absorb. After a time, Yeshua spoke.

"Mai Ker, you look sad."

"Confused," she corrected.

"That, too."

"We lost so much. And you're right," she said, looking just as incisively back at him, "it was a kind of death in here. I know, now. Witnessing death is worse than dying." Her lips trembled. "We lost so much," she repeated in a harrowed, ragged voice.

Yeshua's lips did not tremble, but his eyes became wet.

"But do you want to live, Mai Ker?"

She couldn't speak. It was as if her whole personality in that moment drew inside her, taking fear and hope and love and all her future with it. She was in hiding, like a little child who has lost a parent and felt the world crashing in, and everything about to end. But that frightened little child nodded. Yes. She wanted to live. She wanted what was real, more real than this half-life of broken promises and failed dreams. She nodded again.

Yeshua stood and walked over to her. He took her left hand and raised her to her feet. She didn't cower. In fact, she straightened herself so that she seemed taller than she was.

"I think we desperately need a break, don't you?" he asked her.

Mai Ker nodded.

"Would you do something for me, then?" he asked her.

She nodded again, still mute.

"Would you go over to the house in Pod 4? I've set something there on the porch that I'd like you to get."

She frowned slightly and looked deflated. She shrank to normal size again. She had hoped he was about to give her some great challenge, some great task. Still, she nodded.

"Go ahead," he told her. "We'll wait." He went back and sat.

Mai Ker looked at the others. Without saying a word she walked out of the tent. Yeshua looked around with a peculiar expression.

"Any more cookies, Pam?"

IT WAS fairly dark in Pod 4. They had kept the lights off in the unused pods for years to save energy. Glints and shadows from the overhead lights in #10 carried through the plastic roofs and shed just enough light into #4 so that she could safely walk.

She came near the porch and was startled. In the shadows, the porch swing moved slightly.

Can't be a breeze, she thought.

The swing moved again. A figure was there. A voice quietly broke the silence, causing her to shake from head to foot.

"You know, I've missed you, Mai."

Jimmy stood from the swing. He walked down the steps. The tears Mai Ker had held back a few minutes ago in the tent burst out like a raincloud ruptured by lightning. She stared in disbelief. Yeshua's one word rang like a bell.

"All . . ."

She fell against Jimmy's chest and wept uncontrollably.

Jimmy gave her a few moments before he spoke. He held her shaking body as she gasped in air between loud sobs.

"This is very strange," he said playfully. "Some reunion. I thought you'd be *happy* to see me."

"Jimmy," she said, delight breaking through the tears. "Jimmy!"

He helped hush the tears from each eye with a kiss, then brushed his finger over her cheeks.

"I could not believe it," she said. "It has all been too much. I'm sorry. I could not . . ." She broke off, weeping, an implored forgiveness behind her wet eyes. "But you believed it," she said, kissing him. "You were the strong one."

"No, you know better. You knew my doubts. And since I've been gone, I bet you've been pretty strong, these last months."

BACK IN the tent the Solarians and their guests still sat, low voices carrying on private conversations. Mai Ker had been gone almost fifteen minutes.

"Shouldn't we go on?" Pam asked.

"Is there a hurry?" Yeshua said.

"Sorry. Old habit."

"Maybe we should go look for Mai Ker," Bridget said. She, too, felt impatient and awkward just sitting. "She's been gone a long time. Not sure she's in good shape right now."

Yeshua nodded but said, "She's better, now."

"What did you send her to get?" Bridget asked.

"Her heart."

This set Pam's mind wandering, and the others, too. Then an approaching voice, actually a half-chaotic laugh, caught Sing's ear. It was not far from the tent. Sing's heart did a little hiccup. She jumped up and ran out, almost tripping over Braden's cast. Nathaniel heard it too, but sat frozen, confused, and suddenly afraid. A split-second passed and he heard Sing cry out with joy and disbelief, "Daddy!"

More chaotic laughter, and loud sobbing erupted.

"Daddy?" Bridget repeated in stunned amazement.

Yeshua was smiling like the cat who swallowed the canary. This canary was named Death.

"I love surprises. Don't you?" he laughed.

Jimmy, Mai Ker and Sing, strung together like beads, came through the wide tent door. Their guests had no idea who this was but all the Solarians raced to them and piled around, latching onto whatever part of Jimmy they could catch and hold tight, as if he might vaporize into mist. Sing ran to the crib and brought baby Kai to him. Jimmy pulled one arm free, with great effort, and cradled Kai into one of the happiest hugs of his life. Now he was weeping loudly, too, filled with joy.

Sobs gave way to laughter. Kisses erased tears. Pam and Bridget joined in the fracas of outpoured love, cuddling the man who had been a husband to them, too.

This moment that none had expected overcame the Solarians with near-ecstasy. Even the newcomers were caught up in the momentary rapture. They laughed and smiled and chattered at each other, with no clue who this new man was, but as certain as the Solarians that he was the object of great love.

"Must be someone important," Adrian told Garan.

"Their father, maybe?" Garan replied, reading the jubilant expressions on the children's faces.

Yeshua remained quietly in his chair, unwilling to break in or restrain the explosion of joy at Jimmy's return and such a delightful reunion. As under a flash of lightning, the many broken hearts and torn relationships were being repaired by the true Father's love.

Finally, as the emotions of the Solarians began to calm, Yeshua called with solemnity to the new arrival.

"Welcome home, Jimmy."

"Who—?" Jimmy caught himself and looked. "It *is* you," he laughed as if he had known this man all his life, though he had met him face-to-face just a little over seven months ago. "I wasn't sure Mai wasn't kidding!" Jimmy realized it might be better to shut up just now but he couldn't hold his feelings in. "Well, anyway, thank you!" he called to Yeshua over the excited chatter of his children and wives. He shook his regenerated head in believing-disbelief, touching his own arms to be absolutely certain this was not some kind of magnificent dream. "You're really something," he smiled at his Lord.

Yeshua smiled back, enjoying their joyous moment with them, one more simple outworking of his plan.

"Well," he said just loud enough for everyone to hear, "we have a lot to talk about still, but this calls for a celebration! Pam, if you'll help me, I'd like to make a special cake."

She looked at him, thinking he must be a little crazy.

"I didn't think they had cakes back then. Well, like ours, I mean."

"No," he said, "but I've kept up."

8

Saturday Morning

The celebration of Jimmy's resurrection carried on late into the night. The visitors with Yeshua joined in the celebration as if they had lived their whole life in the Solarium. One thing they had missed most in all their time of waiting, Adrian said, was a grand party like this.

The Solarians awoke this morning to more incredible and fast moving changes. At first, Bridget suspected it was the aftereffects of the homemade wine they celebrated with last evening. But as her head cleared, she realized that what was happening was outside herself, not in her head.

What had appeared as subtle physical changes around them in the previous two days, changes that had started in slow motion, had begun to accelerate into rapid fire. It was as if someone setting off the first rocket of a fireworks display accidentally touched the fuse of every rocket at once. The world OUTSIDE was exploding with new magnificence. Bridget wished she could write down an account of everything she was seeing but she realized that the fantastic details of what was changing so quickly could not be fully chronicled because things were simply happening too fast to keep up.

The most spectacular thing, as she and the others were discovering was that changes didn't just happen, they *continued*. Each morning something new would appear, or something old and lost would be restored, but in greater fullness and perfection than had ever been known before.

This morning, the sunlight pouring in from OUTSIDE was the most noticeable difference. In part, its greater brilliance was because the light purplish hue of the sky had fully dissolved the last couple of days and now had completely disappeared. The sky was so clear that it was almost colorless, except for occasional hints of blue and turquoise. The sunlight had subtly shifted over the last two days. Bridget could not describe, even to herself. It seemed more pure. What she could not see was that this sun was nearing its end and would die not in an explosive supernova but in a quiet transformation that she and the other Solarians would never see.

Until this morning, the light had seemed softer, more warm and welcoming. Today the intensity had changed again. She found herself squinting when she looked straight up through the pods. It wasn't that the light hurt her eyes. In fact, it was as if her eyes had been made to look at this light. But it held a quality of hiding something greater within itself, or behind itself, a secret of the heavenly realms that no human eye had ever seen, or ever could see for that matter.

As she looked up, Bridget felt the weight of that hidden mystery bearing down upon her, but it brought pleasure, not pain or even discomfort. The only word that came to her mind was "glory," though what it meant, she wasn't sure.

She was standing near the door of her bedroom tent, sipping warm coffee. Apart from the quality of the sunlight, what caught her attention most quickly was the rich green color that was spreading across the burnt-out prairie around the Solarium. Things were growing, and quickly. But the green she saw was not a green she knew. It's very hue said "alive." She was anxious to get out and explore, to see what new flora was growing because from this distance it certainly didn't look like anything she recognized.

Mai Ker came over from her own tent. She had just awakened.

"What are you looking at, Bridget?"

"Look OUTSIDE."

"Not sure my eyes can focus that far yet," Mai Ker said dreamily. She rubbed her eyes and tried.

Bridget realized Mai had just spent her first night again with Jimmy. She didn't want to ask but really couldn't help herself.

"What's it like? Having him back?"

"Jimmy?"

"How many men slept in your tent last night?"

Mai Ker laughed.

"Wonderful."

"Thought he'd be up by now."

"No. Still sleeping."

"Would've thought he'd had enough rest by now," Bridget laughed. She looked at Mai Ker. "So, is it like before?"

Mai Ker had to think about this. She was rubbing sleep from her eyes.

"I cannot describe it," Mai Ker said, pursing her lips, a kind of uncertainty in her expression.

"Can't, or would rather not?"

"I cannot. I mean— Alright, this is hard to explain. I was certain I would never see him again, after that awful day. Having him suddenly here—back—it is very strange. But what was most strange was that I did not even think about making love. Never felt any urge."

"Can't imagine that," Bridget frowned.

"Something is different."

"About him?"

"Yes. But me, too."

"Different how?"

"As I said, I do not know. It is like—" She hesitated. "—it is like there is a different kind of love now. Not less, more. Does that make sense?"

Bridget shook her head that it didn't.

Mai Ker considered for a moment. "What I feel toward him is deeper. It does not need sex to express it." She stared at Bridget who was still frowning but trying to understand. "You see?"

"Not really." Bridget thought. "I mean, if Clayton had come back, I bet it's the first thing we'd want."

"Really? Do you think that?"

Bridget reflected for several moments.

"Maybe not," she admitted. Her mind drifted.

Mai Ker looked OUTSIDE finally, pulling her dangling hair back from her face and stretching her back, trying to focus on the distance. But her mind was still INSIDE. Her eyes shifted to Bridget. "Will he?"

"Willy? Atchison?"

"No, will *he?* Will Clayton come back?"

So far, since Jimmy's appearance last night, Bridget had managed to keep this obvious, oppressing question buried deep beneath her consciousness. Under the question in Mai Ker's eyes, it leaped to the surface. Bridget felt a wrenching in her gut as if the breath was suddenly knocked out of her.

"I don't know," she said, feeling both mental and physical pains.

The question was too difficult to even consider. Bridget's mind slowed, looking for a way to bury it again. But she failed.

What would that depend on? Bridget began to wonder. *Jimmy, yes, there was no question. A believer, a very faithful believer. But Clayton?* she fretted silently.

"I don't know," she found herself saying out loud, more quietly. Her whole being recoiled as if she had touched a hot stove. She didn't know the answer.

Mai Ker watched her, seeing what was happening.

"Can you ask?"

"Ask?" Bridget said, returning to earth.

"Yeshua."

Bridget thought, and shook her head. "I'd be afraid."

"Of what?"

Bridget pulled her eyes away from Mai Ker's and stared OUTSIDE again. "The answer."

Mai Ker realized she should let it drop. The joy in her heart over Jimmy made the sadness in her heart for Bridget cut even deeper. Time to change the subject.

Following Bridget's eyes, she looked out through the pod wall, more focused this time. She saw the same strange, new green that Bridget had noticed.

"Pretty. What is that strange color?" Mai Ker asked.

"I was thinking you could tell me."

Mai Ker laughed.

"I am afraid I am a neophyte in this new world, too," she smiled, glad the conversation had shifted away from Clayton Block.

She looked into the distance. Spreading out in wide patches across the blackened earth that had been ravaged by last November's wildfire she saw large swaths of germinating grass and the stems of bushes. Here and there what appeared to be sapling trees were also starting to shoot up.

Then Mai Ker noticed something else. Not only was the quality of the sunlight different this morning, but the sun looked even further south toward the horizon than yesterday. How this could be, she couldn't fathom. But the grid-like beams of the pod roof made easy reference points, like latitudinal and longitudinal lines on a globe.

When she first noticed the change in the sun's position yesterday morning she guessed it was a trick of her imagination. But she also noted its position when they arrived back at the Solarium yesterday afternoon, mentally marking the sun's arc relative to certain pod beams as she stood in Pod 10. The arc of the sun yesterday had been tracking just below the second beam down from the crest of the dome. This morning, though, at the opposite end of the pod, the sun was rising along an arc that would peak somewhere below the third beam by afternoon. Mai Ker could think of no explanation except that the Earth's axis was shifting in relation to the position of the sun.

"How can that be?" she said to herself aloud.

Bridget's mind was still elsewhere. She looked quizzically at Mai Ker.

"What?"

"The sun's arc. Look. It has moved south again."

"I noticed the light seemed different today."

"No, not the light. The sun has changed position. It always changed a tiny bit each day, but not this fast!"

"Position?" Bridget was still at a loss.

"Yes, above the equator. It has shifted really far just since yesterday. It appears to be migrating south toward the equator," Mai Ker said.

"One more change, I guess."

"An impossible one," Mai Ker replied. She re-examined the sun relative to the beams. "Incredible."

"I think we may need to redefine 'impossible,' Mai Ker," Bridget said as she finished her coffee, "and maybe 'incredible,' too."

Bridget looked OUTSIDE closer by, at the prairie that lay just beyond the pod wall. The livelier green was spreading there, also. Then, as her vision came home, she finally noticed that what was happening OUTSIDE was also happening INSIDE. She glanced around the big pod. The crops in here looked more alive than ever before. Several corn stalks seemed to be straining effortlessly toward the pod roof as if lifted by an invisible hand. A field of soybeans looked like a regiment of stiff-backed soldiers, not a bunch of downtrodden hobos. New life was pouring in all around them, unseen, but with very visible results.

WHILE THEY had gotten ready for the party last evening, Pam's curiosity about Yeshua had grown exponentially. Baking a cake alongside one who claimed to be the Son of God was, it seemed to Pam, beyond bizarre. Baking a simple cake with the man who claimed to be the universal savior? *Unbelievable,* was her main reaction. *Shouldn't he be doing something more important?* she kept asking herself while trying not to slop cake batter on her last clean pair of slacks.

Then she had considered the fact that Jimmy, whom she had last seen lying dead in the dirt of Pod 10, was walking around in the tents, playing with his children, still getting hugs by the minute, and cuddling his grandchild whom he had never seen. *What would be more important,* Pam finally understood, *than celebrating that?*

She had also been preoccupied with the presence of their visitors. If Yeshua was not whom he claimed, how could she explain where all these others people came from? They kept laughing and joking with each other, celebrating the fact that they had been "reborn," as they put it.

For poor Pam, though, the more outlandish thing was that Yeshua offered to help her do the dishes after breakfast this morning. They stood by the sink together, him washing, her drying.

"Something is bothering you," he said, scrubbing a pan that had held scrambled eggs.

"It's just, trying to adjust to you being here. And who are all these other people? We were sure everyone was dead."

"Yes, they were."

"You mean, like Jimmy?"

"Dead from the flesh but alive in the spirit."

"I thought that was a just figure of speech."

"It's that, too."

"Do you always talk like this?"

"Like what?"

"Like cryptically, in riddles. Kind of like you're teasing us? Makes me feel stupid."

"Since I am who I am, I suppose it's unavoidable." He set the pan carefully on the counter for Pam to dry. "You're not stupid, Pam. You're just—what is the figure of speech?—just not up to speed yet."

Pam laughed.

"That would be the right figure of speech." She grinned at him. "But how in the world could I ever catch up to your speed?" She wiped the pan dry and placed it on its shelf. Her mind shifted. "What did my daughter mean last night?"

"Piper?"

"Yes."

"Which part?" Yeshua asked playfully.

"That phrase. 'We shall all be changed.'"

"You've read it, Pam. More than once."

"Read what?"

"The Bible."

"Yes, but not all of it," she admitted with an embarrassed look.

"But think, you might remember that phrase."

Pam looked sheepish.

"No, sorry, I don't remember that one."

"Well, not surprising. There was a lot to remember in all those books, huh?"

Pam let out a little chuckle as if to say, "Well, yeah."

"Piper was quoting Paul," Yeshua said. "About the resurrection, and those who would still be alive at that time."

"Those who hadn't died, you mean?"

"Yes."

The light clicked on in Pam's head.

"Us?"

"Yes." He recited Paul's words. "'I tell you a mystery. We shall not all sleep, but we shall all be changed, in a moment, in the twinkling of an eye, at the last trumpet,'" Yeshua said with a sound of triumph.

Pam stacked several plates into their proper cupboard. "Meaning?"

"Meaning that you will be changed, of course."

"I think my eye has twinkled a lot since yesterday," she said uncertainly.

"Paul meant, 'when it happens.' He didn't mention how soon it might, did he?"

"No," Pam shook her head, agreeing.

"People were always in such a hurry. Not everything happens in haste, Pam. That is a modern way, not my way."

Pam took off her apron and hung it over a stool, then picked up her cup of nearly cold coffee and sipped. Yeshua wiped down the breakfast table with his dishrag, tossed it into the sink like a short basketball shot, then sat at the now empty table.

Pam cautiously joined him after refilling her coffee.

"So these others, the ones who came with you. Who are they? Why them first?" Pam asked.

"The first-fruits of the resurrection. But many more will still come."

"When?"

"Soon enough."

"Like Jimmy?"

"Yes, but not all at once. Over days and weeks, at least as we *used* to count weeks."

"You said time would be different."

"I did." He smiled at her childlike questions. "Good breakfast, Pam." He was on his feet. "I'm going to find Jimmy."

Pam didn't dare ask why.

ABOUT AN hour later, Mai Ker also went looking for Jimmy and found him, after a short search, deep in conversation with Yeshua near the corral in Pod 9 where Jimmy was feeding the horses. She joined them and sat on an old, upside-down plastic crate near the corral fence. The men's voices fell off to a hush as she came near.

"What are you talking about?" she asked. "Am I bothering you?" She could tell she had.

Jimmy just smiled. "I'll tell you later," he said.

"I have a question," she said.

Yeshua and Jimmy looked at her and waited.

"The Earth is shifting."

"That's not a question," Jimmy kidded in his usual manner.

"No. But why?" she asked, looking at Yeshua. "The sun position is moving toward the equator. A lot, just since yesterday. How can that be?"

"That is a question," Yeshua said. "The answer is, I am making changes. Improvements."

"But how?" she pressed. "To change the position of the sun, that could not be done." Her expression revealed her disbelief. "To do that, you would have to shift the whole Earth—reset its axis. That's impossible."

"Is it?" Yeshua asked benignly. "If you watch, you'll find the planet is righting itself."

"So the axis *is* shifting."

"The tilt of the axis is changing, Mai Ker. It's becoming more true. When sin erupted ages ago, it affected everything, not just humanity. It affected the planet, and the entire universe."

"You are not serious."

Jimmy listened, afraid to get in the middle of this.

Yeshua's bizarre explanation for the change of a scientific fact that Mai Ker had always taken for granted completely upended her.

"You are serious," she said.

"I am serious, yes. Why does this surprise you?"

"Why does—?" She could not choke out the question. "You're claiming bad behavior knocked the Earth's axis off kilter? That it is used to be different at the beginning?"

"Yes. But I said sin, not bad behavior."

Now it was Mai Ker who was silent, waiting.

"Sin was rebellion, Mai Ker. Rebellion ruined many things."

He waited, she watched him. She was not about to tackle this one.

"You see," he went on, "sin was not just wrong behavior, it was a disease of the human spirit. It bore in deep, like a cancer. It tainted the world around them as much as it injured them. Do you see?"

Mai Ker was frustrated.

"Can we just please talk about the sun?"

"That is what I am doing."

"How could human behavior affect the physical world?" Mai Ker asked.

"The physical world is, always was, an expression on the spiritual realities behind it. Corruption within created corruption without." He could tell neither Mai Ker nor Jimmy understood. "It's hard to grasp at first. Give it time. You'll come to understand." He made a cordial smile.

"Hard to understand?" Jimmy pleaded. "Yeah. More than a little."

"Moral rebellion cut deeply, Jimmy. It bore like a serpent into nature itself, embedded itself in the Earth. The Earth had been created in a perfect axial relation to the sun. When it shifted out of perpendicular, catastrophic changes followed."

"Like what?" Jimmy asked bluntly.

"Jimmy, you are a scientist, how can you not see this? Once you throw the surfaces of the Earth into constantly changing positions relative to the sun's intensity, expose different areas to more or less sunlight on a given day, chaotic weather results. The violent storms you so often had, and what you called seasons. It created an unstable atmosphere."

"Alright, I understand that much," Jimmy said.

"Constant weather havoc is not what the Father designed, weather that was raw and unpredictable. Radical temperature changes. Intense heat, then subzero cold. Torrential rains, then droughts." He looked at them. "You didn't think we *created* it that way, did you?"

Mai Ker, in fact, had thought that. So had Jimmy. What had always been seemed normal since they had nothing with which to compare it.

"Well, yeah, I guess we did think that," Jimmy said, looking at Mai Ker for confirmation. "That was nature, you know?"

"No, it was ill-nature."

"And now you are changing back?" Mai Ker asked, suspicious that maybe this was some not-very-clever attempt at a practical joke.

"It must change back for the world to settle. When it has returned to its original design, order will be restored."

This he said so matter-of-factly that Mai Ker could see from his expression it was no joke.

"No more bad storms?" Mai Ker asked.

"No. Some nice, peaceful rainstorms."

"Wait," Jimmy said as it dawned on him. "No more seasons?"

"Once the axis regains its right position and the sun is stable above the equator, there will be little climate change in a given place. Only the warming and cooling of day and night. If you want a change of seasons, you'll have to travel."

Jimmy looked sad. "Warm summer nights? Snowy, wintery days?"

"Here, there will be plenty of warm nights," Yeshua laughed. "And if you go far enough north, you'll still be able to find snow. Or climb a tall mountain in a few months." He laughed again. "People are so hard to please."

Neither dared reply to this.

"You said the axis-thing, it happened because of sin," Jimmy said, changing the subject back.

"Yes. Rebellion against the Father."

"So, that would mean—" Jimmy frowned at the unexpected truth, "—there will be no more sin."

"Just so." Yeshua said it as if placing a seal on an envelope. "I thought you already knew that, from when we talked before."

"I know, but it's hard to believe," Jimmy said. "I mean, I can't believe somebody won't come along and mess it up." He faked an embarrassed chuckle.

"Have you seen any sin, Jimmy, in my presence?" Yeshua waited.

"Wait, I've only been back a few hours. I'm not a good judge."

"As good as any. Mai Ker?"

She thought. Her face turned into that of a little child looking for an excuse for being caught outside after dark.

She thought some more. What had anyone done in the last 24 hours, the last 48? Everyone was so preoccupied with Yeshua. He seemed always the focus. She thought even harder. Nothing came. She looked disconcertedly at Jimmy.

"He is right, Jimmy. Nothing," she said.

Jimmy tried to make sense of this newest revelation.

"So," he said, "everyone—everywhere—is forgiven? Completely forgiven?"

"I did not say that," Yeshua answered. "I said there would be no more sin. I did not speak about what must still take place for some, to deal with their past."

Mai Ker wasn't sure what this meant, since to her the whole idea of sin was only a vague notion of moderate wrongdoing. Jimmy, however, got nervous again because just minutes before Mai Ker arrived, he and Yeshua had been talking about the fact that Jimmy had taken three wives.

He kept quiet, Mai Ker didn't.

"What do you mean, about the past?" she asked Yeshua.

"Wrongdoing came with a price. It is time for that cost to be tallied."

His simple statement made them both fidget.

"As we were just saying," Yeshua said, looking at Jimmy who was suddenly busy again with oats and feeding bags.

Mai Ker looked at Jimmy. "What about?"

Jimmy moved and hung a feedbag on one of the horses in the corral. A young mare nearby whinnied, playfully stomping a front hoof, wishing someone would saddle her and take her for a ride.

"We were talking about Bridget, and Pam," Jimmy said sullenly, staring down at the bits of gravel ground into the bed of the corral.

"Oh." Mai Ker looked startled, but then confused. "Oh . . ." In a kind of defensive stance, she looked at Yeshua. "What about them?"

"Why I married them," Jimmy answered before Yeshua could. "After you and I were married."

"Explain what you told me, Jimmy," Yeshua said, relaxing against a corral rail.

"I told him I did it, you know, reluctantly. But we were desperate. Everyone was dying, and we had to somehow have more babies." He looked at Yeshua. "And that was wrong, wasn't it?"

"More babies? No. But taking more wives, you knew it was wrong, or you wouldn't have resisted it so firmly." Yeshua gave them a moment for this to sink in. Mai Ker remembered Jimmy's reaction when she and Bridget and Pam first thought up the idea. "But then, I've allowed a lot of people to do a lot of things that were wrong. And look at the wonderful children that came forth."

"Yeah," Jimmy said, "explain that to me."

"About children, Jimmy?" Yeshua said with half a grin.

"No, explain why you allowed people to commit so much wrongdoing."

"Well, that one I can answer very simply. I wanted love more than obedience."

This stopped Jimmy in his mental tracks.

"Obedience never creates love. But genuine love always leads to obedience," Yeshua said.

"Please stop a minute," Mai Ker butted in, since she had missed the earlier conversation between these two. "You are saying what we did was wrong? For Jimmy to marry the others?"

"I am saying exactly that, Mai Ker. But to teach you love, sometimes I had to allow wrongs like that. It was often through the hurts that you learned of healing."

Mai Ker was not at all sure she wanted to hear this but she couldn't walk away, either.

Yeshua had been listening to the pleas of the corralled mare. He walked toward the gate where a bridle, saddle and blanket sat perched. Lifting them easily with one arm, he opened the corral and strode in.

"Enough for now," he said.

Jimmy and Mai Ker weren't sure if this was directed at them or the horse. They watched Yeshua approach the young mare, Ginny, who was more surprised than they were. Both knew Ginny was very rowdy whenever she was ridden.

This should be good, thought Mai Ker.

9

Saturday, Late Morning

"I want you both to understand," Yeshua was saying as finished securing the bridle and threw the blanket across Ginny's back, "but I don't want you to worry about any of this. We are beyond that."

He lifted the saddle over the animal and worked on the cinch. "Yes, I allowed all those things because I knew that eventually the time of healing would come. And it has, this day of resurrection."

"Like the tilted axis of the Earth, the tilted axis of humanity will now be straightened, each bent and broken soul will be righted." He looked at Jimmy and Mai Ker who stood like scarecrows stuffed with straw.

"You two coming, or are you just going to stand there looking defeated?" he laughed.

Mai Ker and Jimmy looked at each other, hurried to the barn for tack, and in under three minutes had their own mounts ready.

Yeshua led them out of the corral and on an easy, plodding ride through the adjacent pods. The other Solarians and newcomers watched, some with confused expressions, others with grins. Everyone kept their distance from the three horses. Yeshua sat atop a very calm Ginny as if she had known the touch of his hands and knees for years. He brushed the mare's neck firmly.

"Your marriages, Jimmy, to Pam and Bridget," he was saying as they rode the walks around the ocean in Pod 12, "I permitted them but they were unnecessary."

He turned his head to them as they followed two short lengths behind him. "The love I gave to the two of you was sacred." His voice was deeply earnest, but not angry. If anything, it held a quiet tone of sadness. "I did not intend for that to be breached."

"We thought it was necessary," Jimmy said, "considering the mess we were in." He wondered if he could in any way defend their actions, or even if he needed to. "Anyway, there were all those Hebrew men with extra wives, back in Old Testament times. So I thought, it must be OK. And, yes, we wanted children more than anything." He stared at Yeshua's back, realizing the outright silliness of explaining anything to Yeshua. "You understand, right?" he said apologetically.

"Better than you," Yeshua answered without sarcasm. "The patriarchs, and the kings, yes, they took many wives, and for the same reason. A lot of children were important, or so they thought, to their survival. Because they did not trust me."

Jimmy pushed his horse ahead so that he came alongside Yeshua. Mai Ker, still antsy, hung back.

"In the very beginning, it wasn't so. There was trust," Yeshua went on, "until the sin came forth." Ginny steered herself toward the water's edge and pulled hard at her reins to get a drink. She spewed out the saltwater as soon as it reached her tongue. "Sin, once born, deepened that lack of trust. It was the first fatality, in everyone. And it wasn't just that they didn't trust me. Knowing their own hearts, they could no longer trust each other."

Mai Ker now pulled up closer, too. On the narrow path, it was a very tight fit for all three horses.

"But you must see, it was hard for us to trust about these things," she said. "After all the death around us. How could we trust anything?"

"Yes," he said.

"And the things Jimmy tried to tell me about you, and the Father. That was so hard, so different to how I was brought up." She meandered through a complex delta of the moods, feelings, and thoughts that she had experienced in those first months INSIDE. "It did not make sense to me. He said you loved everyone. And all I could see was death. I tried to listen, and just accept what he said blindly."

They were rounding the far side of the ocean, the rest of the pods returning to sight beyond the wall of #12.

"Mai Ker, faith was never about blind acceptance," Yeshua told her. "But yes, it did mean having to relearn things you thought you knew about the world." He gave her a kind glance. "I know that was hard. Trust takes time."

They were almost the same words Thomas had spoken to her yesterday in the truck.

"You're right," he went on, "in the culture where you were raised, trust in a single God was strange, foreign. But trust is the core of faith."

Although they were riding slowly, Jimmy's horse was sweating. The circulation system of the pods was being burdened by the extra people and body heat, with only the small open doors of Pod 1 to feed in fresh air. Jimmy felt stifled but he was pretty sure it was not just the air.

"So your people in the Old Testament times, they didn't trust you, either?"

"Don't look at them, Jimmy. Look at yourself, if you want to see a failure of trust."

Jimmy, caught up short, decided not to ask his next question. Yeshua answered it anyway.

"They trusted simple math more than they trusted me. More wives, more kids. Strength in numbers, rather than strength in me."

Jimmy nodded.

"But it deprived them of the kind of love that you two knew at first, that singular, focused love that can only exist between a man and woman deeply tied to each other."

"Pretty tough for Pam," Mai Ker observed, trying not to sound too snippy. "Bridget at least had Clayton."

"True. Once William died, she felt abandoned. More so than any of you."

Jimmy remembered his attempts to make Pam feel the same kind of love that he had for Mai Ker. He and Pam both knew he had failed.

"What you wanted, wider bonds of love, more children, that was not wrong. But how you went about it, that's where you failed."

"And how," Jimmy muttered to himself.

Yeshua ignored it.

"The love of a husband for his wife was not to be violated. Even in extreme times."

Mai Ker was digesting what had been said. Her emotions, now much stronger than ever, recognized the truth.

"Yes, looking back, I knew I was giving up Jimmy. I mean, I was giving up that special thing we had. I guess now—understanding about death—I believe I would rather that we all just died out, rather than violate that love." She was looking at Jimmy with a desire that went far beyond any fleshly feeling.

They had now ridden back into Pod 10 and were moving along the south side, carefully avoiding fields of burgeoning crops.

Yeshua pulled Ginny to a halt, turned, and sat looking at Jimmy and Mai Ker, whose eyes were locked. Ginny pulled at her reins, wanting to move on. Jimmy and Mai Ker were oblivious to the protests she was making.

"Too proud, too bullheaded," Yeshua said.

"Who?" Jimmy asked.

"Oh, everyone."

Jimmy looked into Yeshua's face. The waves of hair framing it were like moving images sketched in sand along the shore they had just passed in Pod 12.

Time to be straight, Jimmy decided. Straightforward and honest.

"I see it was wrong," he said, looking back at Mai Ker. "I never loved you less," he said with all the sincerity he possessed.

He got off his horse and helped her down from hers. He pulled her into a hug and didn't want to let go.

Finally, he turned to Yeshua.

"Give me this much. You could see the future, I couldn't. We couldn't," he said. He glanced at Mai Ker for backing. "And she insisted, you know. They all did."

"I do know that," Yeshua said with a sympathetic nod.

Yeshua spoke quietly to Ginny and without goading, she broke into a gallop as if escaping a race gate.

Jimmy and Mai Ker watched, too surprised to move. What was he doing now?

"Well?" Jimmy asked.

"Why not?" Mai Ker laughed.

They jumped back on their horses and jolted them into a gallop. Halfway around the far side of the pod, Mai Ker's saddle, which had not been cinched completely tight, began to tilt to one side. She braced herself for the fall. But as quickly as she could react, the cinch belt somehow worked itself tight, righting the saddle in the process.

Mai Ker gulped a deep breath as they came to where Yeshua had stopped and sat waiting.

"It's alright, Mai Ker. We caught you."

Mai Ker, still recovering her mental balance from the expected fall that didn't happen, stared at Yeshua. He rode alongside her and visually inspected the cinch.

"You should be more careful with your saddle."

"Always happens when I get in a hurry," she managed to laugh.

Yeshua directed Ginny back to the front and they rode slowly on around the pod back toward the tents. Then, again unexpectedly, he dismounted, dropped Ginny's rein to the ground, and sat on a water-stained bench near the podwalk from #6.

Mai Ker, still shaking a little, joined him. Jimmy was forced to sit on the ground.

"So, about the marriages," he said to them both, "I know you were trying to save humanity from extinction. But you never had that power. It was sin that was consuming humanity, not death."

Both acknowledged what they now understood.

"By marrying, having more children, you thought you were ensuring the survival of humanity. But it was a sinful humanity you were preserving." Yeshua half-smiled, a smile that meant either consolation or wry humor. "Sin was still your master, not me."

"Guess I didn't really consider that part," Jimmy admitted.

"I know you tried, Jimmy, but you didn't see my plan. Remember all those evenings you all sat and debated? Why did it all happen? Why this, why would God allow that?"

Jimmy and Mai Ker looked at each other, feeling now rather foolish.

Were we blind? Mai Ker was asking herself, *even in our love for each other?*

"Yes," she admitted to Yeshua, but also to Jimmy. "We were blind, and desperate."

"You see that you took too much responsibility for what had happened?" Yeshua asked.

Mai Ker nodded.

"Yes, I even felt that at the time. But like you said last evening, we felt somehow to blame. Part of our 'dying,' as you called it."

Yeshua put his arm gently around her shoulders. Her eyes welled with stuffed-back tears as horrid memories of the last months of the final catastrophe tried to come out and play.

"In your desperation, you made decisions that were not yours to make." He looked at Jimmy. "It caused you both to make a terrible sacrifice. Mai Ker sacrificed you, Jimmy, and you sacrificed her, just as surely as if you had used knives."

Jimmy nodded, his own eyes feeling puffy, about to lose control of his emotions.

"Mai Ker, your one love. But for what you thought was necessary, you sacrificed the privacy of that love to try to carry on." Yeshua nodded as if he was agreeing with some unspoken word. "You have my judgment. It was wrong. But you also have my love. I understand why you thought it was necessary. You were trapped and felt this was a way out. More children, who might extend the life of humanity, at least for a time."

Mai Ker looked down. The soil under her feet engrossed her. She cut a small arc into the soil with the toe of one of her makeshift shoes.

"Yes. Even after we made the decision, I could always tell how difficult it was for him," Mai Ker said. She sniffed back the tears and smiled at Jimmy. "But he never put me second." The only tears she now had were expressing the joy of her deepening love for Jimmy.

Yeshua continued with quiet compassion in his voice, holding Mai Ker but addressing Jimmy.

"Pam and Bridget you took for a practical reason, to bear children. I know you tried to love them," Yeshua told him. "But you can't love more than you can love, you can't love what is not true."

"I tried."

"Yes, but Pam and Bridget both knew that you had to try. You abused their hearts, and your own."

Yeshua had struck the nail squarely on the head and Jimmy felt the hammer.

"Well, anyway, it was the three of them who thought it up," Jimmy moaned, still trying to defend what had just been declared indefensible.

"Jimmy, don't blame them. They had their reasons, you had yours. I remember every one of those little scenes you played out. That didn't make it right." He heaved out a sigh that sounded like steam from the vent of an ancient volcano. "This treating women as mere utilitarian things, it was one of the greatest tragedies that entombed mankind." His voice became more stern. "That women sometimes encouraged it did not excuse it."

"But you—" Mai Ker blurted out, on the defensive also.

Yeshua's hand went up as if to stop a lightning bolt.

"I permitted it. I did not approve it." His voice was stern.

Jimmy's and Mai Ker's defenses, confronted with truth, quickly fell away.

"We will leave it there," Yeshua said, his fierceness subsiding. Time runs differently now—but nowhere does it run backward."

"I don't know what else to say," Jimmy said truthfully.

"There is no more you need to say. It is finished. What you sought was good, the means you chose were wrong." He stood, looking at them with tender eyes. "I know the impossible dilemma you were trapped in, something you had never expected. And I know you were driven by love. I don't fault that."

The three were quiet for several moments, moments of the new time that did indeed feel like eternity.

"I guess we should get back to our chores," Jimmy finally said somberly.

"Probably," Yeshua agreed.

There was little conversation as they rode the rest of the way back to Pod 9, except this.

"Why were you always giving us what wasn't good for us?" Jimmy wanted to know. "Letting us go astray?" He looked sad. "I don't get that."

"Made in my image, Jimmy, remember? That's what I do. I make choices. For you, like any children, part of learning good was finding what was not."

Jimmy rode into the corral and dismounted, trying to digest all they had talked about. He looked at Mai Ker, who looked at him, got off her horse, and came over and hugged him again with a new passion, a love that recognized the depth of the sacrifice he had made in marrying Bridget and Pam. All along, she had thought only she had made any sacrifice in sharing him.

Knowing her thoughts, Yeshua smiled as he slung his saddle back onto the fence, his back to Jimmy and Mai Ker.

"Do you forgive me?" Jimmy asked.

"Who is being asked?" Yeshua said.

"You," Jimmy said, still looking into Mai Ker's beautiful eyes.

Yeshua turned.

"I knew your heart, Jimmy, how you resisted the idea. How you struggled and prayed. I forgave you then."

THE NECESSARY field chores were finished up shortly before lunchtime. Through lunch, Nathaniel was whispering to Herald in the most confidential of tones.

After they carried their plates to the kitchen, Herald and Nathaniel came over to Yeshua, who was still sitting in a chair outside the dining tent, finishing his apple juice.

"We're going OUTSIDE. Wanna come?" Nathaniel asked.

Both boys looked like they were asking for the moon.

"I would be delighted." He stood, not quite matching Herald's height, smiled, and said, "Let's go."

"Mom," Herald said to Bridget as they started away from the tents, "we're going to explore."

"I can come along," she said, a bit of worried mother still protruding.

"It's alright, Mom. We'll be fine."

She saw that they simply wanted a few minutes alone with Yeshua. This was next to impossible with everyone crowding around him most of the time, including the newcomers, everyone constantly peppering him with questions and hopes and ideas.

"You lead," Yeshua said to Herald.

Just like their trip down the mountain, Herald suddenly felt larger. He led them into Pod 6 past the huge aviary cage that stood silent and empty.

"Kind of sad here in number six," Herald said as they walked through the pod. "We usually stay away from this one. At least, Mom and Jimmy did."

"It does feel sad, doesn't it?" Yeshua remarked. He looked up along the empty branches of the large, bare tree that rose up through the middle of the cage.

"Sing said her mom told her once how much she missed the birds," Herald said, looking around the abandoned aviary.

"Not much longer," Yeshua said cryptically.

As they passed into the podwalk leading to Pod 4, a small, strange sound stopped the two young men.

Whi, whi, whi, whi, came the sound like air spit through a pinched straw. It came from high above and behind them.

Whi, whi, whi, came the answer of a second voice. Both boys turned and dashed back into Pod 6 again, their eyes shooting upward.

Perched high up on a branch of the big tree in the aviary cage was something neither had ever seen. A small female nuthatch sat, gripping the branch tightly in her talons as she pecked at something near her feet.

"Is that what I think?" Herald asked Yeshua.

"Yes."

"Man, I've only ever seen them in pictures. Does it have a name?"

"Several. Nuthatch is its kind. But this one was named Caroline."

"Oh wow!" Nathaniel said, beaming. "How perfect. Look how little!"

"Don't say anything to your mom, yet, would you?" Yeshua instructed Herald. "I'd like to surprise her, and the others."

A second bird that they had not yet spotted, also a nuthatch, chirped again from a wire across on the far side of the cage, then flew and landed two branches below where Caroline sat. It was similar to her but was more intensely colored. Where Caroline had a thin, black feather scarf at her neck, this one's entire head and neck were banded in black.

Having made whatever sort of greeting birds make, the second creature, a male, started walking, head down, down the tree trunk toward a more stable perch.

"There's two!" Nathaniel cried with delight.

"Her brother," Yeshua said. "Getting his first chance, finally."

"What's his name?" Nathaniel asked, enthralled with the tiny creatures.

"He doesn't have one yet." Yeshua turned to Herald. "Perhaps you can think of a name, Herald. It was your father who named the female."

Herald only half heard, still gazing up at the birds. Unexpectedly, Caroline flew down and landed gracefully beside her brother. The two did a strange little head dance, bobbing this way and that.

"I love them!" Nathaniel said enthusiastically.

"Were they here before?" Herald asked.

"Caroline was here with your parents," Yeshua said. "Your father hit her with his car, almost killed her. He brought her here to nurse her back to health."

"Really? My dad did that?"

Yeshua didn't answer, except for a very slight nod.

"How'd the other one get in?" Nathaniel asked.

"Get in? You mean INSIDE? He didn't. I restored him here," Yeshua said.

Both boys looked at Yeshua with astonishment. He didn't give them much time to remain astonished.

"They'll have a lot of company soon. Come on, are we going out or not?"

"Mom is going to love this!" Herald said.

"Remember, let's let her discover them on her own. I think that would be a nice surprise."

"I can hardly wait!" Herald beamed.

As they headed on toward Pod 1, nearly a dozen more birds of beautiful colors and various sizes began to appear in the aviary. Yeshua had called them as well. They came at his command in much the same way as the angelic creatures of light had rallied to his presence when he first appeared on the mountain.

Yeshua and the boys passed through the Visitors Center and reached the front doors. As they emerged from the Visitor Center, Herald was hit in the face with a new smell.

"What is *that*?" he asked Yeshua.

"What is what?"

"The smell. Well, the taste, really."

"I think you're smelling fresh air."

Nathaniel took a deep whiff, too, and smiled

broadly.

His favorite word came out. "Wow!"

"It's like—" Herald had to think. "—it's like strawberries in cream."

"That's because you love fresh strawberries in cream," Yeshua smiled. "For Nathaniel, it tastes like . . ."

"Like purple grapes, I think. Tangy! Can that be?"

"It wasn't like this before," Herald said. "Even when we had our masks off on Thursday."

"None of you, even your new friends, have ever tasted air as it was meant," Yeshua said. "The air is healing. Renewed in a purer state, and richer." He looked at the boys and said, "Your excursion. Where would you like to go?"

"Just walk, I guess," Herald said. "I love being OUTSIDE."

"Wait, can I show you something?" Nathaniel begged. He was tense with a different kind of excitement.

"What?"

"This way."

Enjoying deep breaths of the freshened air, Nathaniel led them out across the parking lot toward where he and Pam had buried the two guards. He wanted to show Yeshua the small markers they had set up. He had been so pleased that they were able to bury the man and woman after they had lain forgotten so many years in the basement Control Room. But as they reached the spot, Nathaniel jolted to a stop. His young head and shoulders pulled back.

"I don't understand," he said.

"You sound like Herald," Yeshua said.

"What happened?" Nathaniel asked, looking up at Yeshua, then down into the dirt. Sad disappointment pummeled his face. He was about to cry.

Where the two graves had been there were only two empty depressions in the ground. These had filled very slightly with water weeping out of the soil. The markers were untouched. The bodies were gone.

"What are you looking for, Nate?" Yeshua asked very seriously.

"But, I don't get it. We put them—right here." His hands gestured at the empty graves.

"They are not here, Nate. They've risen."

Nathaniel didn't understand. Yeshua took his shoulder and turned him slightly.

"Looking for them?" he asked, pointing Nathaniel toward the building.

Nathaniel's eyes went to the front wall of the Visitors Center where a long bench sat a few yards to the right of the doors. Herald looked, too. On the bench sat a middle-aged woman and a younger man. They were in simple, almost white shirts and pants and soft shoes.

Herald did a double take. He recognized the rusty-reddish hair of the woman.

"Oh my gosh. Can't be!" he said in a muted voice.

"Why not?" Yeshua asked him.

"They were—dead. All dried up," Nathaniel said, his face wrinkled.

"Yes," Yeshua said, "they were."

"But we just came out that door. I didn't see them then."

"You wouldn't have. You weren't looking." Yeshua offered Nathaniel his hand. "Don't be nervous. Come on, let's greet them."

He walked toward the pair, Nathaniel in tow.

Herald followed, hanging back. Since Jimmy's reappearance last night, the events of the past day were growing stranger by the moment. Jimmy was someone Herald knew. These two, however, he had never seen as anything but dried, twisted flesh. It felt like something was creeping up his spine and he decided the best thing would be to just keep quiet.

"This is Tom Kenney and Joanne Garvin," Yeshua said, introducing them to the two boys. "This is Nathaniel Moua-Algood, and Herald Listner-Block. Children of the Solarium."

Nathaniel gaped at Yeshua, then at the two on the bench.

"How do you know them?" he asked, his face perplexed.

"You should say, 'How do you do?'" Yeshua instructed him.

"How do you do?" Nathaniel asked uncertainly.

Herald echoed it.

"This young man helped lay your remains to rest over there," Yeshua explained, his arm firmly around Nathaniel's shoulders so he wouldn't get frightened and bolt.

The two on the bench were sitting comfortably but both seemed a bit on edge, uncertain exactly what had happened in the last half-hour. The last they remembered, they were in a half-state, aware of themselves but certainly dead, surrounded by others who were mostly departed family members and friends. Suddenly, unexpectedly, and with the most peculiar sensations either had ever experienced, they began to feel their flesh again. Their bodies were forming without any intention or aid from themselves. They felt they were drifting from a kind of semi-consciousness in the middle of what seemed an imaginary, walled garden where they ended up on a hard, wooden bench. They felt for the first time in a long time the sense of something solid underneath them, and could smell the air around them once again, although it was a smell unlike any they had known in their first life.

Over several moments, they realized they were not in a garden at all but outside of the Solarium complex where they had spent their final days.

Joanne Garvin slowly collected her thoughts. She looked at the oldest of the three watching her. She knew him. She had seen him somewhere, maybe even recently, although exactly how and where she had "seen" him without eyes was, for now, a complete mystery.

"It was very kind of you," she said to Nathaniel, who she had never seen. "You must have been born after we died." She looked at Tom. "We had been gone a very long time, I suppose, when you found us. We were with—" She looked again at Yeshua, "—with him, I think." She nodded as if convincing herself.

"Yes, you were with me, though I may have seemed different to you then," Yeshua said without further explanation.

"You do look different now," she said, eyeing Yeshua not only with new eyes but with new vision.

He simply nodded.

Tom Kenney had finally oriented himself enough to the new reality around him that he realized he was here, real, and able to speak. He was finally convinced that this was not some faint-hearted, hopeful dream he was dreaming in his last vaguely conscious condition.

"We knew our bodies would just end up lying there," Tom said, "in the Control Room. But it didn't really matter to us. We talked," he said, glancing at Joanne, "and decided it was our duty. To try to stay in touch, and in control, as long as we could."

Yeshua smiled. "Control," he said. "An interesting choice of words."

"Joanne was really brave about it," Tom nodded.

"Well, we knew what would happen, what was coming when I came in for that last shift. We were together at least." She smiled at Tom. "Friends. That made it better." She took one of Tom's hands and gave it a squeeze.

"Ouch," he said. "Careful! When did your grip get so strong?"

Joanne eased her grip. It surprised her, too. She examined her new hand.

"You sacrificed," Yeshua said. "It was kind, and very courageous."

"Our families were gone, see," Tom said. "So it was easier to come to work than to sit alone among those we just buried."

"You served your station well," Yeshua assured them. "You served me well, though perhaps you didn't understand that."

"We just did what we were supposed to," Joanne said matter-of-factly.

Yeshua shook his head.

"You gave all you had left. To you, it may have seemed a little thing. To me, it was not. And to those in the Solarium that you cared about, it meant a great deal."

Tom slowly stood, his feet uncertainly holding beneath him.

"You know, I would love to take a walk," he said like one who has just acquired his sea legs. "A long walk!"

"How'd you do it?" Herald asked, catching his arm. "How did you make it so long down there? When everyone else was dying?"

"Omaha had installed some reserve air tanks for us," Joanne explained, "when things began to look bad. When they knew."

"Knew?" Nathaniel asked blankly. This was all long before his time.

"When they knew the atmosphere had turned poisonous. Mr. Haskins, he wanted to help your parents survive," Joanne said. "So he wanted us here for support. Well, as long as we could."

"The reserve tanks lasted quite a while," Tom added. "The air filtered in through the cooling system. It was a big secret. The tanks would have been stolen if anyone had known. And us probably killed in the process of taking them."

The admiration on Herald's face was apparent.

"That was really brave," Herald said. "For you to come back, day after day. I mean, when you—" He hesitated, but it seemed alright to talk about now. "—when you knew it might be your last day."

"The last days are over," Yeshua said.

"Would you like to take a walk with me?" Tom asked Joanne, offering to help her up.

She grinned.

"I would be delighted, my friend."

10

Saturday Afternoon

Had Jimmy and Mai Ker realized how fresh and delicious the air OUTSIDE was, compared to that in Pod 9 where they were feeding sheep, they would have been out walking, too.

". . . and I have to tell you this, Jimmy. Do not laugh at me, please. But it was all so fantastic, what you used to say about your God. How could I know it would all be true?" Mai Ker said, laughing at herself. "Your Bible stories, they were so perfect, like the fables I heard growing up. Stories that parents told their children to cheer them up."

"Yeah, except the children knew better," Jimmy replied with irony. "Apparently, they were the ones who understood things best. The mystery hadn't been twisted out of their systems yet."

"Yes, like the way Piper always was."

"What do you mean, was? I think she still has that special sense of the mystery of things," Jimmy said.

"I think you are right. You know, I did get more skeptical of things as I got older. Maybe that is why I liked science. When I was little, I saw spirits all around. What was strange was that my parents believed in such beings, but they told me I was just imagining things, or daydreaming."

"My folks, too," Jimmy said. "Worried I was too religious."

"That was very confusing. In the old country they knew these things. They had a longer memory about spiritual powers."

Neither Jimmy nor Mai Ker noticed, but at one side of the pod several glints of shadow and light moved playfully in small spirals above the rabbit hutches. Some of their protective angels OUTSIDE had drifted in overnight, exploring the inward side of this fantastic little world, artificial though it was.

The bunnies noticed, though. Three of them were on their hind legs trying to reach up through the cage wire to touch the strange, wonderful beings that were ever more present in recent hours, like a tide of warm water flooding in around them. At least, that was how it felt to the nearly senseless rabbits.

"But even with the faith I had, you know as well as I do," Jimmy confessed, "at times it wasn't very strong."

"I know," she said. "I remember those talks."

"With all the horrors we saw, I started doubting everything, too. A powerful and just God seemed impossible at that point."

Mai Ker nodded. She had felt the same.

"Anyway," Jimmy said, "with everyone dying, it all seemed so pointless." He examined his arms and torso with his hands, still lodged in a certain perplexity about what was so apparent and real about himself now. "And then, here I am again," he grinned. "Just like he promised."

"So why could I not see it?" Mai Ker asked. "Why could I not accept it?"

"Maybe like Paul wrote. We used to see just shadows, dim reflections, like looking into a dirty mirror. Things are plain now."

"I was so blinded," Mai Ker admitted.

"Sweetheart, I think we all had that malady," Jimmy said encouragingly, giving her a hug. "Our eyes were ruined but so were our hearts. It wasn't just you, love," he said, still holding her. "Like Yeshua said, we were slaves. Worse. We were slaves in the dark hold of a very dark ship. Row, row, row your boat, never getting anywhere." The nursery tune zipped through his mind and got stuck for the next several minutes.

"Slaves to what was hollow," Mai Ker said with an insight she could not account for. "We were so taken up with so much that did not really matter." She looked at the handsome man who had been her husband. "You were in one kind of darkness, I was in another." She took a tighter hold of his upper arms and gave a long sigh. "I will never forget that moment, Jimmy Algood. Even now."

"Yeah? Which one? First time I kissed you?" Jimmy grinned.

"When I heard that awful gasp from you. Before I could twist in my harness, I heard you hit the ground. It is the sickest I have ever felt."

The grin abandoned Jimmy's face like an escaping convict.

Mai Ker had to work hard not to re-experience the full emotions of that instant again.

"My whole body went sick. And my heart. It was the worst, Jimmy," she said with flaring intensity in her eyes. "The worst. Every fear I ever felt came rushing at me, dangling from that rope with me. I saw you down there, laying still, and I knew I had lost you." She pulled him closer and buried her face in his chest. "I wanted to die with you. If Herald had let me go, I would have jumped." She sobbed just a little, but couldn't really cry, now that she could hold her beloved Jimmy again.

He caressed her hair.

"Thank the Lord for Herald. His bravery."

"I am a lucky girl," she said.

"A blessed girl."

She pushed back a little and looked up into his handsome, dark face, which was more alive than she had ever seen it.

"But I didn't know that then. Even if you had convinced me, with all your Bible promises, I would not have remembered when you died. I was bitter. Completely lost."

"We don't have to relive that, Mai," Jimmy reminded her. "Yeshua has promised. It's done. No more pain, and no more dying."

"I know. It made me think, though. How I loved you, then. And when I hold you now, why it is different."

"Oh. So you don't love me now?" he wondered uncertainly. The expression on her face was a mixture of love, pity, happiness, and desire.

"No, silly. That is just it. I do. But it is more than—" She had to reach to find the words. "It is more than love, if you can understand. I tried to tell Bridget this morning. I could not explain it."

"Sit down," Jimmy suggested as he guided her to a stool that sat alone by the end of the row of rabbit hutches. She sat as Jimmy leaned back against a hutch.

"I do know, you know," Jimmy said. He felt impossibly awkward, like a teenager about to dial the phone and ask that special girl for a first date. "I know," he repeated, "I feel it, too, ever since last night. Our first time back together." He thought quietly until Mai Ker looked up and her eyes demanded he go on. "It's like, I love you more than ever. But, now, well— you're more real to me. Does that make any sense?"

"More real?"

"Yes."

She nodded, rubbing a twitch or a gnat away from the end of her nose.

"That is what I have been feeling. We are different now," she speculated. "Different people. Man and woman. But of a different order or something." She struggled to express it. "Almost like a new species." She shook her head, feeling she had lost her mind entirely. "I do not know how to say it."

"So let's not work on saying it, but doing it."

"Yes," she agreed. She gazed at Jimmy's eyes, eyes whose color was darker yet brighter than she remembered. "That seems best."

Jimmy stood relaxed, unmovable. The sheep they had just fed wandered aimlessly around the pen, full now and happy.

"It's not that I didn't feel pleasure being with you last night, Mai. Or a desire for you. I did. But—I don't know how to say it, either. I want you to be perfectly you, and just the idea of having sex would feel weird, like it would violate that perfection." He shook his head, brushing sweat out of his hair. "It feels all mixed up. That's all I know!"

Mai Ker stood and held him again.

"As long as you understand," she said. "You are like that to me, too. It feels like just touching you is somehow a violation of the rules. I do not know why. But it is still wonderful."

"I know," Jimmy said, expressing what he couldn't quite manage. "Last night, it was like . . . well, I thought the first second we were alone I'd want to make love. But the moment we *were* alone, that's the one thing I didn't want. It's like you're now the queen of my world, like you're above me somehow."

"Not quite a queen," she laughed.

"You know what I mean." He held her tightly. The passion in him was different from what he had felt in the past. "You are more beautiful than I even remember. The word that came to me last night was 'magnificent.' The depth of pleasure I feel is from just being near you. Breathing the same air." He drew a deep breath.

Mai Ker nodded, though it was in no way a boast. "I felt somehow radiant being near you last night. I mean, you have been resurrected! I am astonished at you. You! I felt awkward, but I could not say it. I thought you would laugh."

Jimmy did laugh slightly.

"See," she said, "exactly why I said nothing. I knew you would laugh."

Then she did, too.

They were hand-in-hand now, walking back toward the tents in #10 like young lovers on a honeymoon.

"It's like we were kids who have finally grown up," Jimmy mused. "Not physically, but spiritually. It's sure not what I expected."

"But beautiful," Mai Ker told him. "And good."

"It's what he said all along," Jimmy said, thinking of Yeshua's words in scripture. "When we love him, when we love the Father, we begin a new life, and a new connection to each other."

"I am just happy you are here to share it," Mai Ker said, snuggling her head against his shoulder as they walked. "You don't know how much I missed you."

"I know how much I missed *you*."

Their touch was much more than touch. It was an actual connection, a perfect communion of their spirits, as only love at its deepest reality knows.

They arrived by the front of the main tent where several of their guests were gathered, talking with Bridget and Pam. After so many years of forced solitude, the place had begun to feel like Grand Central Station.

Jimmy and Mai Ker both felt they needed to be alone for a while. They agreed to meet each other later by the pool. Jimmy stroked her long, silken hair and tenderly touched her cheek. The connection was so real that a kiss would have been superfluous.

THOMAS HAD gone looking for Yeshua sometime ago after learning he and the two boys had gone exploring. He caught up to them a half-mile down the highway to the east. They were walking aimlessly, talking, enjoying the beautiful day.

"Lord, our friends are peppering me with questions. They're wearing me out. Can you bring everyone together and help them?"

"We'll go back, soon. Join us for a while, Thomas."

Thomas looked just a little impatient but he knew his Lord enough to know they would not rush back. As he walked along with them, Yeshua was describing the boys' future, and what their part would be in his new world.

Thomas listened quietly. After about twenty minutes, measured by the old clocks, Yeshua suggested they walk back. But in just moments, it seemed to Herald and Nathaniel, they were standing in front of the Visitors Center.

"Thanks for taking us along," Nathaniel said as they started through the doors.

"Thank you, Nathaniel," Yeshua said, "I think you took me along."

Nathaniel beamed and Herald laughed.

"I guess I did!" Nathaniel smiled.

When they were back INSIDE Yeshua turned to Herald.

"Herald, would you do me a favor? Gather everyone over at the house?"

"In number four? Sure. Just give me a few minutes."

"Take your time. We're in no hurry."

Herald found the visitors still gathered near the main tent, although Eira had gone off with Sing and Piper to Pod 11 to play with the animals.

A hapless Braden sat by the tents, listening to the mass of women, his broken leg still an impediment to getting around.

Herald managed to assemble everyone and led them to the beautiful old Victorian house in Pod 4. Yeshua was there ahead of them, seated on an evergreen-colored porch chair. Thomas sat nearby, his eyes closed, in a folding chair on the small but very green front lawn.

None of the four elder Solarians had been through Pod 6 yet, continuing to avoid it as they had for so many years. As Yeshua watched them approach, Caroline flew out of a partly opened, upstairs bedroom window and circled the upper story of the house as if looking for someone.

Bridget caught the first sight of her.

"Caroline!" she cried with joy.

The tiny bird, if it heard her, ignored her.

"Oh, my gosh," Mai Ker said, her eyes sparkling. Then she looked funny at Bridget. "Are you sure?"

"Is it?" Bridget begged of Yeshua.

Yeshua chuckled.

"She's sure, Mai Ker. It is indeed your little Caroline. She and a few of her friends have deigned to join us."

As he spoke, another 10 birds, including Caroline's brother, swooped in through the podwalk from #6 and circled up near the roof of #4. A few landed on trees and bushes. Two alighted on the ground near the pod wall. All seemed to be watching the humans intently, although, as with cats, this could have been a clever animalian trick.

Mai Ker spun in a circle, watching them fly and calling to them in bird-like tones. "I am so delighted!" she said to everyone between birdcalls.

Caroline landed on the porch rail just to the right of Yeshua. Her small but active brother flittered down and sat beside her. A little wren landed briefly on Yeshua's left shoulder, spoke a little chirp of something to him, then flew off to perch on the peak of the old Victorian.

While almost everyone's attention remained on the colorful, cheerful birds, little Eira spoke, eyeing the house. She had seen this beautiful, impressive place through the pod walls and could not imagine why no one lived in it. No one had yet offered to take her inside, and she would never have been so bold as to ask, or to wander in on her own.

"Are there real beds in there?" she asked Bridget as she plopped down beside her on the grass near the porch steps.

"I'm afraid they're all over in the tents. We moved them as the children grew."

"I was so hoping to sleep in a real bed tonight," Eira said shyly. "I never had one." She looked embarrassed. "Before." She narrowed her eyes and pursed her lips in thought. "Funny thing, but it's kind of hard to remember 'before,'" she said, essentially to herself.

"Tell you what," Bridget said, "you can take my bed tonight. You'll have not only a bed, but your own tent."

"That would be very nice of you," Eira said. "But you don't have to."

"That's what makes it fun," Bridget smiled. "I don't mind sleeping outside. Well INSIDE, outdoors. I enjoy it once in a while."

"You can have my pallet of blankets that Garan made for me," Eira offered.

"It's a trade," Bridget said.

Eira, whose mother had died giving her birth, slid closer to Bridget. Every few minutes, when her attention wandered from Yeshua, she would look up and smile at this woman she thought so strong and lovely.

Braden, after hobbling in, sat by his mother on the other side. His eyes went to two very large, yellowish-green birds that must have been tropical, he decided, although he had not been very good about this area of his schoolwork. Hearing Eira, he said, "Mom, we could make some more beds. We've got plenty of stuff."

"We'll see," Bridget said.

Despite a low commotion as everyone else was settling, Yeshua heard him.

"Thank you, Braden, but it won't be needed. Not everyone is staying."

This was news not just to the Solarians, but more so to their visitors.

"Why did you bring us here, if we're not to stay?" Adrian asked, plainly disappointed.

"Most of you have other homes, and you'll want to return there before long. Once the newness here wears off."

"We're going home then?" the man named Jacob asked.

"Some," Yeshua answered.

"So, then, everyone is not coming here, once they are raised up?" Garan asked, thinking he had figured this out.

"No," Yeshua said. "Many have already returned since we left the mountain. Most are returning straight to their homelands. Those for whom all is settled." He gave a small sigh. "And there are some I must still meet with."

"Then why did we come here, Lord?" Eira asked.

"To do me a service, Eira. My friends here, those who have lived here for so long, and those who were born here, they would have found it hard to believe that the dead were being raised, without evidence."

The expression on Pam's face said he was right, as always.

"They knew, you see, that everyone had died. They might've thought I was a survivor, someone who managed to escape death."

"Hah, now that's funny!" Thomas said, his eyes finally open, laughing heartily. "Anyway, you could easily have proved them wrong."

"You know I'm not a showoff, Thomas."

Jacob's daughter, Katherine, was sitting by her father on a wooden chair in the yard.

"How will we get home then?" she asked.

"You can walk."

"But it must be miles," Katherine replied. "Maybe hundreds." She looked around. "I'm not even sure where we are."

"I'll direct you. And walking will not be as long as before. Once you have a destination, you'll start and you will find it. Or, it will find you. The travel will go very quickly."

"How Lord?" Jacob asked, his aged wisdom still questioning what already sounded absurd.

Yeshua gave him a friendly smile.

"Things are changing, Jacob. Maybe you've noticed? The world is being regenerated. When you want to go somewhere, the Earth itself will help you. It will come to you."

Most in the crowd, except Thomas, frowned at this.

"What, you mean we just go, and we arrive?" Jacob asked, still skeptical.

Another bird came flying out through the podwalk, a brilliant cardinal with a small seed in its mouth stolen from a bush in Pod 10. It settled in the grass near another bush that looked equally promising.

"Most of these new birds appeared right here, in the Solarium. But that cardinal there," Yeshua said, directing their eyes, "yesterday that one appeared off the western coast of what was once Australia. Which is not, I admit, quite as far away as it once was."

Herald was sure he was kidding.

"That's on the other side of the planet, isn't it?" Herald asked.

"It was," Yeshua agreed.

"But, Lord, everything looks the same, mostly," Adrian said. "Well, except, not many plants out there," he gestured with his head OUTSIDE of the pods.

"Always judging by appearance, Adrian," Yeshua said with an insightful look. "That was always a problem for you."

Adrian, who had had this discussion about his snap decision-making and other failures not long after his death, nodded.

"Old habits, sir," he said. "Got me killed, sure enough."

"New times," Yeshua laughed. "Trust me, Adrian."

"You know I do."

Yeshua smiled.

"I see," Herald said as it clicked, "like when we walked back earlier," he said perceptively.

"Good, Herald," Yeshua said, "explain to everyone, would you?"

"Well, we were out walking," Herald told them, "got maybe a mile or so down the road. I'm not sure. Anyway, we started walking back, just normally, and then suddenly, we were here."

"Here by this house?" Jacob asked.

"No. By the front door of the Visitors Center. But, I don't know how we got there so quick." He snapped his fingers to show them how quickly they had arrived.

"So, you will be able to walk home, even those who were from across the sea," Yeshua said.

"You mean, like that story about you on Galilee?" Garan asked very excitedly.

"No. I mean that the continents are growing together. Where there were oceans, they will seem like small lakes. And sure Adrian, if you wish, you may be able to stand on them."

Everyone thought he was only kidding Adrian, except Adrian.

"Yes, perfect!" Adrian almost bellowed.

Garan tugged at his arm and tried to calm him.

"Adrian, he's still speaking you know!"

Reproved, Adrian quieted himself.

"So," Jacob asked him, "if we think of travel, and think of home, we'll just—be there?"

"No, Jacob, you'll walk as usual. But you will find the end of the journey very close to the beginning."

"I'm very confused," Pam confessed. She sensed everyone was probably hungry since it was getting late into the afternoon, but one question had been bothering her since Yeshua's arrival and it wouldn't leave her alone.

Yeshua looked at her, prodding the question out.

"But, I always thought the world was supposed to end," she said.

"It did," he answered.

Pam frowned. "But here we are."

"Yes?" he pressed her.

Pam went silent with a very puzzled look frozen on her face.

"So, the world *won't* end?" Bridget asked, trying to rescue Pam.

"Bridget, it has. The old world, that age, has ended," Yeshua said.

"I thought Jimmy's Bible said it would be consumed in fire," Pam said.

Yeshua looked at the two women, then at the others, most of whom had the same question in their eyes.

"There are different kinds of fire, Bridget. Think of your training. What sustains both fire, and life?"

She thought a moment but had no ready answer. Mai Ker rescued her this time.

"Air."

"Yes," Yeshua answered. "And the air burned, didn't it? And with it, all life."

Pam, unfortunately, was still stuck on the world ending.

"So, the world was never going to completely end?"

"Pam, why would I obliterate what I myself made?" Yeshua asked her with a compelling look.

"But the Bible . . ." Pam tried to say.

"I realize, in your language it was confusing, but not as I spoke it. In the old language, a thing is at its end when it has reached its fulfilment."

Several dozen passages of scripture flew through Jimmy's mind and a light clicked on.

"Of course!" He looked at Yeshua. "One silly, little word."

"Indeed," Yeshua agreed.

"Seriously? You never said the world was going to end?" Slowly, Pam began to frame the new picture.

"I promised my Kingdom would come, didn't I? How could it come if there was no world of people to fill it?"

He said this as if it was just as plain as the new daylight, but several, even among those who had been raised from death, were still uncertain. Yeshua could see the conversation was getting tiring. They had had enough for one sitting, the day had grown long, and everyone needed to have some food and fun.

"Simple truths," Yeshua said, "they were always the most misunderstood."

"Jimmy has a Bible," Mai Ker said. "I could go—"

"Mai," Jimmy interrupted, restraining her, "I *don't think* we need it now," he said, directing her eyes toward Yeshua.

"Oh. I see," she said, but she didn't.

"Mom," Braden complained, "I'm hungry."

"For goodness sake," she said, "didn't you eat lunch?"

Braden thought.

"I think I was busy."

Yeshua laughed.

"There are still chores to be done, yes?" he asked the Solarians. "We can all lend a hand. And Braden could use a snack."

EVENING CHORES took just as much energy as ever but no one minded because the work was spread across so many hands. It was great fun for the Solarians to have so much help around. They were saddened to hear that some of their new friends would be leaving.

Milking, collecting some green beans that had come in, picking fresh blueberries, and plucking several new eggs from under the hens was actually a treat for their younger visitors. These chores were familiar, like at their homes in the old times, and it helped them feel at home in this strange, modern complex of aluminum and steel and this stuff called plastic.

Late in the evening, long after supper and long after most had found their beds for the night, Yeshua went to walk alone by the ocean in Pod 12.

Jimmy and Mai Ker had been sitting together and watched him stroll away. They followed at a distance. He seemed lost in thought. The two of them walked slowly, whispering, careful not to disturb him.

Here, in the softened light of the pod at night, the radiance of his whole body was more apparent. They couldn't decide if the unusual radiance was actually in him, or around him, or both.

Then he stopped. They looked at each other.

"Should we sneak back?" Mai Ker whispered.

"No. Let's go on," Jimmy said.

They walked on and were soon alongside him.

"It's very pretty here by your little make-believe ocean," Yeshua said.

"Well," Jimmy laughed, "for make-believe, it's pretty powerful. Almost killed Herald, once."

"I remember," Yeshua said.

Mai Ker shot Jimmy a questioning look, but took it as fact anyway.

"I loved walking along the shores of Gennesaret." He noticed Jimmy's look. "Galilee, you would call it." He walked on. "The sound of the waves breaking. It was always soothing and helpful. Like the Earth breathing."

"So, can I ask something?" Jimmy asked. "I didn't want to say it this afternoon."

The three stopped.

"Anything," Yeshua said.

"It's— Well, I know you always have a plan and all. I get that. But I've thought about this since I got back. And I can't figure it."

"Can't figure what?"

Mai Ker looked at Jimmy and urged him on with her lovely brown eyes.

"Why us? Why here? Why were we left, when everyone else was taken?" Jimmy asked with some unease.

"How do I best put this?" Yeshua said, starting to walk again. "You remember my friend Noah?"

"Of course. You don't know how many times I felt like him, stuck in this place."

"I do know. Noah and his family didn't survive the cataclysm because they were perfect. I chose them because they were strong. They were my witnesses to what came before, to what came after." Then, as if subtly pointing out the omission by the Solarians, he added, "That's why they built an altar and worshipped when they finally made landfall. Because they recognized my love, and my providence."

"So, all that time, we were just—witnesses?" Mai Ker asked.

"To what came before, and to what has happened since."

This was not an acceptable answer for Mai Ker. Jimmy, too, was surprised, but neither knew what to say.

"Don't feel insulted," Yeshua added. "You were much more than that. You were the continuity of humankind, from the old to the new."

They walked in silence for a short distance. Then Mai Ker spoke, more satisfied with this thought.

"Continuity. Like a thread," she said.

"A very thin one, yes." He nodded at both of them. "Each of you who came to the Solarium had lived a fairly decent life. But none of you were even close to perfect. Far from it. But that's not why I chose you. You also were strong. I knew you would need that strength to survive in here, to witness the beginning of the judgment. That is what you saw, from INSIDE."

Mai Ker could not hold the emotion in.

"It was very unkind."

"To you, Mai Ker?" he asked. "Or those OUTSIDE?"

"Everyone," she said, guarded hesitation just holding her back from wanting to lash out.

"There is more than one sort of kindness, too," Yeshua said, tacitly acknowledging the truth of what she had said.

"It was brutal, for us in here, at least."

"Yes. I said you were strong. I needed you to be strong. Every one of you. The little ones, too." He knew full well the suffering of all those OUTSIDE, how the Solarians suffered, too, and what Mai Ker and Jimmy were feeling at this moment. "Maybe you can see that the most unkind thing I could have done would have been to leave mankind for all eternity in spiritual death. In the pain of eternal separation, and brokenness."

"Maybe," Jimmy muttered.

"It was painful to allow it," Yeshua went on, "because I know the horror of death all too well. Feeling utterly abandoned, and helpless. Your breath going out for the last time. Yes, I know very well. But it was not unkind. In the end, the greatest kindness is to rescue the brutalized slave, however much he has come to enjoy his slavery."

Jimmy pondered this as they walked.

"Yeah, I guess I do see," he finally said.

"Death was the only real rescue from eternal slavery in a wretched, wicked world." Yeshua spoke as one who knew the most wretched death of all.

"So you protected us here," Jimmy said.

"Yes. John Haskins thought he was protecting you, but it was always me."

"But Lord, you see that it was not just humans you destroyed," Mai Ker said. "It was everything."

He turned and took her in his arms as a father would counsel his most precious daughter who was about to destroy her life with some foolish decision.

"Yes. I wiped the planet clean," Yeshua answered, unfazed. A terrible power was now in his voice, a bewildering look in his eyes. "I allowed evil and destruction to have their way. The whole creation groaning, in childbirth. That is always painful." His looked into the depth of her soul. "Remember?"

Mai Ker unconsciously rubbed her hand down across her chest and stomach. She couldn't bear his look. She pulled away and had to gasp for a breath. He looked intently at her and Jimmy.

"You asked. You now know. I am the one man to have ever known the pain of childbirth, giving life to this new world. A very long labor. Don't think that I have not felt every heartache, every crushing pain. They are all in here," he said, his palm clasped to his chest.

The terrible mystery of these words left Mai Ker and Jimmy speechless. The primordial voice they had just heard frightened even the angels who hovered nearby. Everything fell silent except the quiet, breaking waves that Yeshua so cherished.

He walked on ahead, alone. Jimmy and Mai Ker watched for a moment, then turned back toward #10, hands clasped tightly as if holding each other in life, hoping they had not injured something deep in this man they were only just beginning to truly know.

11

Sunday Morning

No one overslept this morning. Just moments before sunup, there was a loud, chaotic sound of soil and rock wrenching and tearing like an earthquake that was under perfect control.

It was nothing like the quakes that had violently shaken the Solarium months before. To the sleeping Solarians and their guests, this felt more like laying on an old hotel vibrator bed that shook a little too hard, but not hard enough to toss you on the floor.

The rumbling movement woke everyone instantly, especially Garan and Adrian who were sleeping on the ground in Pod 11. Some woke in panic, others with nervous curiosity.

It was mainly the Solarians who were in panic. It felt too familiar, a muted version of the scare they had felt twice before. Jimmy jumped from his bed, breathing rapidly as he froze in place, unsure if he dared move. The Solarium was gently swaying like a giant passenger liner on a rough ocean. He looked out of his tent toward the pod roof and realized it was in no danger of collapse. It had undergone much worse in the past. He relaxed and took a calming breath.

As Herald and Sing found their feet and dashed through their tent door, their eyes locked on the world OUTSIDE. Beyond the pod walls the all-too-familiar but greening landscape was in motion, shifting, rising slightly here, falling a bit there. It felt like they were on ponies of a great carousel carrying them swiftly around and around, making them dizzy, but mostly filling their hearts with childlike pleasure.

"Herald, what's he doing now?" Sing asked loudly. She clung to Herald for stability, even though they themselves were barely moving.

"You're asking me?" he cried.

Both had spotted Yeshua OUTSIDE, alone, walking along a small rise just to the east of the complex, above the depression that carried the Arkansas River. They could just see him through the easterly wall of Pod 10.

Bridget and Pam were suddenly alongside Herald and Sing and joined in gawking, wondering what was going on and worried that maybe they were losing their minds. They stared. The ground OUTSIDE was not supposed to move like the waves of an ocean, but it was.

"Oh, my gosh, that doesn't look good," Pam said with her usual worrisome tone. "What in the world did we eat last night?" she asked, sure the strange vision before her eyes was the result of too much of something.

"Maybe it's the Earth that has an upset stomach!" Bridget said, breaking into laughter.

Pam realized how silly she sounded, but Bridget was sounding sillier.

Jimmy, Mai Ker and their guests were collecting in a clutch of humanity near the main tent. They all saw Yeshua and could not help but watch, although at the moment he seemed oblivious to them and the Solarium, lost in his own world.

Yeshua turned to his right. Several short but blossoming new trees about 100 feet from him appeared to turn in a kind of pirouetting bow toward him. As he walked up a hill rising under his feet, the top of the hill crested higher, then broke and descended. It looked to those in the Solarium as if he was surfing a wave onto an invisible beach.

While all this was happening, new growths of vegetation were appearing around the area. It was like watching time-lapse photography. Plants jumped from the soil in eruptions of energy seen in hungry lions but not in lowly plants. The dead soil around the Solarium, which had shown gradual signs of new growth for several days, was now bursting with plant life. Bushes grew to 3 and 4 feet in minutes, as if supersaturated with life.

Yeshua rode the crest of the hill as it descended to a level and came to a standstill. He turned a slow, full circle, scrutinizing his work.

Fascination filled the eyes of those watching, especially Nathaniel and Braden, who had scooted out of their tent, Braden with great trouble, at the first shaking.

What was happening OUTSIDE, or how it was happening, was clear to no one except Yeshua.

Apparently satisfied with what he had done, he began to walk purposefully, as if following an invisible path, back toward the southerly wall of Pod 10. But walking hardly described it. It looked more as if the soil under his feet was carrying him along, up, a little to one side, then back to a level again as he came closer.

"Almost like that night on the lake," Thomas mused to himself.

"What?" Piper asked.

"On Galilee, that night. He walked right out there— on the water—in a terrible storm. It looked something like this," Thomas explained. He shook his head. "He never stops amazing me."

"Unreal," Sing was saying to Herald, not hearing Thomas.

"Too real," Herald replied. "Maybe it's *new* real."

However it was happening, the landscape around the Solarium was being remolded, though no visible hand was at work. Even as Yeshua walked back toward them, shapes along the furthest horizon were turning ever-so-slowly. The crest of the distant Pikes Peak inched into view, then drew closer as though pulled by a massive rope.

Their brains could not digest what their eyes were witnessing. The great mountain, at least the top of it, could now be seen from INSIDE. Before it had been hidden by the horizon except, as Herald and Bridget had learned, when seen from the top of the taller pods.

Gradually, the shaking lessened. The pods remained perfectly intact even though the rock, soil, minerals, and water under the complex had just been reshaped to a depth of a quarter-mile.

Yeshua disappeared around the front of the Visitors Center but shortly reappeared as he came through the doors of Pod 1.

Eira was standing by the south edge of Pod 10, where she and Adrian had run to watch the amazing display of power. Both had kept their gaze fixed on Yeshua as he walked back toward the Solarium. Eira now ran through the adjoining pods that connected with the inner door of Pod 1, with Adrian close behind her. They nearly ran headlong into Yeshua as he came into Pod 2.

"Lord, that was so beautiful," Eira cooed as he stepped INSIDE, a dazzled look in her eyes.

Yeshua, smiling, took Eira's hand and headed toward the tents.

"How did you do that?" Adrian asked, following behind.

"What?" he asked Adrian innocently, as if he misunderstood.

"That!" Adrian exclaimed, pointing OUTSIDE to Yeshua's remodeling work.

Yeshua looked out, then looked at Adrian's astonished expression. Eira's eyes darted between them. Yeshua started walking again, talking as he went.

"Adrian, how many years did you live in your old life?" Yeshua asked.

"Just short of twenty-three, Lord. But you know that."

"And every morning you got up, and went about your work. The sun rose every day, the trees waved at you, the rains and snows came. The stream from the mountain poured delicious, cold water down through your village."

"Yes," Adrian said uncertainly, missing the point but trying to keep up with Yeshua's pace and his words.

"And did you ever before ask, 'How did he do that?'"

Adrian's face showed a tepid smile that hid his defeat. Eira grinned backward at him, trying her best to make her short legs keep up with her Lord.

"Stepped wide-eyed into that trench, didn't you?" she giggled.

Nodding, Adrian walked around and ahead of them. Yeshua and Eira watched him speed on, exchanging little knowing looks.

The rest of the gathered Solarians and visitors kept a close eye on Yeshua as he approached them, fearing some further innovation here INSIDE at any second. Nothing happened. He simply walked to the tents with Eira and greeted the others with a vibrant smile.

"A very refreshing morning walk," his voice jingled. "Nothing like watching the sunrise, is there?"

Silent faces scanned his. Behind their silence was amazement at what they had just witnessed. In some, it was absolute awe. In Braden, it was fear. No human being, he thought, should be able to wield such power.

"What shall we have for breakfast?" Yeshua asked no one in particular.

"A few fish?" Thomas joked, provoking a smile from Yeshua. "Or, I know! Some mustard seeds?"

Thomas threw in as an afterthought.

"'And you will say to this mountain . . .' Now that is funny, Thomas. At least your humor is improving."

No one else got it. Bridget and Pam looked at each other. Pam shook her head with a, *Probably don't want to know* expression.

"I love this. But I get scared, sometimes," Pam whispered confidentially as she pulled Bridget toward the kitchen tent.

"Like he said. The world is definitely changing."

Breakfast was thrown together quickly, a filling meal of corned-beef hash with lots of scrambled eggs and toast.

The visitors joined the Solarians around the long table, watching Yeshua eat. His escapade OUTSIDE had them mesmerized. They wondered what might be next. There were stares but no questions. It was enough, they felt, to just sit here near this unpredictable man and watch him eat, after seeing the miraculous transformation of the high plains prairie around the Solarium.

"Immanuel," Jimmy murmured to Pam at the far end of the table.

"Huhm?" Pam asked, her eyes focused on her meal, her mind trying to assimilate new realities that were flying in like attack aircraft in large formations.

"Immanuel," Jimmy repeated. "I always thought it was just sort of a symbolic name. God-with-us." He looked down the table at Yeshua. "Nothing symbolic about it."

The quiet around the breakfast table was refreshing. The long talks with Yeshua were fascinating but a burden, too. The Solarians and their guests had so many questions and everyone, so it seemed, wanted everything answered at once.

Now, they began to realize, that was not his plan. There was so much to know, so much to learn. Each question was like watching the infinite knowledge of this God-Man being carved chip by chip off some monolithic stone and spoon-fed to them in tiny, chewable bites. It would go on forever, and "forever" now had a depth of meaning it had never held before.

The deeper problem was that the answers he gave were hard for the kids to digest, and often harder, in a different way, for the adults.

JACOB AND his daughter Katherine tagged along with Bridget to the barn in Pod 9 and were helping her fork piles of fallen hay back up into the loft. Several of the kids playing there yesterday had, as usual, left a mess.

The three worked in silence, their minds running in different tracks.

Half an hour later, Yeshua came into the barn. He grabbed a horse brush and went to work brushing a young colt named Browny in its stall. He had taken a special interest in the horses. Once in a while he spoke to the colt but Bridget and the others paid no attention.

Piper, looking lost but actually following Yeshua at a distance, came and sat on a large stool by the barn door. She, too, was daydreaming, her thoughts a long way off. The spiritual connection she felt for Yeshua since those first moments on the mountain kept her in a quandary, full of questions, the answers to which she knew she would probably not understand. When she heard Bridget speak, her ears perked up.

"Can you explain something to me?" Bridget asked Yeshua hesitantly.

"Likely."

Bridget focused herself on the hay and the pitchfork, keeping her eyes turned away from him.

"Why did you put us all through it?"

Yeshua knew this would be much the same talk that he, Jimmy and Mai Ker had last night. He also knew it was the most troubling question the Solarians had, a question that had built a head of steam INSIDE the Solarium for more than a decade.

"All?" Yeshua prodded her as he had Mai Ker, "or those of you here in the Solarium?"

"Well, everybody, I guess. But, yes, mainly us."

Yeshua drew a long breath, enjoying the lively smells of the barn. He ran the brush deeply through the colt's mane and pulled several loose hairs from the brush.

"You say I put you through it. That's true, I did. But the origin of what you suffered, what everyone OUTSIDE suffered, that was something you put yourselves through." He did not take his eyes off the colt.

"*We* didn't decide what was going to happen," Bridget said. "We had no control over anything. Maybe some of them OUTSIDE did, but not us."

Jacob and Katherine listened closely but kept tossing hay.

"What all of you suffered, the pain and the death, all of that was brought on by sin. That was something you brought on yourselves. No one was without sin."

"Except you," Katherine corrected him.

He thanked her with a nod.

"Sin followed sin," Yeshua said, "sin fed greater evil. A vicious circle. Look back, Bridget. The world had been dying for centuries. And it had to die, so that death itself could be driven out."

"You drove out death by killing everyone?" Bridget asked incredulously.

He brushed the colt's back with long, thoughtful strokes.

"I drove out sin by allowing everyone to die."

This, though bitter, seemed more palatable to Bridget.

"I tried to help Mai Ker and Jimmy see this last night. I know it may not make sense yet, but death was how I rescued each of them from the chains of their own sin."

"It was all so horrible, so sudden. And in here, it was having to watch." Bridget took a long pause. "Knowing, and being helpless." Her mind recoiled again to the day Paul Bishop and the refugees had shown up, then to that other day years later when the Solarian party found the refugees' decayed bodies near John Martin Reservoir.

"Death was a great fright," Jacob interjected, straightening up and resting his pitchfork on the floor. "For me, at least."

"For me, also," Yeshua said unexpectedly. "Even knowing what was beyond, I felt the horror. That weight, pulling me down into unseen darkness, the icy, wretched fingers of the enemy clutching and jerking at my feet." He turned and looked at the others. "I was no different from you, except that for me it was worse, knowing I'd be torn in two." His hands opened as he stretched his fingers. "But I could not turn away from the Father's plan." He wiped sweat from his hair and forehead. "Even I—in my human flesh—felt those moments of cowardice there in the garden. But I knew there was no other way."

Piper's daydream had evaporated and her eyes were glued to Yeshua's hands.

"Couldn't you have just fixed it all? Somehow?" she asked, connecting with Bridget's thoughts.

"I know it's bewildering, Piper," Yeshua answered. "But my Father had a perfect plan from the beginning. It required my submission, as Son and Man. Perfection comes only at the price of surrender."

The others listened, absorbing his thoughts. Piper was off her stool, leaning hard against the rails of Browny's stall.

"You did it on purpose," she said in awe.

"Unless I chose surrender to death, death could not

be conquered."

"I don't understand what you just said," Katherine admitted.

Piper, ever in tune with what mystified others, said, "So that's why we submit to you."

A simple nod was his reply.

Bridget thought he was changing the subject. She jabbed her pitchfork into the wooden floor.

"So all that death and suffering—all that was necessary?" she asked again emphatically.

"For the first world to pass, yes. It was a proving ground. It was often in the moments of greatest suffering that the true questions were finally faced."

Jacob picked up his pitchfork again. The pile of hay on the floor was shrinking.

"I came as a child to become a man, to cleanse man's freedom. To slay death meant a human had to do it. That meant a sacrifice." He looked at Piper and the others as one stating a simple fact. "A *willing* sacrifice." He kept brushing Browny. "None of you had the purity, or the strength."

Thomas came into #9 chewing a piece of cold toast and gravitated toward the barn, also wondering where Yeshua had gone off to. Hearing the end of this conversation and knowing the emotions involved for the Solarians, he hung back, standing near the corral.

"But all those dead people," Piper finally said, taking Bridget's cause. "The ones we saw that day at the campground? It was so sad," she said, her face painted with the sorrow of that day. "I felt so bad for them. It broke my heart."

"Because you have my love in you, Piper," Yeshua said, looking straight at her. "Not everyone would have felt that." He set down the brush and took her hands, like a suitor proposing to his beloved. "That love was strongest when it was most needed."

He didn't explain what he meant, leaving her with

even more questions.

"Every death was sad for me," Yeshua said. "My brothers and sisters, yet my children." He looked at the others, his face stern. "I had to watch, too."

Browny bucked his head slightly. He wanted more of the soothing brush. Yeshua dragged the brush the full length of his back, pulled the knotted hair out of the brush and dropped it onto the barn floor as if it were contagious.

Bridget was hushed, trying to pull her stuck pitchfork up out of the wood. Katherine and Jacob kept working, occasionally looking at each other, remembering how, just after their own deaths, they had peppered Yeshua with these same questions centuries before the end.

They tossed the last of the hay into the loft and sat on small, square stools to rest, overcome either by fatigue or Yeshua's words. Jacob brushed thick sweat from his beard and wiped his hands on his pants.

Bridget got the pitchfork loose and set it aside. She picked up a large push broom and began sweeping the residue of seed and chaff left on the floor.

"OK," Bridget said. "I think I see. But why did Jimmy have to die—so close to the time? Losing him was so hard. For Mai Ker, especially." Though Bridget directed attention to Mai Ker's feelings, she herself had felt the deep hurt, too, the death of her second husband. "Why was he taken like that?"

"It was hard for all of you, I know that," Yeshua said, his voice quiet but unwavering. "Jimmy was taken, as you put it, because he did a careless, stupid thing. He was tired. He should have stopped climbing and rested longer, and he knew that. But he didn't. His life hung by one safety rope and he made a careless mistake. It was no fault but his own."

"But you could have prevented it," Bridget insisted.

"I can overrule the law of gravity, you mean? Yes, but I chose not to."

Piper frowned.

"But why not? Would it have been such a big thing?" she asked. "Why not save Daddy, when you were so close to coming back?" She was visibly troubled.

"Well, first of all, he was already saved."

Piper had to think about this. She remembered her dad's stalwart faith, even when he was upset or distressed. Then she saw what Yeshua meant.

Yeshua walked to her again and drew her eyes to his own.

"Death was never the main risk in life. I let your dad go because I was not worried about him. It was hard for you, I know. But each of you grew through that loss. Loss and hardship were the parents of strength."

Bridget remained quiet. She went and hung the broom back on the wall. Everyone was thinking, all about different things. Yeshua looked at Bridget's back, then spoke to the others.

"Could all of you leave Bridget and me for a bit? She'd like to speak with me alone."

12

Sunday Afternoon

Jacob and Katherine started to leave the barn. Piper tried to hang back but Yeshua pushed her out through the door and encouraged her to go find something to do. She gave him a look of rejection, but followed the other two, who were waiting on her.

"That must have been so hard for you, Piper," Katherine said as she took Piper's hand. "Dad lost me when I was only 28. So I never had to feel what it was like to lose him."

Jacob said nothing but acknowledged her with a fatherly smile.

Bridget had not realized it until Yeshua said it, but he was right. She did need to speak with him alone, badly. Emotions were racing in her and the conversation they had just had only ramped up a mixture of emotions she could not control.

Moments before, as she hung up the broom, her mind had gone to the one thing she most wanted to ask, the one thing she was most afraid to ask.

She turned and looked out of the barn, her eyes following Piper and the others, and let out an anxious sigh.

"Will I ever see Clayton again?" She was afraid to look at Yeshua, to see his lips begin to form the answer.

"We'll see," Yeshua said.

She frowned deeply.

"Every time my father said that he meant, 'No.'"

"I am not your father."

"But you know."

"I do."

"And you'll tell me."

"In time."

Now she was really upset. It could not be a tough question for him.

"How much time?" She felt he was putting her off, and it worried her.

"Not everything happens according to a man's timepiece. We will see. I can't explain this in a way you'd accept right now."

She couldn't hide her emotions. Her arms were shaking.

"I need to know."

"Yes, you do." He walked over to her, taking hold of her arms. "But I don't hurry what cannot be hurried. And there is something important for you to do."

"What?" she asked, feeling the heat and pressure of his hands warming her arms and calming them.

"Pray."

With that, he left her, walking slowly out the door where he nodded to Thomas, then took the side podwalk into #8. He went into the maintenance shed where he noticed the bench saw. He picked up a piece of wood stock, and began to measure it.

Bridget still felt the impression of his hands on her arms. As she came out of the barn and started toward Pod 10, Thomas caught up to her. He had overhead some of what just transpired between her and Yeshua.

"Having a little trouble?"

"Trouble?" she asked, miles away, her heart working overtime, and wondering what it was she was to pray about.

"Understanding things?" Thomas asked as they passed into the podwalk.

"A *little*?" she snipped, still upset.

"I know that feeling well," Thomas said.

"You?" she asked in disbelief. "One of his best friends?"

"Oh, yes. Me."

He stopped her and stood facing her just before they passed from the podwalk out into the gigantic, open space of #10.

"Bridget, give yourself some grace. Don't try to take it in all at once."

"Well, sorry, but I have lots of questions. *We* have lots of questions."

"I know. Who could blame you? I can't imagine how it was here. Being cooped up that long. Not knowing, not understanding. Afflicted by doubts."

"You can't possibly know."

"I have a little sense of it," he smiled. "It was probably much easier for those who just died." He gave her as sympathetic a look as he could muster. "You will understand. Give it time. Right now, to start, just trust the one who made you."

"Easier said than done," she said.

She looked at him, appreciating the fact that he seemed to care what she was feeling. She couldn't tell if Yeshua did or not.

As if he knew her thoughts, Thomas said, "He does care, Bridget. You have no idea. You don't see it now. You will, though."

He gave her a solid squeeze on the shoulder, turned, and walked on ahead.

Bridget stood there, stuck in the podwalk, stuck between what had been and what was happening now, wondering which was more confusing.

BOTH HORSES ran full out, heads bent toward the ground. Nathaniel's horse, Browny, had taken the lead, Yeshua trying to catch up on the back of an old mare named Aunt Louise.

Lunch and afternoon chores were over so Yeshua invited Nathaniel to ride the horse he had brushed earlier. They were rounding into the west edge of Pod 10, approaching the podwalk into #5.

Pam, watching in horror from the front of the tents, yelled at them to stop. She thought it would be reckless to ride through the podwalks, not to mention the concrete being hard on the horses' hooves. And she couldn't imagine how they would get around the pool at this speed. Then she pictured them tearing up the yard around the house in #4, if they headed there next.

Nate and Yeshua were both laughing loudly and the hooves pounded so steadily on the soil that neither heard Pam's bellowed protest.

Sing and Herald were also watching from a nearby field as Nathaniel grabbed the lead. Of course, he had the faster horse.

Nathaniel jerked the bridle in Browny's mouth as they raced toward the podwalk. He started to duck his head so he wouldn't bash it into the top of the doorjamb. But Browny had a different idea. He loved to race, especially against an older nag like Louise, and he knew how to protect his rider. He could not know that Nathaniel was ducking and he knew the boy's head would not clear the door. In an instant, Browny planted his front hooves into the soil like a jackhammer slamming into solid concrete and jolted to an abrupt stop.

Nathaniel went flying. The others watching, which fortunately did not include his mother or father, caught their breath. It looked like Nathaniel would fly headlong into the inch-thick Stellar pod wall alongside the door jamb. At the same moment, though, an almost imperceptible glitter of light fluttered around him and snuggled him up before he could hit the pod. His head rose upright and he landed on both feet, as surprised as a cat tossed out a second-story window. His tennis shoes skidded to a stop well short of the Stellar wall.

Nathaniel was more stunned than anyone. Aunt Louise and her rider lumbered to a stop alongside him.

"They shall bear you up," Yeshua chuckled to himself. He nodded to the creatures, still hovering around Nathaniel, who had caught him in mid-flight.

"Wow!" was all Nathaniel could manage.

Yeshua dismounted and put an arm around his shoulders.

"You're alright?" he asked.

Nathaniel nodded vigorously. "Let's go again!" he almost shouted.

Yeshua laughed at his bold courage and enthusiasm for danger.

Pam, Herald and Sing were running toward them. The angels glimmering around Nathaniel drew back like water running off someone fresh out of a pool. As the other three Solarians approached, they felt themselves walking into a pool of warmth and a shining presence that seemed new in the Solarium, even though the angels had been around a very long time.

Pam immediately understood.

"They saved him!" Pam said breathlessly as she came to a halt alongside Yeshua.

"They did, indeed."

Pam smiled.

"Great friends to keep nearby," she smiled.

"Soon the Earth itself will help protect you. And the angels will stay close as your guardians, now with a free hand."

"Free?"

"No more interference from evil wills."

Nathaniel didn't understand any of this, but he understood the sensation that had run through him, like a mild electrical charge racing up his back.

"Come on!" Nathaniel pleaded again. "Can I try it again?"

Yeshua shook his head.

"Let's not," he smiled.

"Do you mean to tell me that we can't be hurt?" Pam said, incredulity in her voice and more so in her face.

"Oh, little hurts. Stub your toe, maybe, little reminders of our humanity," Yeshua laughed. "But no, no more big hurts. Just be patient."

"This world is getting stranger than I thought," Pam said.

IT WAS late afternoon. Beams of sunlight filtered in through the pod and clothed the Solarium in a bath of rich warmth. All the children, with Herald and Sing supervising, were at the ocean. Kai was on the narrow beach in her small pocket chair that Herald had built.

An afternoon of work in the fields had tired them out and the adults had chased them away to enjoy some playtime. On a day like this the children preferred the warm salt water to the cool water of the swimming pool.

Before anyone headed into the water, however, they gathered around Piper, their curiosity peaked. She seemed off in her own world again, sitting on a small, flat rock with her toes in the sand, lost in thoughts she felt were beyond sharing.

"So, how did you know him, Piper?" Sing asked, going right to the spot where Piper's mind had wandered. She sank down on her knees by Piper and looked hard at Piper's cloaked expression.

"Know him?" Piper asked from far away.

"Yeshua. Herald told me. On the mountain, when you first saw him, somehow you knew him."

The other children came closer, squatting like a little flock of birds waiting for seed.

"I felt I did," Piper said, "but I'd never actually seen him."

"How could you know him, then," Herald asked, "if you'd never seen him?"

"I can't explain, exactly. It's knowing in a different way. A way that's . . ." She searched for a word. ". . . a way that's deeper than seeing with your eyes. That make sense?"

Sing frowned.

"No. Well, maybe a little," Sing acknowledged.

Nathaniel felt just as lost as he did earlier listening to Pam and Yeshua.

"How come everything is so confusing now?" he asked.

"Now?" Sing said.

Braden wasn't really interested and was anxious to get in the water, leg cast and all.

"Yeshua has been talking with Mom and the others. I know he has," Sing told Piper.

"Yeah," Herald said, "They go off with him alone a lot. I wonder if he's asking them things about them-selves, their past. Like he doesn't already know."

"He knows," Sing said. "I know he knows. It's in his eyes."

"His eyes are sure different. Have you seen it?" Nathaniel asked.

Others nodded.

"Not so different," Piper said.

No one could say for certain what was different about Yeshua's eyes, or his face, but none had missed the radiance that surrounded him.

"So, is he going to talk with us like that, too?" Sing asked with apprehension in her voice. "About our past?"

"I'm sure he will," Piper said.

"I'm kind of worried about my turn," Herald admitted hesitantly.

"Well, I wouldn't worry," Piper said. "He's spoken with me a couple of times, privately of course. He said he wants to know my heart."

"Yeah, that first afternoon on the peak, I felt it right away. It's like he sees inside you," Herald said.

"Is it spooky?" Braden asked Piper. He wasn't paying close attention and was absently scraping together a little sand castle that so far had no discernible design.

"No, not like you mean. Actually, it's the least spookiest thing I can imagine. When he said he wanted to know what was in my heart, I said, 'You already know.' He said, 'I want to hear it from you.'" Piper looked at the other children, including little Eira, who had come along.

"That's right," Eira assured them. This was one of the few things she was an authority on.

"Hear what?" Braden asked.

"Are you with him?" Eira said. "He wants to hear you say it. And to say you're sorry for things you've done wrong. And if you want to live under his rule."

"Aren't we kind of already?" Braden wondered, paying a little closer attention.

A wave lapped up onto the shore by Braden's cast, diverted around it, and washed out the west side of his castle.

"I mean," Piper explained, "can you respect him as our king. You have to be in—a hundred percent. Not halfway. Do you see?" Piper was having trouble expressing it but none were having trouble understanding it.

"So, we each have to tell him this?" Sing asked.

"Yes."

"That we think he is king?"

"*Think?*" Piper said with mild sarcasm. "Did you miss what he did OUTSIDE this morning?"

"You know what I mean," Sing answered.

"He's not just a king, you know, he's more." Piper acted like she didn't want to say it.

From nearby, Kai was burbling and chewing softly on her thumb. Sing picked her up out of her little chair and cradled her in her arms.

"More what?" Nathaniel asked.

"God." The word fell slowly from Piper's lips.

"What does it mean?" Sing said, genuinely in the dark. She had no clear understanding of the word, even though her father had so often spoken of God.

"Herald, you explain it," Piper said.

Herald frowned. *Why is it my job?* he wondered.

"Well, I guess, like Jimmy used to say. You know, when he read to us from his Bible. The best I can put it is, God is responsible for it all."

"All what?" Braden asked, his interest finally beginning to engage.

"All of everything. Jimmy said God made the world, so that would mean everything." He glanced at Piper as if for approval. "And he keeps it going, too. Right, Piper?"

"Uh, yeah," she said like this should be obvious. "But he's beyond us, beyond the world."

"Well then Yeshua is not God," Sing objected. "He is obviously right here with us."

"No, but that's the really awesome part," Piper said in a heartbeat. "Remember in Jimmy's Bible? The name Immanuel?"

Herald unknowingly echoed Jimmy's comment at breakfast. "God with us."

"Yes," Piper said, "as a man."

Sing was still struggling. Holding Kai in one arm, with her free hand she brushed back some hair that an overhead fan had pushed in front of her eyes.

"Seems so farfetched," Sing said.

"But look," Piper reminded her, "you wanted to know how I knew him. That's how. I just *knew,* because he's been here with us all along. Before, we couldn't see him. Now, we can."

"Can't we go swim now?" Nathaniel asked. "My head hurts."

"I'm sorry, Nate. I just want everyone to know, he'll

seek you out." Piper was getting animated. "He wants our allegiance." She rubbed at her cheek. "You need to be ready. He wants our love, too, but I don't think he'll accept our love without our allegiance."

The other children had turned inward, wondering what they should do. For nearly a minute they looked at each other, or out over the sloshing waves of their artificial ocean, turning things over in their young minds. For the Solarian children, life had always been strange. It seemed beyond strange now.

"You do it, Piper," Herald said, getting up and wading into the water.

"What do you mean?"

"You tell him, for all of us."

"That he's our king?"

"Uh-huh." Herald was ready to dive in.

"That's not fair," Piper said. "Why can't you tell him yourself?"

"Maybe I can. But after you tell him." He was looking away, toward the water.

Piper stood and went over to him, barely touching his arm. "Why would it be so hard?"

Herald wouldn't answer. Finally, he did, still facing the water so the other children wouldn't hear him.

"Because he scares me. I really like him. But he scares me."

"He's not scary," Piper said.

"To me he is." Herald pictured Yeshua's face, radiance and all.

Piper ran her toes back and forth in the water that was flowing in and sifting down out of sight through the sand. Her lips wrestled each other as she tried to think of what to say to Herald.

Sing came over to them.

"Don't push him, Piper," she said. "I know what he's feeling."

Piper looked at her, then at Herald.

"Alright, I will then. I'll talk to him, for all of us," Piper said. "OK?" she asked Braden and Nathaniel.

They nodded enthusiastically.

"OK, but it won't be enough. He's going to ask you eventually. He's going to want you to declare it from your own mouth."

This shuttered the conversation.

It was not a moment too soon for Braden, who was dragging his leg toward the water. He dove forward. The air in the inner cast helped him float, but kept rolling him sideways. He joggled around like a fishing bobber on a line, fighting to keep his head up.

Piper dove after Braden, hoping he would not drown.

AS THE children swam playfully, Yeshua was having one of those conversations Piper had spoken of, this time with Mai Ker. She and Yeshua were sitting on the porch of the old Victorian again, looking across the lawn, neglected for years but now greening up by the hour.

What had been a very difficult conversation for Mai Ker had just wound down. Both were smiling. Mai Ker's breathing was returning to normal and she could begin to taste again something in her mouth other than cotton. A weight of generations had just lifted off her shoulders.

"Thank you," she said earnestly.

"For which part?" Yeshua asked.

"Well, everything, but mostly, I forgot to thank you for the birds. I've missed them so much!"

"I know you have. You're welcome, Mai."

"Bridget was ecstatic yesterday when she saw Caroline!"

"Was she?"

Mai Ker looked puzzled.

"I thought so. Why wouldn't she be?"

"She was at first. But then it seemed awkward for her. Caroline reminds her of Clayton."

"Oh." Mai Ker watched his face for any hint. "So?"

"So, what?"

"Is he coming?"

"Who?" It was a careful but obvious dodge.

"Clayton."

"Seems to be a common question today."

"Please do not play around about this," Mai Ker said as sternly as she dared.

"I'm not playing at all, Mai Ker. There is much to consider. It needs time."

"Hasn't there been enough time? He died years ago." She considered this remark and her excitement deflated several levels. She began to worry. "You have not decided yet. Is that it?"

"Other things are involved besides my decision, Mai Ker. As you have just discovered about yourself."

She remembered what they had just talked about, her own past, and her years of resisting the very idea of a sovereign God.

"Oh," she said again, "I see."

She stood from her porch chair.

"Can we walk over there?"

"Where?"

"The aviary?"

"Let's."

Mai Ker walked beside him through the short podwalk into #6. There were several new birds besides those they had seen yesterday.

"Wait, where did those new ones come from?"

"Where does anything come from?" Yeshua asked her.

She laughed.

"Very funny," she said.

They spent several minutes walking around the huge open cage as Mai Ker imitated the voices of several birds. Yeshua watched her delighted smiles that seemed to match the bird songs. She was definitely connected to nature in a special way.

"I see why you pursued biological science," he said.

"It was only natural, I suppose. I always loved all of the—" She corrected herself. "All of *your* creatures."

They started into the podwalk leading back into Pod 10. Yeshua, nearly a foot taller than Mai Ker, rested his heavy arm over her shoulders as they walked. She felt considerably taller than usual.

"Jimmy will be happy," he said.

"Yes," she said. "He was usually pretty happy."

"I mean, now that you have come under my reign. He'll be even happier, now. Yesterday, he was worried."

"About me?"

She slowed her steps. Yeshua gave her shoulders a gentle squeeze.

"He has worried for months, Mai Ker. For years, actually. For being such a wonderful person, your heart was very stubborn."

"Yes, I suppose it was. But you changed that, softened it."

"So did Jimmy," Yeshua told her.

As they came out of the podwalk into #10, the waning sun's rays penetrated through the pods sideways creating the image of layers in a cake. The golden rays cast long shadows, highlighting the burgeoning plants running field after field across the great pod. The sunrays and shadows mingled with the subtle glimmering lights of the angels who were never completely out of sight now. What had been the Solarians' protected, miniature world was itself beginning to blossom, with fruit and light and new warmth. Creation, INSIDE and OUT, was showing signs of new vigor and joy.

"Yes, Jimmy will be very happy," Yeshua repeated, as they cut away from the sidewalk and strolled carefully through a recently harvested field of squash. "No more parting between you two."

"What do you mean?" Mai Ker asked, stopping to look at him squarely.

"I mean that if you did not want to be with me, you could not be with him for long."

She looked surprised. He lifted his heavy arm off her shoulders.

"Why didn't you tell me that before? When we talked?"

"I don't twist arms," he said. His eyes bore upon her, going right to her heart. "Committing your life to me had to be a willing decision, Mai, with no hidden motives. It is the nature of love that it can never be compelled."

She nodded, understood, took his hand and began walking again.

"You see why, don't you?" he asked.

She smiled, but her reply was interrupted when she saw Jimmy beyond a fence line at the far side of the pod. She pulled free from Yeshua's hand and ran toward him. Jimmy was bent down, searching for any remaining weeds he might find among some cabbage plants. So far his hands were empty.

Mai Ker leapt on his back like a pillow flung in a pillow fight. They tumbled onto the ground. She laughed ridiculously. Surprised, Jimmy rolled, then lifted her aloft like a large doll, looking up into her eyes. She kissed him, pulled herself closer, and kissed him again.

"Thank you, Lord, for this wonderful man!"

"Thank you, Father," Yeshua said to himself as he walked steadily toward the kitchen tent, looking for a snack.

13

Sunday Evening

Evening dishes were done and it was to be an evening of rest. Pam and Sing had teamed up and made a special cake, cherry flavored with white and yellowish creamy icing, an unwitting rendering in flour, sugar and water of what the Solarium had looked like late this afternoon.

The afternoon sky, cloudless until nearly 6:00 p.m., had darkened to the west. Growing banks of clouds swam toward the eastern horizon, beckoning a hesitant moon that crept slowly into the sky. The giant orb, magnified by the atmosphere, climbed to watch over the planet out of whose womb she had been created.

Everyone, including their visitors, was clamoring for dessert. They were waiting for Yeshua but he was nowhere to be found. The youngsters begged to start in on the cake but Jimmy insisted they wait. He went looking for their king.

To his surprise, he found Yeshua resting on a recliner alongside the pool in #5, his eyes closed. Jimmy hesitated, not sure if he should disturb him. But as Jimmy approached, Yeshua opened his eyes to greet him.

"Didn't know where you were," Jimmy said.

"It is sometimes hard to tell, isn't it?" Yeshua said. "You're all waiting, I suppose."

"For dessert. Pam and Sing have the cake done. Want some?"

"Wouldn't miss it."

They walked back at an easy pace.

"Thank you," Jimmy said, unsolicited.

"For?"

"Mai Ker. Your talk. Thank you."

"I've known how deep the love is between you. It can now grow to fulfillment."

"It just never stops, does it?" Jimmy said.

"Love?"

"Yes."

"It does for those who have only imagined it. But for those who have actually given it, it cannot cease. That's its nature. It is who I am."

Jimmy's mind began to tangle in these weeds and he let it go. He felt so good, and so in love with Mai Ker and their children, that he didn't need to say anything more. Walking alongside Yeshua was enough.

As they walked, Caroline flew out of the podwalk from #6. Jimmy recognized her again. He smiled at Yeshua, who nodded back.

"It's so great that she's back. Will other animals be coming back!"

"Some, those that were special to people."

"Oh man!" He watched the little creature circle over them, then fly northward toward the tents.

The kids had all quieted down some by the time Jimmy and Yeshua reached the main tent where the Solarians and their guests were gathered. Caroline, unseen from inside the tent, had swooped up and perched on the top of it like a sentry. An old habit, still retained.

As soon as Pam saw Jimmy and Yeshua approaching, she cut the cake. Braden hobbled over to be first in line. Cake was his favorite.

They settled into chairs or onto the thick canvas floor. Pam sat on a soft chair near a lamp, her plate and a cup of juice cradled on her lap. Piper scooted toward her on the floor and leaned against her leg. Pam savored a bite of cake. The sweetness clung to her mouth.

"I think we've all died and gone to Heaven," she said.

Yeshua gave her an animated grin.

"Backwards, Pam," he said, sipping milk. "You haven't died, and Heaven has come here."

"I still can't get ahold of that idea," she said. "I've been waiting for so long. To die, I mean. And now, no waiting, and no dying! I can't quite register that."

"You were chosen for that privilege, most of you who lived here." Yeshua looked at Jimmy. "Some not."

Jimmy didn't even blink. His death had been horrible but, he now understood, more than worth it. As followers of Yeshua for so many generations past had discovered, death was a brick wall, but there was a narrow door. One needed only the key.

The room was quiet as everyone softly munched their cake. OUTSIDE the Solarium, the thunderheads had gathered into rain clouds. Gentle flashes of lightning punctuated the sky. Steady rain bathed the pods for the next half hour, then slowed to a steady, misty drizzle that continued into the night.

"Where's Thomas tonight?" Bridget asked. "And Jacob?"

"I've sent them on an errand. Some work to do."

"So just us tonight?" Mai Ker asked.

"Exactly so," he said. "The Solarians, your children, and your new friends."

There was a very brief silence. Piper leaned forward and sat up straighter.

"May I say something? I'm supposed to tell you something."

She had already clued him in before supper.

"Something to say to me?" Yeshua asked, playing his part. He gave her one of those expressive looks they had been exchanging. "Of course, Piper."

"All of us kids, we talked."

The other Solarian children nodded earnestly, except Herald who sat alongside Sing, holding her hand but looking at the floor.

"And?" Yeshua encouraged her.

"We've decided. We all want you to be our king."

"All?" He looked toward Herald, seeing only the top of his head. "I'm glad—" he started to say with a serious tone in his voice.

Herald couldn't stand it.

"The thing is," he butted in, "I don't know if that's right. For me, I mean."

"What's wrong, Herald?" Yeshua asked, again with an encouraging tone.

"Well, there was that time." Herald looked at Jimmy, clearly afraid to go on, but he did. "That day when Jimmy fell. I forgot everyone else, and thought only of myself—playing the hero. I raced up there to get to Mai Ker and got her down. Then I saw Sing." He squeezed her hand. Sniffles started to plug his nose. "I realized," he said choking a little, "how badly I scared her, and how stupid it was. And wrong. To risk my life like that—not even thinking of her. Then I went and climbed the pod OUTSIDE, and I knew it was dangerous, and I knew we were having a baby." He stopped for an overdue breath. "Sing didn't want me to go. But I wouldn't listen. Of course." His voice trailed off.

Sing listened, watching him and holding his hand tightly, but said not a word. Yeshua knew what was in Herald's heart and gave him the opening to continue.

"So this has to do with you accepting me?" Yeshua asked.

"Of course it does! Don't you see?" It was a stupid remark and he regretted it the moment it left his mouth. "I'm sorry, I don't mean that. I just mean, I'm not worthy of you—when I acted so selfishly, playing Mr.

Hero, and forgetting about Sing!" He looked exasperated, thinking Yeshua didn't understand his feelings.

Yeshua knew all too well.

"A very human emotion, Herald. You acted strong, but you felt weak. I once knew that feeling, briefly. The night before they killed me. I prayed for hours so that I could be brave. But really, I wanted the Father to spare me the pain. I felt my human weakness hanging from me like a millstone. So yes, Herald, I do know."

"It's not the same," Herald said quietly.

"No?" Yeshua tried to reassure him. "Herald, the human spirit is weak. Apart from the Father, you would all be helpless." He studied Herald's expression, which was changing to one of compliance and understanding. "Those times when you didn't consider Sing's feelings, both times you were doing it to rescue someone from a danger. The one time—when you and Bridget went out to repair the pod roof—you believed Sing was in danger." Yeshua's voice had become stern, as it had with Mai Ker earlier in the day. "Looking back, now, you think you acted selfishly. But beneath that selfish drive was also a worthy one—your desire to protect Sing, and your unborn baby."

Herald was caught off guard.

"Well, maybe. I guess."

"So?" Yeshua prodded him.

"So, I still don't feel worthy of you. My gosh, I know who you are!" he said intensely. He glanced sideways at Jimmy. "I don't even feel I should be around you!" If Herald had meant anything in his life, he meant this. He would have fled this instant but for Sing's tightening grip holding him in place.

Herald's eyes analyzed the canvas floor, studying each wrinkle and misplaced thread.

"You feel that because you're not worthy, and you're honest enough to admit it," Yeshua answered flatly but powerfully. "But none ever was. Not one."

Yeshua's stern tone began to ease. His eyes narrowed slightly as he waited for this to settle in on Herald.

"We should be having this conversation in private, Herald. But you brought it up, so I'll respect your courage. Son, no one could be judged by my worthiness. No one could live five seconds under that demand. But that's not the way the Father chose. I judge by your heart, your will. That is where I find the real you." He asked Herald to look up. "And that young man I have no hesitation to welcome into my kingdom."

The minutes-long silence that followed this sat like a layer of concrete poured across every person in the tent. The younger Solarian children stared up at Yeshua, mesmerized, but growing to love this man who had been a complete stranger to them three days ago.

Jimmy was watching Herald closely, this fatherless boy he had tried so hard to mentor and love as his own son.

"Is it alright, Herald?" Yeshua finally asked when it was obvious no one else dared speak.

"Huhm?" Herald managed, looking up.

"Is it alright with you, to give me your allegiance, allegiance to a king you are completely unworthy of?" He stared at the boy.

Herald nearly bit a hole into his lower lip, which quivered uncontrollably.

"Yes."

Just having said that word brought courage back into Herald's heart, from where he did not know. The depth of his sense of unworthiness multiplied instantly at least a hundredfold but his courage a thousandfold.

He raised his head further, looked at Yeshua, and nodded hard.

"Yes, Lord," he repeated, clearing his throat.

"Then you are a worthy prince in this kingdom," Yeshua told him. "Ask Thomas sometime. The least worthy is the most."

These words shattered the concrete straightjacket that had confined everyone. Air returned to the tent. A new peace settled over them, except for Sing.

She took her hand back from Herald, who had nearly crushed it moments ago, and got up and walked over to Yeshua's chair. She stood looking at his face. His skin looked more alive than ever with its ever-present radiance engulfing his entire body. She felt she could see inside him. She looked into his eyes.

"It's alright then? For us children?" she asked.

"Well, I have Piper's word, don't I." It was not a question. "Yes, it will be alright." He rubbed Sing's chin. "We may still talk, to make it more real for each of you," he smiled fondly.

"I think I would like that," Sing said. But then an inexplicable sadness crawled across her face and the momentary light in her eyes dimmed. As she fought an unwelcome frown, she said, "But what about Kai?"

"Ah," he said, "there it is."

"What?" she asked, confused.

"The unbounded love of a mother for her child." He took Sing's hands firmly in his own and rubbed them as if bringing life through them back into her whole body. "A love that would trade her own life for her child's." He stood and cuddled her head against his chest. "Don't worry, Sing. Your beautiful little Kai will be with us."

"But she can't decide. Piper said we all had to decide," Sing fretted, burying her face in his thick shirt.

Yeshua, his hand at the back of her head, drew her face back so she could look at his.

"Sing, Kai is fine. She and I have talked."

"She can't."

"Not in your tongue, no."

Sing's eyes opened wider. She looked at him, utterly astonished.

"You talked . . ."

"We did. She loves me. Not yet like she loves you, of course. But she will."

Sing was shaking her head.

"But I'm worried."

"Oh, you worry so much. A true subject trusts her king."

"I trust you. I—I just don't understand."

"And right now you don't need to." He kissed her cheek. "You will in time. A princess grows to know everything about her Father's house, and her Father's ways."

Sing felt they were dancing although they were perfectly still.

This moment that could easily have gone on forever was broken by the graveling sound of Jacob's voice at the door of the tent, where Jacob stood alongside Thomas.

"It's well, Lord. We've brought them," Jacob said.

Suddenly, he dodged his head as Caroline flew in through the door and circled overhead around the tent. She lit on the top of a lampshade several feet behind Yeshua and perched, waiting.

Thomas, also dodging Caroline, spoke.

"Took some searching though."

Bridget, Mai Ker and Pam were staring at Caroline. They were also trying to decide, hoping against hope, if her presence signaled something. All three froze between apprehension and disbelief.

Will Atchison stepped from behind Thomas and walked into the tent.

"Nice place," Will smiled, looking around. "Not what I would've built, of course."

Pam turned, stunned a second time. She rushed as if in a dream toward Atchison, bumping a table and knocking two plates of the cake onto the floor.

"Oh, dear God!" she yelped, reaching Willy. She grabbed his arms and embraced him. "William the 2nd! Dear Lord, I can't believe it!"

"Believe it? See it!" Willy laughed, squeezing her in his best bear hug.

She pushed back, grinning madly.

"You are late for supper," she scolded.

Willy roared his bellicose laugh.

Bridget remained frozen in place, expectant, looking from Caroline to Yeshua, but afraid to hope and afraid to move. She glanced at the door and just as quickly glanced away. Thomas looked back over his shoulder.

"Well?" Thomas said to the evening air behind him. He made a slow, forward gesture with his hand.

Clayton Block appeared in the doorway between Jacob and Thomas, embarrassed and apparently still unsure he was actually here. He had the look of a kid who had just crawled out from under his bed after some naughtiness and was about to get spanked.

Bridget couldn't move. Her eyes, she was sure, had failed, or her mind was playing a trick. She saw a man there, but it could not be Clayton. She tried to say his name but couldn't. Herald saw the sudden anxiety on her face, then looked at the man standing between Jacob and Thomas. He stood and walked to this newest stranger. He could tell from his mother's look alone who this must be.

"Dad," he said with a sense of having just discovered a hidden treasure.

Now Block stared.

"I'm, ah, I'm Herald," his son said.

Before Block could digest this, Bridget finally broke the emotional glue that had held her feet to the floor and rushed to Block. She grabbed Herald's upper arm and squared his broad shoulders to his dad's, trying futilely to brush away tears that were spilling all over her son's face and her own.

"Herald, this is your father," she said, swallowing tears. Then she lunged at Clayton and kissed him for what seemed to everyone in the tent to be an embarrassingly long time.

"Welcome home," Yeshua said to Willy and Clayton, rising to greet them. "You can see, some here have waited a long time for this night. Though they were afraid to hope for it."

"Me, too," Willy said. "Always said, 'If it's too good to be true, it ain't.' Wrong as usual, I guess."

He laughed and beamed his unique William the 2nd smile. His fun-loving disposition was an instant hit with the children.

Jimmy and Mai Ker pressed into the little group as hugs were incoherently exchanged. Mai Ker turned and mouthed a *Thank you* to Yeshua. He just nodded as if this might happen every day.

He then beckoned Thomas off to the side and said quietly, "I sent for three. Where is she?"

"Sarajane? Wouldn't come. Said she'd have to think about it some more."

"Well," Yeshua said, "not unexpected." Disappointment crept into his expression. "It always hurts, when even one turns back."

Mai Ker couldn't hear them but noticed the change in his face.

"What's wrong?" she asked Yeshua, unintentionally quelling the spontaneous celebration.

The others grew quiet. The children's stares moved from the two new strangers to Yeshua. He looked toward the tent roof as if looking through it.

"One of you is missing," he said.

Bridget looked around. Her face was struck with an *Oh, no,* look. "Sarajane," she said.

Yeshua nodded, his face grave.

"I did try. She won't come."

Mai Ker saw the confused looks passing between the elder Solarians and the blank looks on the younger ones.

"I do not understand," Mai Ker said, "why would she not want to come?"

"I won't say," he said.

"You won't say?"

"It is for Sarajane to say."

"But we want her back," Bridget said. "She went through so much. She's like a sister."

"I know that," Yeshua said, adding nothing further.

Block looked at him. Through death Block had come to know Yeshua's face and his great power. The doubts were gone, but confusion remained.

"That's all you're going to say?" he asked bluntly.

"That's all I'm going to say." Yeshua went and sat again. He picked some crumbs of cake from his plate and carefully nibbled them.

A cloak of quiet worry fell over the Solarians, at least those who had known Sarajane. She had often drawn back from them. But why, or how, they wondered, could she refuse such a reunion?

Yeshua saw their despondency and answered their looks.

"It's not you. It's her." He looked at the first- and second-generation Solarians spread around him. "When I spoke with her this afternoon, I had hoped she would come."

"Spoke when?" Jimmy asked. "You never left here today."

"Not that you would have noticed," Yeshua replied. "I did talk with her. I gave her time to change her mind. She hasn't."

"I don't understand. You've been here with us, how could you have seen her?" Pam asked.

"Don't worry, Pam," he answered.

"She is still dead you mean?" Mai Ker asked.

"No, she is raised, like everyone else. But she's chosen to remain alone."

"This does not feel right," Mai Ker said with a hushed voice.

"No, it doesn't," Yeshua said. "Anyone who turns away, it does not feel right for me, either. But choices have to be made. And choices have consequences."

"I do not understand why she would not want to see us again," Mai Ker said, the hurt in her voice palpable.

"As I said, Mai Ker, it's not you. She doesn't want to be with *me*. That's all I will say for the present."

The Solarian children were mystified by this intense exchange about someone they had only vaguely heard of. Except for a few pictures in the Solarium archives, the children had no idea who Sarajane was.

Oddly, their guests seemed to better understand what was going on, as if they had been through something like this themselves.

"But you can change her mind," Mai Ker pressed him, "right?" She waited.

"Change her mind?" Yeshua said, musing as if he had never considered the question until this moment. "What you mean is, can I force her will?"

"Yes. No," Mai Ker stuttered. She remembered their talk earlier in the day. She realized she knew the answer.

He looked at her, then at the rest, including the two men who had just returned.

"Any of you, did I force you?"

"No," Jimmy said solemnly. "We listened to you, but we changed our own minds."

"You more than changed your mind. You altered your will, and thus your future." Yeshua nodded almost imperceptibly. "Sarajane faces the same choice."

"But where is she?" Block asked, trying desperately to catch up with the last few days.

"She's elsewhere," was all Yeshua would say.

Atchison decided to wade in, as he could see the conversation going nowhere.

"So, let me understand. She wants to be alone. And you're alright with that?"

"Alright? No!" Yeshua said too loudly, his eyes widening. "No." He brought his voice down. "I am *not* alright with it. But I must respect her choice as I have respected yours. There are no conscripts in my kingdom."

Pam, almost swallowing the words, said, "So, is she in Hell?"

"One of her own making."

"Hell is real?" Willy asked.

"William," Thomas interrupted, "where have you been?"

This stung Willy like a giant wasp.

"Well, I—" He looked dumbfounded. "You mean . . . you don't mean—"

"He means exactly that, William," Yeshua said more calmly. "You've come here, now, because you made a decision. If you think, you'll remember."

William the 2nd deflated, then nodded purposefully. He stood like a sentry who had been caught sleeping on duty. He dared not look straight at Yeshua for the time being. Their last conversation had involved enough of those eyes to last Willy at least a century. He also avoided looking at his friends. A spot on the gray canvas of the far tent wall took his full attention.

"Oh, my Lord!" Block suddenly cried out. "Look who's here!"

He finally noticed Caroline perched on the lamp where she sat as if this were just any other night in Solarium-3. Block hurried toward her so quickly it spooked her. She spread her wings, flew for an instant, but turned in midair and plopped onto his shoulder, pecking at his cheek.

"Well I'll be . . ." Atchison said, glad everyone's attention had gone elsewhere. "That beats just about everything. Is that really our same little critter?" he asked Yeshua.

"The very same, Will."

Bridget was still beside herself. The entrance of Caroline into the tent followed almost instantly by Block walking through the door had sent her emotions into a complete tailspin. She felt a mixture of confusion, frightened joy mixed with love, surprise and contentment, seemingly disconnected emotions that escalated into a perfect sense of fulfillment. Her heart overflowed, her whole body felt on fire. She hurried after Block and grabbed him sideways, careful not to dislodge Caroline from his shoulder.

"Clayton, I can't believe it! I missed you like a part of my body was gone."

"You look pretty whole to me," he laughed.

She gave him a little sideways shove on the chin, a gesture they both knew meant "I love you despite it all!"

Pam, Jimmy and Mai Ker were chattering with each other like three lunatics at an asylum picnic, each experiencing a rush of feelings like those going on in Bridget. But all the elder Solarians felt one thing in common. They were together again. Except one.

With the new arrivals and an onslaught of stories about the old times in Solarium-3, the younger

Solarians began to feel awkward. Herald finally broke into the commotion.

"Mom, could we take the kids somewhere else for a while?" Herald was still tremendously uncomfortable around the two men he had never met before, even though one was his father.

"Maybe you better stay," Block said to him. "All of you."

Yeshua, as if waking from an evening daydream, nodded haphazardly in reply to Block's remark. The indescribable radiance that constantly surrounded him appeared to have been ramped up six notches.

"So, is Sarajane gonna be OK?" Willy asked Yeshua.

Curiously, this unexpected turn had hit Atchison even harder than the others who had been with her at first. Despite his close friendship with Block and his outwardly humorous disposition, he had always been something of a social outcast as a young man and knew firsthand the sense of isolation Sarajane was no doubt feeling.

"She has isolated herself, Will. I can do no more, unless her heart changes."

Mai Ker's lips were opening to speak but she was cut short.

"Enough," Yeshua said. "If Sarajane is imprisoned, it is a prison of self-condemnation. I've told you I do not override anyone's will. She has been offered a chance. She must make her decision, a decision that will be final."

"How could anyone shun God?" Piper muttered, her whole countenance in pain. She could not accept this simple but disfigured reality.

"Oh, Piper, so many do," Yeshua told her. "We must leave it at that," he said to everyone.

There were several beats of silence, except for a number of quick chirps from Caroline. On the last of these, a second nuthatch, the male, dipped into the tent, circling high near where the center pole supported the roof. Caroline gave Block a last peck by the ear, then launched from his shoulder to join her brother. They flew quickly out into the glowing darkness of Pod 10.

"Now, who was . . .?" Block said in surprise. He looked at Yeshua.

"A brother."

"Huh," said Block. "Didn't know she had one."

"Only briefly," Yeshua said, remembering the tiny stillborn creature lying on the soil all those years ago. "Enough heaviness," Yeshua told them. "We must celebrate the return of William and Clayton! Is there any wine in this great Solarium?" he asked, though he didn't need to.

"Are we going to have communion?" Pam smiled, her sudden excitement breaking the tension that had hung over them like a second tent.

Yeshua burst out laughing.

"Dear Pam," he said, quelling his laughter, "that time is past. Sacraments were a pledge, a mere foretaste. The true bread, the best wine, are now here," he said, gesturing to himself.

Pam's excitement changed to intense embarrassment because she immediately grasped what he meant, owing to the patient drills of a rather insistent, bothersome pastor who had trained her as a child.

"Within me," Yeshua said, "Earth and Heaven are one, spirit and flesh perfected."

"Like Mom said," Piper smiled, "communion."

Kai made a babbling sound from her carrier alongside Sing.

"Out of the mouths of babes and infants . . ." Yeshua said.

His subjects, young and old, were one and all feeling overwhelmed, trying to fit together these new pieces of what seemed a gigantic jigsaw puzzle. He smiled at their earnestness to regain their lost vision of the deep mysteries of creation. So that they would not drown in their thoughts, he broke in.

"Maybe I wasn't heard. Is there any wine?"

Jimmy looked at Bridget and Mai Ker.

"You didn't drink it all?" he said with playful accusation.

"Drank quite a bit after *your* stupid move," Mai Ker said with a pretended glare.

"I bet," Jimmy said, the instant of his fall rushing through his memory, but this time without fear or pain. "Yeah. Pretty stupid." He looked at Mai Ker. "But you didn't drink it all?"

"No, silly," she laughed. "Come on. There's still a large stock in number fourteen."

"Of course, the fuels and fertilizers pod," Yeshua chortled.

Somehow, Mai Ker missed the joke.

"Yes, you know, up high?" Bridget told the Lord, gesturing with her head toward the younger children.

"Wisdom itself," Yeshua said.

14

Sunday Night

Their hour-long conversation was now several hours past. Late evening had crawled into night.

The younger children were in bed. Herald and Sing had gone for another private walk. Bridget, Pam and Mai Ker went with Block and Atchison over to the old house, a visit for old times, talking about all that had happened since the two men had died.

Clayton and Willy brought with them a few vague notions about events from what Yeshua had told them before they were resurrected, preparing them for their return. But only now were they learning details, especially about the children.

Before long, Clayton noticed that Bridget was not really at ease. He took her hand and guided her over into Pod 5 where they stood awkwardly by the swimming pool, facing more of it than each other.

"I worried you wouldn't come back," Bridget said hesitantly.

"Really? Why?"

She turned and studied his eyes as if for the first time.

"It was taking too long," she said, "after Jimmy came back."

"Yeah, I don't understand why, exactly. He said to be patient. Said it had something to do with you."

"Jimmy?"

"Yeshua."

"Wait." She looked at him suspiciously. "You talked

with him recently?"

"Oh, we talked over the years a lot. But when I found out Jimmy had been sent back, I started bugging him about me."

"You talked with Yeshua, while you were dead?" It seemed a step too far for Bridget, though she should have known it.

"Well, sure. OK, I guess it wasn't really talk, since I had no mouth, so no voice. I can't really describe it. You kind of had to be there."

This did nothing to help relieve Bridget's unease.

"I'm not at all sorry I missed the dying part," she laughed. She pressed Clayton. "So, you coming back, he told you it had to do with me?"

"Yeah, the timing, he said."

Bridget looked distraught, then guilty, as she slowly said, "Yeah."

Block saw the hesitancy in her face.

"Can you tell me?" He watched her lovingly.

Bridget felt exactly as she had at the moment she told her mother and father she was pregnant at 15 years old.

"I wanted you back. Jimmy was back, so I knew it must be possible. And I asked him." She hesitated. "That was really bad."

"What?"

"He wouldn't answer."

"Whad'ya mean?" Block asked.

"He said I had to pray."

"Oh, yeah. That was the timing part he meant."

"So I did, this afternoon before supper. For a really long time. But . . ." Bridget's words drifted into silence.

"And?"

"I was afraid," she said.

"Afraid to pray? Or that I'd come back?" Block was stuck, not sure how to go on.

"Both," she confessed with an embarrassed look. "I

wanted you back, oh, I *wanted* you. But then I pictured it, pictured this. And I got scared, because I knew if you came back you'd be mad."

Block thought he saw where this was going so he just prodded her to continue.

"Mad, because I married Jimmy. I betrayed you."

Block collected her back into his arms. He didn't need to see her face. In fact, he didn't want to see her face for the moment.

"Bridget." His voice was soothing but just as strong as ever. Stronger. "Sweetheart, you didn't betray me. I was gone. Till death do us part, remember?"

"I know. But when we married Jimmy, it felt funny. Not funny. You know." She fumbled for words that made sense, fighting her emotions. "He knew why we wanted him to have children with us. My gosh, he was so embarrassed. You should have seen him. He was so awkward, like a little boy getting his first kiss."

"That's Jimmy," Block grinned.

"But we did it right, we were married. He insisted! And I pledged that I would love him. And I did, I really tried." Her assurances felt forced, even to herself. "But never, Clayton," she looked up at him, "did I feel like I felt toward you."

She stepped away and turned her back. She felt closed in and wanted air. "And then when Yeshua said I had to pray, I thought, my gosh, now I've really done it. Not just made Clayton mad, but made him mad, too!" She tried to calm herself out of the memory of those moments with Yeshua. "Then I realized why I had to pray. I wanted you back—and I didn't. I didn't want to face you, Clayton. I didn't"—she swallowed hoarsely—"I didn't want this moment." She nearly cried, but tears would have been false.

Block came up behind her and touched her shoulders ever-so-carefully, as if the slightest touch might tear into her flesh.

"I think there was an apology in there somewhere," he said softly. "Except you don't need to. After I went—died—Yeshua let me know what happened here. Yeah, I admit, it felt a little strange. I couldn't for the life of me figure out why he thought he needed to tell me. 'Course, I didn't understand yet about a real resurrection." He made a simple nod that Bridget couldn't see. "Now I see why he had to tell me."

She turned to him. She looked at him again, the handsome features she had been so drawn to since the day they met. She remembered that quiet evening in the Research Center, their first night Sealed-In, figuring out a name for Caroline. His tenderness toward his little pet had fascinated her.

His face now was certainly the same, yet different. It looked richer, stronger, more invigorated than ever. Three small acne scars from his teen years were still there, but they now looked more like points of light, a constellation of life-stars forming a special pattern that marked him as the true Clayton.

"You do amaze me, Clayton Block." Her smile emerged from behind the fear. "OK, I admit it. I still love you."

He pulled her into his arms again. The warmth of their bodies melted together. They stood like two trees that had grown together in a forest over decades, whose branches, once far apart, were now intertwined and not quite distinguishable from each other's. If they had stood like this into eternity, they would have been content.

"Well, feel guilty for a while if it helps," Block joked. "Just don't do it because of me. Anyway, maybe it's Jimmy who needs the apology."

THE NIGHT had grown long. While the other elder Solarians had been off reminiscing at the old house, Jimmy found himself sitting, half-dozing, just outside the front of the main tent, his partly refilled wine glass in one hand.

It was well past midnight. Through the southerly exposure of the roof of #10, the waning moon broke through dissipating clouds and approached the horizon, bidding Jimmy goodnight, whispering to him that the wee hours had arrived.

Yeshua was nearby, also sitting, leaning against a fence post with his knees drawn up to his chest. Jimmy couldn't tell if he was awake or asleep.

"You never explained," Jimmy said quietly, in case Yeshua was in fact asleep, which he doubted.

"About?" came the quick response. Though his eyes were closed, Yeshua was not the least bit sleepy.

"About how you could have talked with Sarajane. When you never left."

"I don't always explain."

"But would you?" Jimmy looked around. "It's just the two of us."

"It's no secret." With both hands, Yeshua brushed his dark hair around the back of his head. "I just went."

"Went? But you were right here all day."

"To you, it would seem so."

"You were there—and here?" Jimmy was sure the lateness of the hour had jumbled his mind.

"I left for a time, but you would not have noticed."

"When you were by the pool?"

"Then. And several other times."

Nothing was sinking in. Yeshua could tell.

"Jimmy, remember that I said time runs differently, now. And for me, it is unique."

"OK . . ." Jimmy intoned, though it meant nothing.

"At 'times,' as you would call it, I left. But for me, time has never been entirely solid. If you see what I mean."

"I don't, actually."

"I am embodied. In that respect, I'm just like all of you. But I am also *not* like you. Incarnate, but still the Son."

He looked across at Jimmy, whose head was tilted up slightly as if his chin were hanging across a clothesline that wasn't there. Jimmy didn't reply.

"It's not easy to grasp. I'm like you in our humanity, but unlike you, in the Father."

Perhaps it was the lingering effects of that second glass of wine, but this made entirely no sense to Jimmy, either.

"When I've gone somewhere else, as you perceive time, you would not see me leave. Or return."

"Moving in the spirit, you mean?" Jimmy asked.

"No, Jimmy, spirit and body, the whole of me. But the time involved, relative to time here, is different. I might be gone a long while—as you would measure it if you were with me—but here it would seem like just the blink of an eye, the length of a hiccup."

By now, Jimmy's mind was saturated in more ways than one and was approaching incoherence. He felt the draw of a good night's sleep. His eyelids began to fail him. Yeshua could tell, but he knew Jimmy, in that state, would probably understand him better than were he fully awake.

"You didn't think I was *stuck* here, did you?" Yeshua raised his eyebrows toward Jimmy. "Me?"

Jimmy felt his look without looking. He laughed, jarring himself back into sharper consciousness.

"You? No, I don't think you could be stuck anywhere." He laughed again. "But you're real flesh and blood, just like us. How could you be somewhere else at the same time?"

"There's that 'time' thing again. Time is more elastic for me than for you," Yeshua said.

"Doesn't seem fair."

Yeshua smiled.

"Yes, well, my fair and yours sometimes don't line up, do they?"

For an instant, Jimmy's mind felt himself falling from that high beam near the roof of Pod 10, hurtling toward the ground. The image snapped through his mind like a camera flashing in front of him in the dark. He turned his head and looked at the glowing figure lingering there in the dark against the fence post. He realized "fair" was a meager idea made up by humans that had nothing to do with the holiness of the God who founded creation.

Yeshua took pity.

"I can never surrender my nature, Jimmy, my oneness with the Father. How might you put it? Life for me is like living in parallel. Space is more fluid for me, and time more pliable."

"So that's how you did it?"

"Saw Sarajane?"

"Yeah," Jimmy said, the word dropping lazily from his lips.

"We are going too deep, Jimmy."

"Try me."

Yeshua simplified what was beyond mere human knowing.

"In the body, I am self-limited. But my limits are far wider than you could imagine. I move in space differently than you, so I can share myself across times."

"Everywhere at once."

"No, that would be the Father. I am one place at once. Just different 'onces.' Time does not control me, Jimmy, I control *it*."

"You lost me."

"As I expected. Don't worry." He could tell that Jimmy was no longer aware of the wine glass in his hand. "You should get some sleep, my friend. Things are coming. You'll want to be rested."

"Things?" Jimmy lowered his head and was quiet. *Does it matter, after all?* Jimmy was trying to ask himself, though his mind had lost interest in his own thoughts. "I need a new brain," he muttered.

Yeshua almost burst out laughing.

"Indeed," Yeshua smiled.

"You're right, I need some sleep."

"I believe you," Yeshua coaxed him.

Jimmy was now chuckling. "*You* believe *me.* Yeah, that's a good one . . ."

Yeshua took up his own wine glass from where it sat balanced on the grass. There were only a few drops left.

"This is good wine, Jimmy."

"We made it."

"I know. The summer before you died."

"That was a good year."

Jimmy was trying to stand so he could go lay down. It was the last time he would ever feel this depth of fatigue. He worked his way to his unsteady feet and pointed himself toward his old tent, where he would sleep alone, and very soundly.

THE LIGHT rain OUTSIDE had ended and the clouds were fully departed as the night crept past 2:00 a.m. Through the open outer doors, the fresh smell of the night's rain floated through the pods, its freshness circulated through the ventilating system. For so long, the isolated smells of the INSIDE had been all the Solarians had known. Now the cleansing scent of the rain bathed the complex, the dampness settling like a blanket of contentment over those sleeping under the protective pods.

The ancient fear of night and darkness was about to vanish into an invisible place from where it could not return.

The main lights in Pod 10 were turned off and from OUTSIDE the gentle nighttime light they now called The Evening Glow filtered through the thick Stellar pods. As Yeshua had promised, there was no more complete darkness, even though the moon had fully set.

Jimmy rolled onto his side in his bed, sleepily pressing his head deeper into the pillow, dreaming anew about Yeshua's words. *Time is more pliable for me,* Yeshua had said. *Like a tent wall,* Jimmy's dream told him. *Solid, but not fixed.*

A very gentle breeze from the overhead wind fans in #10 ruffled the walls of Jimmy's tent almost imperceptibly. He felt he was in the womb again, sheltered, with only muted sounds around him, the sounds of life about to burst forth. A sense of gentle swaying overtook him as if cradled by an unseen mother in an old rocking chair. Soon, by the hand of Yeshua, he fell into an even deeper sleep.

Everyone else was likewise sleeping soundly at what would have been, by the old measurements, about 4:00 a.m. At that hour, an event none of the Solarians had foreseen came and went in what would have been several seconds, if measurable time had continued during those moments. It was a quaking of the entire cosmos, but not so much a quake as a shaking, as shaking flour through a great sieve. In those incalculable moments, the entire created order was the flour and was being sifted and refined into utter freshness, the stuff of a new beginning. All the many physical changes the Solarians had witnessed the last few days had been a mere prelude, a straightening and sorting out of the old, before a final demolition and rebuilding.

As the transfiguration began, Braden and Kai alone were awakened very slightly, but neither was aware enough of themselves or their surroundings during those brief moments to react to what was happening around them, and in them. Had they been even half-conscious, fright would have taken over, since everything they were, and everything the world around them had been, became for an incalculable instant more mirage than reality.

Here, gone, then here again, as if nothing at all had happened. The entire physical order, along with its hidden underpinnings, hung as if suspended for that moment in a cloud of non-existence. In what would have been microseconds of the former time, a complete cosmic transformation took place. This final transfiguration of the created order happened without anyone here seeing it or feeling it, except Yeshua. He was sitting quietly in a chair in the Meeting Tent as the change began, praying, speaking with the Father. As his eyes sparkled, time and space were instantaneously transformed. The one thing in the entire universe that did not change, that needed not change, was Yeshua himself, for in his own glorified life was the very seed of what had just occurred.

When those in the Solarium would begin to awaken later this morning, things around them would seem the same, at least to start. Then, almost without noticing, they would begin to see colors more brightly as their eyes left the blur of night behind and came into morning focus. For the colors themselves were now different, richer and more vibrant.

Even the dramatic remodeling of the landscape that Yeshua carried out around the Solarium would still appear to be exactly as he had made it yesterday morning. The one exception would be that Pikes Peak had now drawn even closer so that it would look possible to take a broad leap off one of the high pods and land at the foot of the mountain.

During the cosmic shaking they had just slept through, in fact, all of the Earth's continents had shifted, closing toward one another. As Yeshua had promised, the great seas of past ages were now like small lakes or bits of scenery along the edges of a grand, unified mass of dry land, remolded by the Spirit of the Father.

The other change that would become apparent in the coming days was that everything had become more solid. Rocks, soil, and every physical element were new with a substance and reality that humanity had not seen since the first days of the first creation. Even the water was made anew. It would taste far more delicious and they would soon discover that it could also not only support them but also mysteriously protect them.

The Solarians and their guests were about to discover a world they had all dreamed of, a world reaching into the eternal realms where life was indestructible and where death would be remembered only as an ancient legend. But because they were all part of it, the newness around them would at first appear entirely normal, except for a vague sense that something had once again changed, that Yeshua was once again up to something.

The approaching sunrise would bring each one of them a terrific surprise.

15

Monday Morning

Morning seemed to arrive late. The Solarians were sleeping in.

Thomas, Garan and Adrian, however, were up before the sun and took it upon themselves to milk the cows in Pod 9. Fresh milk sounded like an important thing with breakfast this morning. Besides, the milking schedule had been badly disrupted the past few days and the cows were restless because of not being milked on time.

Anastazja was also up and in the kitchen tent searching for bowls and utensils to make scratch-made pancakes and enough scrambled eggs to feed everyone. Working in a strange kitchen was a challenge, particularly since the last one she had used had been built in the old year of 1411.

Anastazja was resourceful and managed. Soon the aroma of cooking sausage and pancakes filled the tent and she was stirring two dozen eggs in a large crockery bowl. Bridget had thawed the sausage last night but when she overslept, Anastazja decided to surprise her.

A delighted smile graced Bridget's face when she finally got up. She walked lazily to the kitchen tent and smelled breakfast cooking. Not far behind her, Thomas and his helpers brought two large jugs of warm milk from the milking pails.

"Can we chill this down in that machine?" he asked.

"Machine?" Bridget replied sleepily.

"That big, white chest standing on end, there. Where you keep food."

"Oh, sure," Bridget said. She grinned at him for calling the refrigerator a "machine," although that's exactly what it was.

"Would you help with the pancakes, Garan?" Anastazja asked.

"I'll help if Adrian will," he said.

"I am happy to help Garan, if he thinks he needs help lifting a pancake," Adrian laughed.

Garan gave him a friendly glare. "I was never taught to cook. I can, I mean. But not sure who would want to eat the stuff."

"Well, this smells wonderful," said Yeshua as he also appeared in the tent. "Some smells never lose their ability to invite, do they?" He sat on a bench near an extra worktable that had been set up.

"Lord, Garan will make griddle cakes for you this morning," Anastazja teased, "but he says you may not like them."

"If Garan makes them, I will force myself to eat one," Yeshua laughed. "Let's have a breakfast feast today!"

Eira bounded into the tent and skipped over to Anastazja by the counter. Since she had been an orphan in the old world, she was still overcoming her shyness around others. Just as she had begun to think of Bridget as a new mother, she had also adopted Anastazja as a kind of favorite aunt.

"May I make toast?" Eira begged.

"With pancakes?" Anastazja droned. She saw Eira was instantly crestfallen and realized that toast was probably all the child felt able to make. "Sure, sweetie. If you're careful not to burn it, dear. Or yourself," Anastazja cautioned.

Eira had not yet operated the large, shiny electric toaster but she had watched for a couple of days and was sure she could master it. She loaded all six bread slots. Once the lever was pushed down, she went to the big, white cooling chest and dug for butter.

One by one, the other late risers drifted in and began to snack on bits of sausage and toast as Anastazja tried fruitlessly to shoo them away and finish the eggs at the same time.

"You all can wait now," she kept saying. "You sleep late, you must wait. Can't rush a good meal. If you can't help, just go sit somewhere." She swatted Nathaniel and Jimmy's fingers away.

Breakfast in the dining tent was a feast indeed. Yeshua called forth a blessing from the Father and they all plowed into the meal. The sausage, pancakes and eggs disappeared quickly but the aroma lingered. The toast went slower, as Eira was having trouble keeping up the supply, scurrying between the kitchen and dining tents.

"I feel so good this morning," Block said from the end of a second table that had been rigged from several boards and two old sawhorses to accommodate their guests. "Must be your cooking, Anastazja."

"Or something more," Yeshua said almost inaudibly. He had been watching the Solarians to see if they had noticed what was new. So far, except for Block's comment, none had said a word.

"What's that?" Willy asked Yeshua through teeth cluttered with scrambled eggs.

"I said, maybe something more," Yeshua repeated. "Clayton feels better than usual today."

"After bein' dead, pretty much everything feels better," Willy guffawed.

"You haven't noticed, then?" Yeshua asked with an innocent look, his eyes scanning the room.

The various conversations toned down and faces turned toward him. As Yeshua expected, it was one of the visitors who had begun to notice.

"Oh, I saw it," Anastazja said, stacking some empty plates at the end of the main table. "Clear as daylight.

Just waiting for somebody to mention it."

Yeshua nodded. He looked from Bridget, to Block, to Atchison, to the younger Solarians, then to the other visitors.

"Very observant, Anastazja," he said. "One has to look with eyes that see, even though you all share new flesh."

Mai Ker looked mystified. Herald looked at Sing, his favorite pastime now as ever. Suddenly, his eyes grew a little wider.

"Oh, wow, yeah!" The three broken words trickled from Herald's mouth like water tumbling backward up steppingstones. "Sing, your skin . . ." He touched her cheek gently.

Sing looked and rubbed her arm, then looked at Herald. She looked closer at her forearm again and saw the change. Her face began to light up.

"Didn't think you could get any more beautiful," Herald said. "Wow," he said again, almost in reverence. "You should see your face."

"Seeing your eyes is enough," Sing said. "They're alive. I mean, more alive!"

The Solarian children looked around at their familiar and unfamiliar parents, who stared back at them. A wave of astonishment rippled across the tables as they tried to absorb what they saw and what had changed. Several of them had looked in a mirror this morning but none noticed the obvious changes until this moment. Put simply, they all now shared the radiance they had seen for days around Yeshua, a kind of aura of light that wasn't exactly light but more of a presence, as if their inner beings now extended slightly beyond the confines of their bodies.

The face of each person bore a vitality that had not been there last night. Skin shone like malleable gold, eyes pierced one another's eyes. Their hair looked like living tissue instead of dead debris. The life-giving Spirit shone out from them and glistened for all to see.

Though many of those present had been raised from the dead, they had not, until early this morning, been fully and finally transformed. In the transformation of everything else, their spirits and bodies had changed, too. Energy, vibrancy, any of a hundred words might describe it, but none now missed it.

As they became more aware and took in this new reality, they realized their bodies felt much better, and not just because of a great breakfast. They sensed new strength, almost overwhelming strength, throughout their whole beings.

"What has happened?" Mai Ker asked. She looked at Yeshua, who was beaming.

"What you have waited for," he said. "True resurrection."

The Solarians and their children who had struggled against the terrors of death for so long INSIDE stared at each other. Then they looked more closely at Jimmy, and Block and Atchison. It was obvious the three were not the same as yesterday. All three had undergone a physical resurrection, yes, but until the changes of early this morning, they had looked perfectly normal. What shone in the three men now, and in everyone else, was an incredible vitality and a handsome, durable beauty beyond their natural appearance of old.

"How can we—" Sing began to say but her thoughts were arrested. She couldn't express the depth of what she felt.

"Too strange," Piper overlapped with Sing. "Not to die—but to live again." She looked toward Braden and Nathaniel. "You guys look older this morning." She turned to Yeshua. "Is that possible?"

"Possible?" he asked with a shrewd look, a twinkling in his eye.

Piper grinned.

Yeshua might have explained but thought better of it right now. What he knew but did not say was that if an eye can twinkle without feeling a moment's change, an entire person, an entire universe, could be transformed just as quickly by the Father who commands all things.

Braden stood and immediately felt taller. But mostly what he felt was no pain in his one leg.

"Hey," he said, startled. He walked away from his chair a few steps. His eyes glittered and a smile spread across his maturing face. "It's OK!" he almost yelled. He looked at his mom, beaming.

"Wouldn't you like to be rid of that cast?" Yeshua asked him.

"But—" Bridget gulped, always the cautious mom.

"It's not actually doing anything," Yeshua assured Bridget, "except hindering him."

Pam was beginning to realize what must have happened overnight.

"You know, I did feel odd when I got up. Not sore and stiff. I am *always* sore and stiff."

"No more of that," Yeshua promised.

"You look younger, Pam," Bridget said. "At least, I think it's younger."

"Neither young nor old," Yeshua said. "Just Pam."

"Mom, help me?" Braden said. He was trying to get the straps loose on the bulky, rigid outer cast that had been supporting his leg for the last week.

Bridget helped him remove the outer cast, then unzipped and peeled off the air splint underneath. In a burst of excitement, Braden jumped up on the table, knocking a pitcher of orange juice to the floor. The pitcher bounced and spun. It was no longer glass, but neither was it plastic. It was clear, solid, unbreakable, but of a new material unknown to man until this morning.

"Whoops! Hey, you guys, look, no break!" he bellowed. "It doesn't hurt!" he said with glee, looking down at Yeshua from atop the table. "Did you take the pain away?"

"I took the pain," Yeshua said, "a long time ago. Today you've received what I gave then."

Everyone except Yeshua was still gawking around, studying each other with new eyes, amazed at the impossible changes wrought in them as they had slept. They saw this morning what few human eyes had ever witnessed, a once "living" person transformed into a regenerated life. Only Thomas, who had witnessed the resurrection of Yeshua generations ago, had seen the glory of what they now saw in each other, new in both body and spirit.

They felt pristine, like souls released from chains. The difference was undeniable, the contrast stark. Without even trying to consider it, they each realized that what they had experienced until yesterday could hardly be called "life" at all compared to the victory of regenerated life that was burgeoning inside them.

Most remarkably, their ability to remember had changed as well. Each was aware of his or her whole past life as though every past moment was still present. But that old life now seemed only a piecemeal collection of fragments, as if every event, thought and feeling of their past could be summed up in a few seconds.

For the elder Solarians, whose lives had extended over decades, finding all their memories compressed in time yet expanded in detail was an odd sensation indeed. Each recollection was there instantly, filled with detailed sights, sounds, smells, and sensations they should long ago have forgotten, or discarded.

"It is fantastic to feel this good!" Will Atchison said to no one in particular but in a more resonant voice than he had possessed before.

Faces around the room all said, *Yes!*

Yeshua had explained to their guests, before any of

them appeared on the mountain last Thursday, that what they were about to experience, simple resurrection from death, was only a first step, the beginning of what would be fulfilled only after a time. That promise they now saw fulfilled.

"This is what he meant, then," Jacob told his daughter Katherine as they sat at the extra table.

"Yes, certainly," she smiled back at her father. "We were merely raised from death. Now the Father has transformed us."

And so, around the breakfast tables, their visitors were trying to contain smiles as the eyes of the Solarians blinked like newborn infants. The expressions on Jacob and the others, now that the cat was out of the bag, were filled with delight and amusement.

"I remember my first day of new life, transfigured life," Yeshua said to the Solarians. "Just as you are feeling. In the Father, I could always see beyond. But it was delightful that morning when my man's eyes caught up with my vision."

"*Your* eyes?" Sing asked. She was searching for understanding with new spiritual eyes.

"When my body was reclaimed—when I myself was regenerated—it brought to light in my flesh what I had known only in the spirit. Death had been doubly painful for me, I who am life itself. But the regenerated life the Father poured into me that morning was so much more than human flesh had ever known. The great surprise was how truly weak I had been before."

"I, ah . . ." Jimmy's words faltered, trying to express the sensations he now felt. *What's next?* he wondered.

Piper moved and sat beside her dad, giving him a tender smile and hugging him.

"All along, Daddy, you were right," she gleamed.

"Are you kidding?" he laughed. "I had no idea!"

Yeshua inhaled deeply again the lingering aromas of

their breakfast. "Life, breath. I was the seed pushed deep into the Earth, into Hell itself, to become the first-fruit of the true resurrection. Look back. I think you can agree, this was worth death as the price of admission."

AS THE morning excitement gradually calmed, Pam and Bridget decided to take Eira, Katherine, and Anastazja to see the old house later in the morning. Eira had been begging for a tour and was captivated by the beauty of it, a place that had seemed to the original Solarians quite an ordinary, old-fashioned house. To Eira and the other guests it was a palace, something imagined while listening to childhood stories.

"What a great privilege to have had such a home," Katherine told Pam. "It is so beautiful. And all the funny little things. The lights that come on in the ceilings. What marvelous inventions!"

The others agreed as they inspected the fittings and fixtures, and the piles of unused linens and other items still stored in several of the closets. Such opulence was beyond anything their guests had known in their lifetimes.

"So pretty," Eira kept saying as she explored every room.

In the room Pam had once shared with Sarajane, Eira was intrigued by the beautiful wooden frame of the mirror on the bathroom medicine chest.

"Why does it sit out from the wall like that?" Eira was curious.

"Well, it opens, see?" Pam said, swinging the mirror open.

To her horror, tucked behind an empty medicine box that had never been thrown away, Pam saw an asthma inhaler. Eira saw it, too.

"What a curious little toy," Eira said, starting to reach for the inhaler.

"Not a toy," Pam said, quickly shutting the cabinet. "Medicine," she said, leading Eira out of the room, "for whatever good it did."

ACROSS THE complex, Piper was giving Yeshua another tour, too, though she doubted he needed one. She had just shown him the large electrical panels and backup battery systems in Pod 13, explaining, as best she could, how the whole system had once failed completely.

"Daddy said it was one of his major 'panic' days," she said very seriously.

She asked if they could stop to rest on a metal bench outside of a storage building in #13 but as soon as they sat, Piper realized she wasn't actually tired at all.

Yeshua stretched out his legs and sat back as if he could enjoy an hour's nap, though he wasn't even faintly tired, either.

"I'm surprised you didn't heal Braden's leg," he said out of the blue.

"What?" she said, looking at him as if he was from Pluto. "What do you mean?

"You had that gift. I'm surprised you didn't use it then."

Piper was uncertain what she could have done about Braden's broken leg. She couldn't tell if Yeshua was serious or if he was just making up a story to entertain her. He answered the questions in her eyes.

"You could have healed him."

"Healed him? How?"

"Use the gift I gave you. You knew it was there."

She reflected for several moments as if prying an old picture out of a discarded scrapbook.

"I guess I did feel that, sometimes, like there was something I should do, whenever somebody was sick. But I was never sure." She looked at him awkwardly. "And I was afraid."

"Of what?" he asked her.

"Of being embarrassed, being different. They would have thought I was weird." She hemmed. "They all thought that, anyway," she added with a more awkward look.

"Yet you healed Sing."

"I did?" Piper said, her mind searching for a connection. She thought he meant something about Sing's morning sickness during her pregnancy.

"My Spirit was with you, Piper, even when you were a very young child."

Young child. The connection clicked.

"That time?"

"Yes. You were both little, Sing was very sick. She nearly left here for Paradise."

The memory sprang back into Piper's mind with exquisite detail.

"Of course, I remember! She was on that big, high table—a bed—in the infirmary."

"You remember it as high because you were so small.

"Mai Ker kept crying."

"Yes, Sing was ready to let go. Your dad prayed. And I sent you," Yeshua said.

"*You?*"

Nearly corporeal images of the scene blossomed in Piper's mind as if she were standing right there in the infirmary, but without the choking fear of that time when she was not quite three.

"Me," Yeshua replied. "They were keeping you away, but you snuck in and gave her a kiss, though it was really from me."

"And she got better," Piper was nodding. She made a child-like frown. "I'm not sure I understand."

"That's alright, it's no longer important. You did what you knew, as a child knows, to show your love for your sister. The brief touch of my Spirit that you brought healed Sing. You gave the gift I gave you."

Piper stared at him, awed.

"I never knew."

"You didn't need to. But, you see, you could have healed others, too. Even Braden's leg."

There was a pause, a question Piper wasn't sure she should ask.

"And Daddy? When he fell?"

"No, sweetheart," Yeshua said somberly. "Not that. That was beyond your gift."

Piper was quiet for a full half minute, wondering how many opportunities she had actually missed.

"Can I tell her?" she asked suddenly.

"Sing? Of course. Whenever you like. I think you'll find, all of you, there are many things you can talk about now. Lost memories, now regained."

"And I never knew."

"Let's walk back, shall we?"

Piper got up, made a dramatic little curtsy and smiled.

"Yes, my King."

SING HAD gone searching for Herald, who had been MIA during after-lunch chores. She found him sitting at a computer in the Research Center, digging through archived files. He was determined to find those old Christmas carols he stumbled across years ago. Something in the words stuck in his mind, something about that first appearance of Yeshua.

He glanced up as Sing came into the Center. He smiled.

"I can't get over it," he said. "You were so beautiful before. But now you're more beautiful than I could've taken in before!"

Sing smiled at the compliment.

"Well, Mr. Handsome, you've changed too, you know."

"What, I wasn't attractive before?" he asked, actually uncertain.

"No, silly. You know what I'm saying. Before you were cute. Now you're gorgeous."

"I don't think men are supposed to be gorgeous."

"Well, it's a very manlike gorgeous."

"So beautiful," he repeated. "Like the paintings, the great art here in the archives. But they don't even compare, not to what you've become." He stared as if he could spend eternity drinking in her beauty. "What's so weird," he said, trying to express something he did not yet understand, "is you're so stunning"—there was an uncomfortable pause—"but I don't feel the same."

"You don't love me?"

"Sing, that love—what we called love—it's feels like an empty word, now." He tried to form the idea. "I *more* than love you now. Do you understand?"

"OK, Mr. Clever, explain what that means."

Herald shook his head, not because he didn't know, but because he could not quite express it.

"It's that—I feel differently toward you. Your beauty, it's like—it demands a new kind of respect. Almost reverence. You see, don't you?"

Sing knew exactly but didn't let on.

"Go on," she said, grinning only on the inside.

"Well," he fumbled, "I'm kind of afraid to touch you. It's like you're too perfect. And I don't have the same desire, like I had. To . . ." He fumbled some more.

"To . . . ?" she prodded.

"For making love," he finally said.

"Hum," she half-blushed. "That's very interesting. Me, too."

Herald looked shocked, thinking only he had felt this.

"You, too?"

"Yes," Sing said. "I love you more than ever, Herald. But not just because of the physical touch. I love what's in you more. That's the best I can say it."

They were both quiet for several moments, not feeling pressed to add to what they had said. Herald broke the silence.

"In some way—and I don't get this at all—but it's like you're new, I'm new, but we're different. And whether together or apart, it wouldn't matter. Do you feel that?"

"Yes."

He frowned.

"But I don't want to miss out on any time with you."

"The way I feel toward you, maybe we were missing out before," Sing said, "even when we were together."

She walked over and hovered over Herald, rubbed his neck and shoulders gently, and leaned down and kissed him.

"So why wouldn't we still have a desire to make love anymore?"

"I don't know. We don't know what's still in store." She drew up a chair and sat close to him. "Yeshua seems to have changed us inside and out. Maybe this is one of those things."

"Well, I can't see how this is gonna work out," Herald said. His eyes looked off into the distance, his fingers fiddled with the keys. "Do you think we'll have any more kids?" he wondered, sounding discouraged.

"I don't know. Yeshua must have thought of that," Sing said, "right? It seems he's thought of everything."

Still distracted, Herald drew her attention to the computer.

"Well, anyway, listen to this."

THE GRAND tour of the old house over, the women and Eira headed back to the tents. Pam and Katherine walked behind.

"What a fine house, Pam," Katherine said, still marveling at the modern world and its strange inventions like indoor plumbing.

"Yes, I loved it. I was sad when we moved. But we had to conserve energy, to stay alive."

"As pretty as the world was back then," Katherine said, "it could not compare to what's here now. When I look out there," she said, gesturing OUTSIDE, "I'm just delighted with the beauty he has made. Have you noticed how intense all the colors have become?"

"You all knew, didn't you? Before this morning, I mean," Pam said, shifting gears.

"Knew?"

"That things would be changing. That we would be changed, our bodies."

"We had hints. Yeshua had told us a little, before he brought us back. But we didn't know when it might happen. I suppose he didn't want to spoil the surprise."

"It surely was that," Pam said.

Katherine was looking out through the pods again.

"No," she said, "the beauty we used to know, in the old times, somehow it was always lacking. Pale and fragile. If you were artistic, you could try to paint it. But the actual beauty of the thing was gone before the paint could dry."

"Yes. I never painted but even taking pictures with cameras, I—"

"With what?" Katherine asked.

"Cameras. Oh, it's a little machine that takes pictures."

"Takes them where?"

"No, I mean, it captures scenes, and stores them." She saw the inquiring look in Katherine's eyes. "I'll show you later. Anyway, even with digital pictures, when you reviewed the pictures in the camera, something was already gone. Like you say, just lost, not as pretty as when as I snapped it."

"Snapped?"

"With the camera," Pam said. "When you clicked the camera."

"They clicked?"

"The old ones did. Never mind," Pam said, as Katherine got more confused in what seemed a pointless conversation.

"Why did they click?" Katherine wondered.

"Look, you could shoot or snap or take a picture. I'll find a camera, easier to show you. And the electronic ones didn't have a mechanism that actually clicked, but they built them to make a sound as if they did. You see?"

Katherine laughed.

"You lived in a very strange time, Pam."

"That's what we used to say about your time," Pam laughed.

They were halfway across Pod 10 and spotted Piper and Yeshua who had stopped at a water faucet to get a drink, cupping water into their hands.

"*There's* beauty," Katherine said.

Pam nodded, watching. "He's so . . ."

"Real?" Katherine asked.

"Yes, and beautiful. With my beautiful little Piper by his side. Seems to just tower over all of us, doesn't he?"

"Even before he brought me back, I always felt that. He was so radiant, when he would spend time with us. His face, his hair, his whole body. Must be what they saw on the mountain that day," Katherine thought absently.

"Pikes Peak?" Pam asked.

"No, a different mountain, in his first appearance. Don't you know the Scriptures?"

"A little," Pam said truthfully.

"When the disciples saw him changed. Remember?"
Pam didn't.

"Moses and Elijah came and spoke with him,"
Katherine said, assuming everyone knew this crucial
event, "before he was crucified."

"Oh." *How did I miss that one?* Pam wondered.

"Wonderfully changed, radiant, and the cloud
covering them." Katherine said as they walked. She
stared across the pod at Yeshua. "The Father was
telling them what was coming. And now, it has come,"
Katherine said.

Pam remained silent, as if she was in a church and
didn't want to disturb anyone.

"How amazing, for him to go through with it,"
Katherine whispered.

"With what?"

"The cross, Pam." Katherine shook her head. "How
he must love us."

THE REST of the day was uneventful, a welcome relief
to the Solarians as well as their guests. With the world
so completely changed, and trying to adjust to the
strength and feelings generated by their completely
new bodies, they needed a breather.

Late in the evening, Yeshua called everyone
together in the Meeting Tent. He sat on a bench at the
front.

"I will be going away for a while."

Jimmy began to speak, worried that another absence
of centuries was about to break upon them. Yeshua
held his hand up.

"You needn't worry. You'll notice I'm gone, but it
won't be for long. I wanted you to know so you won't
be looking for me."

He then held open his arms and without so much as
a word, Braden, Nathaniel and Piper gathered around

him. Herald and Sing held back, though they weren't sure why. Eira began to step forward, too.

"Just the Solarian children, Eira," he said softly to not hurt her feelings. "Sing," he added, "would you bring Kai to me?"

Sing nodded and hurried to her tent where Kai had already been put to bed. Presenting the baby to Yeshua, who cradled Kai in his right arm, Sing stepped toward the back of the tent again with Herald, taking his hand.

"What's going on?" she whispered.

Herald made an *I don't know* kind of face with a shrug of his shoulders. "Just watch," he said.

As if he heard, Yeshua said, "Herald, Sing, I know you're not children any longer, but you are part of this." He beckoned and they both came forward. "Before I go, I want to say something, children." He looked at the youngsters, nodding as if giving final approval to a sculpture he had just finished.

Herald was about to open his mouth, but Sing's hand on his arm restrained him.

"What is it?" Nathaniel asked Yeshua.

"First, I want to tell you I'm very pleased with you. Each of you. You are uniquely blessed because you are the last. And you have labored very hard here with your parents."

"Feels like I'm always last," groaned Nathaniel.

"But now you will be honored, Nathaniel," Yeshua assured him. "You, the six of you, are the last children of Earth."

"Six?" Braden said, looking around. "Five."

"Kai?" Yeshua asked him with ponderous eyes, nodding at the baby.

"Oops," Braden said.

"You are the last, and therefore most blessed. The time of multiplying is finished."

It was as if he had heard Herald and Sing's conversation earlier in the day.

"Your parents, and all the generations, have done as I directed, " Yeshua went on. "They have been fruitful as I directed, peopling my creation. But you six children will forever be honored as the last, the children of the Solarium. In the regeneration, you have become first."

He handed Kai back to Sing, then stood and lifted his arms high enough so that even Herald would be able to pass beneath his hands.

"Receive the Father's love and blessing."

As if rehearsed, they walked one at a time and stood under his hands, feeling those powerful hands come down firmly on their heads. Incredible warmth surged through them as he touched them. Each, having been consecrated, stood aside. Sing stepped forward. Yeshua blessed her and the baby as one. As he looked down at Kai, comforted and quiet in Sing's arms, he breathed a deep sigh.

"The very last," he said, "and the very first. Receive the Father's kingdom."

A quiet burble rose out of Kai's throat and parted her lips just enough to form half a baby smile. Then she dozed off again.

Yeshua stood and gave the children a gracious nod.

"I won't be away long. Enjoy your new rest tonight. This day of great change will bring sleep more delightful that you have ever known."

He made a kind of bow that was no bow at all, and walked from the tent.

16

Tuesday Morning

Through the quiet hours of the night, Yeshua walked back toward Colorado Springs, accompanied by Jacob and Garan. As they walked across the eastern plains toward the hills east of the city, it felt to Garan as if the land rolled unseen beneath their feet. From time to time, Yeshua raised his arms as if drawing the city toward them.

The sun was just beginning to come up behind them as they descended into the valley, where a bustling Colorado Springs had sat, and made the short climb to Manitou Springs.

They found Salah and the others at the park where they had left them. A growing collection of resurrected souls had gathered into a small community that would eventually replace the city.

The newcomers, under Salah's leadership, had created a burgeoning campsite, patching it together with bits of structural materials as they could find. It was very plain so far but they were happy and carefree owing to each other's company.

The transformation of each person's body, as had happened at the Solarium, had happened here as well. They were each discovering the joy of new strength and very different emotions.

Yeshua and his two companions joined them for breakfast.

"Master, we found that old garden over there, from years ago," Salah told him. "Dead as could be. But a couple of days ago, we noticed colors. Then yesterday morning, things really began to grow!"

"Yes," Yeshua said, "the Earth is reborn."

Bartholomew, one of the men with Salah, spoke.

"Astounding, Lord! Early yesterday there were just a few small corn stalks. But by nightfall, look—full-grown corn, ears and all! Never saw anything like it."

"The soil knows its master, I think," Salah said.

"It's just amazing that seeds that laid in the ground so long could ever sprout," Bartholomew said.

"But you are wrong, Bartholomew," Yeshua said. "What you see is from entirely new seed. Nothing of the old is left."

"You should have seen the Solarium," Garan told them.

"The what?" Bartholomew asked.

"Where he took us," Garan nodded toward Yeshua. "Beyond all belief. You have to see it someday!"

"So, I'm curious, Lord," a woman named Marie said. "These new bodies, are they of the same stuff?"

"Do you mean, is your old body still somewhere in the earth, Marie?"

"Yes. Doesn't matter, I suppose."

"Are you making a pun?" Garan laughed.

"It's a good thing to be curious," Yeshua answered. "But even your old bodies, by the time you died, were not of exactly the same stuff as when you were born. They grew and changed more than once, from the womb to your end."

"Oh, surely," Marie said.

"My young mother's body and the one that finally died were certainly not much alike!" her friend named Naomi laughed. Her light brown hair fell around her face like an antique picture frame and set off eyes that shined with age and wisdom, although she now looked little more than 30 years old. "Glad to be rid of that old thing!" she laughed again. "And good riddance!"

"The new bodies I have given you are of the new Earth. The old ones have gone."

Marie nodded. She didn't want to think too deeply about this. She was satisfied.

"What exactly happened, Lord, while you were away?" Salah asked.

"A great deal, my friend. Early yesterday the great transformation took place, which is why you feel as you now do. The universe has been transfigured. Your bodies are not only regenerated, but perfected."

Garan finally asked a question he had held in for days.

"Then why does yours still bear those marks?"

"These?" Yeshua asked, showing them the scars of his crucifixion.

Garan nodded, trembling slightly.

"These are not mere physical marks, but indelible spiritual marks. They go with me into eternity. Call them your sales receipt, for the price that was paid."

Several in the company nodded. For a minute, no one spoke.

"Will you stay with us today, Lord?" Marie finally asked.

"No, I'll be up there." He gestured toward the peak that watched over the city.

"Can I come?" Garan asked, anxious to see again the beautiful panorama from the peak.

"Not today, Garan. I have work to do."

"Still looks like it might be cold up there, Lord," Salah said. "Except the patches of snow that were up there have disappeared."

"Yes, the world is new. Fresh snow will fall in time, at the higher elevations. But the old glaciers have gone." Yeshua looked around. "I will carry a cloak, if someone might lend me one."

Four offers came at once. He chose a cloak from a man name Zebulon that looked especially warm. Its owner, being a thin fellow with little fleshly insulation, found a warm cloak a necessity regardless of climate.

"It came back with me, Lord," Zebulon laughed. "Don't know how. Always kept me warm in the Alps, though. Woven together of lamb's wool and goat hair. Will suit you fine."

"Indeed, it will," Yeshua said, a tone of irony in his voice. He tried it on.

"A little tight at the shoulders, but it's fine." He clasped Zebulon's hand in his own. "I promise to return it."

"Oh, don't worry, sir. I've found two old blankets. Now that's an odd thing, too. Sunday night, they were miserably scorched. When I woke up in them yesterday, looked like they were fresh from the weavers!"

Yeshua just smiled.

"I'll be back at nightfall," he told Salah.

AS HE neared the summit of Pikes Peak, Yeshua pulled the cloak tighter. The sunlight was warm but a steady breeze blew out of the northwest, bringing an unfriendly chill. At this altitude, even with the sun now very near the equator, the temperature at the summit hung around 50 degrees. The peak that had been just over 14,000 feet in height 48 hours ago had grown to just shy of 15,000.

Despite the renewal of the Earth, the ramshackle buildings at the summit remained, just as the Solarium did. The task of clearing and rebuilding was something the Lord knew his friends would want a hand in.

The bomb blasts had caused less damage up here, except for some blown-out glass and several doors thrown out of kilter.

He sat near the south side of the old restaurant on a hand-hewn bench that overlooked the plains to the east. He enjoyed the solitude, speaking with the Father.

He had been there no more than ten minutes when a man came into view, climbing the mountain near the old tracks that had brought cog-railway cars to the summit. The man walked laboriously, looking around suspiciously as if some hunter were following him with a crossbow.

Outwardly, the man looked well-groomed in his dark brown slacks and woolen coat. Worn laced-up boots covered his feet, like those he had worn in southern Europe in the fourth century. He had been a businessman, buying and selling metal goods. He made and lost several fortunes in his home in Gaul, dealing with military men who were always in need of material for new weaponry. His name was Junonius.

Not far from the summit, he stopped to rest. He remembered a trip into the Alps one winter to meet a commander in need of a load of iron. Right now, Junonius felt like that load of iron was in his trousers and boots. He caught an extra deep breath and pressed on, finally seeing Yeshua across the old parking area.

Rather than go around a small bed of tightly packed rock left by the now vanished snow pack to reach the stranger, Junonius decided to cut across. He made it only ten steps before he slipped and buried his short beard into the sharp rocks. Back on his feet, cursing under his breath, he brushed bits of rock off his clothes and picked some from his beard.

Who in the world, he thought, *is so important that I've been summoned up this barren mountain?*

Yeshua stood to greet him. Despite the thicker air, Junonius was panting like a racehorse at the end of a sprint.

"Come and sit," Yeshua offered, gesturing toward the bench. "It's a remarkably beautiful view."

Junonius turned his head slightly east and produced a scowl.

"Would be much nicer if there were some trees to break this incessant wind!" He frowned but took a seat on the bench. "Just why I have been called all this way?"

"To take time to speak with me," Yeshua said bluntly. Before he began, he knew where this would lead.

"Time, yes, never enough, is there!" Junonius grumped. "Talk about what?"

"Your life."

"Life was fine. Till I died. Completely unnecessary. A brick falling off a tower, dropped by some stupid, careless woman! Like to know who built that damned tower."

"The builders did not intend to kill you, Junonius."

"Intended or not, they did!"

"That's not why we're here."

"Well, who are you, anyway?" Junonius examined him through bushy eyebrows hovering over squinting eyes. "And how can you know my name?"

"I am the Lord."

"Lord? Which one?"

"There is only one."

"Look, there are lords on every street. Had five in my lifetime! What makes you lord over me?"

"I'm Yeshua. You knew me by the Latin form, Jesu. We must talk about your future."

"Now hold on, there, my future's just fine. I died, yes, but somehow I'm back. Can't account for it, really. But why question luck?" he brayed.

"There was no luck involved," Yeshua assured him.

"What, then, just fell out of the sky?"

"Actually, you came up from the pit."

Junonius frowned deeper this time.

"Yes, you may be right there. I have a vague recollection—a dark, cave-like place. Just enough shadows to let you know you'd rather be somewhere else."

"Hell. You called it Hades."

"Not pleasant, I can tell you. Glad to be back. Except for this damned wind." He jerked up the collar of his coat. "Now, what were you talking about?"

"Your life, and your future."

"Nothing to talk about. None of your business, my past."

Yeshua nodded, not because he in the least agreed but because he knew this is exactly how Junonius thought.

"Junonius, I've called you repeatedly to enter the Father's kingdom. Each time, you've ignored me."

Skepticism radiated from Junonius' eyes, an expression he had learned through years of practice.

"Look here, whoever you are, don't need your help, or anyone's. I can take care of myself."

"The one thing you were best at."

This was one of many conversations Yeshua would have, knowing the outcome. But the Father's kindness and patience required it.

"Junonius, every chance has been given you."

"Why, then, are you wasting so much of my time?" he demanded with growing irritation.

"It is very simple. Each time I called you, you told yourself you would consider it some other time. But there comes a time when the door is shut and bolted. This is that time."

"And why, pray tell, would this Father give me another opportunity?"

"Because we know your struggles, your family, your handicaps. Like that injury to your left arm that left it limp since you were a boy."

"Now how—?" Junonius' skepticism changed to something more like anger. "Look, don't be talking bad of my old father." He calmed himself. "It's true. I had troubles. And many enemies."

"Yes, you did."

"It wasn't because I didn't try. I tried to be good. But you know the way of the world, a little cheat here and there was needed—to stay ahead."

"Yes, I know the way of the world," Yeshua said, "but we are speaking of you."

"So, you're accusing me of some wrongdoing?"

"Your own actions accuse you. I am settling your account. The Father has placed final judgment in my hands."

"Yes, I remember, I was warned about this in—what did you call it, Hades?—that the world had finally ended. Judgment day had come."

"You're dithering again, Junonius. Tell me your decision."

Junonius pondered. He knew the offer well enough, an eternity in the light and compassion and fellowship of God and his children.

"I don't think you're being very fair to me."

"Fair?"

"Yes, I think a little fairness is deserved," Junonius argued.

"If I was fair," Yeshua said, "everyone since Adam would end in Hell."

Anger rose in Junonius' eyes.

"I died. Wasn't that punishment enough!"

"The only question is how you wish to live."

Junonius sat silently for half a minute, agitated, his breathing ramped up again. A thought occurred to him, a habitual thought he could not drive from his mind. *Maybe there will be something in it for me."*

"What would you require of me?" he asked.

"Two things. Your obedience to me as Lord, and your love as a friend."

Junonius thought, one eye partly shut. His expression morphed into a deeply furrowed frown.

"Give obedience to a total stranger?"

"Well, there is the tragedy, isn't it, that I am a stranger to you."

"What's the cost?" Junonius asked quickly.

"Cost?"

"Yes. How much? Do I have to pay right now? I seemed to have lost track of my money purse," he said searching his pockets.

"The price has been paid. To you, it is free."

Junonius' face said he was not a man to be fooled.

"Me? Take something for nothing?" he demanded proudly.

"I'm offering you a place in my kingdom," Yeshua said. "The condition is that you must pay nothing, and must have nothing with which to pay."

Junonius sat morosely. His look said he was impatient to go. Yeshua had gotten under his skin. In his heart, Junonius knew the wounds of a lifetime of hurts, broken promises, and hard feelings. Buried deep within him was an urge to break free of it all, a new life, a new spirit. But, from long habit, he shook his head.

"Nope, not buying today. You're a pretty good salesman, I'll give you that. But I'm not buying it. I know how to look after myself. Always have."

The door closed, by Junonius' own hand.

He looked out toward the eastern horizon again, wanting to spit. Saliva was bundling up in his mouth, about to drool out.

"New world, you say? Looks pretty dead to me," Junonius sniggered.

Yeshua ignored the remark.

"Take care going back down," he told Junonius. "It will be darker when you get back there."

"I'll be fine. Quite self-reliant, you know."

He stood, looked down his rather protruding nose at Yeshua, turned haughtily, and walked away.

AT SOLARIUM-3 at this moment, the Solarians and their visitors were still trying to adapt to the changes.

The crops in the fields, most planted several months ago, had begun to grow at an even more unbelievable rate, maturing faster than they had ever seen. The fruit of many of the plants was appearing ahead of schedule. Ears of corn and heads of wheat were three times their normal size. One ear of this corn would easily feed eight instead of one.

This meant the Solarians would need to redesign the entire planting and harvesting schedule and rethink storage of crops. How much of all this could they ever use? What could be given away? Should they stop replanting for the time being?

One of the distractions caused by this growth spurt was that some plants were so tall that they obstructed the view across Pod 10. When the Solarians looked out from their tents, it seemed they were not looking over their fields but into a homegrown forest.

The most peculiar thing of the day, though, happened when Braden and Nathaniel invited Adrian to go fishing in their ocean. Having baited his hook with an overgrown night crawler, Braden reared back and cast his line.

The helpless worm flew out over the water, dropped—and bounced.

"What on earth?" Braden cried.

"Whad'ya do?" Nathaniel asked, seeing the worm atop the water.

"Didn't do anything," Braden said to his half-brother.

"How come it won't sink?" Nathaniel wondered out loud.

"Worm's too fat!" Braden speculated.

Adrian laughed. He suspected what was going on. "I don't think it's the worm. Let me see your pole."

He took the pole, trying to figure out how to draw the line back toward shore. He had never seen a fishing reel. All his fishing had been with a piece of thin cord and a small iron hook.

Braden showed him how to reel the line in. Adrian worked the worm off the hook and put a thinner one on. With Braden helping, Adrian cast the line.

The new worm bounced a bit higher than the first one.

"Funny!" Nathaniel laughed.

"Weird," Braden said.

Nathaniel cast his line. The wormed hook hit and skidded on the water but refused to sink.

"It's not your gear," Adrian said, squinting out over the ocean. "It's the water."

"Waste of time," Braden said. "Not gonna get any fish like this."

He took his pole from Adrian, reeled the line back in and took off the worm. He tossed it toward the water. The huge night crawler immediately began to sink when a large fish broke out of the water. Like a lightning strike, it snapped up the worm and hauled it under.

The two boys and Adrian stared, then looked at each other. Nathaniel picked up a pebble and tossed it. It bounced across the water and sat atop a gentle incoming wave that drove it back to shore by Braden's feet.

Braden plucked another unsuspecting night crawler from the cup that held some soil and their bait. He rocketed the worm out over the ocean. It dropped, splashed, and sank.

"Ah, I think somebody's going to have to explain this one," Adrian said.

"I think I know who that is," Nathaniel said.

"Yeah," Braden said, "and he's not here right now."

"Well, it was nice of you fellows inviting me along, but I think our fishing expedition for the day is over," Adrian laughed. "Unless you want to keep drowning worms."

They collected their gear and tackle and headed back to the tents.

YESHUA'S NEXT visitor on the peak had died as a middle-aged woman. She now looked and felt as though she was in her 20s.

She appeared from around a corner of the building at Yeshua's back, although he knew of her approach. Her reddish-brown hair streamed down her back nearly to her waist, over a long, heavily woven overcoat. Though the midday sun was warm, she shivered when she saw Yeshua.

He greeted her and gestured for her to sit on the bench.

"Riona, thank you for coming. Are you warm enough?"

"A lady down below offered me this coat." She looked at Yeshua cautiously, and didn't sit. "You're him?"

"I am."

Her face, although new, bore signs of deep spiritual pain from her old life. She had been imprisoned for adultery in medieval Ireland and had slowly wasted away during six years. She lost weight and her heart weakened. Though her skin became badly infected in prison, she had managed, after her release, to find a position as a scullery maid in a poor house in one of the vilest areas of the city.

"They said you'd be up here. I thought it was just a story," Riona said. "People often made fun of me, told me stories."

"I know. It isn't a story, Riona. If you'll sit there, I'll act as a windbreak."

Riona circled past him and sat and adjusted the folds of the coat, trying to get comfortable. Knowing whom she was beside was the most uncomfortable thing she could imagine.

"Am I in trouble again?" she asked as though she had been dragged again to the warden's office.

"No. I just want to talk."

"I'm supposed to confess my sins again, is that it?"

"Child, you've confessed these same sins so many times, once more would be pointless."

"Some things bother me. Can't seem to put them behind me."

"Like why you went to prison."

"You know about that?"

"And I know about the agony you suffered there every day, yes."

"It was my own fault. I should have known. I was raised right."

"Would you like to speak about it?"

"Too embarrassing."

"I'm not easily embarrassed," Yeshua said with a reassuring look.

She launched into it as if a dam had burst inside.

"It was my doing, I know. But he pressed me," she said, choking down little breaths with tears. "I was the housemaid, a great, beautiful mansion, it was. He was the owner, the mayor of the city—"

"I know all this, Riona."

She tried to compose herself.

"I was just nineteen. I was pretty then, so everyone said. And his wife, well, not to be mean, but she was a hag, belittled him all the time. Everyone in the house, for that matter. Always needed this, or wanted that. Badgered him. Said they weren't wealthy enough. Goodness, they had everything!"

Yeshua listened, nodding encouragement.

"I tried to avoid him but he would catch me in a room making the beds, or cleaning. I resisted him mightily, but then he said my staying on depended on what I was willing to give him."

She hushed back tears that had been cried a thousand times before.

"I was afraid, see. I came from great poverty, and my parents were both gone. I had nothing, and no one, and the old oaf knew that. And I gave in." It looked like a great weight pressed down on the back of her neck. "For a roof, for my food. I couldn't face begging in the street again. I saw what they did to girls in the streets." She let out a deep, pained sigh. She felt ashamed and weak.

"I know you resisted, Riona," Yeshua said. "But why did you turn away from me?" Yeshua asked her gently.

She considered this for the first time.

"Well, I was a sinner, wasn't I? They called me those horrid names and I believed them. I couldn't believe you would forgive such an awful thing." She gulped. "Then his wife found out, and killed herself."

Yeshua took her hand, saying, "It was not your doing, Riona."

She drew her hand back.

"Felt like it was," she groaned.

"That was her choice."

He touched her shoulder and the shivers subsided. She found it hard to look straight at him.

"They came and arrested me. Adulteress, they called me. 'My life is over,' I said. I was so angry I wanted to kill him!"

"I prevented that."

She looked up, and believed him.

"In the prison, I heard his wife had done herself in. I thought, 'I should, too.' Would serve the lout right!"

"I prevented that, too," Yeshua said with a consoling look.

"You wonder why I turned away from you," she said miserably. "Easy. I wasn't worth saving."

"To me, you were, Riona."

"I made no good in the world."

"I know it felt that way, but it's not true. You had a son, a boy who found real happiness after you let him go."

"I had to give him up, sir. Me going to prison. What could he have had from me? Just misery."

"His life was not miserable, Riona. It was delightful in his later years. You would not know, but he helped save many children from starving in the streets in those years."

Riona looked dumbfounded.

"No."

"Yes."

He watched her take this in. He saw the subtle change, the slight realization that she had contributed something worthwhile to the world after all.

"Go on," he said.

"Well, you probably know, my skin got very sick, those last four years in the prison. It made me very ugly."

"Pustular psoriasis."

"I didn't know what it was called but it was ugly, and painful. Like something crawling around under my skin."

"You complained very little."

"Well, then, what was the point? Complaining never did a soul any good. After I got out, I tried to hide it under clothing but you could see people react. Sometimes it smelled." She adjusted the neck of her coat from habit. "No one wanted to hire me, especially if there were children in the house. An ugly, convicted adulteress."

"And the man didn't help you."

She let out a pathetic whimper.

"Him? Help me? Forgot me five minutes after the constable hauled me off. The lout never even showed at the trial. Sent a written testimony. Said I was a tart, and seduced him."

"If it helps, you will never see him again."

"He was not resurrected, then?"

"He was, like everyone. But he is where you will never see him. He is lost in his own darkness."

"Must be pretty dark."

"Yes. He sees one thing only now, the inside of his own soul. For eternity."

Riona was shocked.

"Truly?" Hearing this comforted her.

"But back to you," he said.

"Well, as you say, I turned away. I felt hopeless, and unworthy of you."

"Would you turn back to me, now?"

She looked up at him, a kind of disbelief hovering on her face.

"I can?"

"If you choose. If you will confess that you gave up on me."

Her look of doubt turned to one of reprieve, then relief.

"Then I confess it, Lord!" She looked at him afresh. "Finally, a man worthy of trust. I had begun to wonder."

She gave him a newly embarrassed look. She didn't understand how he could know so much about her, yet she felt she could trust him. How she knew this, she was uncertain.

Like God raising his eyebrows, a light gust of wind blew across the summit. A small, tent-like cloud settled just above them and danced among contrary winds.

Riona gaped at the cloud, afraid, wondering if she should duck beneath the bench. But then the cloud turned to pure light and settled further, clothing her and Yeshua as in an iridescent shroud.

Her eyes filled with tears of joy. She straightened her back.

"I do love you, Lord. I lost faith for a time, my trust just went. But I pray you can still love me," she pleaded.

"Always," was all he said.

"For a long time, you know, I blamed you for everything."

"I do know. But that is forgiven, too. We will put that behind. You can blame me for the glorious life that lies ahead of you," he smiled. "That blame I will take. Receive my forgiveness, Riona, and be whole."

She was on her feet suddenly. As Yeshua stood, she threw herself against his chest. Only his great strength kept them from falling backward.

"I want you to find your joy, all that you missed," he said. "You have made a good beginning."

She continued to hold and hug him as if she could not stand on her own.

"You can stand perfectly, Riona. You have strength beyond what you can fathom, because you have finally stepped through the door of the Father's house. Thank you. I know it was a very long step."

"Longer than my entire life," she cried joyously. Then she said, "I don't deserve this."

"Love can never be deserved, Riona, or it would cease to be love."

She let go of his arms finally and looked out over the panorama of beauty that spread below them, seeing for the first time how glorious the world might be. As she drank in the splendor of the new Earth, Yeshua remained quiet, speaking with the Father.

If only she was last, he was saying.

He took her hand and began to lead her down the road toward the city.

17

Wednesday Morning

Having brought Riona to the company of his friends, Yeshua spent the night in Manitou near the ruins of an old church that had been reduced to a pile of sandstone rocks scorched and cracked by nuclear heat. Not many years before the end, the church had been converted into a glitzy gift shop filled with cheap trinkets that provided tourists with a reminder of their time spent near the beautiful mountains, away from the damning grind they had called life.

Through the night he watched over those who slept. By morning, three lower courses of stone from the old church had been rebuilt, fitted so perfectly together that they held tightly in place with no mortar.

As the company arose and breakfast was readied, Yeshua came and offered his blessing on their meal.

"I'm returning to the peak this morning," Yeshua told Salah. "Thank you for looking after Riona last night. Keep her close until her parents come."

"When will they be coming?"

"In a few days. Encourage her to spend some time today with Jacob. He's a kind soul, I think he will help her learn again to trust."

Salah had met Riona only last evening but could see how nervous she was around others. He went, as Yeshua asked him, and found Jacob.

Yeshua borrowed Zebulon's cloak again, tossed it across his shoulder, and cut across country, avoiding the old roads, making his own short cut up the mountain.

HIS FIRST hours at the summit passed quickly as person after person arrived for judgment. Some had been in Hell for many centuries and had sought to avoid this moment, thinking they were in hiding. In fact, Yeshua had simply left them alone.

Over the course of many days, every person would be resurrected to face their future. What that future would be depended on how they had lived and whether they had known the Lord and followed him, or denied him.

Like Riona, some had wavered in their faith and would now have to make a true decision, once and for all. Others, despite the best efforts of Yeshua's followers, had never even heard his name let alone his promises, and so had died separated from his grace and forgiveness. Still others had known of the Father, revealed in the beauty of his creation and the intricacy of its design, but they had never learned of Yeshua's sacrifice, the price he had paid for them to open the way to true life. But as the Father had determined before time began, each person would have the opportunity of forgiveness through Yeshua, offered now by the hand of Yeshua himself, and the chance to turn and claim Yeshua as Lord of their past, and future.

Many would still refuse. Some hearts had grown so hard that they can no longer turn. Yet with the few who did turn and embrace him, Hell was robbed.

Not every soul faced judgment with fear. Many had known Yeshua and lived as subjects of his kingdom and approached him now with joy, not apprehension. His next visitor was one of these.

YESHUA SAW her approaching from the northern edge of the summit, having found her own shortcut up the mountain, too. She appeared to be about 20, although she had lived nearly 80 years before her death in the final days of the great cataclysm.

She wore only a light, white overcoat with a woolen scarf folded down around her neck. Her formerly gray hair was now a rich brown, framing a face that both knew and expressed love.

When she saw Yeshua, she broke into a jog toward him, coming to rest just a few feet from where he stood to greet her. She straightened her coat and collected herself, as if preparing for the most important job interview ever.

"Welcome, Corine. How was the climb?"

"Delightful, Lord. Wonderful. The air is so fresh up here!"

"Yes, it's much thicker than it was in the old age."

He gestured to the two heavy, wooden chairs. She sat; he remained standing.

"Do you understand why I called you up here?"

Corine smiled.

"They said it's the time of final judgment."

"Yes."

"Well, I've longed for this day! Seeing you after I died was delightful, but still there was the waiting, for the others. This is a day I've longed for, for so many years."

"Thank you for being so faithful. I know that was not often easy," he said.

"Oh, I know, I talked about you every chance I got. Drove people crazy, I'm afraid," she smiled.

"Many of them were crazed already," Yeshua said with complete seriousness.

"Well, I will say, it was more and more of an uphill battle in those final days, when death was everywhere."

"It was an uphill battle from the beginning, Corine, as my very first disciples learned."

She nodded.

"Oh, I know. I had it easy. I wasn't crucified, or beheaded, or tortured, like so many were."

"But you were faithful. And not just in speaking, but in how you lived, how you embodied my word in your caring for others." He sat in the other chair. "The way you cared for the dying, especially at the very end, it changed many hearts. Many you will never know of, even now."

"You're being kind. But if I changed even one, that's enough," Corine said. "It just seemed the right thing. With the terrible brutality—all the atrocities at the end—simple kindness was the only salve, wasn't it? And I had so little. What else could I do?"

"Nothing. But you eased the death of many who have now become my friends. The love they saw in you gave them confidence in me. That tiny cross you always wore loomed very large in their eyes."

Corine choked up a little, looking down briefly.

"I'd have done more—anything—if I had been able."

"Love shown to the unlovely, Corine, that was enough. You turned hearts. You helped them find peace in dying, and grace."

Corine nodded, still feeling she had not done anything unusual.

"Do you remember a place call the Solarium?" Yeshua asked out of the blue.

"Oh, sure, that big research place. It wasn't far from us, you know, just east down the highway."

"A bit east of the farm you and James had."

"Yes. My poor husband. He really suffered. His heart was failing even before the air went bad."

"Only his fleshly heart," Yeshua smiled.

"He went just a few hours before me. I can see it still. We were sitting together in the living room. All the news had gone off the air by then. They were all dead, I suppose. Sad, but a kind of blessing, really.

Didn't have to listen to their silly jabber anymore. We were sitting, it was quiet, and I was reading from the scriptures about your death. And I looked over and James had stopped breathing." She paused, remembering. "He was such a fine, godly man! Give you the shirt off his back, then go buy you an extra!" she laughed. "Why do you ask about the Solarium?"

"Because I've been there since my return. There are some friends I'd like you to meet sometime. You don't know this, but you helped them, too, not long ago. They borrowed some gas from your farm."

"Well, I can't imagine why they would need it, but, welcome to it! Wasn't doing James and I much good, now was it?" she laughed heartily.

"That's the spirit in you I love, Corine," he smiled. "I'll bring you there someday, after everything gets settled down, and you've had time to go wherever you would like."

"That would be fun. Quite a spectacular place! James and I drove over to see it once, walked around the outside. Kind of like a huge fishbowl," she said, looking out over the landscape to the east. "But it was nothing like the beauty you see from up here," she said dreamily.

Rich yellows, browns and greens were erupting as far as she could see details, which, with her regenerated sight, was nearly 40 miles. Not far beyond that, now that the peak was closer to the Solarium, she could see glimmers of light reflected off the domes. "I cannot express how grand it is to feel things so richly, and to see now so clearly!"

He offered her his hand as they stood and walked toward the edge of the parking area, overlooking the panorama below.

"Where you would like to travel first. Home?"

"Not my last home, my first. If it's still there."

"No, the farm where you were born in western Kansas is gone. But that hillside where you used to sit and play when you were little, looking out over the river? It's still there."

"Oh, that would be fun, too! I always loved to sit and watch the river flow."

"Whenever you choose to come back this way, I'll personally escort you to the Solarium."

She looked at him uncertainly, as if he should say it, rather than she ask.

"May I be going now?"

"Go with my peace, Corine. By the way, down in Manitou Springs there's a small community growing. There'll be someone who wants to go with you. I think he'll make a good companion."

Corine's eyes opened brightly.

"And who, Lord, might that be?"

"A surprise."

Corine laughed.

"I knew you weren't going to tell me," she chuckled. "Always liked surprises, didn't you?"

"I think that's fair to say," Yeshua smiled. "But I will tell you. It's James."

"Oh, thank you, Lord!" she said, turning to hurry off.

Yeshua caught her arm. "Thank you for holding fast to the end, Corine."

"Just held onto you," she beamed.

She turned and without a glance back, she hurried down the mountain.

HERALD HAD gone looking for his father and finally found him in Pod 13, where Block was straightening up racks and benches of tools that had been often used by the other Solarians but never properly put away.

Block had come across an open can of varnish, shoved to the back of one workbench. The remaining quarter can of varnish had dried into a chunk of hardened minerals and acrylic in the bottom of the open can. Unbeknown to Block, it was the varnish Jimmy had used all those years ago to finish Block's own coffin. Jimmy had shoved the can into a corner and left it. He had looked at it dozens of times over the years, but never again touched it. That dried-up can had seemed to Jimmy, for reasons he was only now beginning to understand, as a little monument to the life of Clayton Block, a life that had been unfinished, cut short.

"Need any help?" Herald asked Clayton tentatively as he came into the shop.

Block nodded, then smiled.

"I'd be happy for your help, son."

Block was still struck by the likeness his son bore to himself. Herald's disposition was similar to his own, except that Block noticed his son had picked up some mannerisms from Jimmy over the years. *Very natural,* Block was thinking as he watched Herald grab a broom and go to work.

Since the night Block returned, the two had crossed paths repeatedly, but each time it was as if there was an invisible electric fence between them that both were afraid to touch. Although he had never known his father, Herald obviously inherited some of the half-hidden shyness that Clayton had always displayed.

Now that he had found his dad, Herald wasn't sure what to talk about.

"So, were you surprised to see your little pet Caroline?" Herald asked.

"Yeah," Block laughed, "could hardly believe it! She's quite a little creature. I'm amazed she outlived me so long, here in the Solarium. She was so fragile, but there's some kind of toughness in her."

"I've noticed that, in the other animals, too. They seem to know they were made to live. They don't surrender life easily. Even those we killed for food."

"I suppose Yeshua built the will to live into them just like he did in us," Block said. "You know, I nearly killed her. Did your mom tell you that part?"

"No, actually Yeshua told me, Saturday, when I first saw Caroline."

"Yeah, I was just leaving to come here, hit her on the street by my old apartment. Picked her up and brought her along." He smiled, thinking back.

"I can't quite picture you picking a little crunched bird up off the road." Herald laughed, thinking about it.

"Yeah, it's funny, I don't really know why I did that. I was in a big hurry, running late, I was trying to get to Omaha to meet with John Haskins so I didn't get fired before I even started! But when I hit her, I just felt compelled to pick her up. She looked so sad and helpless laying there."

"Well, whatever there was between you and her must have been neat. I saw her fly over to you yesterday, over by the storage shed," Herald smiled. "I mean, really, it was kind of funny, to see her hang around you like that." He paused, thinking, finishing the sweeping. "Mom said you always treated her like gold."

"Caroline, or your mom?"

"Both, actually."

"So, did your mom talk much about me?" Block asked.

Herald didn't want to lie.

"Well, actually, not all that much. I mean she told me quite a bit, mostly how you handled all the terrible problems, back at the beginning. When you all first got here."

"And?"

"Well, to be honest, whenever she talked about you, I could tell she would get really sad. Like it still hurt. She told me how you died so suddenly. Right in the middle of things, when everything was in a big uproar. I think it kind of haunted her."

Block put a few more stray tools away in their racks.

"I guess it would," he said, looking at Herald. His son had inherited his frankness, too, to the point of bluntness. "Your mom is a wonderful woman, Herald. I can't tell you how lucky I felt to have her here with us. With me. And—well, when things started going to heck, she was tough. She struggled, sure, but we all did. She was like a rock to me."

Herald chuckled.

"I would have guessed the other way around." He had created a pile of sawdust and small cardboard scraps in the middle of the shop. "Could you hold the dustpan for me?"

"Sure."

Block grabbed the large dustpan that was kept in a corner and held it for his son to sweep the debris into.

"Mom said you were a great man, Dad," Herald said. It felt truly awkward. He had always thought of Jimmy as his dad, though he was a stepfather. Now he felt a new joy to be able to call his true father "Dad." A large vacancy in his heart now had a roomer.

Block blushed, which, in his new flesh, brought red radiance to the surface of not just his face and neck but his exposed arms, too.

"Did she?" he said, sounding surprised.

"Yeah. Said you treated her and everyone else like gold. Maybe except when you got worked up."

Block laughed.

"Well, we had some hellacious arguments. Things were so chaotic, I guess that was bound to happen. One time, we had a bunch of refugees show up, and your mom and I had some pretty harsh words with each other."

"That's one thing she did tell me. She said she was glad you stood up to her and didn't give in, because I might not have been born."

This grabbed Block by the throat and gut at the same time. He stood looking at his son. Yes, Herald was a miracle baby, conceived almost immediately after Clayton married Bridget and carried to birth months after he died.

"It was a strange time," Block said, his mind running through a whole weed-patch of memories. His eyes drifted through the walls of the shop into a place no one else could see.

"What are you thinking about?" Herald asked tentatively.

"The past. How odd it was that we few were picked to be here, when we had no clue what was coming. How things went crazy and we had to fight to keep our sanity." He studied Herald's handsome features. "And how lucky I am to be back here, with my son."

He reached out and offered his arms to Herald. Herald stepped to him and they embraced.

"Welcome home, Dad."

Once he was able to collect the feelings that were racing through him, Block said, "I'm really glad Jimmy was around for you. And I'm sorry I wasn't."

"Mom never really explained how you died."

"Wanted to spare you from knowing you were related to stupidity, probably."

"So, what happened?"

"I only found out when Yeshua told me, after he received me in Heaven. See, I loved drinking raw eggs for breakfast. The eggs gave me a really bad infection. It killed me."

Herald's nose and lips wrinkled.

"Raw eggs? Sick."

"Exactly the result, yeah," Block could now laugh. "I can't even explain how glad I was when I died. It was much less painful than what went right before!"

Herald put the broom away.

"Well, you're here now. And I'm really glad. So we didn't have a past, but I bet we're gonna have a great future," Herald grinned.

Block, for one of the few times in his life so far, was speechless.

LATE IN the morning on Pikes Peak, a woman appeared from over the northern ridge. She was tired looking, with sandy-gray hair falling below her shoulders. The cotton dress she wore looked new, but she did not, even though she was walking in her resurrected flesh.

Winded, she bent for a moment to recover her breath, although the air up here was now as thick and full as it was at the base of the mountain. Yeshua knew it was not the climb, but the anxiety, that made her short of breath.

She was one he had sought out several times after she had died. Each time, she would cower, her spirit pretending to be wounded, turning within herself. Each time, she had asked politely if they might speak some other time. Any other time.

Though she had professed faith during her old life, and expressed her love for God in countless prayers, Yeshua knew that she did not fully trust him.

Today would be her final chance.

When she saw Yeshua, she stopped abruptly, ducking her head and turning, hoping he had not seen her. She was about to hurry back down the mountain but some feeling chastened her. An unseen arm reached toward her.

She knew she must face this. Mostly, she was just anxious for it to be over. She was certain that an eternal Hell awaited her.

Why not face it? she silently asked herself. *Maybe the fires will burn away this horrid guilt.*

She crossed the wide parking lot to face her judge.

"Well, sir, here I am," she said, still nearly breathless.

"Welcome, Heledd." He pointed to the second chair.

"I think I had better stand."

"I'd rather you didn't."

She felt that being in the dock, so to speak, standing was the only proper thing to do. But she also felt weak, so her decision to sit came easily. She kept her distance, though, shoving her chair backward a foot as she sat.

"We've needed to speak for a long while," Yeshua said.

"I know. I know how many times you came to me before. I give you credit, you are persistent."

"I am."

She looked around suspiciously, wondering if anyone else was near, within hearing. But her guilt was the only thing lurking.

"I don't think you'll want to forgive *me, sir,*" she said dejectedly, her eyes roving over bits of gravel beneath her feet.

"For what?" he asked, though he knew full well.

"What do you know?"

"That we are talking about a murder."

She winced. Her hand went to her mouth, a feeble gesture as if to prevent herself speaking. She looked down at her skirt, still imagining the bloodstains where now there were none. They had once been vivid, dark red, sticky. She had burned that dress.

She nodded, "Yes."

"It was a Friday, in the tavern near Ammanford." He watched her for confirmation.

"Where I lived, yes, in Wales."

"March, 1723."

She stared at him, dumbstruck. How could he know

that?

"Is this some kind of magical trick?"

"Nothing magic. I have a very good memory."

"Well, then you know there was some money missing from the county office. He was the clerk."

"You had been to the office the week before. To look at a birth record, you said."

"Not strictly true, though."

"No, it wasn't."

Her words began to gush forth as from an artesian well.

"He found me—the clerk did—at the tavern. Accosted me about taking the money. Said he'd have me in for it. Grabbed me, tried to drag me away. I carried a knife always, to protect me and—well, before I knew it, it was deep in his belly. He fell over me against the wall, and me screaming—" She was gasping.

"Not a day you want to remember."

"A day I can never forget." Her head felt too large, filling with pressure.

Yeshua waited, and she went on.

"Old Llewellyn the tavern keeper—he was my cousin—helped me shove the body in that big storage closet by the back cellar, and clean up the mess. We dragged him out late that night, before he stank. Stuck him in the grave of an old man who was buried two days before. And no one was the wiser."

"Except one."

"You, sir." Her faced revealed shame.

"It was very evil, Heledd. To kill over a small amount of money, and to heap lies on top of lies. It was very grievous to me."

"I know it was wicked," she said, feeling genuine remorse and unrelenting guilt. "And he had a little daughter, too, such a beautiful little thing. And I took her father, in a rage." She fell quiet. "But, I was afraid."

She was breathing hard again, as if life would just not stay in her resurrected flesh.

"Why did you not repent?"

"Confess, you mean? Oh, my Lord," she gasped, "I knew word would get around. The old priest, he loved his liquor too much. Couldn't hold his liquor much less his tongue."

"Heledd, no one ever confessed before a priest who was not confessing to me. You should have confessed it to me."

"I didn't understand that, sir. We were told—"

"I know full well what you were told," he said sternly. Then his tone softened. "If you had known me better, you would have prayed to me, confessed."

She looked at him, feeling utterly condemned. She fumbled with a bent screw that had torn out of the chair arm when she shoved it back. She blindly tried to work the screw back where it belonged, trying to keep her composure.

She studied his face. Oddly, she saw no condemnation in his eyes. She saw something different, something she had never seen before, a love incapable of words. She realized now how little, in fact, she knew him.

Involuntarily, she gasped in a breath.

"And if I were to confess now?"

"Go ahead."

She did. The black guilt that hung around her like a strangling fog began to lift.

"It was a wicked thing, Heledd. But to not confess it to me, that was doubly wicked."

He stood and came closer. Unconsciously, she brushed hard at the edge of her skirt, looking up into his eyes.

"I can still see that blood stain, too," Yeshua said.

She nodded, still painfully conscious of what was not there.

"Would you like it to be gone?

She nodded again.

"It is forgiven. The stain can go," he said decisively.

The cloud burst. Tears poured forth.

"It was so wrong! So wrong! I am sorry, Lord!" she gushed, about to drown in emotion.

Yeshua helped her to her feet and wiped her eyes but centuries of fear and anger and self-loathing continued to pour out. She used her sleeves to help him stem the salty tide.

"You have been in your own prison a long time," Yeshua said.

"So dark," she said, sniffling in, trying to clear her nostrils. "Trapped, and desperate, I was. I felt so badly, especially for his poor child."

"Tomorrow, Heledd, you will meet her. To apologize."

This jolted Heledd almost senseless. But in only moments, she realized that being able to apologize to the girl who was now a woman was the very thing she wanted more than anything else in this new world.

"Oh, Lord, could that be? Thank you!" she beamed joyously through wet eyes.

"You carried that weight much longer than you needed," Yeshua told her. "But I knew your heart. And I welcome you to my kingdom."

Heledd embraced him. His touch, the touch of this human who was himself God, was medicine that healed her inner wounds instantly, as if they had never been. Light poured into her from she knew not where. The dark spirits that had tormented her fled in terror from this light.

Her damp forearms shivered. Yeshua took Zebulon's cloak from the back of his chair and wrapped it around her.

"When you get to Manitou, would you do me a kindness? Return this to the man named Zebulon?"

"Lord, I would rejoice to carry even your shoes."

He gave her a parting embrace. She clung to him briefly, but he urged her on her way.

"Enjoy this new world," he smiled.

She made her way down the mountain, her new body finally feeling invigorated. The perfect sunlight warmed the cloak around her and, though she didn't know it, her face had become radiant. Her heart beat liltingly as she walked, as if to notes skipping off the neck of a mandolin.

The beauty around her bore in, her spirit fully cleansed and restored. Creation and its angels were singing in the air that bathed her, and finally she was able to join them in the song of the redeemed.

18

Wednesday Afternoon

"Now look here, don't you—!"

The man, Dariusz, had been ranting for half an hour as if he had just been robbed of the cache of precious jewels that he had secreted away in his cellar during the decades of his otherwise pointless life.

He strutted around Yeshua and the parking area atop the peak like a vulture circling its prey.

He lost track of where he was and nearly stumbled over a low rock and concrete wall by the easterly ridge. He teetered, a man drunk with himself. The landscape far below seemed to recede, pulling backward and down. He felt queasy.

"Is—is this mountain—moving?" he demanded. "I'm not accustomed to such heights!"

"Having spent so much time in the depths."

"What are you insinuating, now?" Dariusz sputtered, spitting bits of saliva in the air.

"I insinuate nothing. I only tell you the truth."

"Damnation!" Dariusz shouted to the air. "Stop this mountain from moving!"

"It's not moving at all, Dariusz." Yeshua's voice was quiet, but commanding. "I won't keep you, if you want to go."

"Leave?" Dariusz said it like one in a prison who had never considered such a thing possible. He took small, tentative steps toward Yeshua, stopping a cautious 20 feet away. "But, that's it, you see. I don't even know why am I here. What is this about?"

"About your life, all that you squandered."

"I wasn't good with money."

"I'm not speaking of money."

Dariusz stared at Yeshua, then turned away. He looked toward the distant horizon, but even the sky looked dark at midday.

Yeshua knew that his efforts to draw Dariusz back from the brink of black self-destruction would be fruitless. But the chance had been offered.

From what he felt was a safe distance, Dariusz turned, a skeptical look in his eyes. "I can go?" he demanded.

"You have always been free to leave me," Yeshua said. He released a heart-felt sigh. "What you can never leave behind is yourself."

A scowl spread across Dariusz's face. The skin tightened into an involuntary, disfigured grin, like a piece of rotted fabric stretched too tightly over a broken mannequin.

"Yes, well . . ."

"I'm sorry you're leaving," Yeshua said truthfully.

Dariusz shook his head vehemently. "Well, it won't bother me." He looked out again. "The world was always an ugly place."

"For those with no vision."

"Talk in riddles, that's what you do—as if I'm some damned school child! I haven't the time," Dariusz snapped. "I haven't the time," he repeated, the words echoing hideously in his skull as he strode away.

NEW LIFE continued to spring up around the Solarium in unpredictable ways.

Bridget, Mai Ker, Clayton and Herald were huddled around a small worktable in Pod 10, debating how they might keep up with harvesting plants that were now growing into giants. None had ever seen corn grow like this. Some stalks were over 15 feet tall. Cabbage plants sat in their plots like baby elephants waiting for some kind person with a blade to come along and set them free. Carrot tops were nearly knee high.

"We sure won't lack for food," Block was grinning.

"Is this happening OUTSIDE, too?" Herald wondered.

"Fact is," Jimmy admitted, "I've been so consumed with everything in here, I haven't paid much attention." It was the reverse of his old problem of trying to avoid looking OUTSIDE because everything was utterly dead out there. "Just guessing what may happen next is keeping my brain pretty busy!" he said.

"That has never been too hard to do, Jimmy Algood," Mai Ker teased.

"Do any of you realize that it grew last night?" Jimmy said with an upward gesture of his hand.

He was greeted with puzzled looks.

"The corn?" Mai Ker asked.

"The pod."

The frowns followed Jimmy's hand as it pointed toward the pod roof. His friends began to wonder if a newly resurrected man could still go crazy.

"What?" Block asked.

"Honest," Jimmy said. "I just noticed it this morning. I'm not sure if it happened last night, or sometime before."

"The pod grew?" Block said flatly in disbelief.

"Nine and a half feet, to be precise," Jimmy said with a deadpan expression.

Herald frowned up at the beams.

"Not possible," he said, "aluminum and Stellar plastic don't grow."

"Certain about that?" Jimmy asked. "Come here."

Jimmy led them to a side of the pod near the podwalk into #14, where he had set up a transit earlier this morning. No one had noticed it, since it was buried behind a row of small bushes that were nearly 7 feet tall. The transit was aimed toward the peak of the great pod.

"We all know the height, right?" He remembered his fall. "Me, in particular . . ."

"One hundred thirty-two feet and four inches," Block said. "So?"

"Not anymore." Jimmy waved Block toward the transit. "If you sight using the side beams, struts and cross-members from ground up, my handy-dandy handheld computer tells me that the crest of the pod is now exactly nine feet, six inches higher than it used to be."

Though thunderstruck, no one doubted Jimmy now, but Block still wanted to be convinced. For several minutes, he aimed the transit at various beams and cross-members from the ground up, reading the angles and degrees on the electronic display and calculating distances each time he repositioned the instrument.

Jimmy handed him the small computer which he had left sitting on a bench this morning.

Block ran quick figures. He looked back up. He looked at Jimmy and the others.

"Well, first of all, I can't believe you even noticed that, Jimmy," Block said, smiling, "talk about good eyes. And second, son," he said turning to Herald, "apparently new laws are in play, because—guess what—aluminum and Stellar apparently *can* grow."

He handed the computer to Herald. Herald scrolled backward through the calculations, then stared at the roof.

"Huh," Herald said, truly perplexed. "How come Yeshua's never around when you need him?"

Bridget grinned at Clayton, then shot a smile at their son, whom she could see was finally warming up to Clayton. Whatever the years had stolen from Herald and his dad was quickly being filled in with an affection that was both natural and supernatural.

Mai Ker had sat on the bench. She, too, was looking up at the pod, a question in her eyes.

"Are we going to stay here always?" she asked the group.

"What?" Bridget asked at the abrupt change of subject.

"Are we all going to stay? Is that his plan?"

"Yeshua?" Jimmy asked.

"Who else?" was Mai Ker's quick reply.

"Don't know," Block said. "Honestly, the thought hasn't crossed my mind. My brain's like Jimmy's, playing catch-up."

"We'll have to ask him," Jimmy said, "when he gets back."

Then Jimmy looked around, not sure Yeshua wasn't already there somehow. He remembered their conversation about time being pliable, and different "onces."

"Sometime," Jimmy said, his mind drifting, "remind me to tell you what he said."

"Yeshua?" Mai Ker asked.

"Yeah, about time."

"Time for what?" Mai Ker asked.

Jimmy wrinkled one eye shut. "Never mind," he said.

He knew he couldn't explain, anyway.

EVEN FOR Yeshua, the afternoon had seemed long. Many encounters like the one with Dariusz had run their course. Yeshua craved quiet time with the Father.

Having given away Zebulon's cloak to keep Heledd warm, Yeshua now wore only the shirt and pants he had worn since his return. Though they appeared to be ordinary clothing, they were more like part of his flesh, woven of a living fabric unknown in the past world.

As the sun set and nightfall came on, gentle winds began to crest over the mountain. As the temperature dipped, the fabric of his clothing began to thicken, like an animal growing its winter coat. It would thin, as needed, tomorrow, but for tonight he would stay perfectly warm.

Along the southerly ridge of the summit, a small grove of pine trees had marshaled itself during the last 24 hours, growing, like everything back at the Solarium, at an impossible rate.

The great oddity was that trees were growing here at all, far above the elevation that had been timberline on the old Earth. Still, here they were.

Yeshua leaned his back against one of the new, young pines that was already over 30 feet tall. As he settled for the night and rested his eyes, the supple bark of the pine reached out around him just enough to cushion his spine. The thickening trunk gave a bit, allowing his head to ease into a small, fresh recess, hewn by his presence. The tree cradled his head tenderly, as his mother's hands once had.

Starlight broke out slowly, star winking at star, light bearing out across the entire universe as if from this one spot atop the peak. The thousands of ever-present angels circled as usual, but kept their distance, allowing their Lord his rest, although he would never sleep. The universe hovered in his mind and moved with it, there somehow contained and continued and held in life, as it had been since the beginning, from the very first moment of light.

19

Thursday Morning

Yeshua sat on the edge of a rock face as the new sun rose. The night had moved quickly, as nights now would, a mere blink in eternity.

He spoke with the Father throughout those hours, reflecting on what had happened here yesterday, and in many other places he had visited between his visitors here. At all moments in one place, Yeshua moved lightly through his new world, unbound by the constraints of his old flesh. The Father's timelessness rested within him, eclipsing space and time. Although these immeasurable movements were natural to his God-nature, they were still slightly disconcerting to his Man-nature.

More such encounters would play out until every risen soul had faced him. Like Corine, those who had committed themselves to him in the old age were eagerly going about their new lives, having passed beyond the pains of judgment long before their death.

"Thank you, Father, for those who turned," Yeshua said with raised arms. "And accept my pity toward those who would not."

Yeshua's last visitor here on the peak was a boy named Eulalio who had died at age six, a victim of drowning, when he was accidentally thrown from a ship in the Mediterranean in the Lord's year of 981. His father, the ship's captain, had recklessly taken him on the voyage even though it was the season of unpredictable and violent storms.

"It's good to see you, Eulalio."

The boy had just appeared from behind a row of bushes near the east ridge.

Eulalio looked around. He took in the spectacular view from the peak which had passed 15,300 feet overnight and was beginning to settle at this, its final, elevation.

The boy's black hair capped a darkly complexioned face that framed narrow brown eyes, which at the moment were wider than ever.

"Am I still dead?" he asked when he saw Yeshua sitting, quiet in prayer. "I'm to speak with a man, sir. Would you be him?"

"I am." He offered Eulalio a hand. "I'm heading down the mountain this morning. Would you like to go with me?"

Eulalio didn't move.

"But they said I must speak with God today." He looked around, uncertain of what to do.

"I am the Son. You can speak with me," Yeshua said jovially, trying not to overwhelm this child who would soon be a man.

"I suppose, sir," the boy said, taking his hand.

"But I need to ask you, son, if you are willing to be my subject, and enter my kingdom?"

"You have a kingdom, sir?" This seemed far from believable because the man alongside him, apart from the strange brightness around him, looked so very ordinary. He had no kingly robe, and no crown.

"I do, and you will have a share in that kingdom, if you choose to obey me."

"I'm not very smart about such things," Eulalio said humbly. "My old dad, he was smarter."

"Not smart enough to leave you home that last trip, though."

Eulalio frowned.

"And what must I do, sir?"

"Be willing to follow me, Eulalio, and obey me." He smiled down at the boy. "And by the way, you'll have a chance to see your own father again. He's grown up some, too."

"Then I am with you, sir. I get a kingdom, and my father back! More than I could want."

"You'll find more than you ever dreamed," Yeshua said.

Eulalio suddenly looked embarrassed, and momentarily dejected. "But I have nothing to pay with."

"I have paid your way, son. I do not charge for my love."

This brought a huge smile from Eulalio.

"Excuse me, sir. I've been impolite. I have not asked your name."

"I am known by many. I am Yeshua, the Son. You may have heard me called Jesus."

"It is a beautiful world, this," Eulalio said as they came around a bend of the road and a different panorama opened before them.

"It is, indeed," Yeshua agreed. "My Father is quite an artist."

Patches of greens and yellows and browns spread before them toward the western horizon, burying the blackened soil. Life was overcoming the last vestiges of death.

They came down a sharp hill and saw the shallow remains of Crystal Creek Reservoir below.

"Now that's a sight," Eulalio said melodically. "How pretty. Look how clear the water is!"

"Clearer than ever," his guide said. "We must take a drink when we get there."

As they neared the water's edge, rich sunlight reflected off the water toward the heavens. Light looking down, light looking up.

"Get yourself a drink," Yeshua told his new friend.

"No cup, sir."

"That's why I gave you hands."

Eulalio laughed. It was something his mother used to say.

He dashed to the water, knelt carefully so as not to dirty his new pants, and cupped his hands into the water. The water's surface seemed to resist but he finally scooped some up and slurped it down.

"*Never* had water like this at home!" he called to Yeshua.

"Nor anywhere, since Eden."

"Want me to bring some?"

"I already have some," was Yeshua's strange reply.

Eulalio playfully splashed the refreshing water over his face, then ran up and rejoined Yeshua.

"It's all so beautiful," Eulalio said twice as they walked on through even more lush areas as they descended in elevation.

"Yes," Yeshua said. "And this is just the barest of beginnings." He put his arm around Eulalio's shoulders and walked close beside him. "I'm glad you're with me," he said as they crossed the dam at the reservoir's end and walked toward Cascade. "The kingdom would have been much less without you."

A LUNCH of fresh-cut fruit and vegetables awaited them in Manitou. After eating, Yeshua walked off by himself, to sit on a low rise at the park's end. He sat for over an hour, quiet in prayer. Though his heart was still saddened about those who had been lost, he gave thanks to the Father for the great joy Eulalio and others had now discovered, having answered the Father's call.

As Yeshua sat alone, others of the company sat in a small circle near the center of the park, the ruins of the old city still visible around them.

"Me," Garan said to Jacob, Salah and some others, "if I had planned this, I'd have made sure all the wreckage of the old world was gone by now. He must surely be able to remove it," he added, nodding to where Yeshua sat.

Jacob looked at Garan, then looked at a decrepit building rotting nearby.

"Or maybe he wants us to have a reminder, for a while. Of what went wrong."

"Not likely to forget how bad a mess of the place we made, now are we?" Garan asked.

"Maybe not," Naomi said, "but with new life springing up all around, maybe Jacob's right, maybe we just need a little time to remember."

"Maybe," Garan admitted. "What about the Solarium, Jacob. What will he do with that?"

"Now there is a question," Jacob said. He ran thoughtful fingers through his thick beard, feeling the suppleness of his regenerated skin beneath it. "And if I was you, youngster, I wouldn't ask him."

He clasped Garan on the shoulder, waiting for Garan to look in his wiser eyes. Garan nodded.

"Probably best," the younger man conceded.

20

Thursday Afternoon

Yeshua called to Jacob about a half hour later. Jacob ran to him.

"I'm returning to the Solarium, Jacob. I assume you want to return?"

"Oh, of course, Lord. Didn't get much time with Katherine in the old world, as you know well. Don't want to miss out now."

"We're past those regrets, Jacob. You'll have all the time you want, and you'll both grow beyond those old hurts. Katherine wants that as much as you do."

Jacob nodded. His daughter's early death had been a terrible loss but now he would grow alongside her. He knew, also, that Yeshua would reunite them with his wife, Katherine's mother, when the time was perfect.

"Let Garan know. I think he wants to go back, too," Yeshua said. "We'll start in a few minutes."

Yeshua spent those minutes seeking out Zebulon.

"I see Heledd returned your cloak yesterday," Yeshua said when he found him.

"Yes, Lord, thank you. That woman who brought it, she was very kind. She seems a wonderful sort. You know, she could not stop talking about you."

"The heart that learns to receive forgiveness can hardly be silenced," Yeshua said.

"I wonder," Zebulon said hesitantly, "I mean, I'm wondering if when she goes—I understand she's going to her people soon—if I might be allowed to escort her?" He gave Yeshua a bashful grin that showed this was more than a chivalrous gesture.

"You like her, Zebulon."

"As I said, she seems a wonderful sort of woman. I would just like to get to know her better."

Yeshua knew Zebulon's heart.

"That kind of relationship will be different now, you know," Yeshua said. "The intimacies of old have also become new. You'll discover intimacy with her, but in a much deeper manner."

"Now, let me say," Zebulon chuckled, "I find that intriguing, but somewhat hard to believe." He had no idea how intimacy could be more intimate than in the past.

"You'll see," Yeshua promised. He smiled. "It's a good idea, Zebulon. I'm certain Heledd would enjoy your company." He eyed Zebulon intently. "Remember, you're a new man. You're also my friend. Show her that."

"Do my best."

"You don't yet know, but you'll find you and Heledd have much in common," Yeshua told him.

Zebulon's death resulted from his conviction for murder. He killed a man in a fight outside a small hotel in northern Missouri in 1833, a fight over a woman they both desired. The struggle ended quickly when Zebulon struck the man over the head with a piece of iron from a wagon wheel he was repairing.

A very short trial with the testimony of seventeen eyewitnesses put Zebulon behind a different kind of iron as he awaited hanging. He would have bashed his own brains in on those bars but his courage failed him.

The day before his execution a local parson came, uninvited, to see him. They talked only briefly. The parson admitted he didn't know enough of scripture to find any passage that might speak to Zebulon's predicament. But he did something no one else had ever done. He asked Zebulon how he felt about dying.

"Can't say I like the thought," Zebulon groaned.

"I tried it once," the parson said, admitting that he had once nearly thrown himself into a frothing river over a woman who had rejected him. "The Lord called to me, told me to stop. Told me I was being a fool," the parson said.

"The Lord . . ." Zebulon said, deadpan.

"Jesus."

"You heard Jesus?" Zebulon's eyes narrowed suspiciously.

"Well, not exactly a voice, if you see my meaning. I heard him in my spirit. 'You're my child, don't do this.' It was like a hand was holdin' onto my belt. I leaned hard, but didn't fall." He nodded meaningfully. "That's how he saved me."

"Can he keep my neck outta that noose tomorrow?" was all Zebulon wanted to know.

The parson studied Zebulon's face, a face that in less than twelve hours would be purplish-blue with the eyes bulging out under a gunny sack.

"He could. But no, I don't expect he will," the parson conceded somberly. "Still, you might ask his forgiveness. You did take a life."

Zebulon was impatient.

"I'm not throwin' myself off no bridge, parson. They're gonna drop me through a hole in that chintzy, damned gallows out there," he said resolutely but with uncloaked fear.

"I know, I know," the parson said awkwardly. "I just mean, I was about to fall through a hole, too. If the Lord could grab hold of me, I expect he could grab hold of you."

This ended the conversation abruptly. But through the night as sleep eluded him, Zebulon began to wonder if this distant God could forgive him. Around 4:00 a.m., the words formed silently on his lips, impassioned words, though he couldn't remember five minutes later exactly what he had said.

With the sun barely above the hills to the east that morning, Zebulon was standing weak-kneed on the trap door, the rope around his neck. His stomach, though empty, was in vicious turmoil. He gulped in air, as if it would do any good. But with that last batch of air he cried out, "Jesus, I'm sorry! I know I'm worthless, but please—grab hold!"

That cry was the reason Zebulon was standing here now in the company of Yeshua, the one who had seemed only a long-dead stranger to Zebulon but who had listened to his final, desperate plea.

"So, you say we have something in common?" Zebulon mused.

Yeshua smiled.

"Enjoy your time together. It won't be forever, but it will be well spent," Yeshua said, nodding toward Heledd.

"You know, Lord," Zebulon said, "when I dropped through the trap that day, I was sure you'd ignore me. But I remember, it felt like your hands somehow caught me as I struggled, my weight pulling the noose tighter." Zebulon winked. "Your mercy is very wide, and thankfully, your arms, too."

Yeshua acknowledged him with a smile. He clapped Zebulon across the back as a sendoff, then went to join Jacob and Garan for their journey back to Solarlum-3.

AS THE three men walked along, cutting across the still partially-barren plains of eastern Colorado, sprigs of new growth continued to pop up. Bushes, trees and wild grasses were quickly filling in the barren landscape.

"Was that a rabbit there?" Garan asked excitedly, pointing about 200 yards off to the south.

"A whole family," Yeshua said.

"They look like small dogs!"

"Yes, they're bigger than those you remember."

Not much of use had ever grown in this region. The seeds of the long dead plants had dissolved with the old Earth. In their place, many new varieties of seed from God-knew-where were germinating. Recent rains had watered the regenerated soil, creating new creeks and rivulets.

Unseen by Jacob and Garan, far below the surface, the water table was rising as the Earth's outermost layers began to morph and come alive. Yeshua's new Earth, to many appearances, was the same old place. But it was an entirely new world, supplanting the old, coming to life in ways that had not been seen since the earliest days of the old creation. The stain of sin was now washed from the soil and new life could take root.

"It's wonderful, Lord," Jacob commented nebulously, "all these new things springing up, with no help from anyone."

"They have help, Jacob."

"But you know what I meant."

"Yes."

Curiously, Jacob's legs became more invigorated each mile they walked, rather than tiring. "I have a feeling it will be more beautiful than ever," he said.

"Finer than human eyes have seen in many ages," Yeshua agreed.

They walked another fast mile in less than a minute, effortlessly.

"And what about the others?" Jacob asked with a visible reluctance. He slowed his pace slightly, watching Yeshua's reaction.

"What others, Jacob?"

"Those who are . . . well, not with us any longer."

"The damned."

The abruptness of Yeshua's words jolted Jacob.

"Yes. Them."

"What happens to them, Lord?" Garan asked. He,

too, watched Yeshua closely. It was a question he had wondered about many times.

"They are in a place apart. Separated."

"I know. But where?" Garan pressed.

"It's not as you imagine."

"No?" Jacob asked.

"Where they exist, in deep shadows, is not one place. Each is in his own place, altogether alone."

"So, that image of Hell, the 'lake of fire,' it isn't real?" Jacob questioned.

"Real enough if you're in it, Jacob. Where they have gone, the isolation and shadows, they are drowning in a fire that does not burn outwardly, but inwardly."

Both Jacob and Garan winced at the thought.

"You need not dwell on it," he told them. "Those who have turned their backs are cast out, cast into that fire that swallows the soul, the continuous perdition of those whose own will betrayed them."

"I see," Jacob said, though as yet he didn't.

"So, forever?" Garan asked. His mind couldn't tolerate the thought of such horrid punishment lasting forever.

"It has to be," Yeshua said, stating the obvious. "They, like you, are resurrected. They cannot die. They are sealed in a tomb of self-desolation, a tomb they dug over a lifetime. The gate into that place they have locked, from the inside."

Jacob began to ask a further question, but this was all Garan wanted to hear.

"I'll take your word, Lord."

"I know you will," Yeshua said, striding on at a quickening pace.

Jacob slowed, turned to Garan and took his arm, pulling him to a halt. Garan's face, though renewed, looked momentarily pale.

"You alright, Garan?"

Garan pulled free and stepped back in pace, intent

on keeping up with Yeshua.

Yeshua knew that however he might try to explain why some had turned away and rejected him, the idea would remain intolerable and repulsive to Garan, to Jacob, indeed, to anyone who considered it.

"You were created for life, my friends, in communion with the Father. Everyone," he said, leading them on across the high, greening prairie. "But not every child loves his father."

"But how could anyone—?" Garan began.

"Because *that* is who they are," Yeshua said tersely. "What you choose, you become. Their isolation burns them, yes, torments them. An inferno they would now extinguish, but can't."

"But surely the Father's love would—" Garan began again, but instantly recognized the bleak truth.

Yeshua stopped and turned, seeing the stark realization awaken in Garan's eyes.

"It was the Father's love they *rejected*, Garan. Pride is a terrible prison."

Garan sighed, confounded, staring out across a meadow of prairie grass filling up with wild flowers. The beauty he saw overwhelmed him, but it also helped overcome the indescribable sadness he felt.

"They wanted life only on their terms," Yeshua said with pathos in his voice. "Now, they have it."

Yeshua walked on, Jacob hurrying to keep astride of him. He could see the pain that hid behind his features.

"It hurts you, Lord. Doesn't it?"

"I will always sorrow for those who are lost. I am there alongside them in their despair. But they can no longer sense my presence. No love can reach them."

The air above them seemed to pulse. The Father's light, normally so gentle, bore down on Yeshua, Jacob and Garan as if it might consume them in their tracks.

"Will we be back soon?" Garan nearly begged, desperate to change the subject. He wanted to see only the beauty bursting out around them. It felt as though they had just passed, these last miles, through a deep, forbidding tunnel.

"Not long now, son," Yeshua promised.

BEFORE HALF an hour had passed, they reached the driveway that led into the parking lot of the Solarium. As they approached, they heard young voices, the sounds of play, the sounds of cheer and happiness.

The joyful sounds, so long stifled INSIDE, had broken free. Braden, Nathaniel, Piper, and Sing, joined by their new friend, Eira, were running and playing across the new grass that was sprouting wildly around the Solarium complex. Herald sat watching, cradling Kai on his lap, laughing at the frivolity of his wife and siblings.

The liberating feeling of the seemingly limitless sky above them had unleashed a sense of the awesome size and magnificence of the world OUTSIDE. No longer confined, able to play out in the open any time they chose, the children felt a true sense of what "life" was to be from now on.

Jacob left Yeshua just inside Pod 1 and went searching for food. The long walk and even longer conversation had left him intensely hungry.

As evening drew near, the kids returned INSIDE and settled down to their more usual games. Herald and Sing were holding a private, informal dance on a concrete pad near the east edge of Pod 10, to music they hummed for each other. Piper and Nathaniel played a game on two opposing laptop computers, one they had created themselves, taught by Bridget. It was a game of mountain climbing and dodging snowballs that exploded because of hydrogen and oxygen molecules erratically breaking apart when they hit.

Yeshua sat by himself near the tents, his eyes closed but alert as ever. The rest of the Solarians and their visitors were talking quietly by the front door of the Meeting Tent, learning the stories of each other's lives. Eira was on Bridget's lap. Bridget smiled at her often and laughed each time Eira did. The child's laughter had the sound of light, harmonious chimes and was gently contagious.

As the darkness settled OUTSIDE and the evening glow appeared, Yeshua got up and walked over to them.

"Rehearsing old times?" he asked.

"It's so much fun, Lord!" Eira giggled. "I'm learning a lot! Bridget is so smart."

"There will always be such learning, such fun," Yeshua said, his eyes sparkling.

Jacob took a long breath. "I'm curious, from earlier," Jacob said. "Is it over then? Done?"

"Judgment? No. There are still others. But you needn't trouble about it."

"How many?" Braden asked.

Obviously Jacob or Garan had shared some of the conversation from their journey back to the Solarium.

Yeshua looked down at Braden.

"Don't trouble yourself," he repeated. "It is not your concern." He looked around the Pod, as if searching. "There is one, though." He looked again, waiting. "He's nearby. Perhaps all of you should witness this."

Jimmy stood, looking around uncertainly.

"What now?"

"This is as good a place as any," Yeshua said evasively but with evident resolve.

"For?" Sing questioned him.

"For the one who has caused you—caused everyone—so much misery."

Sing and the other children looked perplexed, the elders less so.

"It is *his* time, now," Yeshua said.

He walked slowly toward a wheat field near the

middle of Pod 10. The others followed him, none with the slightest notion of what was about to happen.

Yeshua held his hands up and slightly forward as if pushing open a pane of invisible glass. "Lucifer, stand before me," he said in a measured but commanding voice.

For a moment there was nothing. Then came a hideous, ungodly noise that that strained across the whole width and height of the pod. It was a distracting, piercing noise unfamiliar to the Solarians and their guests, though it had silently haunted all their lives.

Yeshua, looking very intense, seemed to be staring at nothing. The noise increased, a sound like six or seven thousand cockroaches raging across a wooden floor as a light broke the darkness, all trying to hide in the same crack. There was an indescribable horror in the noise, as though fear and hatred were being wound tightly around barbed wire and torn to their limits.

Then out of nowhere began the strange flashes. They were not flashes in the ordinary sense because they were not flashes of light, but flashes of darkness, like lightning bolts of black emptiness, the jagged arms of some deadly menace. As each raging bolt cracked, it slashed a spasmodic vacuum through the air. Several bolts ricocheted off the pod roof, one careening into the ground not far from Yeshua's feet, burning a 4-inch deep hole.

He didn't move. Everyone else jumped in place, stunned as if by high voltage electrifying the air. The energy they felt around them, though, was not electricity but rage.

Herald, Sing, Piper and Nathaniel were terrified. They ran to their parents. Nathaniel dove behind Jimmy to watch what unfolded. Little Eira clung to Bridget's waist, shuddering violently, hiccupping for air. Braden stood off by himself like a petrified tree, though his eyes were like the lenses of two large telescopes.

The black flashes blasted through the air again as if shards of a black hole were scattering throughout the pod with no definable place or resting point.

For two or three seconds, the entire pod seemed to go dark. The Solarians felt they had been thrown from a blackened beach into a pitch-dark ocean. But just as quickly, the light returned.

Yeshua was standing fixed, the glow around him more brilliant than ever.

"Silence!" he commanded. Then, quietly, "Be still."

The horrid noise screeched away like air escaping a child's ruptured balloon. The flashes of black, spasmodic horror abated in the same moment, rushing into a focal point as a hollow, razor-thin beam that became frozen near the ground just inches from Yeshua's hardened face.

The dark beam seemed inverted, as if turned in on itself. Then it sputtered in some terrible, non-physical pain, barking out one final, terrified yelp.

Bridget, with Eira still clinging, grabbed hold of Clayton. Pam fell to her knees as if steadying herself for another earthquake.

"You're scaring us," Pam whimpered to Yeshua.

"Will we be hurt?" Eira asked a bewildered Bridget.

Then they heard the uncanny voice. It was not a human voice, nor was it a physical voice. There were no sound waves penetrating the air. Yet they all heard it.

"The wrath of the Lamb has come!" it shrieked. "Curse You! Let me be!" it cried out like a sick man dying, trying to vomit. "What do you have to do with me?"

"The time has come," Yeshua said determinedly.

"You have always said so," the voice replied.

"I've sent many ahead of you. You won't be the first."

"Why would I doubt that?" the voice replied with

resonant anger.

"You are angry?" Yeshua asked the creature.

"I am anger itself. You know this! You have felt my wrath, that day at Golgotha." The voice dropped in pitch but became more inflamed. "Once again, you will feel my pain!" The voice was unable to shout, though it tried, the words straining out like the cry of a tortured prisoner.

"I am beyond your deceits and your pain, Satan. You will harm no one!"

There was a sudden movement of a black hollowness not far from Yeshua's face, as if an invisible serpent had whiplashed its tail around him. Still, Yeshua did not move, or flinch.

"Your anger is fruitless. Your strength is gone," he told the creature.

"Oh, but I am angrier than ever! No one will listen! They have all gone deaf to my whisperssss."

"To your lies."

"No one listenssss," it repeated, spewing vehemence at the entire group. "You are revolting creatures— pathetic scales of rotting snakeskin," it howled. "Leave me! Leave me alone!"

"It is not I who will leave," Yeshua said loudly. "Truth is here, they see through your lies, now. Enough! You have made your choice. It is time."

"You have always said so," Lucifer repeated. "You, the One Lord," the voice said, though the words were forced, covering the realization that an eternal torment was about to begin. "I suppose now I must bow before you . . ."

"You have already bowed, to my voice," Yeshua said. "This is that day we spoke of—all those eons ago. You are never again free to cause harm."

"Why not let me play longer?" it asked in a malicious, slithering tone.

"You call it 'play' because you are twisted beyond

recognition," Yeshua said. His forehead furrowed. "I know the pain of what you call your games with your friends. Yes, I know it in my bones and flesh."

"So you say," came the snide reply.

"So many have suffered the pain of your lies. You will deceive no more."

There was another slash of the dark, whiplashing figure. Sing, staring in complete horror, sensed a crisp, demonic smile emanating from the thin, dark beam of nothingness, though there was no face.

"Oh, Lord, please, stop him!" Sing cried.

Piper grabbed Sing and grasped her tightly. Both were trembling but too frightened to cry.

"Will you turn back?" Yeshua asked it, already knowing the answer.

"Me? Turn? For what?" it sputtered.

"For what you have lost."

"But you would rule," it said. "The One Lord."

"I have always ruled."

"Yes." The next words were slow, nearly silent. "But I do not have to obey."

The light around Yeshua grew suddenly in intensity. His whole body seemed momentarily larger, almost a statue of impenetrable substance.

"No. You don't." Yeshua went silent. He waited, though he knew nothing would come of his patience.

Braden, like a little wooden tree walking, had stutter-stepped forward and was holding on to Nathaniel, using him as a shield.

A terrible scream ripped through the air. The torment had begun.

At the scream, poor Braden almost collapsed. Nathaniel bolstered him, finding his own courage, though he had no idea what was happening around them.

"Silence!" Yeshua commanded again. "I am Lord, and I do rule," he said with absolute force. "Your rebellion is over. Depart into your final darkness!"

"I have so grown to like it . . ." the voice growled pathetically.

"I know that, too."

The rest of the Solarians and their visitors were barely breathing, trying to remain invisible, afraid they might somehow be caught or captured by this horror, this invisible but insidious creature.

Their fears were unfounded. Yeshua was in perfect command.

Silence wore on for a full minute. The thin beam of black nothingness then receded several feet from Yeshua's face, backing away slowly, expecting a trap. It sizzled violently as if trying to escape the horror into which it had made itself. The unbreakable snare was springing shut—invisibly—around it and it was helpless, unable to cut the spring.

For the smallest part of an instant there appeared in the center of the beam a flicker of faded light that just as quickly was snuffed out. The beam narrowed into even deeper blackness that folded in on itself and disappeared with a ferocious *snap,* and was gone.

Yeshua had not moved.

Everyone else stared, too stunned to speak. They were not sure what they had just heard, or witnessed.

Piper finally garnered her courage and approached Yeshua, awed by the divine power that enveloped him like a shroud. Then she saw faint tears weeping from his eyes, barely dampening his face.

"What's wrong?" she gulped, herself near tears.

"Great sadness," he said. "He was so beautiful when I made him. The Light Bearer. Such brilliance, and splendor." He shook his head. "Like none other. And it was not enough."

Piper's eyes expressed her puzzlement.

"Enough?"

"The reign I gave him, that he refused. He wanted

my scepter—or nothing." Yeshua shook his head gravely.

"He wanted to take your place," Piper whispered with a wisdom she did not yet fully possess.

Yeshua knelt alongside her. His eyes captured hers. "Yes, child."

Tenderly, as if caring for a small infant, Piper brushed away the faint tears that stained his face.

"Not all creatures who are loved can love," he said.

21

Friday Morning

The shock of last evening's events wore away slowly. After the two younger boys had been put to bed last night, the elders had gathered around Yeshua in the main tent. Everyone wanted to know what they had just seen.

Piper had been allowed to stay and listen. She alone, of the children, had an inkling of who Yeshua had confronted. Jacob, Jimmy and, curiously, Mai Ker, thought they knew but didn't fully understood what had happened, particularly after Yeshua referred to the horrid creature as the "Light Bearer."

Yeshua said only that he had been a great angel. "Only great light could have produced such great darkness."

"I don't understand," Piper said

"Such magnificent light turned outward generates goodness. Turned inward, it produced great evil. He became too satisfied, too full of himself. Everyone else became unnecessary, except as he might use them."

"Even you," Bridget said.

"Even me."

"How could you stand there so calmly?" Will Atchison wondered.

"Because it was the end of a very long battle which I had already won. He challenged me near the beginning. Lucifer demanded uncontested power. We would never give him that."

The confrontation with Lucifer quickly turned the

conversation to other questions, ones that had plagued the Solarians since the great catastrophe took the old world. The ancient enemy of God was now gone, locked in a pit so deep within himself he could trouble no one, but an awful lot of questions remained.

"Maybe I shouldn't ask," Block said, "but why did you let him run loose so long?"

"He wasn't loose. I always held final control, Clayton. I always restrained him, or the damage would have been infinitely worse. From your timeframe, yes, it seemed evil ran loose, as you put it, a long time. But it often provoked great sacrifices in response. Not a bad thing. Those sacrifices, by many martyrs, produced great love, and turned many hearts to the Father."

No one realized it, but Pam, ever one to smooth things over with a good dessert, had snuck out and retreated to the kitchen. She came back with a platter of her most recent cookie experiment. These were her "Cookies of Delight" with a rich, creamy, white fudge center.

"Anyone hungry?" she butted in, trying to break the tension.

The cookies were a hit.

"I don't suppose it matters much now," Atchison said through a mouthful of cookie, "but what happened, exactly?"

"Explain what you mean, for the others," Yeshua said.

"To us. Earth. What did we hit out there, that destroyed the atmosphere?"

"You're right, it doesn't matter," Yeshua said with a keen look into Willy's inquiring eyes.

"But—you mind?" Will persisted, looking around. "I'd like to know. I think we'd all like to know."

"Do I mind? Not if you don't." Yeshua also looked at everyone. Their eyes were glued to him, especially

Piper's. She had only heard about the terrors of those final days secondhand.

"Go on," Bridget encouraged him, "please."

"It's a bit complicated," he answered. "Let me see if I can put it in a way you'll understand." He pondered his next words. "You're wondering what happened, but also why. 'Why' is fairly simple. It was the beginning of the final judgment, the judgment you brought entirely on your own heads."

Atchison went to work on his next cookie.

"OK, but how?" Block asked.

"The Earth struck an ancient void in space, and in time." He saw this did not register. "It did this three times. Once, on my day at Golgotha. Once, on May thirteenth of the year you first arrived here. And once again, on a night only some of you remember."

He waited. A light flickered in Jimmy's eyes.

"That night of the meteor shower! Remember?" he asked Bridget and Mai Ker. "When we found little Herald staring OUTSIDE. There was that great blank in the sky?"

The two women nodded, remembering it.

"Just like that May, before you came here to the Solarium," Yeshua said.

Pam had unconsciously set the large cookie platter on a side table and drifted into a chair. Everyone's eyes remained fixed on Yeshua.

"For millennia that void followed you, the worst plague of all," Yeshua said, "a gaping wound in the cosmos—waiting."

"And what—do I want to ask?—caused this wound?" Atchison asked, carefully wiping his mouth.

"Sin," Yeshua answered. "The great rebellion. Beginning with Lucifer, and cascading down through every rank of creation." He softened his tone. "To each of you."

No one replied. No one dared look sideways.

"I drew the universe out of nothing, into order. Sin ripped that work backward. It slashed a hole in the fabric of my creation. A hole into the abyss of nothingness."

The blank stares changed to befuddled stares.

"And that's what Earth hit?" Atchison asked.

"Yes. You hit nothing, a void in the cosmos."

"You are not, sort of, making a joke?" Mai Ker asked.

"This cannot be in the least funny, Mai Ker. The Earth hit *nothingness*. That void ripped through the atmosphere, triggered all the static-electric activity. It would have split the Earth if my hand had not intervened. But the damage was done. Earth spun past it, but the atmosphere was mortally wounded."

"You could have fixed it," Piper said without the slightest hesitation.

"And what then, child? Watch the human race continue to deteriorate for a few more centuries? A few more millennia? You were fruitful, yes, you had filled the Earth with souls but also with sin." He looked at Piper. "What good would have been served in waiting longer?"

Piper frowned, searching for an answer. She found none.

"Why didn't we see it coming?" Atchison pressed him.

"Why didn't you see *nothing* coming?" Yeshua asked. "I said, it's complicated. Even now, it may be beyond you."

"Try me," Willy said.

"Your scientists didn't see the event coming because there was, literally, nothing that could be seen, or measured, or mapped."

"You said this was caused by sin," Bridget said, "so why didn't if affect us sooner?"

"It was outside of creation. As the OUTSIDE was to you, here in the Solarium. Sin opened the crack—like that, up there," he said, pointing to the repair Herald and Bridget had recently made. "A small wound, but in time, deadly. That opening, though very small at first, allowed chaos back in when you struck it. The final terrors of the end began. In fact, they began in part the day I died, when Earth glanced against that void the first time."

No one touched this comment.

"And the third time?" Jimmy asked. "The night of that meteor shower?"

"I intervened. Or all of you in here would have died, too."

Quiet ruled for nearly a minute. Atchison gently rubbed the top of his forehead as if his brain felt hot from overuse.

"And this 'nothing' tore up the atmosphere?"

"It began a chain-reaction that, as you all discovered, could not be stopped."

"We stopped it in here," Bridget reminded him.

"Actually, Bridget, I stopped it in here. Your attempt—venting all the bottled up air—it was brilliant, it helped, but it would not have sufficed. I intervened then, too, to restore the balance so your air could stabilize."

"You?" Mai Ker said, dumbstruck.

"Always thought that trick was a little too good to be true," Atchison said.

"Why? Why save just us?" Block wanted to know.

"A simple choice, Clayton. I have always preserved a remnant. Whenever my people failed me, when they turned against me, though they all deserved death, I preserved a remnant. A witness, for the future, against them."

"We were the remnant," Pam said pointedly. "Of humanity."

"Of the past, yes. You, the children, and this," he said, gesturing around the huge complex, "remain as the last witness of the desecrated world that I have redeemed."

Mai Ker was still trying to understand the physics involved.

"This void we hit," she said, "describe it, please."

"It will make no sense to you."

"But it makes sense to you?" she asked him.

"Perfect sense."

With all her confidence in her abilities and intelligence, Mai Ker was willing to let it rest. Will Atchison, with much less confidence in his own abilities, wouldn't.

"A void. You mean, like complete emptiness."

"Well," Yeshua answered, "not emptiness as you mean it. Human comprehension of 'empty' is simply an impression of things missing. My divine comprehension allows me to know it more exactly, as what preceded anything that could be missing. You see?"

"Not in the least," Will grimaced. "And someday, remind me to stop asking stupid questions."

"We should stop," said Pam. "My head aches. Can we go?"

"Anytime you like," Yeshua said. "No matter."

"Great pun," Bridget laughed, pushing back into her soft chair. She was sure Yeshua was having fun with them, now.

"Sweetie," Pam said to Piper, "come along and get ready for bed. It's getting really late."

Piper was in no mood to leave but she was exhausted. She would talk with Yeshua another time, when she was rested. She nodded, went over and kissed Yeshua's cheek, and followed her mom to their tent.

"I'm sure you're all tired," Yeshua said, gracefully giving them an excuse.

Atchison held up one finger to stop others from leaving.

"Could you just describe a little more what it is we can't understand?"

He got several cold stares.

"Let's talk some other time, Will," Yeshua smiled.

BRADEN WAS the first up this morning, awakening a little after 7:00 o'clock. An idea had pestered him as he slept and he couldn't wait to find Yeshua. It was great, Braden thought, having someone this smart around, a "know-it-all" who actually did.

"Why is it taking so long?" he asked as he and Yeshua sipped freshly chilled orange juice.

"What?" Yeshua asked with pretended ignorance.

"Everything being made over?"

"This is good juice," Yeshua said.

"You can't tell me?"

"I could. But let's not be in a hurry. Let's let the Earth grow, as you do."

"And—I've been wondering, too—did you fix my leg just when we took the cast off, or before?"

The constant inquisitiveness of the children, not to mention their parents, made Yeshua laugh.

"You're full of questions this morning, Braden."

"Always am."

"That's not at all a bad thing, son."

Jimmy was behind them pouring some cereal for himself.

"I'd like to know, too," Jimmy said.

"About his leg?" Yeshua kidded, although he knew.

"No. The rest. Why is everything happening so slowly? I thought you'd just do it like"—he snapped his fingers—"that."

"It seems long, does it?" Yeshua asked, again not answering.

Jimmy began crunching the dry cereal without

looking for milk.

"Don't you have one of those magic-stick things?" Braden asked.

Yeshua chuckled.

"A wand, huh? You've been reading the wrong books, I'm afraid." He laughed again. "To you, it seems things are happening slowly, but not to me."

Jimmy wasn't about to go there, "the time thing" again. He changed the subject. "The air looks a lot clearer," he said, looking out through the tent door. "Almost a turquoise."

"Beautiful, isn't it? The atmosphere was very sick. It, too, is regenerated," Yeshua said.

"Daddy told me it got really bad. Before," Braden said. "It killed people."

"Yes," Yeshua said, "but that's over, Braden."

Jimmy sat down by them, still munching.

"Oh, something came up, too, while you were gone," he said. "Seems like Pod ten has grown somehow. Gotten taller." He watched Yeshua closely.

"Is that right?" Yeshua said innocuously.

Jimmy couldn't help himself.

"Well, we both know steel and aluminum and plastic don't grow," he said.

"You're certain we both know that, Jimmy?"

What Jimmy knew was that he was no longer certain of just about anything.

"Nevermind."

"Braden," Yeshua said, "I wonder, I have plans for this morning. Would you like to come along, help me work?"

"Can Piper come?"

"If you'll find her. I think she may be sleeping in."

Braden dashed off to find his half-sister.

WHILE BRADEN rousted Piper out of bed, Yeshua went and found Bridget. She was with Block in the

Comm. Center in Pod 2. Bridget was at a console running diagnostic programs on the Solarium systems, making sure they were not neglecting necessary maintenance. Block was at a nearby console playing a game of hide-and-seek with a computer.

"Morning." Yeshua rolled a chair near Bridget and sat down. "Clever machines that we made," he said.

"Oh, so you had a hand in these?" Bridget laughed. "I kind of thought the devil might have designed these things, just to irritate us."

"No, I gave men the knowledge. Lucifer just latched on to it—like everything else."

He watched Bridget click away at the keys, her mind reprocessing what the computer spit out at her. She felt his eyes. She turned and looked at him.

"Is there something else?" she asked.

"Our talk on Sunday in the barn, about why I allowed so much suffering. Did we finish that, or is there a loose end?"

"No," she said truthfully. "I get it. I'm OK."

"And there's nothing else bothering you?" Yeshua pressed.

Obviously there is, she thought, *or he wouldn't ask.* She looked at Block. Yeshua's eyes followed hers.

"Clayton can stay. It involves him, too."

"What is 'it'?" she asked.

"A day when you and he and the others were here in the Comm. Center, your conversation with John Haskins. Remember? When he told you the truth?"

How could I forget? Bridget thought. The memory leaped instantly into her mind, the scene agonizingly clear. The hurt, anger, and tears were cemented forever in her memory. Then she remembered one particularly awful moment.

"Um. Yes." She looked at Block. "Remember what I said to him, Clayton?"

"To Haskins? You said quite a lot, dear."

"One thing in particular."

"I'm already playing hide and seek with the computer. I can only play one version at a time."

Yeshua had rolled his chair between them.

"John finally told us. He was trying to say he was sorry. I was really—" She caught herself and chose a different word. "I was really angry. I got in his face on the monitor. I said, 'Remind me to write you a forgiveness card at the end of eternity.' I'll never forget those words."

"They made quite an impression on John, too," Yeshua told her.

"Yeah. I'm sure they hurt." She stared at the computer screen for a moment, wishing John Haskins' face might appear. "I wish I could tell him I'm sorry."

"I wish that, too," Yeshua told her.

TWENTY MINUTES later Braden and Piper followed Yeshua through the Visitors Center, then OUTSIDE. They walked casually toward the riverbank. The pure air and sunlight delighted Yeshua as much as it did the children. The sun had nearly reached its final latitudinal position, which Yeshua was certain Mai Ker had already noticed and logged.

"Do you think we might want to make some more changes?" Yeshua asked the children, looking around as if he had just walked into an old house in need of remodeling. "Braden thinks things are happening too slowly."

"What kind of changes?" Piper mused.

"What would you do?" He looked at both kids. "What would improve this?" He gestured at the landscape, across the river and toward the horizon.

Braden's answer was quick.

"Herald told me how beautiful the mountains are," he said, pointing toward Pikes Peak. "I'd like to live on a mountain!"

"Really?" Yeshua said innocently.

"I'd like to be by a nice, quiet lake," Piper said. "Guess we can't have both, though."

"We can't?" Yeshua asked as though terribly disappointed. He studied the terrain, then looked back at the Solarium. "Let's see, you have a pool, and an ocean. A mountain with its own lake," he considered, "that might be very nice."

The children were wondering why he would tease them like this, but their wonder was upended as the earth beneath the Solarium began to jolt and move.

It was not an earthquake, but a regulated shifting, like that morning when Yeshua was out here alone. The Solarium began to rise with the soil but there was no damage, miraculously, to the structures.

Piper and Braden watched in stunned silence. Those INSIDE the complex looked up trembling, fearing the worst, as the whole complex began to be uplifted. They looked out toward Yeshua and the children, then just beyond to where the river channel seemed to recede and drop. In reality, the river remained in place but the land above it was rising.

Piper squatted toward the ground to steady herself, as if she was astraddle a headstrong pony.

"We'll be hurt!" she cried out.

"Nothing will hurt you, daughter. The world is just growing a little," Yeshua said calmly.

Braden had grabbed hold of Yeshua's lower arm like it was a tree trunk.

"The world can't grow!" Braden protested, wishing now he had kept his mouth shut at breakfast.

"But you can?" Yeshua laughed jovially. "Everything can grow. It's the nature of the world."

As they spoke, the river valley continued to fall away rapidly below them and the mountain forming under their feet kept rising at an alarming pace. It was somewhat like an earthquake but more like being on a funhouse floor, the boards shifting forward and back beneath their feet.

The noise of this process sounded like a hundred wrecking balls sequentially broadsiding the Hoover Dam while six cathedral carillons pealed their largest, discordant bells. But nothing was damaged, only enlarged. Several rocky shoulders and ridges broke out into the open near what had been, just moments ago, the smooth riverbank. The river itself widened dramatically as it passed out of sight below them. The Solarium complex remained unchanged, except that two more of the pods grew slightly in height, a fact no one would notice for another week.

In the midst of the upheaval, thousands of the strange angelic creatures came crackling up out of the soil as if they were doing the excavating. They spun in the air into a kind of mystical carousel, turning slowly over the whole area like a crown of stars. Eventually they poured together into a tight cluster and came to rest at the feet of Yeshua. The wrenching of the land eased, the tremendous noise subsided. With a slight bow he acknowledged the angels—and they were gone.

The new mountain they stood on settled as if going back to sleep. It was nothing like the great peak that stood near the horizon, where Yeshua had first appeared eight days ago, but it was now 400 feet above the water that meandered more slowly down the widened river.

Braden still had a lock-grip on Yeshua's arm, his young eyes blinking, trying to clear, certain they had just been tricked. Piper straightened up, standing behind him as though he was her shield.

"Watch carefully. Someday you can help with these things," he told them. "When you've grown yourselves." Then he pointed Piper's head toward their right.

So entranced by what had just happened in front of them toward the south, Piper and Braden missed the fact that simultaneously a broad, deep basin had opened in the ground just west of the Solarium. What had been the fallen-in ruins of the rebuilt Bent's Fort were gone, swallowed into large rocks in the bottom of the new basin. As the two children stared, the ground circulating around the rim of the basin like a lethargic whirlpool finally rattled to a stop.

"Your lake, Piper." Yeshua drew her from behind him.

"It's just a hole," was her confused reply.

She was obviously not given to exaggeration. The 45-foot-deep basin was at least 600 feet across.

"I'm expecting rain," Yeshua said.

Braden took a few cautious steps toward the edge of their new mountain so that his feet were just touching the wide rock ledge that hemmed the new ridge overlooking the river.

"Awesome," he said expressively. Then he felt dizzy. Piper ran for him and pulled him a step back.

"The Father's handiwork always is," Yeshua said. "Enough, for now. Why don't you two play a while? I think I'll look for a snack."

He started for the door of the Visitors Center. Over his shoulder he said to the children, "Watch that drop off. It's steep."

Jimmy and Mai Ker had come running and almost collided with him rounding the corner of the hall into the Visitors Center.

"What in the world happened?" Jimmy asked breathlessly. "Another quake?"

"No, some remodeling for the kids. They're fine, Jimmy. I cautioned them."

"But what *happened*?" Mai Ker begged.

"Braden wanted a mountain."

"And—you mean, you can just *do* that kind of thing?" she said, her mouth gaping.

"You will, too, in time. I promised it long ago. No one believed me."

"But a whole mountain—!" Jimmy was saying, starting to follow him back INSIDE, still in disbelief.

"And soon a lake, for Piper."

Mai Ker turned and was about to run OUTSIDE, but saw the children through the clear hallway wall, laughing, playing, and tossing rocks over the edge. She spun back and followed Yeshua.

"Don't worry," Yeshua told them, "I was careful not to damage anything. Except those old electrical lines that fed in from OUTSIDE? You could say they're permanently disconnected."

They crossed through the podwalk from Pod 3 into Pod 10. Two whippoorwills swung in through the podwalk from #6 and circled the three, then followed along above Yeshua as he headed to find his snack, likely some of Pam's newest treats.

"How are we going to live like this?" Mai Ker questioned him emphatically. "Things suddenly changing all the time!"

"Not much changed, really," Yeshua assured her.

"*We* have changed. I am still trying to get used to this new body you gave me!"

"I know."

"Can we slow down?" she asked.

"The changes?"

"Our feet," she said, dragging to a halt.

"Yes." He stopped. The two birds stopped, circling, then flew back to the podwalk into #6. "Let's go sit by the aviary, shall we?"

He led Jimmy and Mai Ker into Pod 6. Several of the other Solarians were coming toward them but he held up a hand that directed them away. Bridget and

Clayton had come out of the Comm. Center and headed out to check on Braden and Piper.

"Everything's fine," Yeshua called to them, as if mountains shooting up underfoot was as normal as a sunrise.

He took a seat on a small bench by the huge aviary cage. Jimmy and Mai Ker dragged two wrought iron chairs alongside him.

"Incredible," Jimmy said, astounded but not winded.

Through the pod walls they saw Braden and Piper walking back toward the Visitors Center, hand-in-hand. Both children looked exultant, no doubt wondering what miracles might come tomorrow, and the next day.

"What did you want?" Yeshua said to Mai Ker.

She hesitated.

"Why must the whole world change?" she asked feebly, not sure she had a right to pose the question.

"Why not?" Yeshua asked.

"It does not seem necessary. The world was very beautiful as it was."

"It many ways, it was. But it was damaged, remember, dying. And there is beauty you have not yet seen."

"I do not understand this," Mai Ker said.

"Just as I gave you new flesh, I'm giving Earth her new flesh."

This made less sense yet to Mai Ker.

"Mai Ker, sin didn't just damage humans, it damaged the Earth itself."

"'Cursed is the ground because of you,'" Jimmy quoted.

"Exactly," Yeshua answered. "Space and time were torn, but the Earth, too, had long ago been wounded. It, too, had to be redeemed."

"Meaning?" Mai Ker asked.

"What had been bartered away to your ancient enemy had to be purchased back."

This Jimmy understood.

"The cross," he said.

Yeshua nodded soberly. Mai Ker looked at Jimmy, then at the Lord. She wondered if anything was beyond his control.

"How did you do that?" she asked, trying to steady her mind and her hands. "Out there?"

"I willed it." He gave her a contented look. "Be ready, Mai Ker. There's more to come in the months ahead. The world is coming back to life."

22

Friday Afternoon

By late morning, Yeshua was finally alone, walking along the edge of the artificial ocean in Pod 12, speaking with the Father. He had just returned from another of his unnoticed absences from the Solarium, the judgment of an unusually angry man named Reuben.

They had stood on a low hill in what had been southern Germany, overlooking a small country lake.

"Why," Reuben demanded, "can't you just leave me alone? After all, I've never bothered you."

"I remember several times—once when you were in grave danger in the war," Yeshua reminded him. "You cried out, 'God help me!'"

"Yes, well . . ." Reuben searched for an excuse. "Just a figure of speech."

"You've spent your life convincing yourself I don't exist. If I don't exist, how can I leave you alone?"

"You're trying to be too clever. If there was a real God, he'd have come himself."

"And what then would you *see*?"

"See?" Reuben frowned, jerkily rubbing his nose as if a fly were pestering it. "Look, I don't know how you managed to bring me here, but I wish to be left alone. I have extremely important things to think about."

"Reuben, unless you turn, I am the last soul you will ever see."

"Well and good! People were always such damned trouble," Reuben swore. He turned abruptly and stomped into a thicket of tall bushes by the lake's edge.

Back now at the Solarium, Yeshua could still see every crease in Rueben's scowling face, and the despair written there. *Such a brilliant mind,* he said to the Father, *yet unable to see truth.*

Yeshua came to a particular spot along the shore. He remembered the day Sing and Herald had come here, when he had saved Herald by Sing's hands. It would have been easy enough to let Herald drown. But the depth of love that had grown between Herald and Sing was important during that deathly time. And Yeshua had determined that beautiful little Kai would be the last new soul to be called into his kingdom.

OVER IN Pod 10, Willy and the other elder Solarians, with the help of Katherine, Jacob, Garan and Adrian, were watering some fast-growing melons and vegetables. Willy could almost taste the sweetness of the new melons. The group was discussing how soon the new fruit would need to be harvested.

Savoring the imagined taste of new melons, a peculiar question struck Atchison.

"Here we are," he said out of the blue, "so, what's over there?"

"Where?" Block asked.

"Under those grave markers over there, old buddy." He pointed to the small, white-fenced cemetery where the two of them, Sarajane, and eventually Jimmy had been buried.

Block released his grip on his nozzle and the water dribbled to a stop.

"Willy, only you could even think up such a stupid question," Block laughed.

"Why's it stupid?"

"Don't even want to think about it," Block answered, shaking his head at Will's craziness.

"Well, we're *here*, so"—Will shut off his hose, too—"aren't you even a little curious?"

Bridget looked at Atchison with revulsion. "Will, that is so completely gross," she said, remembering all too clearly the burial of each coffin.

"But there's gotta be an answer, right?" Atchison asked everyone.

"Would be kinda interesting," Block finally admitted, always one for an adventure. He checked around to make sure none of the kids were nearby.

Bridget came over to them.

"You're kidding, right?" she said, keeping her voice low. She looked horrified.

"You won't find a thing," Katherine said, unprompted. Her new hearing was acute.

"Whad'ya you mean?" Willy asked.

"You're here. There won't be anything in those graves."

"How can you know that?" Mai Ker asked Katherine.

"You're you, aren't you?" she asked Willy and Clayton. "Can't be in two places at once."

"But those were just dead bodies," Block said. "Carcasses. Not this," he said, gesturing to his new stronger, radiant body.

"But they *were* you," Katherine replied.

"Well, there's one surefire way to find out!" Willy said, grabbing a nearby shovel and walking intently toward the little cemetery.

Caroline and her brother were hovering high in the pod. She had been watching the group work, observing, as far as her Aves wits would allow, how odd human beings looked. When Willy entered the cemetery, her brother headed back for the comforts of the aviary, but Caroline, with the humanlike curiosity she had developed, fluttered down and perched on top of a short fence post, twitching her beak at Atchison.

With a smile toward Caroline, Block hurried to one of the sheds for a bigger shovel and a pry bar. Everyone else followed Willy to the graveyard. Four markers still stood in their places. William Atchison, Sarajane Haug, Clayton Block, Jimmy Algood.

"Isn't it odd Yeshua never said anything about these?" Bridget observed as they walked through the short gate. "It's not like he could've missed them."

"No," Katherine said, "because he knows. I'm telling you."

Willy was over the graves, already digging. His curiosity in overdrive, he started with his own. Clayton added his shovel. Jimmy stood by with the long pry bar.

Clayton's shovel struck the coffin lid first. They bent and quickly cleared the dirt off.

"Are you sure about this?" Mai Ker asked with unease, standing back at what she hoped might be a safe distance.

"Sure as I can be, considering," Willy said.

Jimmy leaned down and used the curled tail of the pry bar to wedge the lid loose. He was sweating, and not from heat. He worked slowly, apprehensively.

"Oh, for cryin' out loud, people," Willy said, jumping into the hole. He kicked dirt away from one side of the coffin with his boots to make room for his now-larger-then-ever feet, bent over, and yanked the lid free.

There was no smell. There was no debris. There was nothing at all except what looked like old cleaning rags shredded by mice and other vermin.

"I'll be—" Willy started to say.

"No you won't," Bridget cut him off.

"Now that is *not* what I expected," Willy said, his head wobbling meaninglessly.

"Incredible," Block said, looking into the empty, almost pristine coffin.

But the men weren't satisfied with one coffin. There were three more. They dug open the graves, cleared the coffins and pried them open. The same thing. Shreds of clothing, deteriorated remnants of small items they had placed in the coffins. No bones, no rotted flesh. No bodies.

"You can go search the whole Earth, if you want," Katherine told them with an "I told you so" tone. "Won't find a single human grave anywhere that's not empty." She looked around. "Why didn't you believe me?"

"Some things are still a little hard to grasp," Mai Ker admitted for the rest. She became more confused and sat down on her heels. "So, these new bodies of yours—are just the old ones?"

"No," Katherine said, "it's like what happened to you, dear, Sunday night. These new bodies have replaced the old. Whatever might have been in these coffins last week doesn't exist anymore. It was consumed when these resurrection bodies took their place. Patterned on those first ones, but perfected. Do you see?"

"Yeah," Jimmy chimed in, "just like you and Bridget, and Pam, and Mai Ker—and the kids. You were all changed, right? Where's *your* old body?"

The perfect sense of it clanged like the single toll of a bell.

"I guess it was too simple and obvious to see," Mai Ker said, wondering if her methodical reasoning had turned to jelly.

"That's funny!" Bridget laughed. "I never even wondered what happened to my old body."

"That's 'cause you don't think like me," Will Atchison said, causing an encompassing smile on Bridget's face.

"Thank the Lord!" she laughed.

PIPER, NATHANIEL, Braden and Eira, out playing, came running past the cemetery not long after the adults went back to their watering.

Nathaniel saw the piled up soil. The coffin lids had been placed back but the graves left open. The low dirt piles around the graves looked like a perfect playground to the kids. They quickly transformed the formless heaps of earth into two small fortresses, though no enemies were in sight. Soon a riotous dirt clod fight was underway. Braden nailed Piper in the head with a hardball, but it bounced away like a balloon off a ceiling.

The older Solarians were finishing their work in the melon patch. Not having to dig weeds actually made the work fun. The vines were so thick that they had to be slogged around so the plants wouldn't strangle each other.

"So, what do you think? What's next?" Bridget asked.

"I expect anything's possible," Block said. "He *is* the one who made it all. I guess he can remake it however he wants."

"But growing mountains up under our feet? That seems a little over the top," Mai Ker commented.

"Literally!" Jimmy teased her.

She gave him a look. "You know what I meant, Mr. Wise Guy."

"I've seen a great many wonders in my time," Jacob commented. "Miracles never do cease."

"Some might argue," Jimmy said, eyeing Bridget.

"Not anymore, Jimmy," Bridget replied. "The miracle is, I've been allowed to outlive my doubts."

The four children, already bored with their dirt pile fortresses, came to watch the elders."

"How come you guys dug up those graves?" Eira wondered curiously.

"Probably mining for something," laughed Nathaniel.

"I feel everything is becoming wonderful," Eira said. "Look at how everything grows!"

"Yeah, plenty of food in our future," Block said, looking up at a bunch of corn stalks that were approaching 20 feet in height, and picturing how they might harvest these.

"I hope so," Nathaniel said. "I can't wait to see what's next!"

"I remember, in the scriptures," Pam said dreamily, "it said we'd walk streets paved with gold."

"Probably just a symbol, Pam," Mai Ker said. "You know, like how a city could be perfectly beautiful."

Without them realizing, Yeshua had returned from his walk and was standing not far behind the children.

"If you'd like golden streets, you could certainly have them," he said. "There will be plenty of gold."

Everyone turned at the sound of his voice.

"What do you mean?" Block asked.

"Gold can grow, too. When sin came, the precious things of the world hid, deep in the Earth. Far from the hands of the wicked men who would covet and misuse them."

"But gold and silver and things, they were always deep in the Earth," Bridget said.

"You're sure of that, Bridget?" Yeshua asked, giving her an inquisitive look.

"Guess I'm not sure of anything," she confessed.

"In the beginning, many precious minerals and gems were on the surface, too. The ornaments of my creation."

"You speak as if they were alive," Mai Ker said.

"They were, though not biologically," Yeshua said.

"What do you mean?" Atchison asked.

"All things were created to live. Sin was killing the Earth. The blood of Abel—of so many others—tormented the soil. The precious things fled deeper underground."

"You mean, like, they buried themselves?" Braden asked, incredulous.

"Yes. Fleeing sin, they burrowed into veins in the Earth, in mourning. Gold, silver, emeralds, rubies, all that is precious," Yeshua watched their reactions. Even now, they were having troubling taking him at his word. The children, though, listened with rapt attention.

"Such things were there for the taking in Eden," Yeshua assured them. "The walls of the great garden were encrusted with precious stones and gems."

"Oh my gosh," Pam said, "just like the New Jerusalem I was talking about!"

"Jerusalem is here, Pam," Yeshua said.

Several of the company looked around, then peered OUTSIDE. Intuitively, Pam looked down at herself.

"You mean—us?" she said.

"I mean exactly that. You are that new and holy city, you and all those who have come back to me," Yeshua said.

Pam beamed. Finally, she had gotten something right. Little goose bumps prickled her arms and back.

"Pretty smart, Mom," Piper smiled.

"So all these gems and precious minerals—they'll just leap out at us?" Block laughed. "Impossible!"

"Something is impossible?" Yeshua asked with a glint in his eye. "Clayton, you're a scientist. Tell me, what's the atomic weight of, say, iridium?"

"Don't know its weight. Its number would be . . ." One eye squinted.

"Seventy-seven," Bridget helped him.

"Yes. What's next in line?" Yeshua asked the group.

"Not sure," Block said.

"Platinum," Herald said.

"You *have* been studying after all," Yeshua joked. "What's its number?"

"Seventy-eight," Mai Ker answered.

It felt like a pop quiz.

"Its weight?" Yeshua prodded her.

She thought. "I did know all these, once. I think, maybe, it is one hundred ninety-five point-oh-eight. Yes?"

"It is. Your memory is improving. What comes next?" Yeshua asked the others.

"That's easy. Gold," Block said.

"Atomic weight, one hundred ninety-six point-nine-seven," Bridget laughed. "That's one even I memorized!"

Yeshua smiled as if in triumph. His look said he expected them to have gotten some grand point. No one had.

"So?" Mai Ker said.

"I assumed you would see," Yeshua said. "Well, a small matter."

"We're missing something, aren't we?" Jimmy asked.

"Ask him to show you," Eira whispered to Bridget.

Bridget hushed her.

"Ask him!" Eira prodded a bit louder.

Bridget's eyes asked him.

"A small change, that's all that's needed," Yeshua responded, "a few bits of matter, a proton, a neutron, an electron, massaged here or there. And instead of iridium, there is platinum. Instead of platinum, there is gold."

He saw their doubtful expressions.

"Show them!" Eira said loudly with great enthusiasm.

"A demonstration, yes. Follow me."

He walked to where the children had built their forts over the open graves. The others followed.

"Come on," Adrian whispered to Garan, "I'm not about to miss this!"

"Braden, son, could you hand me your shovel there?" Yeshua asked.

"Not really mine," Braden said uncertainly, grabbing the shovel he had used in building his fort.

"Honesty is growing, too," Yeshua smiled. He took the shovel and stepped into the sandy soil between Willy and Sarajane's empty coffins. Ignoring the coffins, he shoveled deeper alongside Willy's. Earth kept sifting back into the hole. He set the shovel aside and dug deeper with his hand until he brought out a shiny little object clasped between his fingers.

"What's that?" Thomas asked.

"As I remember it," Yeshua said to Clayton, "when you buried Will, you put a ring back on his finger."

Block was astounded that Yeshua could know this detail, but he recalled it perfectly.

"An old wedding ring. A gold one."

"You put that old thing back on me?" Willy asked, chagrined.

"Well, you're the one who kept it!" Block said only half apologetically.

"Let's not fight, children," Bridget teased.

Yeshua held the object up. It was a man's ring.

"Wow," Block said, truly beyond himself. "That's the same gold ring!"

"Not gold," Yeshua said.

"What?" Atchison and Block asked in unison.

"Platinum."

"Why, that beggar jewelry store guy—he told me it was gold," Willy said.

"Looks gold to me," Block said.

"You're not a woman, Clayton," Mai Ker said.

"Not gold," Yeshua said, "but close. An easy mistake, Will. So, what happens if we change it just a little?"

He pressed the ring into his palm and closed his hand around it, squeezing it gently. He placed his other hand over the first for a moment. He opened his hands.

There was no longer a ring, but a nugget.

"Gold?" Block asked stupidly.

"This time, yes," Yeshua smiled.

"Can I do that?" Willy asked enthusiastically.

"No, Will. Not until you're ready."

"When's that?"

Yeshua gave Atchison a brotherly smile.

"Could be a while, William."

"Wait a minute," Bridget said, something dawning on her. "How come Will's ring wasn't in the—box?"

"That's more difficult to explain." Yeshua looked around at them. "Do you really want to hear?"

Remembering last night, Bridget shook her head and the others joined her.

Yeshua stepped back down and dug his hand deeper into the soil. He pulled up a blob of soft mud.

"What that?" Garan asked.

"Mud, dumbbell," Adrian said.

"But not ordinary mud," Yeshua said. "This used to be a bit of Clayton Block."

Block felt a wave of queasiness trench through his stomach.

Bridget laughed loudly, then stared at Yeshua.

"You're—" Bridget stopped. "Wait. You're serious?"

"I would not joke about this. Dust you were, Clayton, and to dust you did return."

"Never looked better, old buddy," Atchison said, only half stifling a spasmodic guffaw.

"And we don't want to know why *that* was not in the coffin, do we?" Block asked those around him. "Didn't think so."

They didn't notice that Yeshua had pressed the mud in his hand into a tighter lump. He closed both hands over it, holding them shut longer this time. Then he opened his hands.

"Un-be-lieve-able . . ." Willy mumbled with a radically altered mood.

"Awesome!" Braden chimed in over him.

"May I?" Mai Ker asked.

"Certainly," Yeshua said, offering it to her.

She took the large, hard nugget in her hand, which dropped an inch.

"I think it is gold."

"Pam wants streets paved with gold? A symbol, yes. But why not?" Yeshua said.

"How did you do that?" Nathaniel asked, dazzled.

"I'll teach you."

Block was laughing at himself, feeling more foolish than he had since he had been raised from death. "Turned me into gold, huh?"

"Nothing wasted, Clayton. Nothing left behind," Yeshua said.

23

Saturday Morning

The rain started overnight. It poured heavily during the early hours of the morning, washing the land around the Solarium with freshness. As before, the delightful smell of the rain filtered in through the open doors of Pod 1 and refreshed the air throughout the complex.

Piper was the first awake this morning. As her eyes listlessly opened, she smelled the newly alive scent of the rain. The rain could not be heard INSIDE, even though it continued to pour OUTSIDE. But there was no mistaking that smell, even for a child who had only smelled it a few times since the permanent opening up of the Solarium.

She jumped from her bed and ran barefoot through the pods, galloping through Pod 6, where Caroline and her brother and several other cheerful, early risers greeted her with chirps and questions about why there was no fresh seed in the aviary feeders.

Piper barreled through the next podwalk into #4 and around the west side of the old Victorian. She hurried to the pod wall, pressing her hands against the Stellar plastic, looking west. The huge basin that had opened yesterday was filling. It had a long way to go but she was thrilled. A few more rainstorms like this and she would have her lake.

She danced a little backward, playful circle, her heart beating in step, then looked out again. She wanted to run out to the lake but figured she would get yelled at if she went dashing out in this downpour in her nightclothes.

She ran back to the tents and found her mother still deep in sleep. Piper knelt by her bed, breathing as blissfully as Pam, and started gently nudging her mom's arm.

"Mom, it's working! We're going to have a lake. A mountain lake!" she said, her voice got progressively louder, skipping up a pitch.

Pam, unsure if she was dreaming, smiled at the melodic draw of her daughter's voice. This was the child who was never to be, who had become such a blessing to everyone in the Solarium. Pam opened her eyes and focused on Piper's sunny, beaming face. It had even more of a glow this morning.

"What, honey?" Pam asked from the land of incoherence.

"The lake Yeshua made. It's filling up!"

"It rained?"

"Still raining, Mom, can't you smell it?"

"I guess I can," she said lazily. "Sorry, sweetie, in this new body I sleep more soundly than ever." She saw that Piper could not contain her excitement much longer. "You want to show me, don't you?"

"Yes! Please! Come on."

Pam pulled on her housecoat and tried to keep up with Piper, which, remarkably, she was able to do. She looked up to see sheets of rain bathing the Solarium. They reached the westernmost edge of #4 and looked out.

"It will be very pretty, sweetheart," Pam said. "I always thought I'd like to retire in the mountains, and here we are on one. Now a lake, too! I'm glad you asked him."

"Can we go out?"

"It's pouring, honey. Let's wait until it lets up. Probably shouldn't get too close to the edge right now," she said. "Looks like some of the bank is washing away into the lake."

"It will be perfect," Piper chimed.

"Yes, I bet it will," Pam said, hugging Piper and kissing the top of her head, which, because of a growth spurt since Monday, she now could barely reach.

THE WORLD around them continued to change, heal and grow. The Earth itself had begun to grow, slightly but steadily, like a chubby baby that was finally starting to take on its true shape.

Mimicking the lump in Yeshua's hand yesterday, everything around them was becoming more solid, more real, both INSIDE and OUT. New trees were growing across the formerly barren high plains, some as thick forests, some spread around and ordered neatly as if planned out in a park. What had been unique about a few species of the old world, the great redwoods and other giants, would now be true of most. Had Yeshua not ensured open, grassy areas among the trees, the sky would have completely disappeared from view in many regions because of the great height of the new trees.

For Jimmy, that would have been a great loss. As he had noticed, the air was now a light, rich turquoise color, which made for spectacular sunrises and sunsets more beautiful than even the greatest artists ever imagined. When the sun rose on a clear morning, it looked like the eastern horizon had been set ablaze by exploding tubes of yellowish-green and golden-blue oil colors, splattering the brightening sky.

Strangely—or perhaps not—the trees in the complex seemed content to grow 8 to 10 feet and stop. Here Yeshua had exercised restraint. In the interest of preserving the Solarium as a testament to the past world, the trees would stop growing before they began to force themselves against the Stellar pod roofs.

These new sights and realities were all the more enjoyable to the reborn humans because, as they discovered over a period of days, their resurrection bodies possessed much sharper, clearer eyesight. They could see clearly to great distances in a way that was like looking at the landscape through a powerful telescope. Such ability was disconcerting at first, especially for Herald who had never known how poor his eyesight had been before.

It was not only physical objects that were becoming more visible. With some amount of chagrin, the Solarians and their friends began to notice that they could see the spiritual, inward nature of each other that had been completely invisible before. It was as though their regenerated spirits were exposed through the tissue of their reborn flesh so that they were never sure, at any moment, whether they were looking at the outer person or the inner. But oddly, when they looked in a mirror, they could not see their own inner spirit.

Last evening as several of them sat reading, Yeshua was watching Bridget and Clayton leaning together in a corner, deep in private conversation.

"Your soul is showing," Yeshua commented to Bridget.

"Is that what it is?" she asked.

"What was always visible to me, now you can see, too."

"A gift that could be a curse," Block said.

"There is no more curse, Clayton. It will be a blessing, always."

Clayton looked at Bridget with a deeper love that he had ever known and realized Yeshua was right. Their love was growing beyond the fleeting affections they had felt in the old world.

"Why can't I see my own self, when I look in the mirror?" Mai Ker asked, looking up from an old hardbound novel.

"You'd be self-conscious. And you're growing beyond that," Yeshua said.

"This new world sure is pretty," Will Atchison said, gazing at Pam. "What gets me is being able to actually see the air. And, I have to tell you, that was a little upsetting at first."

"Yeah," Block agreed, "it's like I used to feel scuba diving."

The others knew precisely what he meant. The density of the air against their flesh was like a bath, with even the slightest movement. To breathe was to eat, to wave an arm was to stir the ocean.

JUST BEFORE midday, Yeshua unexpectedly called the Solarians and their children apart from the visitors and gathered them again around the porch of the old Victorian in Pod 4.

"We must finish what we began Thursday night," he said as they all settled into chairs or onto the grass.

"Haven't we talked enough?" Pam asked, worried they were about to run another mental marathon.

"There are some questions lingering. I want all of you to feel resolved about what happened—after you came here."

"But the children—" Bridget started to say.

"No, I want them to hear. They should learn why their lives began as they did. In here, in such a strange time."

Bridget still looked hesitant. Herald and Sing, she wasn't worried about. Braden, Nathaniel, even Piper, she wasn't sure of. Kai, snuggled beside Sing in a cotton blanket, looked happy in any case, grinning uncontrollably as babies do.

"You're sure?" Bridget asked.

"These questions are weltering deep inside you, Bridget. Perhaps so deep you don't know. But they are deeper yet in the children, nearly in their blood. I want them to know that this strange world they were born into—it was my doing, not yours."

Bridget's mind eased slightly, though she still wasn't sure this was a good idea.

"What were we talking about?" Sing asked. "We've talked about so much the last few days."

"About what happened, before you were born, honey," her mom said. "When Earth ran into that—whatever-it-was in space." Mai Ker turned to Yeshua, waiting.

"Why don't you explain it?" Yeshua said to Mai Ker.

"Me?" she asked, flustered.

He nodded.

"Well, the universe had been damaged—near the very beginning. Is that right?" She looked at Yeshua for approval and got a nod to continue. "Just before we came to the Solarium. And Earth collided with this—void, this vacancy. And that damaged the atmosphere. That is why everyone died."

"Nearly everyone," Yeshua reminded them.

Nathaniel was watching the grownups, curiosity stuck in his face.

"You mean, if you guys hadn't been in *here*," his quickly maturing mind realized, "with different air, then, we wouldn't be here. Any of us, I mean," he said, gesturing at the second-generation Solarians.

"Yes," Mai Ker said.

"Whoah. That's kind of scary," Braden said.

"We get all that, Mai Ker," Herald said. "I want to know why."

Out of the corner of his eye, Block saw Caroline fly into the pod. From old habit, she flew to the upper bedroom window that he had always left cracked open for her. It was shut. He made a *kitch-kitch* sound with his teeth and she flew to him, perching on the arm of the wooden chair next to his wrist. In half-a-second, she hopped on for a ride. Block moved his arm like a swaying tree branch.

"That is so neat," Piper grinned. "How did you train her?"

"Seed," Block laughed. "She wasn't too picky," he smiled. "It's so great to have you back, little lady," he told Caroline, stroking her feathers gently.

Nervous about all the new, littler people around the porch, Caroline took flight, circled the roof of the house once, then disappeared through the podwalk into #10. Surely there would be some food there somewhere.

Will Atchison ventured onto thin ice.

"I think we left off the other night somewhere around, why didn't you stop it all? The air crashing, I mean."

"Because it was the time determined by the Father. The time of the end, of judgment," Yeshua answered. "Sin had to be expunged. Death had to take its final toll."

"Yes, but we had to watch it all," Bridget reminded him. "I spent a lot of nights angry with you because of that," she confessed.

"I know, Bridget. And I've forgiven you. I know the horrors you witnessed. I had to watch, too, remember."

"It must have been so terrible," Sing said.

"For some, yes," Yeshua admitted. "For those who rejected me, death was a terror indeed, a monster waiting to consume them, the irresistible, final reality. But for those who had tasted my kindness, the cup of my salvation, death was no terror and no mystery. It was a welcome release from a dying world, a passageway leading to me, and now—as you see—to new life."

"The Father must have been pretty angry with us humans," Atchison said, controlling the drawl in his voice so as not to sound sarcastic.

"The Father's wrath is not anger as you mean it, Will. It is righteousness but without passion. Justice without craving. It flows from his holiness, the demand that the consequence of every act of sin and hatred must be borne, and its full penalty paid."

"But you did that, I thought," said Pam, frowning slightly. "You died in our place."

"Yes, but you still suffered the earthly consequences of your sins. For most, that included the pain of physical death. What I paid rescued you from spiritual death, the death that lives forever, permanent separation from the Father's love. That debt I paid. It was from that unrelenting death that I saved you."

Pam was deep in thought. She raised her head, a question rolling around in it like a disobedient pinball. She looked at Yeshua, wondering if he were a lion who might bite her head off at what, after all his assurances, she was about to say.

"It still bothers me."

To her relief, he didn't pounce. He said calmly, "Does it?"

"For everyone to be taken like that," she said too loudly. "And all the needless suffering at the end!" she cried, suddenly caught again in the terrible emotions of those days.

Yeshua didn't answer immediately. He let the flames in her subside.

"The pains of sin were deep, Pam. Its consequences were brutal. But physical death was not the worst thing that could happen to someone." He managed to give her a smile. "I am a testament to that, am I not? And your other friends?" he asked, gesturing to Will, Clayton and Jimmy.

Pam nodded. Her mind, limited by the bounds of her own mental horizon and unable to see the sweep of history through divine eyes, still wanted a different answer.

"There must have been a better way," she insisted passionately.

"Better? That's an interesting concept. A 'better' way to die? Let's see, maybe water again. But then drowning is just suffocating under water, isn't it? And I did promise I wouldn't flood the world again."

Pam looked into his eyes. She could see, too late, where this was going.

"I could have stopped restraining the insanity and let more of those devastating missiles be fired off. Millions more would have died slowly over days and weeks in excruciating pain from radiation poisoning— like those refugees who came to the Solarium that day," he said, touching a raw point. "I could have struck everyone on Earth with their own personal lightning bolt! Quicker. Unless it didn't actually kill them. And far from painless." He paused, a deadly serious expression on his face. "Tell me, Pam. How would you have done it?"

If a pin had dropped ten miles away, everyone would have heard it.

The question doused what little fire was left in Pam's heart. Suddenly, in stark contrast to the tugs of her emotions, she saw the truth. Worldwide death was worldwide death. The means, in the end, were incidental. And now, sitting by her risen friends, she knew death had been defeated.

Yeshua did not interrupt her thoughts. After a time, he spoke quietly.

"Every death was ugly. Do not think I don't know."

The nearly silent intensity of these words caught everyone up short.

Pam swallowed a gulp of saliva that had pooled behind her lips as she ground her teeth. Hesitantly, she looked up. There was no fearsome, raging lion, here. She saw the pain in his eyes. She had seen it before, in the eyes of those refugees, staring in at them through the pod walls, begging for shelter. That little boy, with his pencil and notebook, trying to make sense of what was incomprehensible, while the Solarians stood there, safe, refusing to help them. Dying men and women and children, denied their last chance. The truth burned Pam like electrocution. It was not a question of what she or the others *might* have done. It was what they *had* done. They had condemned others, to save themselves.

The realization nearly crushed her. She would have counted it joy if the great pod overhead had collapsed in on her in that second.

Jimmy had kept silent, but in Pam's face, he recognized what she was thinking. The others did, too.

Jimmy turned toward Yeshua, hardly able to speak. His words crept from a powder-dry mouth.

"Maybe you just should have stopped it all—at the very beginning."

"With Adam, you mean? Or Cain? When?"

"I don't know," Jimmy said like a sulking child.

"No!" The word fell like a hammer. "Once the rebellion began, we had to let it play out. To do otherwise would have violated the very wills the Father had created—and overthrown the entire fabric of the created order!"

They were sure the voice they now heard was the Father's voice. Yeshua looked from person to person.

"Pam—all of you—do you not see that human freedom is sacred? To overrule it would be the unmaking of creation. The gift of will—of choosing—it was the golden thread that bound everything else together. And still does."

Pam nodded, in unison with Piper, Nathaniel and Braden.

"To angels, yes, to humans, I gave a share in my sovereignty. You were, and are, to rule alongside me. Listen to me!" He made sure he had every eye, especially the youngsters. "The rebellion—as you realize after seeing Lucifer Thursday night—did not begin with Adam. The brightest and best of my angels turned on me. It was he who tempted humankind from the beginning, to lead them, too, into rebellion. You all fell so easily. Everyone. I alone withstood him."

"Then why did you ever make him?" Nathaniel genuinely wanted to know.

"For the same reason I made you, my child. To have life, to experience my love. But to create one who can love is to create one who can hate."

Atchison regretted that he had ever brought the whole thing up Thursday night. He squirmed on his lawn chair, trying to bite his tongue, but his curiosity again overran his common sense.

"So, you *chose* to let all those people die," he said, rubbing a non-existent pain in his neck. "Millions."

"Billions." Yeshua said bluntly, with hard, set eyes. "Tell me, Will, which of them would not have died, in time?"

Atchison felt as stupid as he had in his drunken days.

"Point taken."

"No, it was not easy. It was not pleasant." Yeshua's voice held the controlled hurt of a father whose beloved child had run away. "The atmosphere was dying, the ancient chaos flooding backward into creation. It was the Father's choice to let that age of corruption die with the poisoned air." Several quiet moments ticked by. "In the beginning, the Father gave breath. Now, breath was taken away. No more painful than many kinds of death. Much less than some."

"A kind of a poetic ending," Bridget said in a hushed voice, though she was far from understanding the full implication of what she had just said.

It was obvious there was nothing else that could be said. Everyone sat quietly, the new spiritual glow that attended each of them shimmering brightly, the new light inside them seeping out.

Braden, now several inches taller than he was just days ago but still young in heart, had a deeply perplexed look frozen on his bright features. He got up and came over to Yeshua.

"Did I die?" he asked, actually unsure.

Finally, Yeshua laughed again.

"In a different fashion, yes," Yeshua smiled. "When the cosmos was changed, the old into the new." Yeshua gave him a gentle hug. "You slept through it."

Sing laughed, "We all did."

"Much less disrupting to do it while you slept," Yeshua said.

"Beginning to think I slept through my whole entire life," Will Atchison said.

Yeshua nodded.

"You had a lot of company, Will."

24

Saturday Afternoon

"Anyone hungry?" Anastazja called loudly from Pod 10. She was clanging a large soup pan with a metal spoon as a dinner bell.

She had seen the Solarians follow Yeshua into Pod 4 and decided to take charge of lunch. They had been gone so long she was afraid everyone else would be starving before the natives showed up.

"No meat today?" Will Atchison asked when he arrived a few minutes later, first in line at the door of the kitchen tent. The familiar smell of hot lunches was missing.

"I thought about frying some steaks for lunch, but you're getting a bit low," Anastazja said. "I thought you would want to conserve it."

"No need for that," Yeshua said as he came in and went to the counter for a glass of water.

"Not many animals left," Willy said, "to butcher."

"No need for that, either," Yeshua said. "Just as you are now alive, the animals will live, too. They'll repopulate for a while, but we won't need to sacrifice them anymore."

The word "sacrifice" caught Willy off-guard.

"Never thought of butchering as religious," Willy said.

"You didn't live in that time. The killing of any animal was a sacrifice, an offering from the creation. The Father commanded it so that men might discover the sanctity of all life, the sacredness of the blood you share with other creatures." He drank down half-a-glass of delicious water.

"Huh?" Willy said, thinking. "You know, maybe so," he said, snatching a dry cookie from a plate near the stove. "Every time I went hunting, every deer I took—I kinda felt that, kind of a loss. Yeah, a sacrifice. The world giving something up, for me."

"What's on?" Pam asked as she, too, came into the tent. "No meat today?"

"Gonna have to restart this conversation, Lord," Willy chuckled.

Anastazja had laid out a lunch of cold sandwiches and cut-up fruit. Plates and cups in hand, they migrated to the dining tent. The long table filled quickly, along with the second, temporary one they had set up. Their stomachs could tell it was well past lunch hour.

"So, you were saying?" Atchison asked Yeshua with raised eyebrows.

"I was telling Will, meals will be a little different now."

Several of the Solarians looked at their sandwiches, which looked completely familiar.

"Different?" Sing asked.

"Yes. We will have some new foods."

Several half-sandwiches, apple slices, and cups hung in mid-air and it got quiet.

Anxiety rose in Jacob's face. "Lord, you're not going to take away my favorite foods?" he asked with apprehension.

"No. Not in the least. But we will eat anew."

Perplexed expressions appeared around the tables. Food was so basic to life. A wave of nervousness swept through everyone except Yeshua. Bravely, Adrian spoke up for the others.

"You promised a great banquet in your kingdom, did you not, Sir? I suppose," he looked down at his partially emptied plate, "well, maybe that was just symbolic?" His tone and question were both tentative.

"Man, I hope not," Block said, taking a quick, large bite of ham sandwich just in case.

"Let him talk," Jimmy urged the others.

"In the regeneration, life is preserved," Yeshua told them. "The animals as well. You will still take produce from them, eggs, milk, the gifts they provide you. But, they cannot die any more than you can."

Up to this moment, it had not occurred to anyone that death had been conquered for any creatures except themselves.

"Now that's a fine how-do-you-do," Atchison bantered in his best Oliver Hardy fashion.

"Wait, but plants die naturally," Bridget said.

"No," Yeshua corrected her, "plants die unnaturally. All life was created to live. Even plant life will not die. All flora will continue to grow and regenerate itself, and produce fruit and seed, to fill the Earth again." Yeshua spoke, his mouth half full, clearly enjoying the fact that he had more good news to impart.

"But, that cannot be," Mai Ker said with a confused look. "The plants—well, they would eventually take over the Earth!"

"Except, what you have yet to realize," Yeshua said patiently, "is that they will only produce sufficient seed to fill what is not yet filled. They have their own rules."

Mai Ker thought a moment. "Of course. I am so stupid. Even in the old world, plants would not overrun themselves and choke themselves out of existence. Overfill an area, I mean, with their own kind."

"No, they wouldn't," Yeshua said with a knowing look. "They, unlike humans, have always known their limits."

"Well, there aren't many animals left anyway," Pam commented, knowing the exact, edible animal population of the Solarium.

She had not taken into account the fact that birds

had begun to return, Caroline, her brother, and several other species. Nor had it dawned on her, or anyone one else, that Yeshua could just as easily bring back any other creatures he chose.

"Some species will repopulate," Yeshua said, "others will simply return."

Pam's mind went to a favorite pet dog her family had when she was a girl. Yeshua smiled before she spoke, knowing what she was seeing.

"Yes, and some creatures who were pets, who bonded with humans, you will enjoy again."

"Caroline," Block smiled, wondering where she was at this moment.

"Barkie?" Pam asked excitedly.

Herald look at the unexpected grin on Auntie Pam's face.

"Barkie?" Herald said as if in pain.

Pam looked embarrassed. "My puppy, Well, I was very young."

Mai Ker, her training in biology surfacing, smiled as she spoke.

"Of course, how obvious this is. It would not be right if we should live but they should continue to die."

"No," Yeshua smiled. "On the other hand," he said, shaking his head meaningfully, "I—like all of you— love the taste of grilled fish and roast meat."

Lunch had ground to a complete stop. All this talk of animals and food had, ironically, dampened appetites. Everyone waited, assuming Yeshua would explain. He didn't. He dug back into his own sandwich and grabbed up a large slice of apple.

"Holy cow," Willy hooted, breaking the tension.

"Very funny, Will," Yeshua said, cracking half-a-smile, apple bits glistening between his teeth.

"Only William the 2nd would even *dare* think of a crack like that," Block cackled.

"No more hamburgers?" Nathaniel whined.

"Something better," Yeshua said, setting down what little was left of his sandwich. "You'll just have to wait to taste it."

This was like lighting a fire in a box of tinder.

"Lord, don't leave us hanging like that!" Katherine pleaded.

"I said, wait to taste it. I didn't say you'd have to wait to know. Clayton, over in crop plots four-seventy-one to four-eighty-eight, you'll find some new plants. I set them in overnight. It'll take them a day or two to mature."

"And these are . . . ? Block asked.

"Something you've never seen before."

"This should be good," Jimmy said, about to get up.

Mai Ker grabbed his arm and yanked him back onto the bench.

"Better than good," Yeshua promised. "The fruit of these plants will be our meats. These are more alive than what you knew before as plant life, but not quite animal. You'll see the difference. You just won't taste any difference."

"I'll know," Block said. "I'm an incorrigible carnivore."

"Trust me, Clayton, you won't be able to tell any difference. These plants will be melon-like, pumpkin-like, many varieties, but each tastes like a meat we loved."

"How awesome is that!" Herald said.

"Thank you, Herald. And it's not just the taste. The texture, the smell, the feel, everything, you'll believe you're eating animal flesh."

"You can do that?" Eira asked from her seat by Bridget, her eyes lighting up.

"I can."

"Wait, so, steaks and ribs with no slaughtering?" Bridget considered. "No hours of cleaning animal guts, butchering, wrapping?"

"Steaks. No ribs."

"I'm in," Bridget grinned.

AFTER LUNCH, Mai Ker noticed Pam had disappeared. She looked around the pods and found Pam cleaning the living room in the old house.

"Hey, Pam. You OK?"

"Sure."

"I thought the conversation at lunch might have put you off."

"No, not really. I'll cook whatever the Lord gives us to eat."

"So, why the sudden cleaning binge? I mean, here?" Mai Ker asked.

Pam gave her a distracted, unintelligible mumble.

"It was the discussion before lunch, wasn't it?"

This time Pam didn't even mumble, but she nodded.

"Why is this so difficult for you, Pam?"

"I don't know. I guess I still question what he did. Or how he did it. At the end."

"Pam, he is God. We must let him be God."

"Yes, there's my problem." Pam let the well-used dust cloth in her hand hang limply. She plopped down on the arm of the sofa. "I guess I still want the world to run the way I think it should." She frowned, but then smiled. "Thanks, Mai. You have been such a Godsend, such a dear friend. I could *not* have gotten through these last months without you, and Bridget. I'm such a weakling sometimes."

"We are all weak sometimes. At least you're honest. I think you have had trouble asking for help, though, when you needed to."

"Yes, I was never very good at that," Pam grimaced. "I was always the one in my family who tried to hold everything together, you know? Make everybody happy. Kind of be the peacekeeper when the family wars broke out." She sniffed. "I mean, even here. What was my one job? Relationship Maintenance Coordinator? What a laugh!"

She did. Mai Ker joined her.

"Yes, I can see you, solving everybody else's problems. And ignoring your own." Mai Ker gave her a gentle hug. "Some wars were not worth fighting, Pam. Sometimes you just have to let your feelings bleed a little, get the poison out of your system."

"You'd think, as a nurse, I'd have known that," Pam smiled with a sigh.

"A difference in knowing, and doing," Mai Ker said wisely.

Pam nodded.

"Can I help you?"

"Clean? Sure, thanks." Pam looked around at her progress so far. "It needs a little pick-me-up, don't you think? And I've been thinking. I want to talk to him, see if he might let me stay."

"Stay? Here?" Mai Ker asked, completely surprised.

"Yes. In some way, I feel I belong here. I've kind of grown to be part of this whole place. Or it's part of me. I'd like to stick around for a while, if he'll let me."

"There is one way to know," Mai Ker said. "Be bold. Ask him."

Pam nodded again. "Yes. I think I will."

THE REGENERATED sun bore down through the Solarium onto the roof of the shop building in Pod 8, warming the shop more than usual. The morning clouds had broken by early afternoon, said goodbye to one another, and cleared away. The giant air-conditioning units had kicked on, circulating cooled air throughout the complex. The unused pods had finally been reopened, each having received a thorough cleaning with the help of their visitors.

Inside the shop, Yeshua was helping Block, Jimmy and Bridget build new chairs. With the extra company, there were not enough chairs in the dining tent and meeting tent, and they were getting tired of shuffling them around. Yeshua had sketched out a new chair design that, at least on paper, appeared nearly indestructible.

Piper was hanging around the shop watching, but doing nothing useful.

"So, I'm curious," Jimmy was saying, "when I checked the main bank of storage batteries this morning over in number thirteen, even with all the equipment in the complex running, the batteries showed next to nothing in electrical drain." He looked at Yeshua, who made an evasive nod. "The solar panels and generators are feeding them the same current, and we've got more stuff running again, but the batteries don't seem to notice." Jimmy wondered if the batteries had been re-created along with everything else.

Yeshua shrugged.

"If you were to disassemble one of those batteries—which I would not recommend—you'd find new metals in their guts," Yeshua said. "A newer technology. You'll figure it out, in time."

Jimmy watched with fascination every move Yeshua made. This man, the perfect man, if such were the right term, moved as if he was slightly disconnected from his surroundings. But to watch him handle the lathe was like watching twenty faux-mermaids do an intricate water ballet, in midair. Material moved in his hands with a grace that made it appear nearly alive and responding to his touch.

Jimmy felt clumsy by comparison. He felt this more than ever as he bumped two furniture screws onto the floor.

". . . and you'll understand more as years pass," Yeshua was saying. "As your spirit develops, you'll understand the physical world better, how the spiritual realm controls and animates the material form of things. Your first parents were able to see that. Until they fell away."

Piper, also studying his movements, felt inspired to help.

"All I care is that I can see *you*," she said, taking a piece of sandpaper in hand and going to work on a newly fashioned chair seat.

"The essence of things was never visible to merely physical eyes," Yeshua said, turning a wheel of the lathe methodically. "Back then, your spirits were darkened, so the world seemed dark."

"It sure did," Block said as he drilled the leg of a new chair to accept a cross-spindle. "Guess I didn't have very spiritual eyes," he admitted.

"No, you didn't, Clayton," Yeshua said. "The cause of so much grief for you."

Yeshua and Block had discussed this before, at great length, just after Clayton died. Block hoped they would not revisit it now. He let the electric drill wind to a stop, waiting. Yeshua said no more about it.

"Even before," Piper said, "there were signs, though."

"Signs?" Yeshua asked, as if he had no idea what she meant.

Piper's imaginative mind was painting out a picture of the world as it used to be.

"Things coming back to life each spring," she smiled. "All that had ended before I was born, but I remember listening to the grownups talk about how it used to be. Plants would seem dead in the soil all winter, then pop back to life."

"Yes, rebirth," Yeshua nodded.

"Like a hidden message," Piper asked.

Yeshua nodded again. "Wise beyond your years, Piper."

"A message?" Jimmy asked.

"The seasons gave hints, so that the light of hope

was never fully put out," Yeshua said. "Eternity was always on display."

Piper worked her sandpaper across the chair seat, watching with a keen eye as the wood grain seemed to blend into a silken-like finish. Her mind was still working, too.

"Will I be stuck like this, now?" she asked, indicating her small frame, although it was not as small as it was a week ago.

"No, dear," Yeshua smiled, "you'll grow, to your perfection. You will be a lovely woman."

"So the children *will* grow up?" Bridget asked.

"Not just the children. All of you."

"Hadn't considered that," Bridget said, pondering how she might look in several thousand years.

Yeshua knew her thoughts. "You must each reach perfection. You'll grow, you just won't grow old."

"Would you please tell Sing?" Jimmy asked. "I think she's worried she'll be changing diapers forever."

Yeshua laughed loudly.

"Kai won't be left out. I know exactly the woman she will become."

"I used to think the world was so strange," Piper said, almost to herself. "And all along, it was even stranger than I thought."

WITH SIX new chairs sanded, Piper strolled back to Pod 4 to check the progress of her lake. Runoff from the recent rain had brought the lake to nearly a quarter full.

As she came back around the house, she stopped. A flicker of light high up caught her eye. One of the angels, seemingly alone, drifted near the roof of the house. This time she saw the creature more clearly. She remembered what Yeshua had said about having spiritual eyes.

"I can see you better," she told the shimmering

creature.

"As well as I see you," the angel said.

"I'm Piper. What are you called?"

"I am called the Least One."

"You don't have a name?"

"That is my name."

Piper looked intently.

"I don't understand. Are you small?"

"You could not measure me with every length and span you possess in the Earth."

"Do you . . . live here, now?" Piper asked.

"We cross your time and space often, but pass beyond it, too. I, my kind, we exist in the heavenly realms."

"The sky, you mean?"

"Far behind the skies, Piper, in the realms of the One."

Piper watched the subtle movement of the lustrous, indescribable light with fascination.

"Well, by that, I guess you do look small."

"Not small. Just the least."

A gentle, fragrant breeze from out of nowhere brushed Piper's long, dark hair back from her face. She calmed her hair along her shoulders with one hand.

"I think I see." She asked the obvious. "Why are you here?"

"We watch. This is our work. Your race is reborn and I am here to watch you.

"Us Solarians? Or our friends, too?"

"No. Over you, Piper."

The light drew swiftly down toward Piper and a little to one side. It seemed to turn, or bend, but Piper couldn't tell.

"Just me?"

"Just you," the Least One said as if Piper were the most important thing in the universe.

Piper felt on fire. A hot shiver leapt up her spine but

was painless.

"You are—" she stuttered. "You're *my* angel?"

"Yours."

The glittering light drew even closer.

"Are you afraid?" it asked.

"A little," Piper said. "But I kind of feel good, too."

"Part of my work," the Least One said. "To be his light around you, and protect."

"Are there more?"

"More?"

"I mean, for Mommy, Daddy, everyone? Do they have someone, too?"

"Yes, for a long while, now."

"Since Yeshua returned?"

"Years before that."

Piper reacted with an astonished expression. Even though she was in tune with spiritual realities around her, she had missed the angels until that recent night by the ocean.

"They never said anything about you," she said, speaking of her family.

"They didn't see us."

"No," Piper said. "Me either. We weren't looking."

"No," the Least One said. The subtle light solidified into almost tangible form, like an invisible hand being offered to Piper. "It was I who spoke to you by the ocean that night."

Piper was startled again, but then clarity came.

"Of course. I know your voice." Then she wondered. It sounded like a feminine voice. "Are you a girl or a boy?"

"Neither. To you, I would sound like your mother, to others, something else."

"Yes." Piper wondered. "Can you can hear my thoughts?"

"Only if you allow me."

The light moved back slowly, as if not to impede

Piper.

"So you came here that night, over the ocean?"

"Far before that. I arrived when you were conceived."

It took several moments for this to sink in. Piper reached a hand toward the light but felt nothing.

"And the others?" Piper asked.

"When your parents and the others first came here, some of my kind were sent to watch over them."

Piper felt overwhelmed.

"From the beginning? Oh my. And they never saw."

"They saw, but did not recognize us."

"Well," Piper admitted, "even I had trouble that first time."

"Yes, but the Father's Spirit has always been strong in your heart. You could see me that night because you were skilled in faith."

"Seeing is believing, you mean?"

"Believing is seeing," the Least One replied. "The Lord Yeshua's Spirit gave you gifts. Faith was one."

"I don't mean to be rude," Piper said, "but this is going to kind of creep me out."

"Creep?"

"Oh, it's just a saying. Bother me. If I know you're always—hovering?"

"I will only let you see me when you want to see me."

"Really?"

"Yes."

To prove it, the light was gone.

Piper ran to tell her mother, wondering, even now, if she would be believed.

25

Sunday Morning

Despite the fact that new "meats" were growing in their fields, last evening Yeshua had said they were welcome to finish eating whatever was still in the freezers. "Nothing should be wasted," he reminded them.

The problem, he warned, would be that once they tasted the new meats, they would have no interest in the old ones. "You have never tasted a steak, or fish, or broiled chicken like what you will taste now."

They had already discovered this was true. Just after sunrise, Jimmy harvested the not-quite-mature fruit of two of the plants Yeshua had shown him that would replace pork. Katherine ground the fruit up like sausage and cooked it up for breakfast, along with several very large omelets.

Will Atchison nearly drooled, sniffing the aroma that clung in his mustache as he finished the sausage.

"Now that is *real* good," Willy drawled, slowly leaning his head from side to side as if to make the flavor hang on his tongue longer. "Even in old Kansas City, meat-capital of the Midwest where I was born, they *never* put out anything like this!"

"Meat capital," Block said, chewing his slab of omelet. "Well, *that* would explain it."

"It?" Atchison asked his good friend.

"Your brain cells."

Laughter careened around the breakfast tables.

"Everything of the old Earth was corrupted, even the flavor of foods," Yeshua said. "Except the lamb, that night, my last Passover."

"You like lamb?" Sing asked, wondering how anyone could.

"Oh, I like it especially," Yeshua said with a knowing look. Only Piper, Pam and Jimmy got the hint. "A foretaste, friends, of my great banquet to come."

"When's that?" Nathaniel asked, anxious to sign up for any banquet Yeshua had in mind.

"When all is ready," Yeshua said, leaving everyone dangling, an all-too-common occurrence in these days.

AS THE regeneration of the Earth continued and it once again began to flourish, Yeshua gradually revealed more of what was to come.

He and Block had escaped dish duty and were back in the shop in #8 varnishing the last two new chairs.

" . . . and this boggles my mind, that the Earth is actually growing, too," Block was saying.

Yeshua dipped his brush into the varnish.

"How long will that keep up?" Block wanted to know. "I mean, what if it gets too big?"

"It won't. It knows its fixed limit. When it reaches that, it will stop."

"You amaze me. Standing here, working on a chair. But seems like you're working on the universe in the same breath."

"Confusing, yes. A bit. From the moment of my incarnation, it has been like this. When I was very little, of course, my human wits held me in check at times. I had to grow, too, strange as that sounds."

"Strange isn't the word."

"Little by little, the Father revealed to my human mind what our divine mind always knew."

"Kind of like being schizophrenic, huh?" Block wondered.

"Not at all. I was always at one, always whole. But

my human faculties had to grow, just like yours will now."

Block did not have to wonder at this. He felt completely incapable of growing fast enough to understand the mysteries that kept exploding like time bombs around him.

"So, I know I shouldn't ask this," Block said, hesitating, "but how much did you understand? The first time?"

"Everything. It was a matter of human awareness merging with the divine knowing in me. It's not really possible to explain, even in the Father's tongue."

"So you actually did know just how you were going to die. And, well—when?"

"I did."

Another question arose in Block's mind that he could not account for. It had never occurred to him before, but here was his chance to ask.

"Your first life—I mean, before you died—you were truly perfect?"

"Yes. But I was the sin-bearer, remember. On my shoulders, I carried the disease of all mankind."

"How do you mean?" Block asked, figuring he wouldn't understand the answer in any case.

"I never sinned, Clayton. But I could have." He put down his brush and sat on an old work stool. "Are you sure you want to hear this?"

"No, I'm not. Go on."

Block had unconsciously set his brush down, too, lopsidedly across the pail of varnish. Yeshua met his nod.

"I never sinned, but being human, I could have rebelled. Bearing my divinity in human flesh made every temptation that much more difficult."

"I would have guessed it made everything a breeze."

"Many thought that, because they didn't see the truth. Being God, bearing human nature, it made temptation not easier, but worse. All power was in my hands. Lucifer knew that, when he came at me in the desert."

Block reflected on this, watching the varnish congeal on the chair he had been working on.

"You mean, like when you're near the top of the mountain, you have the longest way to fall," Block said. He had no idea why this image popped into his mind.

"Yes, you do see. I was at the very top, always. Any slip was a fall into utter oblivion, for me—for the entire race. The entire cosmos, for that matter. Carrying the weight of others' sins was like carrying a leaky kettle of boiling oil over my head every day. Every instant. Intolerable." He chuckled to himself, shaking his head. "And they wondered why I went off alone to pray so often."

"You never dropped it, either."

"I came very close, remember. That night, in the garden."

"Yeah, but you were immune."

"Immune? How little you understand the mystery of my life, Clayton. Listen. I was strong, but not immune. That was the test. At any moment, I could have turned, and chosen sin. I, the Son, came as man. The Father put before me the same choices he gave you. If I had not been tempted like you, like everyone—and withstood—I could not have become the lamb of the sacrifice."

He looked at Block who was obviously wrestling with this.

"How could the Son of God have sinned?" Block asked insistently.

"Son of Man, too, don't forget. I'm not simple like you."

Block still shook his head. "Guess not."

"Do you see?" Yeshua asked him patiently.

"I see only how little I understand. I just hope you show me the kind of patience from here on that you showed me in the past."

It was as heartfelt a statement as Clayton Block had ever uttered.

Yeshua stood, picked up his brush, and went back to work.

Block took hold of his brush and found it had begun to stick in the pail. He soaked it in the varnish and slowly drew it along several back slats. The varnish clung to the fine grain of the walnut they had used.

He had never, in his first life, thought too deeply about any of this. Jesus, as he had known him then, had been a mythical figure, a storybook character who was too perfect to be true. Now, watching Yeshua apply varnish, Block began to recognize how short he had sold the one who was working alongside him.

"And even your best friends turned on you," Block said, trying to reassess what few details of the whole story he actually knew.

"Yes." He looked at Block, though his brush kept moving. "What would you have done, Clayton?"

Block didn't have to search long for this answer.

"Would've run like a scared rabbit," he said frankly.

"Sin makes men cowards."

Not gonna argue that one, Block told himself. He smoothed out several drips on the back slats of the chair. One problem drip kept wanting to run off the end of a slat, angling this way, then that.

Yeshua reached over with his brush and deftly caught the droplet, sweeping it gently upward where it thinned and disappeared.

LIKE MANY children her age, Piper was having trouble putting out of her mind the one thing her mother had warned her about yesterday. It was not that she was intentionally disobedient, just curious.

The sun shone brightly OUTSIDE as it crested overhead. While everyone was busy with chores and various projects, she quietly skipped out unnoticed through the Visitors Center and hurried toward her lake.

She found it much fuller than yesterday. More runoff and underground seepage from the rain had found its way into the lake, bringing it up to nearly half full.

Piper had not completely forgotten her mom's caution about getting too close to the edge. She was very careful as she walked closer to what would one day be the lakeshore. Along the inner rim, she could see jagged rocks and broken soil that formed the craggy wall of the lake basin.

Her eyes caught a momentary sparkle of light glinting off something about a hundred feet away, halfway between the water level and the top of the basin. For a second, she wondered if the Least One had followed her.

I suppose she would, Piper thought. Then she realized the glittering was not her angel but a very sparkly something embedded in the Earth. *He said the gems would come back up,* she remembered. *Maybe it's diamonds!* she thought with a thrill.

For Piper, diamonds were the things of story books read on a digital screen, classic books John Haskins had made sure to feed into the Solarium archives before his death.

I wonder what they feel like? Wonder if they really have little faces inside? she mused dreamily.

Unconsciously, she had edged toward the future shore, her eyes fixed on the glittering objects, trying for a closer look. She came to a spot just above the sparkling gems and leaned forward, not realizing that with her increased height her center of gravity had shifted. Her left foot settled onto a piece of rock that was no longer attached to its neighbor.

Her shriek could not be heard by anyone in the Solarium, even though the outer doors were standing open. It might be hours before anyone noticed her missing.

She fell violently, her head smacking a large rock and bouncing outward, as she inverted and the weight of her legs and torso carried her head-over-heels into a fast slide. One arm struck a patch of mud that covered a jagged piece of rock, wiping the rock clean. She flipped into the water head first, so shaken she could not even catch a breath. Her eyes stayed open, against odds, as the beautiful daylight filtered down through what seemed to be 5 feet of water, but was in fact only about 16 inches.

One thought struck her. Yeshua had promised they would not die. Had he lied?

Her mind was reacting to this dreadful thought when, without her willing it or in any way helping, her body popped to the surface like an over-filled beach ball. She began to struggle but only for a second before she realized she couldn't sink again if she wanted to. Her only buoyancy was the bit of air she had gasped in after coming up, but she bobbed there like a rubber ducky in a child's tub, not smiling, but unsinkable.

She laughed hilariously.

She felt her head, a little sore where it hit the rock, but no blood. Her elbow that had wiped the mud off the sharp rock also felt perfectly fine.

She laughed more.

"I'll swim every day!" she hollered to the sky.

"But you should be more careful," the Least One said to her from somewhere above.

Piper looked up. The sun bore down brightly, not a cloud in sight. She thought she could see the Least One toward the edge of the water, maybe 25 feet above her, but wasn't positive.

"Now, why would you let me have a stupid fall like that?" Piper asked.

"I'm to watch. You're my charge, not my robot." The short, thin shaft of light which Piper had now fixed in her sight descended slightly into the basin so that it showed more clearly against the backdrop of rock and mud. "I would have intervened if it was needed. But I know the Earth will not hurt you, and the water is safe."

Piper scrambled up the side of the basin with little trouble. The Least One rose, too, remaining at a distance, but followed Piper back into the Solarium.

She went immediately to find her mother and apologize.

"What in the—?" Pam said when she saw Piper's clothes sopping wet, a golden-like shadow emanating from them into the air around her daughter.

"Sorry, Mom. I got curious."

"You didn't," Pam said with a thud.

"Yeah." Piper gave her mom a soggy hug. "I won't go by myself again. But—this is the really crazy part, Mom—the water makes you float!"

With all the seemingly magical qualities of this new world, which were in fact not magic at all, Pam had ceased to be amazed.

"Why would that not surprise me?" she asked, hugging Piper tightly, warming her from the slight chill of the evaporating water in her clothes. "Let's see," she said aloud to her daughter, "you won't die, and you can't really get hurt. Now you can't drown. What's a mother going to worry about?"

"I guess you can finally worry a little less, Mom," Piper laughed.

Pam pulled her daughter closer, her own clothes soaking up some of the wetness.

AFTER LISTENING to a fuller rendition of her

daughter's most recent adventure while Piper changed into dry things, Pam collected the wet clothes and took them to the laundry tent.

Bridget and Mai Ker were there, washing towels that had piled up far too quickly with all the company. Jacob was helping fold dry towels, being careful not to get strays from his beard wrapped up in them.

". . . so you'll just have to ask him," Bridget was saying to Mai Ker. "I don't really remember enough about it."

"Well, I suppose it does not matter anymore," Mai Ker said.

"What's cooking?" Pam asked.

Bridget threw Pam a look as she walked in with Piper's wet clothes.

More laundry? Bridget moaned inside.

"Well, I was a little confused, Friday afternoon," Mai Ker said. "You were talking about gold streets or something, and Yeshua said something about a new city," Mai Ker explained, condensing a 10-minute conversation.

"Yes," Pam, said, "he said, we are the new city. All his people."

"City of Peace," Jacob commented absently.

"You understood that?" Mai Ker asked Jacob.

"Oh sure," Jacob said. "I always took it that someday we'd all go live over there. You know, where the first Jerusalem was."

Bridget and Pam nodded. Mai Ker wasn't sure of the geography.

"But here we all are!" Jacob said with a broad smile that might have lit a coal mine.

It was odd to see one who had died at age 96 grinning like a five-year-old. Pam joined his grin, looking at Mai Ker.

"See, Mai?" she asked.

Mai Ker didn't.

"We'll, dear lady, as Yeshua said—and I admit he's cryptic at times—*we* are the new Jerusalem," Jacob explained.

"But Jimmy always talked about it, like, coming down out of the clouds."

Jacob could hardly contain his temptation to burst out laughing.

"Dear Mai. Do you remember a day—not long ago—you were standing, and I think maybe trembling quite a little, on a high mountain, covered in a huge cloud?" His smile broadened further. "And who all descended out of that cloud?"

"Even more obvious," was Mai Ker's instant reply. Now she was smiling. "I always make simple things so complicated."

"Why else did you go to college?" Bridget laughed.

"Except, I didn't come out of that cloud," Mai Ker said. "Am I part of this city, too?"

"Of course," Jacob said with fatherly, open arms. "Wherever Yeshua rules, there is Jerusalem."

"What's cooking?" Jimmy asked, appearing in the doorway.

Mai Ker jumped a little. "Jimmy, please do not sneak up like that!"

"I wondered where you were hiding. Thought we could take a walk."

Mai Ker looked at Bridget and Jacob.

"Do you mind?"

"Go for a walk, Mai Ker," Bridget said. "Give your brain a rest."

26

Sunday Afternoon

Two hours later, Pam found Yeshua nosing through the kitchen tent, looking for his daily treat of her oatmeal-raisin cookies. Fortunately, one thing that had always grown well INSIDE, even in the old world, was a large, extensive grapevine, from which Pam had often dried raisins.

"Thank you," she said to him, "life is so amazing."

"Thank you," he said, holding up three cookies.

"I feel so stupid about things at times."

"You're not stupid at all Pam. You have a great heart. You just need to learn things you've not learned yet. Good news, you have lots of time."

"I've been wondering," she said, taking a cookie herself and putting the cover carefully back on the cookie bowl. She rinsed her hands in the sink and tied on her apron, intent on making some very fine dessert for everyone this evening.

Yeshua sat on a stool by the makeshift kitchen counter, waiting. It was obvious Pam was fretting, and he knew why.

"What's bothering you?"

She pulled another stool near him. She rubbed her fingers across her cheeks, which felt overly warm.

"It's about here."

"Here?" he said with the slightest of winks.

"The Solarium."

Yeshua smiled at her, nodding.

"Will we stay here? Always?"

"You can leave any time you'd like. Any of you."

The thought disquieted Pam.

"I was afraid you would say that."

"Why afraid?"

She looked awkward and embarrassed.

"For so long, it felt like a prison. But now, well, I'd like to stay."

"Is that so?" he asked, as if this was news to him.

"Yes. Sounds goofy, I know. But it's become my home. I actually think it's beautiful in here. A whole little world, all in one place." A smile in her heart crept onto her face. "Not to mention a very beautiful new mountain lake for my little girl," she added with delighted eyes.

"Yes," he said. "Nice addition."

"Is that wrong? I mean, is there something wrong with me?"

"No. But I do seem to remember a day . . ." He let her finish the sentence.

". . . when I was beating my skull against the door of Pod 1, screaming to get out." She could still feel the cuts and awful headache she had afterward. "You saw that?" She thought. "Never mind. Stupid question."

"And now you want to stay. Perfectly natural."

"Really?" Pam could hardly believe her ears.

"There's no reason you can't stay. As long as you like. Eternity takes a while." He chuckled. "And you can always change your mind."

"A woman's prerogative?"

"A human's prerogative."

"It's strange that I feel so fond of the place. But it kept us alive."

"I kept you alive. But, yes, I used the Solarium."

"I feel like—don't laugh at me . . ."

"You've noticed I like to laugh," he smiled.

"But don't, please. I feel somehow that I owe this place something of myself, now. Because it sustained us.”

“Yes, the Father set it apart. It has become a holy place.”

“That’s it, that’s how I feel. Like a great cathedral,” Pam said.

Yeshua looked as if he were thinking her request over, though of course he already had.

“I think it would be delightful if you stayed, Pam.”

“I can visit other places, though?”

“Of course. Any time you like.”

“I’d like to move back into the old house. It’s so beautiful.”

“That would be good.”

“I’d be, kind of like, the caretaker, wouldn’t I?” Pam asked, her mind beginning to run in new tracks, which, until now, she had forbidden it to do. “It would be a sort of vast museum.”

“Without the skeletons,” Yeshua laughed. “A monument of what was,” he said, looking out of the tent into the great pod. “And, thank the Father, what is no longer.”

“I’m so glad about this!” Pam jumped up and hugged him.

“I have to warn you, though,” Yeshua said without breaking a smile, “sometimes the roof leaks.”

She burst out laughing. He stood, holding her, looking with delight into her eyes.

“You have become a truly exceptional woman, Pamela Hansen.”

She quickly went to a refrigerator, beginning to dream up tonight’s dessert. She suddenly stopped and turned.

“Oh, I forgot. I’d like Piper to stay with me, of course.”

He looked at her with a solemn question in his eyes.

“That is a different matter.”

“She’s my child.”

"Was."

"Still is," Pam said with every motherly instinct still fully intact.

"In a sense, yes. But she is my child, first. And I have a particular plan for her. And I know she will want it."

Pam slowly closed the refrigerator door, crestfallen. Piper was still a child, at least to her, even if she was growing very rapidly all of a sudden. Then it dawned on her that with Yeshua around, Piper was probably maturing inside even more quickly than on the outside. She looked back at him.

"You have a plan for her?"

"A very special one."

Pam looked at the floor, then slowly raised her eyes to Yeshua.

"Well, like you say, she is yours first." Pam said it with a wrenching feeling, as if giving Piper birth a second time. "She was my prayer-begotten child. It was only because of you that I conceived."

"The Holy Spirit still works wonders," Yeshua said. "And we *are* talking of eternity." He came over to Pam and took her hand. "She can stay here as long as she wishes. Just know, one day I will call her, and she will go."

"You are the Lord," Pam said.

AS EVENING crept in and daylight faded into the evening glow as far as sight could carry the eye, Jimmy and Block went back to the woodshop to put the finishing touches on the new chairs. Will Atchison tagged along.

"So how long do you suppose we'll need these?" Block asked Jimmy.

"Don't know."

"You gonna stay here?" Block asked him.

"Don't know."

"This conversation's gonna get boring real quick," Atchison said.

Jimmy retightened the screws securing two chair legs.

"Where would we go?" Jimmy asked.

Block looked at him, then Atchison.

"Where would we live?" Will asked.

"Houses, I suppose," Block answered.

"How? There going to be lumber yards popping up soon?"

"Hadn't thought that far ahead," Block admitted. "Still trying to get used to being alive again."

"Maybe we'll harvest lumber just like before," Jimmy suggested. "Sure are plenty of trees popping up, if not lumber yards."

"What's holding you here, Clayton?" Will asked.

"Not sure. Bridget and I have talked. We realize, it's a new time, we're no longer married, not in the sense we were. And we both feel there's other places we'll each want to go."

"Not necessarily together," Jimmy said.

"Yeah."

"Yeah, Mai Ker and I, we've had the same conversation."

"I'm thinkin' I might want to hang out with Pam a while," Atchison said. "Kinda got short-changed the first time around."

The other two men nodded. As with many all-male conversations, there were long gaps of silence when no one felt any urge to speak.

"How're the new chairs coming?" Yeshua asked as he came into the shed.

The three men nodded at the chairs, each other, and Yeshua.

"I see," Yeshua said. "Deep thinking going on."

"Well," Jimmy said, "yeah, we're thinking, if we move away, where would we live? Have to build new houses, I guess."

"Could take a tent along," Yeshua said with half a grin.

"Funny," Jimmy said.

"Serious?" Block asked.

"No, of course you'll want houses. But then, what's the hurry?"

The men knew there was none.

"And the houses you build now will work differently, of course," Yeshua added without explanation.

"Of course," Atchison agreed, though he didn't know what he was agreeing with.

"You are builders," Yeshua said. "One of my great gifts. Imagine, design, and build. 'In my image,' remember?"

"Materials?" Block asked.

"Before long, Clayton, there will be more trees than you can shake a stick at. Pun intended," he smiled. "And I'll help you make new kinds of tools. Much better than the crude things you've cooked up so far."

"Power?" Atchison wanted to know.

"Of a kind you don't yet know," came the answer.

"We'd need help," Jimmy said. "I'm really better with computers than this kind of stuff," he said, gesturing at the chairs.

"I'll be anxious to help. I would have built a beautiful mansion for Adam and his bride—if they hadn't gotten out of hand so quickly."

"That's a joke," Jimmy said, "right?"

"Why would you think that?" Yeshua looked at them. "You were given the Earth to be my stewards. To tend it, use it, to be sovereign over it—and its creatures. That has not changed, nor ever will. Don't worry, Jimmy. With new knowledge come new skills."

"I always wanted a brick house," Jimmy told him. "Not that stick and board construction."

Yeshua smiled.

"Do you remember something about this place, Jimmy?"

Jimmy drew a blank.

"You noticed a pod getting bigger?"

"Oh, that," Jimmy said as if this was a minor oversight.

"The homes you build will be like that. They'll help you, they'll find their own perfection. It is all in how you design it. And the materials."

"Huh," Will responded, "guess we should'a guessed that."

"You can have bricks, Jimmy. Once I show you how to properly make them."

"Well, maybe—" Block began before Yeshua cut him off.

"Too much talking. Time for some recreation."

"Nate was begging to go riding earlier," Jimmy said.

"Alright. Let's find Braden. A good horse race sounds like just the thing," Yeshua smiled.

THE TALK about new houses and exploring their new world carried through supper and into the evening, as the Solarians and their guests gathered in the Meeting Tent visiting, reading, and just relaxing quietly together.

Word had begun to spread that the Solarians, some of them, at least, would be moving. This sparked interest among their guests. Might they be allowed to stay, instead? The Solarium was spectacular, beyond their most imaginative dreams. The visitors could easily be happy here for eternity, or so they felt today. Plus, they didn't share the memories of the horrors that went on here.

While Garan and Adrian were avidly debating this possibility, Yeshua had been in the kitchen teaching Braden and Nathaniel, who had both survived the horse race unscathed, a simpler way to freeze ice cream. The kids presented the creamy results to everyone, served in small teacups. Sing even fed a little to Kai with her fingertip. It was an instant hit with Kai, not quite two months old.

Yeshua wiped a blob of bright green ice cream from the corner of his mouth.

"One of man's truly great inventions," he teased. "Of course, I provided the cows."

Everyone laughed, but an air of nervous anticipation hung over everyone's head this evening. Was some important event about to take place? They had begun to expect the unexpected.

"You all want me to tell you about your future," Yeshua finally said.

Mai Ker, who was deeply embroiled in her novel, paused and looked up.

"We've had some very long chats. I understand. You'd like to know everything all at once. Tonight, if possible. But there are things I will only share at the right time. And mostly, I'll talk with you individually. There is a plan for each of you, but you will each help refine it. Just be patient."

"The one thing I was always weak on," Adrian said.

"I will wait forever, if I can wait here in this beautiful place," Eira cooed.

"Remember," Yeshua told them, "time will pass differently now. There is no rush. I made you to enjoy life, and to fully enjoy, you must not rush. You are still unlearning your old ways. Some of you unlearn slowly."

"Ah, that would be me, I'm betting," Will Atchison said, raising a hand that was still broad but not as bulky as it used to be.

Block grinned at him. Blessedly, certain things had not changed.

"Most of you will want to be with your families and close friends from before. And for some of you, love must be relearned. Your families were not always a refuge of love."

Several knowing looks went around.

"And new houses," Block added, what little he knew at this point.

"Homes that will amaze you," Yeshua promised. "Havens of peace after all. Not like before."

"My own house?" Nathaniel asked.

"One you may share."

Sing finished her ice cream and gave Kai one last taste.

"Lord, I—" Sing began.

"Yes, Sing, I know. This is the right time, to explain about yourselves." Ears perked up. "How you will grow," he added.

"Feeling pretty well full-grown already," Will said, his hands on a stomach full of a fantastic supper of plant-grown steak, not to mention Pam's special dessert and now the kids' ice cream.

"None of you are done growing, not for a long time, Will. You always thought in terms of months, years, birthdays, aging. But that is past. Now you will judge growth in spiritual dimensions, depths instead of breadths, and heights of a very different kind."

"I sure want to get bigger," Braden said boldly.

"You will, Braden, beyond mere size," Yeshua chuckled. He looked around the tent. "Your souls will soon outgrow even these new bodies, but not in the way you expect."

"I'll be thinner?" Willy asked, a cute grin behind his teeth.

"Leaner in flesh, fuller in spirit, Will. Many left the old world before—like Jacob, here—at a very advanced age. Others died in infancy. Everyone must now grow to be complete. Some who appear young in physical stature will grow in the stature of the spirit," he said, with a subtle glance toward Piper. "And yes, Sing, Baby Kai will catch up, never fear."

"No more diapers?" Sing said, thrilled.

"Another six months or so. Believe me, she'll grow much faster than you will want her to."

Sing winced at this truth. Despite the drudgery, she loved mothering her little girl and, except for the darn diapers, she didn't want that to end.

"There is no past to fret over, no death in your future," Yeshua said. "The Father has made you to live richly. You'll have work to do, but it won't tax you as it used to. It'll bring you joy, the fruit of your labor will be sweet."

"I thought you'd just kind of hand everything to us on a platter," Herald said quite seriously.

"But that would mean no sense of task, and creating things, and no sense of accomplishment, Herald. That would be a very dull, tedious eternity, wouldn't it?"

Herald thought, then nodded. Like his father, he thrived on being active. He actually felt relieved, knowing they would still have purposeful work to occupy their days.

"So no hanging around on a cloud playing harps all day and night?" Bridget laughed. "I love music, but I can't *imagine* anything more boring."

"Harps are lovely, temperately used," Yeshua smiled. "Like too much of anything, they can become torturous."

"Especially on the fingers," Anastazja remembered, having once tried to learn the hand-harp as a girl.

This drew laughter around the room, coupled with a corporate sigh of relief. Yeshua looked around at his reborn children.

"You know, I'm tired of talking. The voice can be just like a harp. And I promised Piper she and I would go for an evening walk, out to the lake. Any of you are welcome to join us."

"Don't get too close to the edge," Piper said, playfully grinning at her mother.

27

Monday Morning

Only Jimmy and Block had gone walking with Piper and Yeshua last night. Stars glistened brilliantly as they enjoyed the freshest night air ever. The still-mysterious angels glittered above them, though tonight they seemed random in their movements, not forming any discernible swirls or patterns, as if beginning journeys of their own.

A pleasant smell rose off the new lake as they came near, the result, Yeshua said, of new species of flora already growing in its depths and along its shores.

"Thank you," Piper said to Yeshua.

"You're welcome," he answered, knowing she meant the lake. "A simple gift. Your gift to me all these years was your love, and your trust. This is my token, in return. To express my thanks to you."

"It was hard sometimes," Piper admitted, "when I couldn't see ahead. Not knowing, you know?" She felt her newly regenerated, undamaged heart throb a couple of times. "Especially when Daddy died." She glanced over her shoulder at Jimmy, walking by Block. "I wavered then. I was afraid."

"I know," Yeshua assured her. "But trust, it's like your new lake here. You look into the water, you know there must be a bottom, but you can't see it."

Piper nodded.

"But the deeper you go," Yeshua added, "you find it. Love of the Father is like that. You have to go deep."

Piper's smile was barely visible in the illumination of the evening glow. She had seen the bottom of this lake, before it began to fill. In some way, though she could not really see ahead in those dark days after Jimmy died, she had seen the bottom of the Father's love. It was, she knew, what drove her to push Bridget to go up the mountain that day. An irresistible love reaching out, drawing her forward.

"Now you've done it," she said with a chuckle.

"What is that, dear?"

"Every time I look into a lake now, I'll be thinking of the Father's love."

"Is that a bad thing?" Yeshua smiled.

Jimmy and Block were talking about the new solar panels, those they had built but never installed. Hooking up more panels had stirred a small controversy the day before yesterday, about whether they should abandon electricity altogether as an ancient technology. Surely, Jimmy thought, Yeshua had something better in mind.

"So, what do you think, Lord?" Jimmy now asked.

"More solar panels?" Speaking with Piper, he had also been listening to Jimmy and Block chatter. "An awful lot of things will go by the way if you stop using electricity," Yeshua said. "How would you run all the equipment in there?" he asked just as if it were a real question.

"But it's still dangerous, right?" Jimmy asked. "Or has that changed, too?"

"There are several ways to generate low but useful voltage that you hadn't discovered before," Yeshua said. "Once I show you, there'll be no more risk of burns or electrical shock. As you already discovered, toward the end, brilliant lights and many useful machines can be made that use very low voltage—if made the right way."

Piper listened disinterestedly, looking up at Yeshua

and smiling, her eyes drinking in the magnificence of the man. She noticed she didn't have to raise her chin quite as far as she did a week ago, although she knew she was far from fully grown.

"All that waiting," she said, a sense of mystery unfolding behind her words, "it was worth it, wasn't it?"

"So full of questions tonight, everyone." Yeshua smiled at Piper, then turned to Jimmy and Clayton as they chattered on about solar panels. "When I said you'd have useful work to do, I didn't mean you needed to discuss it all night and day," he told them.

A welcome silence fell around them. The water was quietly kissing the rock and soil around the edge of the filling lake, water seeping into soil, soil drifting into water. A dance. One of millions going on around them.

They had circled the lake basin and were nearing the doors of the Visitors Center. Yeshua turned to Jimmy and Block and said, "Why don't you hook up those new panels tomorrow? You both seem to be at loose ends."

He and Piper laughed loudly.

THIS MORNING after a breakfast of rolls buttered with a delicious new dairy spread Pam and Anastazja created, a small crew of Jimmy, Block, and Mai Ker went off to Pod 13 to pull the new panels out of storage and start on their installation.

Bridget made them wait long enough for her to do some switching around in the Comm. Center so they didn't blow up the main computers during the rewiring.

The urgency they felt about installing the new solar panels was mysterious, since they knew they might be leaving the Solarium for good before long.

Mai Ker was finally able to put her finger on why they felt the need to do it at all.

"It is like what he said yesterday, about completion.

It would not feel right to me, leaving here with something we had started but left undone."

"You're right," Block told her.

"As usual," Jimmy smiled.

Mai Ker's beauty was beginning to overcome him again, much as it had when he had first met her, in those early days INSIDE. What aging she had experienced before he died was now reversed, or simply gone. Being able to see her beautiful, loving spirit emanating from her restored flesh was almost too much for Jimmy to take in. Beauty, he was only now realizing, was much, much more than skin deep.

"When you think of how we began here," Block ruminated, "all those years back—well, who would have ever thought? The whole time, his magnificent plan was playing out—right in front of us—and we missed it."

"Too busy scrambling to stay alive," Jimmy said.

The word snagged in each mind simultaneously, and they each knew it.

"Alive," Mai Ker said. "We never understood what that could mean, did we?"

"Nope," Block said, using a vise to reshape a metal bracket that would hold one of the solar panels.

"It is still a mystery to me, how he worked it all out," Mai Ker said.

"What do you mean?" Block asked.

"Well, I know he explained. Still, I wonder if we will ever completely see how he orchestrated everything."

"Everything?" Jimmy asked.

"History, Jimmy. Events, lives. Our lives."

"Um," Jimmy nodded, a tape measure hanging loosely from his hand. "Yeah. I think you're probably right."

"As usual," she joked.

"Well, for my part," Block told them, "I am

sufficiently overwhelmed with information to keep me thinking for a good three or four thousand years, to start."

He began drilling holes into the new bracket to accept bolts that would hold it to the side of the panel.

Without warning, an incredibly ear-piercing, explosive blast of sound cannoned through the pods, the Stellar plastic reacting as if from another nuclear blast. Block jerked his hand, jamming the drill bit momentarily against his other wrist, but with no damage. It left not even a mark on his new, resilient skin.

"What in the world?!" Jimmy yelped.

Shaken, Mai Ker flew out the door of the work shed into the pod. Across the other pods, she could see everyone in sight had stopped, frozen, looking up, around, everywhere, trying to figure out what had just happened.

Will Atchison came jogging from the shower tent where he had been shaving, his newly refined stomach line barely protruding over the edge of a bath towel wrapped around his midsection.

"Holy cow!" he barked, this time not in humor. "Who did what?" he called loudly.

Moments later, he saw Piper and Yeshua walking toward him from the podwalk out of #3, returning from the Comm. Center in #2. They were jostling and laughing at some private joke.

They reached the tents. Jacob and Katherine were standing outside the main tent. Katherine, waiting for an answer from Yeshua, was distracted by Atchison's newly refined physique, glowing from within.

"Well now," Atchison drawled, looking at Piper and Yeshua, "I'm thinking, from the looks of it, you two seem to know something about that awful racket a minute ago."

"Piper?" Yeshua nudged her.

"OK, it was me."

"How," Atchison asked, "could a little lady like you make that kind of horrendous noise?"

"The last trumpet," Piper said, as if her meaning should be apparent.

"The what?" Atchison asked.

"I told her, Will, it was simply an image, a symbol—to announce the end of the old world, the beginning of the new. But she insisted, said even if it was just a symbol, shouldn't we have it anyway? So, *I*," he said, defending Piper, "I said, 'Certainly, why not?'"

Bridget had joined them, as had Jimmy, Mai Ker and Block who had run nearly full speed across #10, expecting some tragic news or unplanned disaster. Pam emerged from the laundry tent, still deep in washing towels and spare clothes.

"So, she said it was way past time, I should blow that last trumpet," Yeshua was saying, "but I said, 'Why don't you?' Bridget was done in the Comm. Center, so we went over and I showed Piper how your intercom and speaker system can be computer-rigged to produce a very credible trumpet-blast."

"Credible?" Atchison asked loudly as if this were the understatement of the past century.

"I'm sorry," Piper said to everyone, "It's true, I did insist. I really had no idea he could do that with our speakers. Not that *loud!* Scared me to death, too."

"I think we'll have to work on some new figures of speech," Pam said gently, taking Piper in her arm. "It's OK, honey. No harm."

"A good thing these new eardrums of ours are bulletproof," Atchison laughed as he walked back to finish shaving.

THE INSTALLATION of the new solar panels was finished quickly because Garan and Adrian went over to lend the crew a hand, mainly out of curiosity to see how such solar "machines" could work with virtually no moving parts.

Yeshua returned from another walk outside, the quiet time he cherished with the Father, although they were always speaking, even when he was in the midst of the others. He found the work crew, their job finished, putting away tools and equipment in Pod 13.

"Guess we won't need those old bike-generators anymore," Jimmy said, relieved. "Sure won't miss the boredom of those bikes," he added.

"Maybe they were a good lesson," Yeshua said, "on what's really necessary in life."

The group arrived at the kitchen, hunting for a meal.

"Anyone hungry?" Bridget asked as she sat finishing a bowl of soup.

"Always," Block told her with a hug and a kiss.

Bridget dished up soup for everyone from a large kettle she had warming.

"Look, I know you guys felt you had to do all that with the solar panels, but I mean, what's the point, really?" Bridget asked as they ate. "Maybe we should just shut this whole place down. Completely."

"Except that some will be staying," Yeshua said as he searched a drawer for a butter knife.

This was news. They immediately wondered whom.

"Don't worry, none of you," Yeshua said, knowing their thoughts. "Pam has asked to stay. And Piper will remain with her, for the time being. And Jacob and Katherine have asked to stay a while, too. They love it here."

"Hard to imagine," Bridget said quietly, her mind racing through years of treacherous memories.

"So, it's good we hooked all that stuff up," Block said.

"Very good," Yeshua answered. He opened the refrigerator and pulled out the bowl of thick, chewy spread Pam and Anastazja had whipped up before breakfast. It was made from one of the new plants mixed with cream, and tasted like honey and finely ground cashews. He drenched a piece of bread with the stuff. "The Solarium will be here a long time, a museum to past ages. Pam will be caretaker, with Jacob and Katherine helping. And I'll bring others. They can't run this place without help."

"It was always a challenge even for seven," Bridget said.

The mention of "seven" sparked another pang of conscience over Sarajane.

"Your new solar panels are a stopgap. New energy systems will need to be built," Yeshua said. "Electrical equipment will wear out, eventually. What I've planned won't."

"Nuclear?" Mae Ker asked.

"No, Mai Ker. Nuclear was too primitive—and it was like children playing with matches. You never discovered the true dangers of it. The energies I mean are far beyond that, far more subtle. Being a biologist, you'll find them rather fascinating."

"Well, I have some catching up to do with the kids," Jimmy said, excusing himself. "I've missed months of playtime." He washed breadcrumbs off his hands and darted out the door.

"So," Mai Ker asked, "what about the rest of us? You said you have a plan?"

"Let's you and I talk," Yeshua said. He offered her his arm and escorted her out of the tent.

A FEW hours later, three of their visitors collected what few things they had brought with them and prepared to leave the Solarium.

"Glad you came here?" Garan asked Adrian.

"The most amazing time I've ever had. And I've had some pretty amazing times!"

"When he asked us to come with him that day, to the mountain, I couldn't figure out why he chose us," Garan admitted.

"He had a reason, I suppose. Maybe someday he'll say."

"Maybe someday we'll realize we don't need to know," Garan said, packing a small bag of souvenirs the Solarian children had given him.

Adrian was going with Anastazja, bound for a new home in central Europe near a river that now flowed with pure, rejuvenated water. Members of their families would gather and meet them there, Yeshua promised. This first of their many new homes would be built from the remnants of an ancient orphanage. It was no longer needed, Yeshua said, since there were now no orphans.

Garan was bound for a small town in western Asia that he had never seen but where he had ancient, undiscovered family roots. There he would meet generations of ancestors who had been long dead before he had been conceived.

"Safe journeys," Bridget told them as hugs went around among the Solarians and the three.

With words of blessing from Yeshua, they left, each beginning an adventure even greater than their visit to Solarium-3.

"They'll be fine, Bridget," Mai Ker told her with an encouraging arm around her waist. "Yeshua is sending them where they'll be happiest, for now."

Bridget noticed Eira had not come to say goodbye. After a few minutes, she saw Eira standing off at a distance by the corner of a tent, like a child left behind when the circus has moved on to the next town.

Bridget went over to her. Eira was sitting on the ground, modeling some short pieces of string into artwork on the grass.

"Hi, Eira. Didn't you want to say goodbye?"

"It's hard for me." She didn't look up, her little

fingers still shaping pieces of string.

Bridget had grown very close to Eira. She felt real sadness at the thought that Eira might leave, too.

"I wonder if Yeshua would let you go along with me, when I go?" Bridget said.

Eira's eyes lit up.

"Really?"

"Unless he has some special place for you. We can ask."

Eira jumped to her feet, excited, thrilled, bubbly and happy all at once. She grabbed hold of Bridget as though they had been mother and daughter forever. Since her own mother had died giving her birth, Eira had never had a connection like this. She loved it.

"I don't know my plans yet, Eira. But I would be truly delighted for you to be part of them," Bridget smiled, kissing her forehead.

The hug lasted a full minute, then they went looking for Yeshua.

ONE OF many surprises for the Solarians was that the fruit trees in Pods 10 and 12 had all suddenly come into full bloom. Usually, depending on their variety, only a few would produce fruit just once or twice a year. But in recent days, small fruit had appeared on nearly every tree and some would be ready to harvest within the week.

"How come all the fruit trees are producing all at once?" Herald asked Yeshua as they and Bridget collected two baskets of ripe peaches from a single tree. "Clayton—Dad, I mean—found two huge grapefruits yesterday."

"The Earth is newly alive. It will produce in all its fullness," Yeshua answered. "Every day there will be something to harvest. In here, and out there. You'll never lack for food. Nor will the animals."

They brought the fruit to the kitchen to wash and cut

some of it up. Mai Ker and Pam were making pies. Jimmy was washing out several large storage containers to hold all the fruit.

Bridget was piling six very large peaches into a colander. "Everything is producing—fruit, grain, everything—at lightning speed."

"And?" Yeshua asked as she hesitated.

"Well, what about us?" She paused. "Will we be fruitful, too?"

He knew the question and where it was leading.

"No. As I said before, the Father's kingdom is complete. Kai was the last child of Earth."

"So," Will Atchison asked in his usual bold manner, "you mean, no more . . ." He wobbled his head side-to-side.

"Those old passions and desires were given to you for a reason, so that you would be fruitful. Fortunately, it was one of the few things you did well," he said. "But sin infected them, too. Most never knew genuine love because they could not distinguish its truth from the physical desires."

"I can testify to that," Will half-mumbled.

"Like so many wonderful things the Father designed, sexual desire was abused and twisted. It often brought more harm than blessing."

Will gave a knowing nod.

Bridget could not help thinking of her pregnancy when she was 15 years old. Her own life testified to this painful truth.

"Love will now be perfected, and there is no more need to procreate. So, no, you will not have the kind of physical relations you had before. But intimacy will be much deeper."

Atchison was watching Pam as she made indentations in a piecrust with a fork.

"Now that you say it, I have noticed something different," he drawled.

Pam turned and looked at him, the fork pausing in midair.

"What would that be, Mr. Atchison?" she asked playfully.

"Only that, ever since I came back from being dead, I've felt many fresh desires, but not one was for you-know-what," he grinned at her.

"I am a married woman, Will Atchison," she smirked.

Yeshua said patiently, "Until parted by death."

In the brief hanging silence, Jimmy reacted as if he had been stuck with a cattle prod.

"Of course!" Jimmy said, a brilliant light blinking on. "That's it!"

"That's what?" Mai Ker asked.

"If I hadn't died, I'd still have—well," he grimaced toward Yeshua, "three wives."

"Only part of the reason I allowed you to fall that day, Jimmy," Yeshua said. "The main reason being, you acted stupidly going up there in the first place."

Jimmy frowned.

"If you had listened to Bridget, and simply gone OUTSIDE, you might have tested the air and found there was no need to patch the pod roof at all."

Bridget gave Jimmy a little mischievous smile.

"Well, I didn't figure that part out, either, before Herald and I made such a dangerous climb up the outside," Bridget said.

Jimmy was still frowning. Pam, always running to the rescue, changed directions.

"So, then, Jimmy and I, or even Will and I, we won't have any kind of intimate relationships?"

Yeshua looked genuinely surprised.

"Pam, you've already had moments of unusual intimacy with both of them since they've returned. Haven't you?"

Pam considered this, then nodded thoughtfully, thinking of several such times.

"And was sex involved?"

Pam shook her head, even more thoughtfully. During several private moments with Will, and several others with Jimmy, she had experienced with them a kind of love and caring and acceptance beyond what she had ever felt from either of them in their former life. Even now, looking at them both, she held a love for them both that surpassed any mere feeling she had experienced before.

Oddly, no one was actually surprised by any of this. Even Herald had already discovered a deeper intimacy with Sing.

"Your own body and spirit are healed in such a way that true intimacy can occur without the self-centered desires that often mixed with sexual intimacy," Yeshua said. "You'll experience physical and spiritual desire now as one thing."

"Sounds mystical," Mai Ker said.

"Indeed," the Lord replied. He smiled. "Sexual intimacy was like baby steps. Now, you will run, your desires grounded in the realm of the Spirit."

Mai Ker had drifted over and taken hold of Jimmy's arm. She was looking at him with new eyes.

"Many never experienced the kind of love that exists between myself and the Father and the Spirit. Growing into that love is now your vocation, and why you were made in our image. When you discover it, you will not look back."

He took a whole peach from those that had been washed. Taking a large bite, he gave them a nod, and left the tent.

28

Monday Afternoon

A man walked unnoticed out of the podwalk from #5 into the westerly edge of Pod 10. Block and Bridget were a short distance away, cultivating the soil around several burgeoning new "meat" plants.

Yeshua was sitting on the ground near the tents, playing some sort of game using peach pits with Braden, Nathaniel and Eira.

"So this is what it looks like, from the inside," the man said.

Bridget and Block both turned, reacting to the unknown voice.

He looked to be a stranger, someone, they guessed, who was traveling by and wandered in out of curiosity. Anyone would have. But as Bridget straightened up to greet him, she caught her breath. His face was familiar, if not readily recognizable. She knew the face but couldn't place it.

Then it hit her.

"Oh, my Lord." It wasn't an exclamation, but a prayer.

"Yes, Bridget?" Yeshua called from across the pod.

"Paul Bishop," the man said, offering her his hand.

She wanted to run. Block, still bent over, stood and froze. Even without the tattered fatigues, Block recognized him instantly.

Bishop was the leader of the band of refugees who had come to Solarium-3 seeking refuge years ago, during the final days. Two hundred and twenty-seven souls, including Bishop, had begged for their lives, dying from poisonous air and radiation burns, and the Solarians had refused them. It had been one of their most agonizing days INSIDE.

"Lord," Block called to Yeshua, "I think we could use your help over here."

"No, you don't," Yeshua called back, pretending to be too busy with the game.

Bridget looked at Block. They couldn't just walk away. Not this time. Here was the last person they ever imagined seeing again, standing in front of them, his hand still extended in a gesture of friendship. Thankfully, there was no longer anger on his face. The two Solarians felt paralyzed.

"I recognize you two," Bishop said, lowering his hand. "Though you look a little different."

"And you," Bridget said, hopeful she didn't sound rude.

"A fellow named Thomas found me several days ago, said I was to travel out here. Said I was expected."

"Well, I have to admit, not by us," Block said with an extremely awkward smile.

"Welcome to our home," Bridget said, a feeble attempt to make amends.

"Looks different," Bishop said, looking around. "It looks more alive. And—believe me—it looked pretty good before," he said with a little laugh.

His attempt at humor unfroze them and broke down the wall.

"I'm glad you came," Block told him sincerely, finally reaching out and retrieving his hand, "though, I'm not sure exactly what to say."

Bridget offered a handshake next.

"Then let me say it," Bishop said. "I said I hoped we'd never meet again, because you wouldn't want to hear what I'd say. I'm sorry. I apologize for that. It was insidious." He let go of Bridget's hand. The awkward smile had migrated to Bishop's face. "When I wrote those words, I knew you'd probably never get over it. But I expect you understood. We were dying off, one by one, and I was angry."

Bridget had set down the hoe she had been wielding.

"Could we sit?" she asked, gesturing to a couple of benches between two fields.

They watched Bishop looking around as they went to the benches.

"Yes, it's quite a place," he said, in awe of the size of this main pod. Equally awesome, his eyes told them, was the height of the plants growing here now.

As they sat, Mai Ker saw the stranger from another plot where she was picking sweet corn. She started toward them, though it appeared she wasn't sure if she should approach or not. Halfway there, she recognized Bishop and jolted to a stop.

Block looked at Bridget, still uneasy, hoping she would take the lead. Bridget got the hint and tried to be diplomatic.

"So, I guess none of us ever expected this moment, did we? Look Paul, I can't imagine how painful that day was for you. For all of you. And I don't know if you can understand how hard it was for us," she said, feeling the tears and pathos of that dreadful day wanting to come back.

Mai Ker came up behind Block and stood, silent, listening.

"Oh, I kind of do," Bishop said. "Even then, I knew—though I didn't want to admit it. Believe me, I saw it in your eyes, what was going on in here." His pained expression changed to one aged by wisdom. "We were all trapped. Out there, in here."

Bridget began to reach for Bishop's hand again, but then abruptly stood and grabbed him up into a hug as if he were a long-lost brother. She held him tightly for several moments. Flabbergasted, Bishop put his arms around her and held her, too, though he looked very uncomfortable.

"Not sure I deserve this," he said awkwardly. "Please," he said, pushing Bridget off a ways, "I hate to see a grown man cry. Especially when it's me."

Bridget laughed, finally letting him go. She stepped back, trying to compose herself. The tears on Bishop's face were different this time. These were tears of happiness, relief, and forgiveness.

Block got up and put a hand on Bishop's shoulder. Their eyes met as friends.

"It took a lot of courage for you to come here, Paul."

"I had to. Unfinished business, I'd say. I'm glad Thomas found me." He looked at Mai Ker. "Just came to say I'm sorry," he said to her.

Mai Ker felt no need for words. She came around the bench and gave him a brief hug, then a small kiss on the cheek. She made a little bow to him, affirming, as Block had, his courage in coming.

"You were a soldier, weren't you?" Mai Ker asked.

"Yes."

"A warrior," Mai Ker added. "I could tell."

"And at times a coward," Bishop confessed.

"Do you know where your friends are," Bridget asked, "the ones who came here?"

"Don't worry, they're all fine. Well, most of them. A few went off somewhere, not long after we were raised. I gather from what Thomas said, we won't be seeing those four again." He looked thoughtful. "Just as well."

"I wondered where Thomas disappeared to," Block commented.

"Said he was running a few errands for the Lord," Bishop laughed. "I'm an errand," he laughed more heartily, which provoked smiles from the Solarians.

"You've got to come meet Jimmy and Pam and Willy," Bridget said.

She took Bishop's arm as if escorting him to a dance. He was more than willing to join them.

"I can't stay long. Have some other business, too, I'm afraid."

"You've got to stay at least overnight!" Block insisted. "Yeshua's with us. You can see him again."

"Here, too?" Bishop said in wonder. "Sure gets around." Bishop had already had a private meeting with the Lord not long after being resurrected.

"I expect he does," Bridget said.

AFTER TRACKING down the other elder Solarians, they gathered everyone in the Meeting Tent, where Yeshua had been hiding himself the past several hours, deep in prayer. He had actually left twice during those hours, although no one would have realized this, even if they had been with him in the tent.

As the others entered, Yeshua looked up and smiled.

"Glad you made it, Paul," Yeshua said.

"I know you," Herald said after Bishop was introduced. "At least, I feel I know you. Jimmy talked about you a lot."

Bridget eyed Jimmy keenly. "Thought we had agreed that subject was off-limits in school, Jimmy."

"Yeah, well, you know how inquisitive he is. He and I were talking," Jimmy said sheepishly, "and it wasn't in school, so, technically, I didn't break the rule. He kept asking what happened that day."

"Jimmy said you were probably the bravest man he ever met. Even though it was through a plastic wall," Herald told Bishop.

Bishop was embarrassed by this but gave Jimmy a grateful nod. The others could tell there was a flood of built-up emotion bubbling inside him.

"Man, I don't know how you did it out there. I can't tell you what a coward I felt like," Jimmy said.

"Maybe we were all cowards, Jimmy," Block said. "We had a chance to survive in here," Block said to Bishop, "we knew the danger in opening the pods. And we put ourselves ahead of you, and your friends." The shame on his face intensified. "And any chance you had."

"A tough choice," Bishop said. "But you know, the next day when we settled into a campground at a reservoir near here, I got to thinking. I was still fuming, but I realized I would have done exactly what you did, if I'd been in here."

Bishop's admission brought welcome relief to the elder Solarians. Pent-up emotions flowed from each of them in quiet sighs, except for Will Atchison, who was gone before the events took place.

"You wouldn't know me, Paul," Will drawled, "I died before you guys came along. But I heard about it, from the boss, here," he said, nodding toward Yeshua. "When I found out we were all coming back from the dead, I asked him if maybe he could arrange a little fix-up session for you all, like this."

Pam looked at Will.

"You set this up?" she said, completely amazed.

"Yes, ma'am, I did," Atchison said, pleased with himself for having thought of something so worthwhile. "Wasn't sure about my other friends," he told Bishop, "but I knew my buddy Clayton, here, would be pretty torn up over what he did. And yes—just for the record—if I hadn't croaked off before you arrived, I'd have done exactly like Clayton."

Bishop listened, then gave Atchison an appreciative smile.

"Thanks to the Lord," Bishop said, acknowledging Yeshua with a side-glance, "there was a longer-range plan. We were just all too preoccupied with ourselves to see it."

"I wonder how many people through history would say the same," Pam said.

Bishop glanced again at Yeshua, who was still sitting toward the back of the tent with his mind apparently somewhere else, although he was deeply interested in what was playing out.

"And," Bishop told them, "the other thing I realize now, if you *had* opened those doors," he looked around the tent, "these beautiful children of yours probably wouldn't be here."

"We didn't even know there would be children," Mai Ker said with brutal honesty. "We were only thinking of ourselves that day."

"Someone knew," Bishop said, looking toward Yeshua, whose eyes were closed. "Thank God."

SEVERAL OF the Solarians, followed by Braden, Nathaniel and Katherine, gave Bishop a grand tour of the complex. As he walked, Bishop realized how precisely the complex had been designed to support only the original team members. He saw now what a tragic mistake it would have been to try to house and feed the 200 some souls who had come here with him. Even if they might have prevented contamination from the OUTSIDE air using Pod 1 as an airlock, the complex could never have supported that many people and maintained the delicate air balance the Solarians had fought to reestablish.

Finally, intrigued during his tour, Bishop agreed to stay overnight, on the condition that they allowed him to take a hand with afternoon chores so he would not feel like a burden.

When evening arrived, with supper settling in their stomachs, Bishop shared a fuller account of the refugees and what had brought them to Solarium-3.

Still gathered around the large tables in the dining tent, the Solarians, their children and their remaining guests listened intently. Yeshua left to take a walk.

They found Bishop's story engrossing, in part because of the great distances the refugees had traveled when many of them were starving and sick.

Most of the group, including himself, Bishop told them, had come from the East Coast. But as they moved west, hoping the air might be better in the Midwestern states, the traveling enclave gradually grew. A few from Ohio and Indiana joined them.

As they travelled across central Illinois, others who had fled south from Chicago found them. The air had putrefied around Chicago and its suburbs more quickly because it was such poor quality to begin with, and the riots and killings spread rampantly. These Chicago refugees banded together with Bishop's clan, working west, searching without any real hope for somewhere they could hide and maybe find fresher air.

One of the newcomers from Chicago suggested a place in Missouri, off of the old I-44 interstate highway southwest of St. Louis. There, the man claimed, there were huge limestone caverns near the town of Sullivan that his family had visited once. Deep underground, he hoped, the air might still be breathable. Parts of the caves had been humanized, with concrete floors and electric lights, the fellow remembered, although they knew the power might go down at any time. It would make an ideal hiding place from all the crazed killers running loose.

That is where the refugee band headed.

When they arrived at the caverns a day and a half later, they found two problems. First, several hundred other people had the same idea and had beat them to the place. Second, there was no food to be found anywhere for miles. Every grocery and gas-stop for 50 miles around had already been looted.

Bishop and his group debated staying, but Paul knew that if they tried to squeeze in underground with those who were already in the caves, they might end up eating each other.

His growing band of refugees pressed on. They were now more than a hundred and seventy-five souls. One of the newest to join suggested the air might be better to the north since, despite the atmospheric changes, cold fronts moving down from the Arctic Circle might bring purer air.

They began to work their way north and west across Missouri, then followed the Missouri River north, knowing it originated somewhere up in western Montana. Surely, they hoped, the air in that part of the country might be a little better.

What changed the plan was a chance discovery.

After crossing the Missouri River by Nebraska City, several of their company ransacked an old diner near the river's edge, scrounging for food. In the greasy kitchen, a woman happened to notice an old newspaper clipping tacked on a bulletin board. The article, several months old, was about a man named John Haskins who, unbeknown to the refugees, was the second cousin of the diner's owner. The article described the company Haskins ran, a big corporation in Omaha that had built a magnificent, airtight research complex in southeast Colorado.

Bishop studied the scrap of smudged newspaper the woman brought back, along with no food. Despite an elaborate description of Solarium-3, the exact location of the place wasn't mentioned.

There was little debate this time. They pressed north to Omaha where Bishop managed to track down the headquarters of Life-Line/New World Exploration. Here they found John Haskins and four other employees barely hanging on to life.

After some threats to one of Haskins' assistants, Paul Bishop managed to learn the exact location of Solarium-3. Bishop and his people began the long trek west.

Across eastern Nebraska and north-central Kansas, they stole enough gas to keep their vehicles running, along with what bits of food they could scavenge or steal. The journey moved much slower than they had hoped because so many of them were already sick or dying from radiation poisoning. They buried several along the way.

Eventually, they made it across the barren reaches of southwestern Kansas to what was left of Dodge City. Here they found the leftovers of what could have been a shootout with Earp, Masterson and Holliday at the helm, but on a citywide scale. Bodies were everywhere. The stench was horrid.

The refugees didn't linger, even to steal more gas. What food they found was rotting, so they moved on. A few of the group were so sick they asked to be left alone to die. The cumulative effects of nuclear fallout they had encountered around St. Louis, Kansas City, and Omaha continued to plague them. More fallout had fouled the soil through eastern Colorado, carried on winds from some of the same blasts the Solarians had witnessed.

Nearly a month after they left Omaha, starving, living on watery soup and molding bread, they reached Las Animas and found their way along the river to Solarium-3.

"By the time we got here," Bishop told the Solarians, "we'd pretty much given up hope. Then we saw this place—and everyone's heart leapt. Finally, we thought, a chance." He looked at the floor of the tent. "I guess that's why I reacted the way I did that day."

"I wish there had been a way, Paul," Block told him. "But I was lucky. Didn't live long enough to really have to deal with it."

"I did," Jimmy said. "I lived with the guilt of that day for a long time. I think it was only after Herald and Sing were born that I reconciled myself to it. You're right, Paul. They likely wouldn't be here if we hadn't been so hard-hearted that day."

"They were hard days," Bishop said. "I sat out there at night, thinking. I would have killed to save my friends—and myself. In fact, if we'd gotten in, I can't swear there wouldn't have been some killing."

"When the food and air ran short," Bridget said, finishing Bishop's thought.

A somber Bishop looked around at their faces, especially the children's. "You did the right thing," he told them. "When I saw you bury one of your own a couple of days later—I guess that was you, Clayton—I realized, the end had come. We each had to face it in our own way."

Herald had listened to the whole account intently, as had Piper.

"We found you, you know," Herald said. "Well, I mean, what was left."

"No, I didn't know," Bishop said with curiosity.

"We had to go OUTSIDE, because of a leak. And we started exploring. We got as far as John Martin Reservoir."

"It was awfully sad," Piper said, squinting, remembering.

"Don't know how long they lasted," Bishop said. "I died two days after we got there."

"We said a prayer," Pam said. "It seemed pointless." She looked at Piper with a barely concealed smile. "Now I know it was the right thing."

The awful memories cleared like breaking clouds from Piper's mind. As she looked at Paul Bishop, she understood many things she had not, up until this moment.

"May we?" Yeshua's voice said from the dining tent door.

"Mind if I join you?" a second voice said.

The elder Solarians instantly recognized that voice.

Pam turned. Mai Ker jumped from her seat and stood, stammering.

"What? Well, I—!"

"Well, now, it's about time, young lady," a grinning Will Atchison said, rocking back on his chair.

In the tent door, holding Yeshua's hand tensely, stood Sarajane Haug. Very much alive, and looking very pleased to be there.

Yeshua's eyes sparkled.

Pam rushed to Sarajane and they embraced.

"We thought—" Pam searched helplessly for the right words. "We thought—!"

"What she means is," Atchison said as if addressing a naughty child, "we thought you weren't coming to the party."

Sarajane, dressed in a long, simple, lavender cotton gown that she would never before have been caught dead in, smiled beautifully. Her dark hair was richer, fuller, curling yet flowing, and her dark skin glistened. She looked willowy, not at all like her old figure. But it was, without doubt, the true Sarajane.

Matter-of-factly Sarajane said, "I didn't think I was coming here, either."

Still in the doorway, Yeshua embraced her. She wasn't sure how to respond. She still felt the appalling intensity of a conversation they had just three days earlier. Yet he was warm and welcoming now, as if he had completely forgotten.

"Thank you for being patient with me," she whispered.

"Thank you for being patient with me," Yeshua responded, as he let go of her.

"Your mother's death was not easy for you. I know it left a deep scar."

"Still no excuse for how I acted," Sarajane told him. "And how angry I got with you."

"Anger can grow a deep root," Yeshua said. "It has now been cut." He kissed her on her cheek. "You need some time with your friends," he said as he walked away.

Her other old friends gathered around, anxious to welcome her. Sarajane wept tears of joy. The children watched it all, trying to understand the relationships they had never witnessed and the many emotions billowing around them.

"I don't know you," Paul Bishop said, getting up and introducing himself. "I just came here to apologize."

"Guess I need to do some of that, too," Sarajane said. "Sorry, you guys. It wasn't you," she told her friends. "I do love you all, and I'm sorry I left like that, so abruptly. You never knew about my asthma—well, until it was too late, anyway."

"Oh, Sarajane! I'm just so glad you're here *now*," Pam said affectionately. She held Sarajane's hand, unable to let go.

"We had some long talks, Yeshua and I. But it was me. Issues about my mom dying. I felt responsible. Instead of looking for a cure, I should have been there holding her when she died."

Bridget touched her shoulder, then leaned her head against Sarajane's.

"I am so glad you're here!" Bridget said, tears of joy welling in her eyes.

"I spent all those years wrapped up in myself, and in my guilt. I know I pushed you all away. I won't anymore," Sarajane promised.

"The good news is," Will Atchison said with a depth of seriousness completely foreign to his character, "we have all the time in the world to get to know each other better." He hugged her and Pam and Bridget tightly. Then they passed Sarajane from Solarian to Solarian like a newborn, so that everyone, including the children, got a hug.

Throughout these happy moments, tears of joy poured from Sarajane, bathing her face in their love and friendship.

THE REST of the evening grew into another party, as it had to. With some of their visitors gone, Solarium-3 began to feel more like it had at first. In its first life, the Solarium had become a home for seven souls who for much of their own lives had felt like social driftwood. Now it was a true haven, a reminder that God's love could overreach even the most desperate loneliness, and could bond hearts and minds into a family whose origin was in the Father himself.

For Sarajane, meeting the Solarian children was a singular delight. Despite her obvious feelings of awkwardness around them, they adored her. It was exciting to meet a real doctor, even though her skills were no longer needed.

They danced and partied and carried on as if they were all children again. Herald and Sing cued up music from almost every period of history from the computer archives, which made for some interesting if not crazed dance combinations.

Yeshua, who reappeared in time for the celebration, produced a large bottle of what they assumed was wine. Everyone got a taste, including the kids.

"Finest 'wine' I ever tasted," Jimmy grinned toward Yeshua.

"Yes," Yeshua laughed as if joyously intoxicated, "my Father thinks so, too."

No one else understood.

"Should the kids be drinking this stuff?" Bridget asked.

"Oh, by all means," Yeshua laughed. "Give them more! New delights are abounding."

It had not a trace of alcohol. It was, in fact, a bottle of what Yeshua had told Jimmy about several days ago. Tonight, as Yeshua popped the cork, he had whispered to Jimmy, "This is the water I promised you."

Jimmy had laughed loudly and downed his first glass in three swallows, deliriously happy.

As the evening wore late, the kids and half the adults faded one by one off to their beds, visions of God and new life and glory filling their dreams.

Yeshua drew Clayton Block off by himself.

"I have something I'd like you to do, Clayton."

"Now? But I'm really enjoying myself!"

"Now. It's something you would be best for."

Block settled down, and listened carefully. Yeshua gave him some simple instructions and some not-so-simple directions.

"Be back by morning, Clayton, if you can."

Block nodded, went and found a jacket, and quietly left the Solarium. The few that were still dancing, including Paul Bishop, didn't notice him leave.

Yeshua rejoined the party, and did his best to dance with Sing, Herald, Katherine and Jacob in a great circle. They kept bouncing into each other. No one seemed to mind.

29

Tuesday Morning

It rained again overnight. As she had each morning, Piper ran to see the progress of her lake and was delighted to see it filling. A few more good rains and she would be able to dive from the shore without bashing her head.

Jimmy and Mai Ker went early to Pod 11 to feed the sheep. Yeshua, who was always up before the others, went with them and was talking with two rabbits in a hutch.

The animal herds and flocks were still small but Yeshua promised they would grow much larger. Many would be released OUTSIDE. Since they would no longer be a food source, they would be allowed to graze and roam freely.

"Won't that be a problem someday?" Mai Ker wondered. "Won't the herds get too large?"

"They know their proper limit," Yeshua said. "When they reach it, they'll stop reproducing. Built-in instructions."

"Like, in their DNA," Jimmy said.

"New DNA, Jimmy, just like all of you. Except, it's not actually DNA anymore." Yeshua tossed the comment off as insignificant as he left the pod, leaving Mai Ker and Jimmy hanging, staring at each other.

As Jimmy shook feed into the rabbit cages, a calico cat tried to poke its nose into the process. Jimmy firmly pushed it away.

"Not now, Hijinks. You'll get yours later."

"Can I help somehow?" a voice said from the podwalk.

As with Block and Bridget yesterday, Jimmy and Mai Ker were startled. The difference was, they *knew* this voice.

John Haskins stood in the doorway of the podwalk, a cordial smile on his face. He had walked up so quietly that neither had heard him. But Yeshua had long expected him.

Jimmy and Mai Ker knew he must have been resurrected like everyone else. But what in the world, they wondered, was he doing here?

"John," was all Jimmy could manage.

His face looked younger than what they remembered, and certainly less haggard than when they had last seen it on their video monitors in those final days. But it was, no doubt, John Haskins.

"Thought I should pay a visit. Been a long time," Haskins said apologetically. "Sorry I was a little slow getting here. Had some other stops Yeshua wanted me to make."

Bridget came boiling through the podwalk. She had seen Haskins crossing through pod 10.

"John," she said like an echo.

"Bridget," he said with a little nod of his head.

Bridget stopped a few feet away from him, unsure what to do next.

"How about we go over to the house and visit a while?" Haskins sounded hesitant, unsure how he was being received.

"Sure," Jimmy said. "Of course, old house or new?"

"The old one. I came in that way. It's more private."

"What about the others?" Mai Ker asked.

"Could we keep it small," Haskins asked, "for now?"

The three agreed. Quietly working their way along

the northerly edge of #10 to not attract attention, they made their way to the podwalk into #3. But as they passed by the door of the Research Center, they noticed Sarajane sitting at a computer console. She saw them, too.

"Well, look who's here," she said, coming to the door.

"Hello, Sarajane," Haskins said.

"I'm actually glad to see you," she said. "I need to apologize."

Haskins was now the startled one.

"*You?*" he said.

"Where are you four going?" Sarajane asked.

"To the house," Mai Ker said.

"May I join you?"

"Well, I suppose," Haskins said uncertainly.

"So," Sarajane said as they seated themselves on the front porch, "I do want to say I'm sorry, John."

"But—" Haskins began, obviously thrown off balance. "Sarajane, I don't understand. You were . . . well, you were already gone, when they found out."

"Yes. But I suspected. When you had Jimmy and me run those special tests, early on. Then my breathing started going haywire. I knew something had to be up. I also figured, whatever it was, you must have known."

"Pretty perceptive," Haskins said.

"That's why you hired me."

"Then, I don't understand. Why do you need to apologize to *me?*"

"Because, for one thing, I hid my asthma, on my medical records. But mainly because when things started going wrong—when I knew the air was bad—I used to sit here and curse you at night for ever hiring me."

Haskins looked stunned. He had come here to apologize to the team. And here was Sarajane, apologizing to him.

"Anyway, I knew it had to be really bad. Why else all the secret messages to Clayton? I got really angry, you keeping us in the dark all that time. I cursed your name so many times I lost count. Pam, God bless her, she tried so hard to save me. It was futile. I tried to just suck it up and pretend I was OK. I didn't want to upset everyone else, more than they already were." She took a deep breath. "That last day, I wanted to curse you again. I couldn't get the words out."

Bridget, Jimmy and Mai Ker sat listening, stunned. Sarajane had never let on that she knew she was dying.

"Didn't see any reason to freak you all out," Sarajane said. "That's why I kept lying to Pam."

"I wish we had known," Mai Ker said.

"Well, I lied in the interview, made sure you didn't know, John, not until after we were INSIDE. Even snuck my inhalers in. When I started getting worse, I let the OUTSIDE doctor know, but he promised to keep it quiet. I felt bad about all the lies. I felt I let you guys down. I was a doctor, life and death was my business. I just wasn't ready for my own."

There was quiet.

"That's just how we felt OUTSIDE," Haskins finally said, "that we let all of you down in here. But the struggles toward the end were ghastly. I meant what I said. I really did envy you. Cooped up, yes, but you had a chance. I debated for days about coming out here, joining you. I could've made it happen, of course. But I realized the risk of opening the pods. Might kill all of you. In the end, I couldn't do it."

The Solarians waited, knowing he wanted to say more.

"I'm sorry I lied, too. See, I knew before Seal-In. The military guys clued me in, but swore me to silence. Insisted that I not tell you. I guess they figured if you found out, you'd panic, and want out."

"Guess they were right about *that*," Jimmy said.

"So, I had to keep a lot from you, all those months. That was just wrong. I hope you'll forgive me."

"Forgiven, John," Bridget said earnestly. "And I apologize for what I said."

"What was that?"

"You don't remember?"

Haskins thought a moment. "No, guess not."

"Well," she said, "I remember it exactly, I'm sad to say. But I don't want to repeat it. Something about a forgiveness card at the end of eternity."

Haskins chuckled, "Well, yes, I do remember now. Actually, it was pretty clever, Bridget. As insults go." He reached over and took her hand. "Glad we didn't have to wait that long."

Bridget felt the mutual apology as their hands touched.

Jimmy's mind had run done a different track.

"You know, John, it was pretty miraculous, how you set this whole thing up. I mean, knowing the air problems before we came in—which, let's face it, you couldn't control—it went pretty well, if you think about it. Lots of mad scrambling, yeah. But we survived." He looked at Mai Ker and gave her a foolish grin. "Well, for a while, I did."

"What do you mean?" Haskins wondered.

"Never mind. You don't want to hear. Just another stupid move by J. Algood."

"You're right, it was miraculous, though I didn't see it at the time," Haskins said. "Here I thought I had the perfect plan, the perfect Solarium, the perfect project. Money pouring in from investors, even had my retirement all planned out. And all the time, a whole different plan was at work—that *none* of us knew." He chuckled. "Retirement. What a hoot! Hey, where's Clayton, by the way? I want to see him, too."

"He's . . . well, I'm not sure where he is," Bridget said. "He missed breakfast. Off on some project, I guess."

"I see he communicates about as well as ever," Haskins laughed.

"No," said Bridget smiling, "actually, much better."

"Could we take a walk around the complex some more?" Haskins asked. "Like to see what you've done with the place," he laughed.

"You gave us our first tour. Guess we can do this one," Sarajane said.

They started with the house.

"May look a little empty," Bridget warned Haskins. "We did some moving."

As they started in the kitchen door, Yeshua walked up to the bottom of the porch steps. He smiled at Haskins. He had spoken with Haskins by Pod 1 before anyone else had seen him.

"Sarajane. Could I see you over in the Research Center?"

She looked at Haskins, then nodded.

"Sure."

As the others began their tour, Sarajane walked with Yeshua to the next pod and into the research building. Even as strong as Sarajane was now feeling, she almost fainted. In the chair she had left not forty minutes ago sat her mother.

"I believe you know this young lady, Adanna," Yeshua said to the woman.

Sarajane, who had last seen her mother pale, thin, and in excruciating pain, saw before her a woman of beautiful dark skin, a radiant complexion, and joyful, smiling eyes. Tightly fibered Liberian-descent hair adorned her head like a crown. Her mouth was curling at the corners, trying to contain her emotions.

Sarajane ran and fell at her feet, hugging her knees.

"Mom!" she said, pleading for forgiveness.

"My beautiful child," her mother said, taking her daughter's face gently into her hands. "More beautiful than ever, it seems," she added, seeing the glow that enveloped Sarajane's countenance and radiated from her whole figure.

Sarajane turned her head toward Yeshua.

"How did—?"

"She came to me as she was dying, almost in her last breath. But mostly she was pleading with me for you."

Sarajane shook her head for wonder and buried her face again into the heavy-weave fabric of her mother's new skirt, weeping tears of joy.

Yeshua stepped quietly away and left the Research Center. He wandered to the aviary to see how the new bird population was coming.

NOW THAT the Solarium was to become a museum, Sing and Herald took it upon themselves to go and clean up the Visitors Center, which was still a mess since having been ransacked years before by Paul Bishop and his friends.

Herald stood pondering the smashed-in front of a display case that still held, under a thick layer of dust, richly colored souvenir books with pictures of the Solarium complex. The largest was titled, *INSIDE and OUT*.

"Wonder if any of that replacement glass in supply would fit this case?" Herald wondered aloud.

"Yes, I think there's some 6-foot glass sheets in that small shed, you know, in the very back of number thirteen?" Sing said.

Herald put his hand against the remaining corner of the broken panel of glass indicating where they would need to replace it. Herald knelt.

"We just need a large enough piece to fill from here to here—" His hand abruptly stopped. He stared, dumbfounded. As he moved his hand from the broken fragment in the upper corner toward the bottom, the broken edge of the glass seemed to move with his gesture. As his hand stopped, the glass pane had grown back into place, perfectly refitting the full front of the case.

Herald stood, speechless. He tapped the glass, which made a unique sound that said it wasn't glass, but some other substance, harder and clearer than crystal.

"What in the world—?"

"What?" Sing asked, her back toward him as she swept debris out of a corner.

"Look," Herald said, his voice echoing his disbelief. She did.

"What did—?" She frowned. "How did you do that?"

"I don't know! I just moved my hand across where we needed to replace the glass, and—well, there it is. Fixed!" He still could not believe his eyes. "Stranger and stranger."

Sing ignored him, assuming he was pulling her leg. She went back to sweeping. As she bent to sweep debris into a dustpan, the small gold ring she wore on her fourth finger scraped lightly against the hard tile flooring. She emptied the dustpan into a large waste can and walked to where Herald was still standing, the startled look still frozen to his face, gawking at the newly repaired display case.

"Where did you get that so quick?" Sing asked him.

He was shaking his head. "I'm telling you, I didn't go anywhere! I just—look—I just put my hand here," he indicated where his hand had started, "and moved it down this way, and the glass—or whatever it is—it just filled in beneath my hand."

Sing looked at him wondering why he would make up something this stupid.

"All by itself?" she asked.

"No, I just pull glass out of the air like this in my spare time," he said, exasperated.

"Herald, I like practical jokes, but this one's *really* dumb."

"Sing, I'm not joking! You saw me, I didn't go anywhere, didn't get anything, no glass, no tools. I'm telling you, this piece of—whatever—just fixed itself!"

She still didn't believe him.

"Show me," she said, pointing to a broken snack case several feet away.

Herald walked over, unsure if he even wanted to try to repeat this. He hesitated, then placed his hand against a broken piece of glass that still clung in its place at one side of the case's front framework. Slowly, doubting anything would happen, he moved his hand from the right to the left side of the area missing glass. As he did, the broken edge of glass seemed to follow his hand and filled itself in, perfectly. A crystal clear, full sheet of the new material now covered the front of the case.

Herald stopped, afraid to move his hand, afraid of what power it might now wield, and irrationally afraid the new pane might shatter if he removed his hand.

Now it was Sing who was dumbfounded.

"Impossible," she muttered, her head cocking sideways.

"I think that's a useless word now."

"Alright, I believe you. Unreal! Just don't do anything else like that, OK? Until we talk with Yeshua. He's got to explain."

"Something, maybe, about our new bodies?" Herald wondered.

"You are asking me?" she said with a look.

Herald stepped back a foot and motioned to the repaired snack case with a gesture that said, "Stay."

He went to work, instead, cleaning up a damaged pop machine. The paint on one side had been marred deeply with some blunt instrument when the refugees tried to break it open. While Herald took a rag to polish up the machine, Sing went back to sweeping, picking up in the corner where she had left off.

As she swept the broom over the spot where her ring had barely scraped, her eyes grew wide as if some hidden creature were emerging from the floor beneath her. With the first stroke of the broom, the tiny residue of gold that had come off her ring spread. She swept over the spot again, her eyes wider in awe. The gold widened like gold plating, except, as best Sing could tell, it looked like the whole surface she had just swept was turning to solid gold under her feet.

She jumped back as if standing on something sacred.

"Herald," she whispered hoarsely.

Herald didn't really hear her because, at the same moment, as he rubbed the polishing rag across the battered pop machine, the damaged paint instantly repaired itself, again following the motion of his hand.

"Herald?" Sing called again, a little louder. "Come here, please! Now!"

Herald pulled his eyes from the pop machine to turn and look at her. Her face was afire with astonishment.

"Look," she said, pointing, but not looking down. "I think I just did that."

Herald went to her, knelt, and rubbed his hand across the smooth, golden surface that was now about 5 feet across.

"Be careful!" Sing barked, "it might—stick or something!"

"How in the world—?" He looked up at her. "What did *you* do?"

"Swept?" she herself wondered.

Herald looked at the broom, then at the wedding ring on her finger, a spare ring that had been her mom's. He looked closely and saw a very slight abrasion mark on the side of the ring where she had accidently scraped the floor tile.

"Can't be," was all he could muster.

Before he could move, Sing decided to take another swipe at the floor with her broom. The area of gold grew, startling Herald who jumped to his feet.

"Stop, will you! Wait!"

"Yeah," Sing said, "wait till everybody sees this! Is this perfect, or what?" Sing laughed, dancing several steps across the golden floor. "Streets paved with gold," Sing remembered. "I thought they were kidding!"

Herald joined her laughter.

"Come on, we got to find someone and tell them."

Sing flung the broom aside, which skidded across the floor leaving a wide, golden swath behind. Herald grabbed her hand and was about to pull her toward the hallway when the front doors of the Center opened and Clayton Block walked in, in the company of a woman they had never seen.

"Hi Son, hi Sing," Block said. "Do you know where your mom's at, Herald?"

Herald's mind was off in the far reaches of the universe and he had to think for a second.

"Mom? Let me think. Last I saw, she was over in the rec. area in number five."

"Who is this?" Sing asked, stepping forward politely and offering the stranger her hand.

"I'm Erica," the woman said.

"It's kind of a surprise," Block said. "Come along if you want."

"Oh, well, we've got some surprises of our own," Herald laughed. "Come on, let's go!" He was bursting to tell someone of what had just happened, certain no one was going to believe it.

30

Tuesday Afternoon

Yeshua was still sitting on a bench by the aviary cage, singing to the birds. Two more nuthatches had appeared, one female, one male. Caroline would soon lay eggs. Her brother would also have offspring.

Yeshua watched them fly, and perch, and play among the branches high up in the open aviary cage. Birds would be birds, and bees, bees, until the populations of both had recovered around the world.

He leaned his head back against the pod wall behind the bench and rested his eyes. To appearances, resting, but at work elsewhere, as always.

He opened his eyes in time to see Block coming down the hall from the Visitors Center into Pod 1. The woman Yeshua expected walked alongside him, followed by Herald and Sing, hand-in-hand and looking very excited.

The woman with Block looked about 30, with sandy-brown hair that was done up in loose curls atop her head. She was much shorter than Block, about 5-foot-7, but had a familiar-looking figure. Her smile, in fact, was one that Clayton Block had recognized instantly when he first saw her.

The four of them came into the Solarium, through Pods 2 and 3. Through the clear walls, they spotted Yeshua on the bench in #6.

As they approached him, Yeshua was looking up at the 45-foot dead oak tree that was the centerpiece of the aviary cage. Cut down whole, stripped of its bark, and set here in concrete, the dead oak had provided perches for the many birds that had first inhabited the Solarium.

Though dead and rootless all these years, in the last two days the tall oak had come to life. Fragile new shoots were stretching out of the formerly dead branches, meaning that underground, new roots were pushing down into the soil beneath the concrete floor of the pod. Buds were appearing on the tips of every new shoot. Thin bark was beginning to form. In just over forty-eight hours, the oak had grown seven feet, as Pod 6 and the aviary cage also grew taller to accommodate their grand, wooden resident.

"I found her," Block said as they entered #6. "This is Erica."

"Yes, I know," Yeshua said. "Welcome, Erica. I hope your journey was not too long."

"Miles and miles," she said, "but somehow they flew by." She gave Yeshua a hug as if they were the best of friends.

"Yeah, it's really something, this new travel—the land kind of moves along with you," Block said. "I'm guessing we could reach nearly anywhere in just a few days."

Yeshua smiled at his exuberance.

"So, where is she?" Erica asked.

"I expect she'll be along shortly," Yeshua said vaguely, obviously in no hurry to go anywhere. "I so thoroughly enjoy these little creatures. Fascinating to watch, aren't they?" he asked, indicating the various birds flying about both inside and outside of the cage. "And the music of their voices. Delightful."

Different voices were heard as the group giving John Haskins his tour came through the podwalk from #4.

". . . and you remember the aviary, right?" Bridget asked Haskins, stepping into the pod across and behind the cage from Yeshua.

"I sure do," Haskins said, pointing to the iron-framed aviary cage. He looked inside it. "And that huge tree." He did a double take, seeing dozens of buds on the tree. "Odd. I thought it was *dead* when we brought it here," he said, his eyes expressing curiosity.

Block saw Haskins and couldn't decide if he should run to greet him, or hide.

"It was," Yeshua said of the great oak as the group with Haskins came around from the far side of the cage. "It too, is reborn." He looked at Block. "You never saw it before you arrived here, but it came from a spot very near where you used to live, Clayton."

Block looked doubtful.

"Clayton!" Haskins said, finally spotting him.

Block took courage and walked over, grasping Haskins' smaller hand in his.

"John, good to see you," he smiled. "Awkward, but hey, still good!"

He broke down and wrapped Haskins in a loose hug. With Block's new strength, Haskins felt like a stuffed toy in his arms.

"Thanks, Clayton, been looking for you since I got here."

"Been away." He stepped back. "I have to say, John, I'm surprised. Didn't think you'd be coming here."

"Actually, I asked. Yeshua wondered if it was too soon, you know? But frankly, I wanted to come. I didn't want a hundred years or so to run by without us catching up." He looked at the concrete floor for a moment, then back up. "And making amends."

"Well, I appreciate your honesty," Block said, "we do need to spend some time, don't we? I was mad as—" He caught himself. "I was really angry some days, but it was a blessing you brought me here. As terrible as it turned out."

Haskins gestured at Yeshua.

"I think *he* brought all of you here. And it was a lot

less terrible than OUTSIDE, if that's any consolation."

Block's expression agreed. He looked at Yeshua.

"So, what were you saying about the tree?" For the first time, he, too, noticed buds breaking out everywhere along its branches.

"That it grew up very near where you once lived. Do you remember, John, where it came from?"

"Not sure," Haskins said. "One of our planning team had it imported from another state."

"Do you remember which?" Yeshua asked.

"Seems it was Wisconsin, maybe."

"Exactly. It was cut from a forested area not far from your old apartment up in Plover, Clayton."

Block wondered if Yeshua was making a joke, but his face showed he wasn't.

"Really?" Block replied, intrigued.

"A fact, one of the millions of seeming coincidences you could never have seen in the old world. Just days before it was cut down, this tree cradled your little friend Caroline the night she was born, and her brother stillborn. A few days before you smacked her with your automobile."

Block stared at Yeshua, incredulity sweeping his face.

"Can't be," Block said, finding it hard to believe.

"But it is."

"Wow, some kind of coincidence, huh, Clayton?" Bridget said.

"As you grow," Yeshua said, "you'll learn there are very few true coincidences in the Father's plan.

As they looked at the tree, Caroline flew in through one of the podwalks, circled into the cage, and landed on a high branch next to her brother and his new mate.

All this time, Erica had been standing to one side, slightly behind Block. The group with Haskins finally noticed there was another stranger among them. Bridget's eyes locked on her, staring, then crinkled with a question.

"Have we met before?" Bridget asked.

"I'm Erica." The woman appeared to mean that this was self-explanatory.

Bridget frowned. "You look a little familiar. But, maybe not."

"Actually," the younger woman said, "Erica is the name my adoptive parents gave me."

Despite her renewed strength, Bridget felt a shudder of weakness in both her legs. She also felt that her heart, though nearly perfect now, might stop. She took hold of Jimmy's arm to steady herself. She looked sick, but Jimmy knew this was impossible.

"Oh, Lord," Bridget mumbled. Another prayer. She turned, shooting Yeshua a half-elated, half-terrified look.

Yeshua nodded.

"Your daughter, Bridget."

Bridget's pulse quickened. After a second of hesitation, she rushed to Erica, about to clasp her into a hug, but then held back.

Block studied Erica, standing face-to-face with her mother.

"The spitting image, I'd say," Block said.

"I knew you instantly," Erica said to her mother.

"How could you?" Bridget asked, astonished.

"Her daughter?" Mai Ker whispered to Jimmy, not following this.

"Wow," was all Jimmy could say. "This was worth waiting for," he smiled.

Bridget had broken into happy tears. Erica, momentarily taken back by the emotion overwhelming her mother, took her into her arms. For that instant, the daughter played mom.

"How did—? Where did you—?" Bridget tried to say to Block, realizing Clayton had brought Erica here, but words were not coming easily.

Block went over and steadied Bridget.

"He sent me, last night. Tell you about it later," he said.

"I think the two of you might enjoy some private time," Yeshua said, gesturing to the others that it was time to go.

"Would you—? Would you like to take a walk?" Bridget asked Erica, the first full sentence she had managed.

"OK."

Bridget broke the hug and offered Erica her hand.

"Can Clayton come along?" Erica asked.

Bridget thought only a half-second.

"I'd love that."

"I feel like he belongs," Erica explained.

"Yeah, he does." She offered Block her other hand.

The three walked into #10, then made their way slowly to Pod 12, to the old spot where Block and Bridget used to find rest and solace. They sat together near the water's edge. Block, whose feet had travelled some 900 miles round trip since last evening, took off his shoes and stretched out his long toes.

The walking proved easier than the talking. Bridget looked at Erica, then at Block.

"What did you two talk about on the way here?" she asked, trying to skate around the thinner ice.

"Lots," Erica teased. "Mostly you."

So went the ice.

"And what did Mr. Block, here, tell you about me?"

"Oh, quite a bit. Lots that I never imagined, even though I wondered about you all the time."

"You did?" Bridget asked, awash in a world of new emotions.

"Bridget," Block said lovingly, "come on, talk with your daughter."

It was the one thing Bridget had wanted more than anything else for as long as she could remember. Now, the moment had arrived, a complete, impossible surprise, and Bridget felt mute. She took a breath and tried.

"Well, the main thing is, I want you to know I loved you. Always. It wasn't that I didn't love you, sweetheart. That's not why I gave you up."

"I know," Erica said with grace. "My folks—my adopted parents—they explained all that. That my real mom was very young."

"It was very complicated. Your father, he had," Bridget searched for something not completely damning, "other commitments. That's all I'll say. I was young, and terrified. I never planned to get pregnant. When I found out, those next few days, I thought I'd lose my mind."

"Thought you only did that when you met me," Block grinned.

"Can you believe it? He died, but his humor hasn't changed a bit," Bridget told Erica with a laugh. She recomposed herself. "Anyway, I only had one close friend, a girl at school, the only one I could confide in. She convinced me I had to tell my parents. Then I was more terrified. But she walked home with me that day. She actually told them for me, while I hid in my bedroom."

"How old were you?"

"Fifteen. But, emotionally? A lot younger. Sure not ready to be a mom. Gosh, at 33, when Herald came, I wasn't really ready."

Erica nodded. She herself had married young and had a child when she was just 19 years old.

"Yeah, I know that feeling," Erica said.

Maybe, Bridget realized, they had a few things in common.

"Well, after my dad got over wanting to rip my head off," Bridget said, "he and my mom actually were pretty good. My boyfriend insisted I get an abortion.

No way. I knew what was in me."

"How can I say how *happy* I am about that!" Erica smiled.

Bridget smiled back. Erica had been an absolutely beautiful baby, and was now an equally beautiful woman.

"So I said, no, I was having my baby. I even thought, for a couple of months, I'd quit school and raise you. But I was pretty immature. So we decided— Mom and Dad and me—I'd have to give you up." She took a long breath and let it out with a longer sigh. "Hardest thing I ever did in my whole life," she said thoughtfully. "Worse than the labor pains."

Block, sitting alongside Bridget, took her hand. He saw the deep emotion in her eyes. Years of silent regret were giving way to relief and healing joy.

"I'm so glad I didn't listen to my stupid boyfriend."

"Mom. What you did was right. That's why Yeshua asked me to come, so you could hear me say that. You gave me a great life, letting me be adopted. I had a wonderful new mom and dad. They'd tried to have a baby, but couldn't. I became their princess," she smiled. She leaned over and hugged her mom. "You gave them the best gift anyone could give. You gave them a child to love, when they had lost hope."

Bridget bit her lips hard, swallowing an overwhelming mix of emotions she felt might choke her.

"Kinda like I felt, when you married me," Block said.

Bridget squeezed his hand and kissed him. Erica sighed, watching.

"My adoptive parents loved me deeply, Mom. They raised me right, gave me a great childhood, a great life." She looked tenderly at Bridget. "But I never forgot I had a real mom somewhere."

"How much did you know?" Bridget asked.

"I knew your first name. That's all they would tell me, said that was best. They were right. Otherwise, I'd have run off looking for you, and a life that wasn't really mine. And I would have missed the one I had."

Bridget's lips trembled again. She smiled at her lovely, grownup daughter.

"It took me a long time to go on," Bridget told her. "I was depressed for ten months. I swore I'd never be that careless again."

"Except when you accepted that little paper ring. Right about here, wasn't it?" Block laughed.

Erica got the joke as Bridget gave Block a look.

"Funny guy you married, Mom," Erica said.

"You definitely are your mother's daughter," Block laughed again.

"Then one day I was reading news on the internet," Erica told them. "I saw a story about the opening of this place, Solarium-3. And there was your picture. I felt I was looking in a mirror. The first name was right. And I just knew. I was so proud of you, that you were in this fantastic place!"

"Oh, I wish you had contacted me."

"I tried, but it was too late. You guys were locked in, already. I called the main office in Omaha. No contact, they said. Believe me, I tried. No dice."

All that was over and done, Bridget knew. The world was new, and her lost daughter was here beside her.

"See Mom, as I see it, Yeshua knew all along how this would work out. He had a perfect plan. You ended up here, where you were needed. You have a wonderful son with this radiantly handsome old man here," she smiled, "and another son with Jimmy, right? And I had a great life, and my own family. And now, after all the turns and changes, here we are, together." It was like the last verse of a love song.

"Yeah," Bridget said, stitching things together in her mind like a patchwork quilt.

"What might have been, what couldn't be, and what was have finally come together. What could possibly be better than this moment?" Erica asked.

She took her mom in her arms and they embraced again, feeling the closeness they had known at Erica's birth.

THE SOLARIAN children, along with Eira, were having trouble keeping track of the new faces that kept showing up. But by the time Erica turned up, it was beginning to feel normal to discover new relatives or other connections with people they had never seen. Herald and Braden, in particular, were thrilled to meet the sister they never knew existed.

As Bridget was introducing Erica to the children, she came to Eira.

"Eira, this is my daughter Erica, who . . ." Bridget stopped, with the sudden realization. "Isn't that odd?" she said to the Erica, and then to little Eira, who had acted as if she were Bridget's daughter almost from the moment she arrived.

"What?" Erica asked.

"That your names are so much alike." Bridget looked at Yeshua. "Alright, so is this one of your 'coincidences'?"

"Not a coincidence, Bridget. A plan."

The other newcomers intrigued the children, too. They all loved Adanna, Sarajane's mother, who seemed to want to mother every one of them. Sarajane herself was a stranger and she seemed altogether different from the few stories the children had heard about her when studying the history of Solarium-3.

Paul Bishop was pleasant enough, but kept his distance. He knew he was an outsider and didn't feel like imposing himself into what seemed like a close-knit, extended family reunion.

John Haskins, however, mixed right in and impressed the kids thoroughly. He was like a walking encyclopedia of everything to do with Solarium-3, not to mention -1 and -2. His many stories entertained them for three hours and could have gone on for days.

"THIS HAS been quite a day," Block told Yeshua as they finished chores late that afternoon and washed mud from their hands at one of the washtubs in #10.

"Yes. The beginning of many."

"What do you mean? Who else is there?"

"Several billion," was the answer.

Block stared.

"I don't really want to meet your whole kingdom, Lord. Just those I knew."

"Beyond those who lived at the end, Clayton, there were centuries of others before, remember. Nations, histories, a whole line of Solarium-like civilizations, just larger. And they all have a story. In time, you'll find you'll want to hear them all."

He dried his hands and rolled down his sleeves as Block kept scrubbing.

"But think of the time involved."

"What I think is that you haven't quite captured the idea of eternity yet, Clayton."

"Well, no. Probably not. It's just beyond me."

"That's why you must live it. It grows on you. Eternity is not empty. It's filled with new relationships, new history, innumerable dreams turning into true realities."

"Yeah, I guess," Block said, shaking water from his hands.

"You're always hungry, Clayton. Where is your hunger for others?"

He had not thought of it like this.

"I was always kind of a loner."

"In my own way, so was I," Yeshua said.

"You had to be."

"Except I was never actually alone." He handed the towel to Block. "Billions of souls, Clayton, each one with a story, a life. Didn't you ever wonder, walking around a large city, 'What do all these people actually do?'"

"Yeah. Didn't know the answer, though, so I stopped wondering."

"Now you'll know."

Washed up, they joined the others in the dining tent.

"You'll never believe what happened to Sing and Herald, Lord!" Braden said exuberantly. "Tell them!"

Herald and Sing fairly fell over each other's words trying to describe what had occurred in the Visitors Center earlier. Yeshua listened, nodding. Block had trouble understanding exactly what his son had done with the glass.

"Just—like that?" Block asked Herald.

"Just like *that*," Herald said, slowly moving his hand through the air.

"What kind of a world have we stumbled into?" Pam asked herself aloud.

"I don't think you stumbled, Pam," Yeshua laughed.

"Can we have another party tonight?" Eira asked excitedly. All the new faces seemed to warrant another celebration.

"I already have something planned," Yeshua said. "But it's tomorrow."

"Ohh," Nathaniel whined.

"I will be *so* glad when he is done growing," Mai Ker whispered to Jimmy. "Such a handful."

"Yeah, hah!" Jimmy teased. "I remember you dangling at the end of a rope, once. You can be quite a handful, too!" he said loud enough for everyone in the tent to hear.

Mai Ker playfully jabbed him in the ribs, which he

barely felt.

Pam, Katherine and Jacob had made a large supper. A third small table had been wedged in at one side of the dining tent. The "meat" was fresh from the new crops, several of which had fully matured by this morning. Pam was cheery as she set two large platters on the main table.

"Roast Chicken, roast pork. No muss, no fuss. Thank you, Lord."

"You're welcome."

"And," Katherine said, coming to the table with a very large pitcher, "we have more of that special drink for everyone tonight." She gave Yeshua a wink.

Jacob and Pam had taste-tested a chilled pitcher of the new water while getting supper ready. Several glasses had made them feel so youthful that they felt they could go OUTSIDE and run a couple of laps around the Solarium.

"Um," Yeshua said, taking his cup. "The water of life!"

31

Wednesday Morning

Braden was a little slow to catch on. He took a big swig of the new water from the bathroom sink after brushing his teeth. Teeth no longer needed brushing, but it was habit.

"Why does the water taste funny now, Mom?" he asked Bridget as she brushed her hair.

"Funny?"

"Yeah. Tastes *thick*."

Bridget filled her cup and drank, smiling.

"Yeah, it is great," she smiled at her younger son. "You'll get used to it."

They heard Piper calling for Pam as she came running with fresh excitement from a short walk OUTSIDE.

"Mom!" Piper hollered loud enough to wake the few who were still sleeping.

She had not gone to the lake this time but to a flat, rocky overlook near the southerly edge of their new mountain. Since she would be staying here with her mother for now, she was getting more curious about their new surroundings.

"Mom, the trees, you've got to come see!"

"Trees?"

"OUTSIDE! Come on!"

"I have some sewing, sweetie. Can we go later?"

"Mommm . . . !" Piper whined in an uncharacteristic way. "Come on, you won't believe this!"

Piper's insistence convinced Pam that she did need

to see whatever it was. She followed her daughter out through the entirely golden-floored Visitors Center to a spot where the upper plateau of their new mountain overlooked the river. Where before there had been a gentle river valley, there was now a spectacular gorge. It had deepened even further since Yeshua first made it.

"Look!" Piper said, directing her mother's attention.

Pam looked cautiously over the edge. One thing her new flesh had not yet completely overcome was a persistent fear of heights.

Not 50 feet below them, the tops of a whole grove of new trees spread broadly. But these were not trees of the old world.

Atop what otherwise looked like a typical elm or maple, the branches fanned out in an astonishing form. The top of each tree resembled a wide hand, held open as though offering something up to the sky.

As Pam watched, the tree tops slowly closed, as if taking something in hand, then just as gracefully reopened, slowly and purposefully, stretching their uppermost branches like fingers stroking upward across the cloud-strewn sky. Pam imagined the hand of a harpist strumming a sacred chord.

The real beauty was that Pam could almost hear the music, although there was no sound, only the solid-feeling wind cascading over the mountain's edge and down through the grove of trees.

"It's like God's watering them with the wind," Piper said with a radiant smile.

"Yes, it's sure beautiful."

"But I wonder if it's really the wind," Piper said. "The trees seem to move on their own."

Pam watched and agreed. They watched for another ten minutes. The motion of the trees was entrancing. More than a hundred trees filled the grove, which had not been there three days ago. The top branches had reached 60 to 70 feet in height. The strange, branching crowns had formed only last night, beginning their orchestral-like movements this morning as the sun rose.

Further down, along the now more rugged riverbank, some of the old trees that had once lined the river had regrown as well. They were ordinary looking, elms and maples scattered among some scrub oak.

Pam wondered if Yeshua himself had planted the new grove as a kind of signpost, a welcoming banner for the Solarium, the one place on Earth that had preserved life in its womb.

Block had been out running this morning, enjoying the delightful morning sun and crisp air, and jogged up behind Piper and Pam as they watched the unusual trees.

"Just ran the plateau, then down and back up," he said. He had barely broken a sweat. His legs, with bones and musculature vastly improved over the old Clayton, felt just warmed up. He experienced none of the cramping he would have suffered in his old body after an hour's run. "Great views up here, huh?" he smiled, turning in several directions. "It's a nice jog down that path there to the river, and great exercise coming back up!"

"I probably couldn't make it," Pam said.

"Oh, you'd make it, all right. And you'd feel great! Pretty amazing, these new bodies." He looked at Piper. "So, this mountain was your idea?"

"No, the lake. Braden asked for the mountain."

Block smiled, "So, Bridget had another bright son!"

BLOCK'S ASSESSMENT of his new body was only one tiny element of the fantastic realities breaking out day by day around them. Many, like him, had expected some kind of existence after death. Few ever imagined a world so real as this, more real than anything before. Most had imagined only a vague, disembodied afterlife, floating in some nebulous heavenly "country" that was no country at all. That was how Block remembered death, but death was now merely a faded shadow that had disappeared under the brilliant sunlight of this new world.

For Block and the other Solarians, the realization that the Father had planned all this from the beginning was just starting to sink in. Amusingly, it was Mai Ker who was most enthusiastic about the nature and physics of the recreated world, a nature cleansed of all evil and rebellion against its creator. Raised in her traditional Eastern culture, she had expected death and then an endless cycle of reincarnations, dying and being born over and over, unless one could find some door of escape from existence itself. For her, the magnificence of this resurrection world, without having to die even once to enter it, was an unimaginable gift.

She began each day thanking the God she had struggled so hard to believe in. She thanked him for his love, for giving her Jimmy and their beautiful children, but mostly for his great patience with her. She still remembered how bitterly she had cried out against God when Jimmy died so suddenly. But Yeshua had now cleansed that memory, too, and all bitterness was gone.

WILL ATCHISON finally managed a private conversation with the Lord, which, in these days, was next to impossible.

". . . and you can always come back to visit," Yeshua said. He had told Atchison that he was sending him to see his parents, both of whom died in the cataclysm while Will was locked in the Solarium.

"Kinda feels like being put in the brig, again," Willy said, "but in reverse."

"It would be good for you to see them, Will. You had so little time with them in those last years."

"Thought that was your doing."

"With your help. I orchestrated circumstances. You made the decision to come here."

"Think my old mom and dad are that anxious to see the kid, huh?"

"They're not old anymore. But you'll recognize them."

Willy, however, pleaded.

"See, Pam and I didn't get much time together, either, did we?" He gave a little wink. "You know—of course, you know—I was pretty keen on her there toward the end. If I just hadn't buzzed off like I did, bet we might have been married."

He gave Yeshua an imploring look. Before he died, his affection for Pam had never gotten far beyond the puppy love stage. Meeting her again had rekindled his affection, although it burned on a much deeper level. He kept pressing, trying to persuade Yeshua to let him stay.

Yeshua listened patiently, barely able to conceal a smile at Will's persistence.

"You might have been an attorney, Will," Yeshua said, cracking a grin.

"Nah, I'd'a smacked 'em all first day in the courtroom," Will said, grin-less.

Yeshua laughed and relented.

"Alright. I know your heart, Will, and I know Pam will be happy if you stay a while. You'll have plenty of opportunities to spend time with your folks. Or, of course, they could come and visit here."

"Now *that* I bet'cha they'd love!" Will said. "Thanks," he said, embracing Yeshua.

Will ran to find Pam.

IT WAS decided. Everyone but Pam, Piper, Willy, Jacob, and Katherine would soon leave Solarium-3.

Mai Ker, Jimmy and Nathaniel, were going first to what had been California to be reunited with several members of Mai Ker's family, those who had come to know the Father and had bowed to the sovereignty of his Son. She learned, though, that her father would not be there to greet her.

Even before Yeshua told her, she had known this in her heart. Her father had always clung to the old animistic beliefs and many times, when Mai Ker was little, had openly scorned the name of Christ.

Eventually, the three would move on to see Jimmy's family. Though no longer husband and wife, they were still bonded spiritually and would spend much of their new life together, Yeshua promised. They would also spend long periods of time apart, though, in order to build new friendships.

"You have eternity, after all," Yeshua said. "You may not believe this yet, but even apart, your love will only deepen. Love which has lost all possessiveness is the truest."

"Your love is the truest," Mai Ker said earnestly.

"But yours was unique, Mai Ker, you and Jimmy. A special love that few couples ever discovered. The tragedies you two lived through tightened the bond. And you both have very caring hearts."

"His heart didn't seem so caring that one day," Mai Ker said, looking at Jimmy.

"When Paul Bishop and his friends showed up?" Yeshua shook his head. "That's where you're wrong, Mai. It was the tenderness of Jimmy's heart that cut him so deeply that day. He and Clayton stood firm, yes, but it was killing them. It was Jimmy's love for *you* that kept him from opening those doors."

Jimmy just listened, nodding. Mai Ker studied his so-familiar face, wondering what mysteries still lay behind it, waiting to be discovered.

CLAYTON BLOCK, along with Bridget and Braden, were getting ready to travel to his birthplace in a restored community near Denver, Colorado. Eira, an orphan in her old life, would go with them. Erica, too, planned to travel with them as far as Denver. In time, she would return to her adoptive family to meet great-grandparents she had never known.

Only a few of Block's family, Yeshua warned him, would be there when they arrived. Like Mai Ker, he would not see his father again. His mother, who had died alone during the cataclysm but had been a follower of Yeshua for many years, was waiting, anxious to see her son again.

He would also be reunited with his younger sister, Barbara, who had died a few years before he came to Solarium-3. That reunion Block waited for with great expectation. He and Barbara had never been close in childhood. She had waded into alcohol and drugs at an early age and had become distant from the family. But she had been healed in the resurrection, Yeshua said, and they now had a chance to restore their relationship.

Block swept through countless memories of his past, then hit a sidetrack.

"What about—?" he began, but before he could finish the thought, Yeshua nodded.

"Michele? Yes, you'll see your first wife again. And she has someone she'd like to introduce you to, Clayton."

Block looked at Yeshua curiously, then it hit him.

"Really?" he asked with a broad smile.

"Yes. The son you lost in childbirth, when Michele died. You'll be able to watch him as he grows up."

Block felt like he was in a time warp, but he realized time might feel like this from now on. In a gesture completely out of character for the old Clayton, Block grabbed Yeshua in a hug of friendship. He felt he was embracing the brother he had never had.

"You have a very deep hat with a whole lot of rabbits!" Block laughed, releasing his hug but holding on to the arms of the Lord, beaming at him.

"No magic. Just the threads of life coming back together," Yeshua said.

EVEN THOUGH weeds no longer existed, Baby Kai was growing like one. She was already walking, a toddler walk, and Sing was thrilled. She and Herald would not have to carry Kai all the time on the journey they were about to begin.

They were heading into the mountains west of Colorado Springs. Herald's afternoon on Pikes Peak had made such an impression that he decided it would be fun to do some real mountaineering.

Though still nervous about traveling so far from her home, Sing had developed an intense interest in everything to do with the OUTSIDE, what had been a foreign land to her all these years. Their trip west into the mountain ranges would be the greatest adventure of her life. Helping Kai up mountain roads and trails, she realized, would require special patience, but Sing found her patience was growing as fast as her daughter's attempts to walk.

The mountain ranges, Yeshua said, were still changing and shifting, becoming not only more beautiful but more easily navigable. He suggested the three of them settle for a while with some new friends they would find in a high plateau region that had been called South Park. A large enclave of regenerated mankind was growing there, many returning from death as they had died, young people who were still maturing. Herald and Sing would feel at home there, as would Kai.

"The cloud of the Father's presence that you saw on Pikes Peak," Yeshua said, "will often appear in the South Park valley. It will become a place of worship."

"Wait till you see this," he told Sing. "I can't even describe it. It's really spectacular."

"And there's plenty of room to spread out up there," Yeshua told them. "I have to warn you, though, most of the new immigrants will be living in tents for a good long while."

"Guess we're used to that!" Sing laughed.

"The temperatures have moderated," Yeshua added. "You won't be uncomfortable, even at night. It's very pleasant and beautiful."

"You talk like you've been there," Herald said with a questioning look.

Yeshua's eyes sparkled.

When Herald first heard of South Park, he assumed it must be a gigantic place with slides and swing-sets. When he looked up old satellite images, he discovered it was a very different kind of park, a glorious, high-mountain valley butting up against several magnificent peaks to the west.

"There, one day, Kai will find a perfect place to offer continual praises, and many others will join her," Yeshua said, although neither Herald nor Sing were entirely sure what he meant.

SARAJANE AND her mother, Adanna, decided to head for Minnesota. Adanna had been raised in the south suburbs of Minneapolis before moving with her young husband to Rochester to work in maintenance in a hospital there. Sarajane was born there but remembered little of it since the family moved again when she was four to Santa Fe, New Mexico.

Now Sarajane would see her hometown again, or what remained of it. She was a nostalgic person at heart and, before winding along the paths of her new life, she wanted to retrace some of the steps of her first life, simply to remember, to see where she had been and how she had grown up. Her mother was more than happy to make this journey. She, like Sarajane, was fond of remembering the old times.

"Lord, the world is so much more amazing than I ever guessed," Sarajane said while she and her mom rooted around, finding Sarajane's belongings that were stored away in the old Victorian house after her death. "So much more to the world than I ever knew," she added. "In medicine, I thought we had it pretty much all figured out. But there's so much still to learn."

"And no end of time to learn it," Yeshua smiled, leaning against the windowsill in the room Sarajane had once shared with Pam.

Sarajane was especially intent on finding the family photo album, which, miraculously, Yeshua had preserved intact when the old world had dissolved into the new.

"There it is!" she exclaimed, pulling the album from a box in the top of her old closet.

"Thank you for answering that prayer," Adanna said, watching as her daughter quickly thumbed through pages of the scrapbook.

"About Sarajane?" he asked.

"Yes."

Sarajane looked up.

"What did you pray for, Mom?"

"That you would be safe, after I died. And not too crushed."

"I was pretty sad. I did feel crushed."

"Crushed down," Yeshua said, "but not forsaken. You had an important role, Sarajane. You needed to come here."

"Don't see that I really did much," she said honestly.

"You don't know?" he asked.

"What?"

"Your determination, there in the infirmary, just before you died—that's what inspired Pam. She was breaking down, and panicking. You turned that around. One night in her prayers, I put a picture into her heart— a picture of you on that infirmary bed. And your wanting to get up and help. Your sheer determination helped Pam go on. And so Piper was born. And so Sing was healed. And . . ." He stopped. "I'm rambling. You get the point."

"So, I helped save Sing, because of Piper—neither of whom was even born yet." Sarajane reflected on this. "But you know, on that infirmary bed, I just felt like a useless sacrifice to this place, to modern technology."

"Some sacrifices speak powerfully, Sarajane."

She understood, and was grateful to finally be able to call him Lord.

"WE'RE GOING soon," Braden hollered across the main pod to Yeshua as he returned from his visit with Sarajane and Adanna.

"Is that so?" he called to Braden.

Braden ran to him on feet swifter than ever, no evidence that he had ever had a broken leg, let alone just a few days ago.

"Yes! Mom says we're going up to a place that was called Denver. To see Clayton's family."

"And that's alright with you?"

"Oh, I'll love it! Clayton is so great. He said he'll show me around where he used to play as a kid."

"He'll find it changed."

"That's what's exciting! We're gonna try to find some of his old hangouts."

Yeshua smiled at Braden's new joy and excitement for life.

"Keep this joy, Braden," he told him. "You were made for this."

"The world is so big, isn't it?"

"And getting bigger."

"I can't believe you just yanked this whole mountain up out of the ground. *Kaablam!* That was so awesome!"

"Not hard to change what your hand made in the first place," Yeshua said.

He corralled an exuberant Braden in one arm and they walked to the tents.

WHILE THE others were laying plans and packing for travel, Yeshua worked much of the day planning the special banquet, a going-away party for most of the Solarians.

Several last packages of frozen meats were brought from the freezers in Pod 13 to be used up. New meats from the fields were harvested during the afternoon with Jacob and Katherine's help. Vegetables, corn on the cob, potatoes of several varieties, gigantic fruits from their orchards, were being prepared under Pam's watchful eye.

"We want it to be just right," she said to Yeshua as if telling him something.

Four large pitchers of the new water were being chilled in the refrigerator, along with two bottles of new wine that were made last night by Yeshua's own hand.

Pam, with Piper close by, helped him with the preparations. John Haskins and Paul Bishop were invited to stay for supper, since both would be leaving in the morning. Yeshua told them he considered them part of the Solarian "family."

"Adoptees, maybe," Haskins had smiled.

"It's an awfully gracious invitation," Paul Bishop said to Pam, as he hung around the kitchen, finding small bits of freshly cut vegetables to snack on.

"He wants you here."

"Feels awkward, but I wouldn't miss it," Bishop replied.

John Haskins felt awkward about staying overnight, but having made his peace with each of his Solarium team, he felt a little more at ease. Always the practical one, two celebrations in two days seemed a lot. But he had not yet fully learned the ways of Yeshua the Anointed.

32

Wednesday Afternoon

The children, including Herald and Sing, would have helped prepare the feast, but realizing they might not see each other for a long time, they tried to spend as many of these last hours together as possible. This was the only home they knew. A new world awaited them, and many new experiences. They realized they would not be the same the next time they returned.

The youngsters spent the early afternoon playing cards and computer games, then launched a major hide-and-go-seek marathon throughout the fourteen pods.

Around 3:00 p.m., they began to slow down. Eira had just been found hiding, the last and the winner, in a small, empty seed barrel in Pod 13.

The most natural thing to do, the Solarian children decided, was to have a final swim party. They hurriedly changed into whatever swimwear they had. As ever, nothing fit well, but they were no longer in the least self-conscious. They had to improvise a suit for Eira, one worn by Sing when she was younger.

They headed for the ocean, coaxing Mai Ker and Jimmy along as chaperones. This was the first time they had gone swimming since Yeshua transformed the Earth's water.

As the bunch arrived at their favorite swimming spot, Piper concealed a smile. She knew what was coming. She had told the other kids about falling in the lake; she just hadn't mentioned how the water had saved her.

Nathaniel climbed the tallest rock and leapt. He was trying for a cannonball dive, but instead of creating a huge splash, he went only about 6 inches into the water, bounced like a rubber ball off of concrete, and landed several yards away, flat on his back but unsinkable.

The laughter was riotous. The other children started jumping in. They tried to dive under, with no success, bobbing like little rubber rafts.

Nathaniel floated on his back for a few seconds, then rolled himself over and swam further out, floating almost perfectly on the surface. Braden caught him, pounced on his back and made Nathaniel his seahorse, paddling large circles around the other kids. Braden tried making the horn sound of a big ship, but never having heard a real ship's horn, it sounded pretty weak.

Yeshua followed along to join them. Piper, dripping wet, snuck up to him as he was taking his shirt off.

"You did this to the water, didn't you?"

He nodded, the corners of his eyes crinkling.

"What do you think?" he asked.

"I think it's a riot! Everyone loves it."

Sing was laughing, splashing but floating. Herald joined her in the water. He found that he could stand in deeper water as long as he kept his footing. The moment he brought his feet up, his whole body began to float.

"Too funny!" Piper said to Yeshua. "I'm going back in. Come on!"

". . . well, go ahead, try it," Herald was saying to Sing.

Sing looked dubious. Herald pulled off his T-shirt and handed it to her.

"Here. Use it like a raft, if you want. She won't sink, I promise!"

Sing helped Kai toddle to the water, spread the T-shirt in the shallows, and got Kai to lay down on it. She floated perfectly. Sing walked out deeper, guiding

Kai's T-shirt raft. As long as her feet remained on the sand under the surface, she was able to cut the water.

Finally, always ready to experiment, Herald pulled the shirt from underneath Kai. She kept floating like a baby-shaped air mattress. Herald laughed, kissed her on the head, and swam away.

Sing tickled Kai and she cooed. A burp came up and a baby smile curled across her little face. Kai rolled, babbling playfully and stroking her arms, as if she had been swimming for years. She circled her mother. In between several happy babbles, she clearly said, "Father," smiling broadly.

Sing stopped. Yes, her baby was growing too fast, and already walking. But talking? Kai was not quite two months old.

"Herald," she called, "your little girl is calling you!"

"Her other Father," Yeshua said from the beach, where he had stripped down to a pair of baggy shorts.

"What?" Sing called back.

"She was thanking the Father, for protecting her."

"Unreal," was all Sing said, though this was about as real as things get.

As Yeshua strode toward the water, everyone watched him. Against the dark-blue shorts, his skin seemed alive with an even purer light than normally shone through his complexion. Then, astounding everyone, as he slipped into the water, his skin became even more radiant, the color of blue-gold fire at the base of a flame.

He had no trouble diving deeply under the surface. He disappeared from view for several moments during which everyone held their breath, although they knew he could not drown. He emerged a hundred feet out and swam back toward them at a pace that made the rest of them look like absolute weaklings.

Then they witnessed the most amazing thing yet.

As his hands and arms broke from the water

approaching the shore, the scars on his hands looked as if they were on fire. Heat, or light, or both, blazed from them so brightly that it seemed the scars would burn away in an instant. Normally just barely visible, the scars looked like lightning flashing in the water, as if the water had connected them to some unbearable electrical charge. The small, irregular marks in his skin, though perfectly healed over, gave the impression that they went much deeper into his flesh.

"Oh, my gosh," Mai Ker said from the shore where she sat by Jimmy, "look."

For less than five seconds, as Yeshua raised his arms, reaching out of the ocean, the broken streams of water running back off his hands turned the color of blood, flowing from the wounds that were no longer wounds.

As he stepped onto the shore, the brilliantly burning scars, including those on his feet that had been hidden underwater, began to fade to a yellowish-green.

Everyone watched, speechless and in awe. As he toweled off and sat on the sand, the jagged scars returned to their normal appearance, as if someone had slowly turned down a light inside him. Yeshua himself paid it no attention, as if this happened every time he bathed. In fact, it did.

Braden ran to him from the water.

"How'd you do that?" he asked in complete wonder.

"What"

"Turned colors like that!"

"It just happens," was Yeshua's unruffled reply.

"So, the water, this is why our worms wouldn't sink that day," Braden guessed.

"The day you went fishing, when I was away?"

"Yeah."

"Yes. There's more to this new world than meets the eye, Braden. You'll find the water protects life, even the fish."

"But not the worms?" Braden asked, confused.

"Well, the fish do have to eat."

"Fantastic!" said Braden as he crashed back into the water.

Sing laid Kai on a towel on the sand, where the baby continued to chatter baby talk mixed with a few grown-up words. She then went and knelt by Yeshua, trying to look nonchalant.

"So, my little girl can already talk," she said, stating the obvious.

"All have language, even infants. And we all share one language, now," Yeshua said, looking off into the distance, far beyond the far wall of the pod.

Trying not to be obvious, Sing watched the circular marks on his hands finish drying. She vaguely remembered Jimmy telling her and the other children about how Yeshua died, but her memories of it mysteriously seemed to have gone.

"Is that how it happened?" she asked him, "there?" she added, gesturing at the marks.

"Yes. Very large nails."

"That must have been really awful." She felt she might cry, but couldn't.

"Worse than awful. It's amazing how inventive men became with their brutality."

"Why?" she asked simply, almost choking on the word. "Why did you allow it?"

"It had to be done. Sin had enslaved everyone, all of humankind. A slave can't free slaves. Only the freeman."

Sing nodded, sensing the love Yeshua held for her and her family.

"You know—well, of course you know—Herald and I really love each other, a lot. But I never felt before what I feel from you."

"Love is my very nature, Sing," Yeshua said. "It's why I made you. It underpins the entire created order."

"But, I thought Daddy said the Father made us."

"The Father and I are one. In me, you see him who cannot be seen."

Sing drew a long breath. She exhaled slowly, wondering, and wishing.

"Could we just sit here forever?" she pleaded softly.

"We could," Yeshua smiled. "But we won't."

Sing watched as Herald came up out of the water. Once her husband, he was far more, now, more a part of her than ever. She looked at her mother and father sitting nearby, probably in a spot they had sat many times, looking at each other as she was now looking at Herald, and Yeshua. Life was finally starting to make some sense, despite all her complaints.

She leaned over and hugged Yeshua tightly around his shoulders. He laid his head against hers.

"It was well worth it, Sing," he said, knowing her thought.

She needed no explanation.

An overwhelming sensation came over her, not a feeling or anything that could be called an emotion. It was as though life itself suddenly swallowed her whole, the most powerful moment of her existence. She knew that it was because she was so close to this perfect man.

Forcing herself up, she went back to Herald, who was lounging by Kai on the sand. Sing put her arms around them both. So strong, now, she felt she might crush them. She released her grasp, and tenderly kissed each of them. Their new bodies touching felt as one.

"You're my heart, Herald, you and Kai."

Yeshua had lain back on the sand. His eyes were closed. He was breathing very slowly, like one conserving air. Mainly, he was just enjoying this same moment, which for him mingled with his own eternity. All the things that had seemed impossible had come to be, and it was glorious, and good.

Several birds circled overhead, Caroline among

them. As she swooped low over the crowd of swimmers, although birds can't smile, the gentle animal spirit within her did. Her people were dancing in water.

Although this had been the place of her death, she did not fear it. Even as a witless creature, she knew in her own flesh the love of the Father and his protection that would now hold her in life.

She made a sweeping turn and led her fellow pilots out of Pod 12. The one face she sought, Clayton Block's, was not in sight. She knew if she kept searching, she would find him and maybe a pile of delicious seed.

TWO HOURS of swimming and play in the more solid water was enough. Jimmy and Mai Ker rounded up the kids to get ready for an early supper. No one needed to be called twice. They dried off and headed for the tents to change. As they dressed, the aroma of the fabulous meal floated out of the kitchen tent, filling their nostrils from 50 feet away.

Yeshua and Piper left ahead of the rest and were already shuttling between the kitchen and dining tents, helping Pam, Jacob and Katherine with the final preparations.

The rest of the Solarians and their guests dressed in the best clothes they had. Block and Will Atchison noticed that their old threadbare shirts were no longer threadbare. Either the woman had repaired them somewhere along the line, or the Father was also an excellent tailor. Paul Bishop borrowed a tropical-looking shirt from Atchison.

Yeshua, dressed in a new robe they had not seen before, greeted each of them at the door of the dining tent.

"Come and sit," he said.

Bridget, the first one to the tent, said, "Only after you."

He shook his head vigorously.

"No. Tonight I will serve."

Bridget knew better than to argue.

The others came in and were seated at reserved places identified by little place cards that Piper had carefully inscribed with their names. The extra table made enough room for Adanna, Erica, John Haskins, and Paul Bishop.

Two glasses highlighted each place setting, one filled with the new water, the other with special wine Yeshua had made from that new water.

"It just beats me how the water is so much more solid, but it goes down much more smooth," Willy said.

"Smoothly," Pam corrected him as she returned to the kitchen.

"New physics, William," Yeshua said, "water gives life, and it also protects life."

"I'm still confused about something," Braden said with a petulant look, his mind shifting from swimming to traveling. He didn't want to be confused forever, and it was beginning to look like he might be.

"What about?" Yeshua asked, pretending not to know.

"About how you can be here, but somewhere else, too."

"Yeah," Nathaniel chimed in, "me, too."

Yeshua set down a bottle of wine and beckoned both boys. He knelt as they came and stood by him, one each under his raised arms. He drew them close.

"I just don't get why you're so different from us," Braden said.

"For one, I bear these scars," he said, nodding toward his hands, "so that you won't have to." He rustled Braden's hair. "And yes, I can go other places, but you'll always find me close when you need me. Now, go sit," he said, shuttling them back toward their chairs.

Pam, Jacob and Katherine carried in the last of the hot food on large trays and in serving bowls. When the food was in place, Yeshua finally took his place, eyeing the magnificent supper.

"Looks like quite a feast," Atchison said, smiling at Yeshua.

Pam came and sat by Willy, who pulled her chair toward his. He wrapped a bulky arm around her, whispering softly.

"See, this is it, really, why I wanted to stay. It's your cooking," he grinned, before breaking into a bellowing laugh.

Pam leaned over and kissed him, joining his laughter.

"I always knew it was the cookies," she said.

Everyone else was quiet, expectant. Yeshua nodded and was about to offer thanks to the Father. He was interrupted by Herald.

"Wait, Sing and I have something special. Well, kind of a present, I mean. But—you'll all think it's corny, maybe. But could we?" he asked, looking earnestly at Yeshua.

"Should you ask your parents?"

"I think we better ask you."

Yeshua winked at the two young people.

"Whatever you think is best," he said.

"Really?" Herald beamed. "Ready?" he whispered to Sing.

"Think so. Come on," she whispered back.

She nudged Herald to his feet and took his hand to follow. They went around to the end of the long table nearest Yeshua. As Herald straightened up taller than usual, Sing brushed a lock of her flowing, dark hair back behind one ear.

"Don't laugh," Herald instructed everyone with great earnestness.

Sing hummed a hesitant starting note. They both sang. Herald's voice had improved enormously in recent days.

"Hark, the herald angels sing, glory to the newborn King . . ."

They sang quickly through the whole verse, trying to look something like the angelic lights that were at this moment swirling above both the Solarium's pods and the tent roofs.

". . . glory to the newborn King!" They stretched the last note.

Applause went around the tables. Mai Ker laughed aloud. Jimmy smiled broadly.

"Thank you, children," Yeshua said, "very beautiful." He was about to pray again when Sing cut him off.

"Wait," she said. "We learned it all."

"Really?" Yeshua said, knowing full well they had. "Learned it all? That must be some kind of first," he laughed.

"Would you like to hear the last verse?" Sing asked, looking thoroughly embarrassed.

"Please. Go ahead."

"Mild he lays his glory by," they began again, Sing breaking into an alto harmony above Herald's baritone melody, "born that man no more may die, born to raise the sons of Earth, born to give them second birth . . ." They both took a deep breath, anxious to finish it perfectly. ". . . light and life to all he brings, hail the Sun of Righteousness, hail, the heav'n-born Prince of Peace! Hark the herald angels sing, glory to the newborn King!"

As the no-longer-young children finished, some of Yeshua's angels had passed through the tent roof and circled above the head of each person around the tables.

Sing and Herald's song, joined by humming from others, whisked upward into the creatures of light above them. Voices that none of the Solarians yet understood, save Piper, broke out in a gale of sound, a delirious yet orderly chorale. After a full minute, as the joyous tones began to intensify, the angels all became suddenly still, as if the entire movement of the heavens themselves froze in place, in silence and awe. The new Earth resonated in the silence, at peace with the invisible realms, as Yeshua's children came into perfect consonance with the heavenly creatures above them.

Without realizing it, each person in the tent found they had risen to their feet, as if moved by some irresistible, unifying force. Clayton Block began to speak, feeling compelled, while his own angel hovered in a flame of fire above his head.

"Lord!" he boomed in a tone that could have shaken the Earth loose from its invisible foundations, "you *deserve* our praise! You've kept every promise." The words surprised him, the power behind them mystified him, but he knew it was the Spirit of Yeshua himself.

Each Solarian, elder and child, and each of their guests, fell as if choreographed to one knee as one body, a tribute to their King. The spiritual fire over Block's head spread like a wildfire in dry stubble, skipping over every other person. The angels began to swirl in ecstasy, silent in movement but loud in praise. In consummation, human and angelic spirits wove together into a tapestry of prayer, obedience, and divinely given love, heavenly bodies and human bodies wrapping in concert, the fire of God's Spirit knitting them together.

Joyous singing began again, but it was a new song. Everyone joined in. But this time there were no known words, only praises of God's infinite glory in speech that he alone could interpret. A mysterious melody none had ever heard was sung in perfect unison as if they had practiced it every minute since the beginning of time.

As they remained kneeling, Piper's eyes went to the angelic creatures swirling above them. To her amazement, she saw not only those inside the tent, but above it, and above the OUTSIDE of Pod 10. Without her seeking it, Yeshua gave her a treat, a deeper spiritual vision that went beyond what even her new physical eyes could have discerned.

As she watched layer after layer of the angels circling out into the distance, some began to swirl into smaller circles. These circles transformed into portals—hundreds, then thousands—of every shape and size, hovering both nearby and at great distances.

Through these portals, Piper witnessed a miraculous vision. Through each opening, she saw others like herself and her family and friends, gathered around other tables, some large and some very small. But astoundingly, as she looked at each room and group, there was Yeshua, standing by their tables, too, as if he was everywhere in addition to right here. How this could be, Piper could not begin to imagine.

From each portal, she heard, though not with her physical ears, the same kind of joy and prayer that was rising up from within the great pod of the Solarium. Those gathered elsewhere, some sitting at their tables, some standing, some bent on one knee just as she was at this moment, were offering song and praise.

Every moment is this moment, Yeshua had said.

Piper began to see. Her mind struggled but stretched. She realized that what she was witnessing was the glory of Yeshua spreading across the face of his new Earth. These others whom she saw, like herself and the other Solarians, were now citizens of that spiritual realm that existed before space and time where they touched each other and Yeshua in perfected communion with the Father.

Piper took a deep breath. She felt more alive than ever, but she couldn't speak, let alone sing. Her eyes went to Yeshua, who was looking back at her, an indescribable twinkle in his eyes.

Yeshua rose from his place, a brown folding chair that during the music had grown into a solid, carved throne of blood-red carnelian. It sat on a base of radiant, crystal-clear sapphire.

Braden looked up, dazzled by the sight.

"It's so beautiful, Lord!" he shouted like a young warrior charging into battle. Then, in a quieter but intense tone he said, "I love you."

Yeshua smiled, closing his eyes, turned inward in prayer. What blessing was made was between the Father and him alone. His eyes opened, newly alive.

He stood there, still and silent. He looked at each person and angel, the Father's satisfaction gleaming on his face. He nodded his head purposefully, some deep emotion filling his whole body.

"So it is, from the heavens, from the Earth, from under the Earth, the true voice of praise."

They all remained silent, breathing as one, feeling the energy of Yeshua's lifeblood pulsing through their own veins. They waited, still on one knee.

"Please, rise, sit," he said.

One by one, they took their seats. The angels continued a graceful spiral, like planets orbiting their sun.

"You begin to understand, my good friends," Yeshua said, "you see how my plan has been working, through the centuries, through millennia. You've asked many questions, and many remain. Be patient. You've lived barely two weeks of eternity," he laughed. "Time will bring understanding. You are growing to your perfection, the great Kingdom I have surrendered to the Father."

The sheer power emanating from him in these moments might have consumed them if he had not restrained it. The children, especially, seemed overcome, except for little Kai who was laughing a delighted baby-laugh that said the entire purpose of the universe had just been revealed.

Glimmers of new recognition came. Those who had known each other for years began to see the others' true souls. The children saw the spiritual bonds that tethered them to each parent.

Unnoticed, Caroline had circled into the tent a short time ago, called by the music and teased by the subtle movement of the angels. She fluttered down from behind onto Block's shoulder, then hopped and settled on the crest of his right hand. She had just left three eggs in her nest and was hungry. She pecked at Block's hand as if there should be seed there, some tiny pod hidden between his fingers that she could crack open.

Block, in a world of his own, lovingly stroked her tail feathers. He realized in this unrepeatable moment that his love for Caroline went far beyond Caroline, and came from somewhere far deeper than himself. He recognized in her tiny, nearly weightless body the full weight of creation, the mystery that lies beneath all that has been made. Gently, he stroked her head. Her feathers seemed to be aglow this evening.

". . . and this new world could not have come except for the life each of you accepted," Yeshua was saying. "Your choices, your actions—though you will never fully see—have brought the kingdom to its fulfillment."

Bridget saw in a heartbeat what she had not grasped until this instant. "We were each a link, in a chain."

"Yes," Mai Ker added, "joined." She looked across at Jimmy, whose eyes were fixed on hers. They had looked at each so often but now saw each other truly for the first time.

"You didn't always know your part," Yeshua said, "but you each played a defining role. Creation is not a story, it is life, made for you and all who have returned to fill my kingdom. We travel in the unmeasurable times now, the times that were always meant to be, the great Sabbath."

Piper's sky-blue eyes looked around from face to face. Her words came like music.

"The marriage feast of the Lamb," she murmured reverently.

"Yes, the cosmos is regenerated, the true temple complete. You," Yeshua said to them, "are my new creation."

His whole figure and clothing became luminous with a pulsing radiance like the strange cloud that had clothed Pikes Peak fourteen days ago.

Herald looked up to see a golden-yellow light emanating from Yeshua's face, like the sun ascending through the clouds of an early morning rain.

"Dad," Herald whispered to Clayton, who was still preoccupied with Caroline, "look."

Block did. He saw the brilliant light that should have overpowered them all but instead drew them in. Even Caroline seemed mesmerized by the light.

"Well, whatever happens," Block said, "I'm so thankful to have my little Caroline back. What a joyous surprise!"

Yeshua's voice danced.

"Oh, my friends," he said passionately, "you have touched only bits and pieces of the mysteries of life. Immense joys and pleasures await you. There are still *many* more surprises!"

Author's Note

The Last Trumpet

—Then I saw a new Heaven and a new Earth, for the first Heaven and the first Earth had passed away . . .
                    —John to the Seven Churches, 1st century AD

The *Solarium-3 Trilogy* is fiction. I wrote it because it seems an awful lot of modern Christians (not to mention non-Christians) live as if the promises of Jesus throughout the New Testament will never actually happen. This trilogy simply asks, *What if they did?* Are his promises just happy myths to make life bearable, or are they *true?*

I'm prepared for the barrage of criticism that is certain to fly. I'll be accused of not following the Bible. I reply, first, I've not tried to write a slavishly "literal" account of Christ's return because I doubt there are three Christians on earth who could agree on what that literal scenario would be; and, second, I've tried to paint only broad stroke renderings of *some* New Testament promises woven into a *fictional*—I say it again—account of what his return might look like. If I have erred, even if only fictionally, I pray the Lord will be forgiving.

I will have succeeded if readers are inspired to go to the New Testament itself, with their preconceptions set aside and their blinders off, to re-examine the Christian hope.

I've employed a lot of symbolism. Some will have

guessed, for example, that Solarium-3 represents the earth, third planet of our solar system, which is—to this moment at least—God's Solarium, his incubator of things to come. Symbols must be read as such, *not* as factual descriptions.

Please—I warn again!—do not take this trilogy literally or try to concoct some new cult around it. Jesus said no one knows the day or the hour of his return. That would include me. If we can't know the time, we certainly can't know the mechanisms by which God will ultimately bring down the curtain on this present age of a very corrupted world.

What I *am* certain of is that God knows, he holds the plan, and Yeshua the Messiah holds the key. If you want answers, look to him.

This trilogy is merely an extended parable, a teaching story. *It's fiction, not prophecy.* Trust me, the Last Trumpet will sound much more clearly.

—For we know that the whole creation has been groaning together in the pains of childbirth until now. And not only the creation, but we ourselves, who have the first-fruits of the Spirit, groan inwardly as we wait eagerly for adoption as sons, the redemption of our bodies. For in this hope we were saved.

—Paul to the Christians at Rome, 1st century AD

About The Author

JOHN R. SPENCER grew up in Kansas and Colorado, and holds a degree in English Literature from the University of Northern Colorado, where he was, for two years, editor-in-chief of the campus literary magazine *NOVA*.

In addition to writing, he has enjoyed a diverse career as a police detective, emergency medical technician, coroner's investigator, social worker, and community corrections supervisor. He has also worked as a dramatic director for several community and children's theaters in Colorado, Wisconsin and Illinois.

The father of three grown children, he lives with his wife, Candice, in Eastern Iowa.